STON

MESA

SAGAS

First Torrey House Press Edition, November 2017
Copyright © 2017 by Chip Ward

Published by Torrey House Press
Salt Lake City, Utah
www.torreyhouse.org

International Standard Book Number: 978-1-937226-85-5
E-book International Standard Book Number: 978-1-937226-86-2
Library of Congress Control Number: 2017938006

Cover art by Patricia Priebe-Swanson, www.patriciapriebe-swanson.com
Cover design by Alisha Anderson
Interior design by Larry Graham Clarkson

STONY

by
C H I P   W A R D

MESA

SAGAS

TORREY HOUSE PRESS

SALT LAKE CITY · TORREY

To my grandchildren

LUNA WAXWING

BOOK ONE
(the recent past)

AND THE

NEON MONSTER

Chapter 1

There are many versions of how that Fourth of July celebration in Stony Mesa, now known as the Apple Days Riot, unraveled but all agree that it started when Otis Dooley hit Bo Hineyman square in the back with a fresh horse turd. Splat! And the rest is history.

Bo's stallion was handsome enough to lead the parade but was placed by parade organizers at the rear because his rider was not nearly as handsome or well-liked. Bo's sensitive ego was somewhat massaged when he was given a flag to hold and the organizing committee described his role as the "grand conclusion." So when the turd-startled horse bolted forward it crashed through the high school marching band, upended a chain of sequined cheerleaders, galloped through the Boone County wiener dog club, crashed through the boy scouts in their best brown shirts, and sent a ripple of alarm and confusion rolling from the back of the parade to the front.

The skittish horse then stopped short in front of the Daughters of the Stony Mesa Pioneers float. Hineyman was thrown forward and landed in the large gingham lap of Dee Hardsmith who was representing a pioneer settler sitting in a rocking chair. Bo rolled off the float and hit the ground. A moment later he was growling obscenities and charging Otis Dooley.

What happened next and who hit who is a matter of who tells the story. The tuba player in the high school band remembers a horse's chestnut chest in his face and a bystander remembers a tuba hitting him smack on the bridge of his nose. The members of the Boon County wiener dog club remember stepping on their wieners and the dogs remember getting stepped on. A surge of screaming and frantic ducking was followed by yelling. Pockets of scuffling erupted among the crowd but the main action was at the rear of the column where bystanders had to wrestle Bo and Otis away from clawing and choking one another.

Separated and held in check by four volunteer firemen, one on each of the combatant's arms, they leaned forward and shouted. Otis accused Bo of deliberately turning his horse's rear end toward Otis who was standing on the side of the street enjoying the festivities when a juicy green bomb exited the nervous steed, splattering his pants. Bo, in turn, promised to leave Otis penniless and begging for mercy. It was pretty clear there would be none.

But perhaps it is best to backtrack to the beginning. Why Otis Dooley was so ready to take offense and throw that turd is more important to this story than the chaotic consequences of its return trip. The feud between Otis and Bo had been simmering for a long time and that plump green missile merely marked the boiling point.

Let's start with Bo Hineyman, a rich man with an unfortunate name, more so since his rump was plump and girlish. When visiting his ranch in Stony Mesa he fancied himself a cowboy and favored those loose-fitting jeans so popular with pear-shaped aging boomers. He covered the elastic stretch band with an elaborately tooled leather belt fastened by a silver and turquoise buckle the size of a dinner plate.

The buckle, his tailored western shirts, and an immaculate Stetson hat cost more than most of his Stony Mesa neighbors made in a month. There was no telling what he wore when visiting his houses in the Caribbean and in Virginia, just outside of Washington D.C., where he bribed and cajoled venal politicians to do the bidding of his rich clients. Maybe he dressed up as a pirate when on his yacht and maybe he wore a musket and three-cornered hat when in Virginia. Nobody in Stony Mesa knew because nobody ever visited him there. He had few friends in town but had purchased much goodwill from local contractors, vendors, artists, taxidermists, and any other local who had something to sell. If townsfolk were critical of him they kept it to themselves because money was tight in Stony Mesa and they couldn't afford to be cut off from Hineyman's largesse.

Bo's birth name was Richard Boris Hineyman. If his last name alone wasn't bad enough, his first names made his situation worse. He tried using Richard but people always shortened that to Rich Hineyman, which elicited jokes, and much worse was Dick Hineyman. His middle name was given to him by his father in memory of Bo's grandfather, Boris Hineymanskaya, a Russian immigrant who made the family's original fortune long ago by supplying other immigrants to sweatshops in New York City. Boris shortened his surname when he arrived in America so that his status as an immigrant would not be so obvious. Unfortunately, his command of English was not great at the time and he did not understand that "hiney" was slang for the human butt and, thus, his descendants would be the butt of many jokes.

Richard Boris Hineyman made Bo out of Boris and although it didn't match the dignity and respect he felt he deserved, it sounded friendly and down to earth, qualities that helped him sell whatever he was selling at the moment. Whatever charm the name conveyed was wasted on a man who had only three modes: he was either seducing you or totally ignoring you, unless he perceived you as a threat or as an obstacle, in which case he resorted to his bully mode.

Bo raised thoroughbred horses on his cattle ranch, or rather his ranch hands did because The Hineyman, as they called him, only flew in on weekends. His ranch was a place he visited, often with clients who were impressed with how the man they knew in the city, who arrived at meetings in a limo and dressed in thousand-dollar tailored suits, was also this earthy cowboy guy. At least it appeared so to clients who had never actually touched a horse or been any closer to the American West than a national park vacation or a movie. Bo hired real cowboys to work his ranch estate but didn't associate much with the local folks, as his valuable time was invested in corporate clients from big Wall Street firms that most of the good people of Stony Mesa had never heard about. There wasn't much profit in neighbors so Bo ignored them unless he wanted something.

It was harder for his neighbors to ignore him, however, since a few years after developing his horse and cattle ranch he built the biggest saloon and restaurant Stony Mesa had ever seen. The Bull and Stallion was a hobby, or perhaps a stage where he could pretend he was not just a well-dressed whore for hedge funders and credit card companies, but a laid back country and western dude with a stable full of thoroughbred horses. Local women were hired to wear skimpy cowgirl outfits, cowboy hats, and holsters with fake six-shooters. The menu featured steaks and beer with corny names that Bo made up himself. The Betty Sue Cheese Burger cost eighteen bucks and it was the cheapest item on the menu. Most of the kitchen help couldn't afford to eat there.

Stony Mesa sat on a sage-covered bluff above a river valley floor. It was aptly named. The valley that rolled out beneath vermillion cliffs was polka-dotted with black basalt boulders that had been pushed off the neighboring mountains by glaciers eons ago. Try to dig a foundation for a house on top of that glacial debris field and you will hit pods of stone whales clustering beneath sand and sage waves. Stony Mesa was almost impossible to farm. Enterprising pioneers planted orchards on the shoulders of the thin river that meandered through the town but pasture land was scant and the soil too sandy. They called it Poverty Meadows in the days before you could market scenery and make more money by putting a retired dentist on the land than by putting cows out there.

Stony Mesa was the edge of civilization for most of its hundred-year history. It was far from other communities and perched on the rim of a vast basin of redrock canyons just a few miles downstream. The mail was delivered by mule until the 1950s. The town got indoor plumbing, paved roads, phone service, electricity, and television within living memory. Prompted by tourists who became apoplectic and hyperventilated when their cell phones could not pick up a signal, cell service had only recently been enhanced by the addition of a cell tower disguised as a gigantic flagpole. It stood on the bench above the Six Shooter Motel. Residents could see Old Glory from most vantage points in town. Even so, Stony Mesa was on the edge of technology's reach. Venture five miles down the road and you leave the digital realm and enter the primordial world of silence where one must navigate by one's senses alone. A GPS device may tell you where you are in a maze of wilderness canyons but it doesn't tell you how to get out. The county's search and rescue budget was often overdrawn.

A handful of families endured by running cattle on public land and growing fruit to sell to miners in the next county, fifty miles away. Homes were modest and the general store had a front porch where tourists on mountain bikes rested, sipped lattes, and soaked in the quaint atmosphere. The town hall was barely more than a closet and the post office was in the back of a gift shop. There were three motels in town that opened seasonally but they had fewer than thirty rooms each. In the past few years a couple of bed-and-breakfasts opened and there were two RV parks. There was a single restaurant and a couple of places to buy burgers and ice cream except in the winter when everything closed down. The town's most memorable feature was not its enterprises but the thick and venerable cottonwoods that lined the road through town and cast welcome shadows in July.

The Bull and Stallion Saloon was so out of scale with the rest of town that it made the adjacent buildings look like munchkin architecture. Out front was a neon monstrosity that flashed and pointed at the saloon. The marquee in the middle of the blinding beast announced specials on steaks and beer. Above the marquee shined a row of dancing bison that changed colors and pulsed incessantly. On the very top of the structure some thirty feet up was a crown of light so bright that townsfolk joked it could be seen from outer space. But the place provided jobs waiting on tables, serving beer, and cooking various kinds of meat for tourists, so most residents conceded that although it looked like an invasion from the planet Neon, it was one more draw for tourists in a town that depended on seasonal traffic to survive economically.

Stony Mesa was a gateway to a national park that drew a million tourists annually to its honey- and bone- and amber-toned canyons. In all seasons but winter they stumbled from tour buses, transfixed by the wonders of light on stone. Several times a year motorcyclists missed turns on the twisting two-lane blacktop through the park, mesmerized by a landscape of naked rock in pastel shades unlike anything they had ever seen. They discovered abruptly that the buff-colored rocks and faded sagebrush were not nearly as soft as their colors suggested. The more fortunate visitors carried away cameras stuffed with digital beauty that would inspire them long after they had departed.

The trick was to get the tourists to stop along the way. By winter the tourists would be gone and the town shut down. Many of Stony Mesa's residents would leave for warmer destinations, too. Those who stayed would have to drive twenty miles for a jug of milk. There wasn't a traffic light for a hundred miles in any direction. So you had to make your nut while the traffic was heavy.

Bo discovered that doing business in Stony Mesa was cheap and easy. There were few rules and the ones that had been passed couldn't be found since the storage shed where the town's records were kept burned down when lightning struck a nearby pinyon tree. If there had been rules, they would be hard to enforce. Stony Mesa didn't have a real cop, just a dummy that sat in an old police car parked on the side of the road at the entrance to town. People saw the cop car and the figure sitting inside and they slowed down. When they realized the policeman was actually a mannequin they often stopped and took photos. Locals referred to the dummy as Officer Parker Dolittle. There were no lawyers in town and people generally shopped and did their banking "up-county" in a town not much bigger than Stony Mesa. The nearest Walmart was fifty miles away over a mountain pass that could be treacherous in winter.

Tourism and recreation kept Stony Mesa going while the rest of Boon County raised cows and grew alfalfa for cows. Some timber was cut and milled locally but most of the nearby forests were protected by the feds. There was a uranium boom long ago and some old-timers hoped mining would come back but it never did. Greasing the skids with county commissioners on any project Bo wanted to pursue was easy. Any questionable enterprise could pass unquestioned by commissioners starved for revenue and desperate to create jobs for the children of large families, including their own, who had to move away to find work. Most of the local politicians had never seen so much as a power-point presentation and were impressed by a man who dressed and talked like them but swept in on a private jet. Stony Mesa was easy pickings for a man of Bo Hineyman's power and stature. Until, that is, he crossed Otis Dooley.

Otis was mayor by default. Nobody else in the town of a few hundred wanted the office. There was no pay and little status attached to a job which was widely regarded as thankless. Being mayor meant that your neighbors constantly complained to you about low water pressure, barking dogs, and abandoned trucks in weedy yards. Then there was Crazy Kitty who was convinced that the new laser-read water meters could monitor her political and sexual activity. Most people in town cringed at the thought of that last bit of unwanted information. Kitty binged on Fox News and had a rude streak whenever she sensed the black helicopters were about to land.

There was not much that could be done to keep Kitty from endlessly bringing up her complaints about the water meter conspiracy at town council meetings and so most of Stony Mesa's citizens stayed away. There were other eccentric people in town who were also tolerated but not pleasant for a mayor to handle. Like old Ezra Pitts who liked to roam town at night looking into lit windows with binoculars and Theda Bringhurst who kept two dozen cats in her small cabin that smelled like a litter box. Otis had concluded that Stony Mesa was too small to have more than one town idiot so they had to take turns.

There were several competent people in the community who could be mayor but they lived outside the town's narrow formal boundaries and so were legally unqualified. A small retirement and second home community had sprung up on the outskirts of the village. The few retirees who actually lived in town moved there to relax and escape such mundane matters as refereeing squabbling neighbors and keeping the town's one fire truck running. They could care less what happened on Main Street.

Except for that sign in front of the Bull and Stallion. The sign was an affront to all who lived there. Otis Dooley hated that sign more than anyone. Otis was an amateur astronomer. His days were consumed by plumbing and carpentry but his nights were devoted to stars and Stony Mesa had more stars gleaming in the night sky than almost any place on the planet. Far from a city and sitting beneath black-shouldered mountains and rimmed by tall canyon walls, Stony Mesa had almost no ambient light. The desert air was dry and clean.

On most nights one could easily see an awesome lattice of pulsing light divided by the faint phosphorescent trail of the Milky Way against an obsidian black sky. Otis converted a small cabin behind his home into an observatory for a large telescope that was his pride and joy. He named his telescope Spock after the television character in Star Trek.

Otis might be on his knees with dirty hands during the work day but at night he could shed his coveralls, sit back and squint through Spock at the sublime heavens. Most nights he floated out of himself and into a universe of stars, galaxies, planets, comets, and nebulae. He marveled at the vast array of color. Yellow, red, and blue are most common but the deepest views Hubble allows reveal giant clouds of interstellar dust and gas that shimmer like the inside of a lustrous abalone shell. During the Perseid meteor shower, scores of shooting stars slid across the summer sky. Full moons were so bright he needed sunglasses to look at them.

There was always something new to see and yet the night sky had fixed points that had been emitting light for a billion years. In fact, he knew that the light he saw when he looked up at stars had been traveling toward earth for so long that anything he might see through Spock today actually happened before he was born, maybe thousands of years ago. The scale of time and space was humbling.

When Otis mapped the heavens with his eye, he saw the same night sky that the ancient Pueblo Indians saw. To think that he was linked to the mysterious strangers who had littered Stony Mesa's landscape with arrowheads, shattered pottery, and shards of stone tools was humbling. A black stump of petrified wood sat by his doorstep, creviced with crystals and marbled with orange, red, and yellow veins. To think that when that stone stump was a green and living tree the night sky was much the same as the sky he was looking at right now, well, that was more than humbling, that was mind-boggling. But knowing that he was here now to participate in this amazing universe was also inspiring. I may only be alive for a moment, he thought, but this is my moment.

As he stargazed he became a participant in the grand human quest to pierce the invisible and perceive the secrets of the universe. Squinting through a microscope at the hidden microbial world or squinting through a telescope at galaxies beyond the cave of the naked eye, one was opened to wondrous life and infinite possibility. It was this curiosity, this need to know the world beyond the physical limitations of our species, whether we mapped the stars, DNA, or the bottom of the ocean, that made us worthy of our unique place in the order of life, Otis thought. When he put his eye to Spock, he took part in the grand pageant of civilization. There was a kind of dignity to it. Compared to that, neon was just a gaudy trick at best, a reckless cataract of light made by fools to blind the enlightened.

Such reflections about time and space made Otis Dooley modest, grateful, and reverent. The balm of his nightly skywatching also helped him to be a good and generous neighbor, a dependable and honest worker, a patriot who was even willing to take on the tedious and thankless job of Stony Mesa mayor.

On the first night that the sign in front of the Bull and Stallion was lit, Otis retreated from a day of low-back pain and aching fingers to his telescopic lair. He sighed, swung his barreled lens skyward, and pinched his face into the eyepiece only to discover that his beloved night sky had faded under the celestial bleach emanating from the saloon's pulsing sign.

He was immediately thrown from his nighttime zone of awe and reverence into the arms of a bottle of bourbon that he hid behind the observatory wall. They woke up together the following morning. After a restless afternoon of grieving and steaming, it was clear. He'd be damned if that rich faux-cowboy Bo Hineyman would wreck his precious view of the stars. And as the town's duly elected mayor, it was his duty to confront the offender.

He marched into the Bull and Stallion. Hineyman stood at the kitchen door reminding a couple of waitresses to greet customers with "howdy partner." The night before, Kimmy Jo Roberts greeted a handsome and very buff male customer with a big smile and a salacious

"Bang! Bang!" Bo overheard her. Now, he was telling her that the six-shooters were a part of a costume that might make some people, all the French people and the tourists from New York, for example, a little nervous. No need to draw attention to them. Kimmy Jo stole a glance at her cousin Starla Huggins and rolled her eyes while Bo's head was turned. She started to make the sign for crazy but ended up fingering her hair when he turned her way.

"Oh, and never hand them the menu before telling them there's a selection of fifty beers to be had." He tried to smile to soften the criticism and come across as a good guy after all. It was a heavy lift for Bo as it required pushing his cheeks up against the tide of a perpetually furrowed brow.

Otis couldn't wait. "Bo, that electric bonfire you call a sign is ruining a precious resource." Diplomacy was not Mayor Dooley's strong suit.

"What resource?" Hineyman huffed.

"The night sky, you moron!"

"What?"

"People come from all over the world who have never seen the Milky Way, heck, never seen more than a few stars. They look up and they are awestruck. When they go home they tell all their friends who want to come here and see the same, maybe even eat a bison burger at your damn saloon. But when that sign of yours is on all they see is a bunch of friggin' buffalo dancing, the word 'steak' over and over, and a big red arrow pointing at the door." His anger was peaking. "It's an abomination! Damn thing needs a dimmer switch!"

"The only thing dim around here, Dooley, is you. That sign cost me fifty grand. It has state-of-the-art digital controls, the whole works. It's about time someone stepped up the hand-lettered crap that passes for signage here. That arrow doesn't point to my door, knucklehead, it points to the future!"

"Oh bullshit, Bo, it doesn't fit here and neither do you. Do you think you can just push in here and take over the night sky—own it?"

"I don't have to stand here and listen to some squat gnome who cleans grease out of pipes for a living. Get out of here before I call the police!"

"We don't have any police. You ain't in your office in Washington now, dickhead."

"We have a Boon County sheriff and if ever you walk your sorry ass into this establishment again, I'll call him. Now get out!"

The two men were mindful that they were arguing in a public place so they politely refrained from shouting. They delivered their insults through clenched teeth and red faces. A bystander may have mistaken them for contestants in a vein bursting contest.

Otis left as he was ordered to but the following week he wrote a guest column in the county's weekly paper. It read, "Our pioneer ancestors who settled Stony Mesa were rugged individualists but they understood that nobody can stand alone in a wilderness like ours. Neighbors stepped up and built an irrigation system that still keeps our desert valley fertile. They built a school, a town hall, and a church together. They understood that as tough and self-sufficient as a person might be, he still needs a community to make life good. It is our turn to step up and keep Stony Mesa from being gobbled up by the highest bidder."

Bo Hineyman was never named but everyone understood who Otis was talking about. Bo was livid. He called his lawyer, Brad Rugby, and asked if he could sue for defamation. "Are we aiming to win or just teaching him a lesson?" asked Rugby.

"Teach him and any other hick motherfucker who wants to mess with Bo Hineyman that they better not start," he replied. Rugby chuckled and said he would get right on it. Intimidation and Harassment were full partners in Brad Rugby's law office. Bo hired them often.

A week later Hineyman's horse pooped on Otis's shoes and Otis returned the moist bomb to its rightful owner. The feud was out in the open for all to see.

When Bo Hineyman's strangled body was discovered two weeks later, Otis was the prime suspect.

Chapter 2

Luna Waxwing tried not to tremble. Her voice cracked when she spoke so she stayed silent and pretended to be brave. The bulldozer with its enormous gleaming blade looked like a wall bearing down on her and a dozen compadres who sat chained together in front of the mining site gate. She noticed how the cobalt blue of the desert sky reflected in the mud-spattered blade that was about to chop and crush her. As the yellow monster closed in, she caught a fleeting glimpse of the maniac who was jerking levers back and forth in the bulldozer's cabin. He wore a white helmet with a faded logo. The blade dropped and the helmet disappeared behind it.

The bulldozer growled forward and the crowd gathered at the tar sands protest screamed and waved their arms frantically, imploring the driver to stop. Some covered their eyes or looked away. Luna stifled a sob and whispered, "Please, God, no!" a moment before the machine stopped inches away from the chained protesters.

When it was clear that the dozer operator meant to scare them, not kill them, the protestors resumed their chant; "Tar sands no! Drexxel go!" Jacked up by the near slaughter, they shouted louder. Sheriff Taylor saw how the charging dozer infuriated the large crowd that had made the arduous trip to support those blocking the mining site with their bodies. He trotted over to the dozer and grabbed the sleeve of the man in the white hardhat. He ordered him to get down before he made the situation even worse. The driver walked away but not before flipping his middle finger at the chained demonstrators.

Most of the protestors had been camping nearby at High Hollow Springs for two weeks. The strip-mining had not begun but heavy equipment had been moved in so that the site could be prepared. The road would have to be upgraded and a parking lot for work vehicles scraped out. They needed a warehouse for supplies and equipment, an office, a repair shop, a pad for fuel tanks. And that was just the beginning. Eventually the mining site would be an industrial island squatting in the center of the once-wild Seafold Ledges with massive pipelines radiating out from a gouged and scoured landscape. It takes a lot of infrastructure to scrape a thousand acres raw and then boil the soil into oil.

The Seafold Ledges Tar Sands Alliance was a loose grassroots group that aimed at drawing attention to the toxic and water-wasting nature of tar sands production. They had a website and a Twitter account, an office in a converted storage shed, and an ad hoc staff that conveyed compelling information about the massive amount of water that would be needed to process the tar sands and the scary brew of toxic chemicals that would go into the soil and eventually into the groundwater. They posted photos of the apocalyptic destruction of northern Canadian landscapes wrought by strip-mining the tar sands there. They had demonstrated against the project at several public appearances of Drexxel's corporate officers but this was their first act of civil disobedience at the tar sands mining site itself.

Luna took three deep breaths to calm herself. She exhaled slowly and checked to see if she had wet her pants. Dry so far. Her confidence returned, she reviewed the reasons she found herself on a dirt road thirty miles from the highway, joined to a chain-link fence with twelve people who shared her noble convictions but at the moment looked like a discarded charm bracelet of disheveled campers.

The Seafold Ledges was a remote landscape of broken cliffs and wide arid valleys that could only be reached by primitive dirt roads. You had to swallow a lot of dust to get there. The dozens of archaeological sites that were scattered across the high desert testified to a time before cows and sheep replaced elk and bison and the ancestors of today's so-called Pueblo people could hunt and gather there.

After the original human inhabitants left, the Ledges saw few visitors: the occasional cowboy looking for stray cows, a few geologists who found fossils and mapped the tar sands below the Ledges, and a team of Army surveyors looking for a place to blow up bombs and practice war. The Sea Ledges was never adequate for their needs, an also-ran in America's epic race to exploit its deserts.

A couple of times each fall, van loads of college students visited. They would burst from their dusty vehicles, their knees cramped from the long ride, and blink at the bright sky. Many had never experienced a sky so blue. They would be led by their professor to areas rich with fossils where they could paw and poke at the layers of rocks that were uplifted and exposed like the pages of a book. The ledger of the Ledges told a story punctuated with mollusks, trilobites, walking fish, and dinosaurs, a kind of evolutionary braille embedded in stone. In the winter, ice and wind scraped across the bare pinnacles and made a mournful song unheard by all but antelope and bighorn sheep.

Deserts are generally abused and abandoned or simply ignored. That was true for the Seafold Ledges, too, until humanity's insatiable appetite for oil meant that even dirty tar mixed into sandstone was valuable. The fossil fuel industry had already picked the low hanging fruit and technology made possible the recovery of oil from even the crappiest scraps in sand. Suddenly, the Seafold Ledges held something that was wanted.

The Drexxel Development Corporation had bet that tar sands were the next big thing. They had been to Canada and the same land-scape laid to waste that horrified ardent conservationists was a source of inspiration to the Drexxel team that surveyed the massive strip mines there. The scale was mind-boggling and they speculated that the profit to be made in a world addicted to carbon was limitless. A Drexxel scout told his employer that the Sea Ledges could be "better than Alberta." They surveyed the empty landscape of the Ledges and dreamed of trucks the size of buildings moving the raw material of the world toward their bank accounts.

Drexxel's scouts were leasing land and buying mineral rights in places like the Seafold Ledges. Most of it was public land, so leases were cheap. But their plan to dig up thousands of tons of sand and then boil the gooey crude out of it faced major hurdles. One, squeezing oil out of rock is expensive because it is also energy intensive—it would take almost as much fuel to produce the fuel as the fuel produced. Two, they needed a way to get the product out—a pipeline was another big and complicated expense. And finally, there were those crazies with their signs about pollution and global warming who showed up at every pub-lic meeting, chanting and yelling and now, damn it, chaining themselves to the mining site gate. Mining had not begun but the big machines were on hand to prepare the site and that cost plenty. Tar sands mining is marginal and risky enough without adding in such unnecessary delays. Something had to be done about those eco-freaks.

One by one the thirteen chained protestors were separated from each other by bolt cutters wielded by Sheriff Taylor's deputies. They were arrested for trespassing and resisting arrest, read their rights, and carried one by one to vans, the one police van in Boon County and another borrowed from the senior citizen center. A deputy named Eldon Pratt found the entire operation baffling. Who were these crazy people, he wondered, and what are they doing so far from the highway? Why are they so mad? There is nothing wrong with mining, without mining there would be no cars. How do they think they got out here?

Eldon had only been out of Boon County a few times in his life, mostly when his uncle took him cross-country in his truck to deliver shipments of refrigerated meat. They didn't tarry along the routes they followed and Eldon was left with the impression that the rest of America looked like truck stops, which were pretty much the same from one place to another. His fellow Americans were motorists just like him. The people he saw shuffling in and out of rest rooms or feeding coins into vending machines loaded with Red Bull, Slim Jims, and Snickers appeared to have no history, regional accents, political opinions, food preferences, sexual orientations, and so on. In truck stops, diversity is mostly in one's imagination and Eldon wasn't strong in that area. So this bunch of his fellow Americans chained to a gate and chanting incomprehensible slogans struck him as weird.

He whispered to Sheriff Taylor, "Look at that guy over there. He has those dreadlocks you see on TV. Can we cut his hair when we get him to the jail?" Sheriff Taylor frowned at him and turned away. Eldon didn't suggest it to be cruel, he was just curious.

On the way back to the Boon County jail, the vans became mired in mud twice and sand once. A recent thunderstorm left soupy washes in its wake and while crossing one of them the van borrowed from the senior civic center slogged to a halt and stopped. It wasn't designed to navigate four-wheel-drive roads and the clearance was too low. The prisoners were ushered out of the van and stood on an adjacent bank watching Taylor and his deputies try to rock and push the van through a fresh bed of sucking silt and clay.

The sheriff and his deputies slipped and swore, grunted, flailed, pushed harder and failed again and again. The arrested protestors watched the show for several minutes and then looked at each other, shrugged, and left their dry perch above the wash to join in and push the van free. Eldon reached for the handle of his revolver but they waded into the mud with such good cheer that he was confused. They pushed together with all their might and the deputies found themselves sorting out a confounding mix of suspicion, surprise, and appreciation. The van broke free and climbed the embankment, a cheer went up, and the prisoners climbed back into the van without being ordered to do so, carefully scraping mud off their shoes and boots first.

After that, the prisoners conversed freely and asked questions. They learned that the wife of one deputy was expecting a baby girl any day now and that Eldon Pratt recently won a trophy at the county fair for roping steers. The deputies learned that their prisoners included a retired professor, a garlic farmer, a concert violinist, a microbiologist, a computer programmer, an electrician, a nurse, and Luna, who described herself as a "budding rainbowologist." By the time they were delivered to the county jail, Eldon's confusion was complete. As the prisoners were escorted to the jailhouse door, he stammered, "Good luck," then blushed and fell silent. He hoped the other deputies didn't hear that.

The county jail was not designed for more than a handful of occupants. It was mostly a holding pen until the accused could be transported to a larger facility fifty miles away. Sheriff Taylor apologized for the crowded conditions. He and his men had never witnessed a protest or arrested so many people at once. They once busted four people when a fight broke out at the county fair during the demolition derby but that was the previous record.

Police work in Boon County consisted of ticketing speeding motorists, issuing DUIs, settling domestic disputes, rescuing stranded hikers, and rounding up horses that got loose and ventured too close to roads. The accidents they responded to were few and far between but tended to be gruesome given the high speeds that desert drivers are accustomed to, the unforgiving landscape of rocks and ravines, and the too frequent presence of deer, elk, and cows in the middle of roads at night. The previous week Ula May Bostick superglued her husband Frank to the toilet seat and beat him with a broom handle for having an affair with Myra Gundy. That was about as exciting as it got in Boon County. Compared to that, the tar sands protest was epic.

The morning after the protest, Gif Hanford called Orin Bender. Gif was the foreman on site. He'd been out of work for months after a shoulder injury and looked forward to a long, secure, and lucrative run as a field manager with Drexxel's tar sands project. The prospect of losing that because a bunch of loonies with dreadlocks and backpacks got in the way was alarming. His sister's kid had cancer and he was helping her pay medical bills. There was credit card debt and he owed child support. He had too much at stake to let a bunch of damn freaks stop work. He knew that the suits who ran Drexxel avoided embarrassing confrontations with the public and would try to PR their way around any ensuing controversy. No, Gif thought, this calls for someone who knows how to play hardball. Orin could do that as well as anyone Gif knew.

Meanwhile, the thirteen ardent members of the Seafold Ledges Tar Sands Alliance were whiling away in the Boon County jail. They were crowded together in a single holding cell while Sheriff Taylor figured out what to do with them. He called and consulted with the county attorney, Lawton Hatch, and argued that keeping them cost money he hadn't budgeted for and there were not enough cells to handle them according to state standards.

To make room for the new inmates, he considered releasing Ike Mooney, who was arrested the day before. Ike was a driver for the state fish and game workers who were poisoning and draining Circle Bluff Reservoir to scour out invasive populations of zebra mussels and bass. Ike was supposed to haul a load of dead fish to the landfill but stopped at a tavern in Junction and got soused instead. He ended up at the home of his ex-wife's boyfriend, Cecil Barney, who arrived home later to discover a truckload of stinking fish piled up against his garage door. The sheriff felt it would be best to keep Ike until he was completely sober and give Cecil time to calm down. He could release the woman they called Meth Head Mona but she'd only be back tomorrow.

Lawton Hatch interrupted him. He was adamantly opposed to an easy release. "These are the same damn people who shove every federal law protecting endangered species down our throats and keep us from getting jobs and getting rich by tying up oil and gas so we can't get to it. I intend to make an example of them, not coddle them!"

So the prisoners stayed while the lawyer who volunteered to represent them bargained over charges and bail with Lawton Hatch. Luna Waxwing had three days to reflect on the events that put her into an orange jumpsuit several sizes too large and landed her next to a cell-mate named Mona who had lost her teeth to meth. Mona was caught shoplifting cigarettes, her tenth offense. Luna had lots of time to converse with Mona and the others in the lock-up who were not there for protesting the strip-mining of the Seafold Ledges. She wanted to hear their stories. On day three she had a revelation.

"I get it!" she told Mona. "Addiction, alcoholism, self-sabotage, laziness, rage—they're not just bad behaviors but ways we withhold our participation from a world that makes no sense, that cannot sustain us psychologically or spiritually."

Mona cackled, coughed, then reached down into her jumpsuit to scratch her crotch. "You sure is funny, girl!"

Mona notwithstanding, Luna thought she was onto something. She herself had succumbed to drugs, failed, and raged because she just couldn't belong to the program that her teachers and counselors, her mom, and her peers handed her. Why accept a way of life that is coldly competitive, even predatory? Why is it so important to own things, to have more, always more? Are the so-called successful happy?

In her teens, she looked around and saw judgmental hypocrites in charge at every turn. Greedy pigs wrote the rules. And the rules were imposed in an ass-backward way that offended her. Pink hair was criticized but it was okay to flaunt a diamond that was mined by workers who were essentially slaves. You were mocked for being a vegan but it was okay to eat calves that were trapped in huts and overdosed on milk so their flesh was pale and tender. People give their dogs Christmas presents and then eat ham from a pig that is every bit as intelligent and sensitive as their pets. Stealing millions from widows was punished lightly if you wore a fine suit and silk tie but rob beer from a liquor store and you could be killed, especially if you were born black or brown or red. It was all so transparently bogus and contrived to her but nobody else agreed. Lose the attitude, they told her. Liz, don't be such a downer. Grow up!

Her search for a North Star to guide her took her to church where, again, the contradictions were ripe. Killing a fetus the size of a thumb that had no relationship beyond its host was a sin but it was okay to bomb cities full of whole people with parents, siblings, neighbors, and co-workers.Masturbation was a sin but the addictive consumption of wasteful bling passed for normal.

"I can use my two fingers to get off," she told the pastor, "and you use your wallet, so my pleasure has a smaller ecological footprint than yours." The pastor was both baffled and alarmed. She was asked not to attend the youth retreat that summer and so she left the church and never returned.

She didn't stand a chance, Liz Waxwing with her poems and paintings, her guitar and her hand-colored scarves, her notebooks covered with drawings of fairies, horses, and snakes. To top it off, the American Way was boring. Boring! She rejected it.

At seventeen she was busted a second time for a purse full of pot. She failed to appear at her court hearing and a warrant was issued. Unfortunately for Liz Waxwing, a cop was sent to serve the warrant just minutes after Liz dropped three hits of the best acid she ever had.

Unfortunately for the cop who served the warrant, Liz was lean, supple, and so tripped out that she thought she was being abducted by an alien from outer space. She was pretty sure the shiny thing on his chest said "Pluto." Ummm, maybe "Polite."

When the blue uniformed space monster stopped to eat a whopper and fries, she managed to slip her cuffs and squeeze between the metal netting separating the back seat from the front. There was just one way out, she reasoned. I must steal this car and escape.

She was easy to catch, especially after she turned on the siren and lights. At ten miles per hour, a speed she considered dangerously fast, she was only a few blocks away when a cop on foot managed to reach past her and grab the keys.

She was appropriately contrite after the LSD wore off. Her father, whom she had not seen for years, paid for the best lawyer he could find and several teachers came forward to testify that Liz was a bright, creative, and sensitive girl who could be redeemed. The judge sent her to a wilderness therapy program in Boon County, far away from those hippies and punks who were a negative influence. Years later, Liz returned to the back-o-beyond desert that was once the scene of her exile, this time to sit in front of a bulldozer while chained to a gate.

Jay Paul Ziller was arrested, too. He went by the name Hip Hop Hopi, a reference to a maternal grandmother who was half Hopi and his childhood in Oakland where his parents taught in an inner-city school. They named him after a character in a Tom Robbins novel. It could have been worse. His sister was named Rosy Dawn and he had a brother named San Gabriel after the mountains his parents were camping in when they conceived him. Most people called him Hoppy.

Throughout his inner-city upbringing, Jay Paul Hip Hop Hopi Ziller expressed a primal urge to rush straight into danger. This tendency may have been reinforced by the frequent need to defend himself and his sister in schools where they were, ironically enough, a small white minority. Although their best friends were non-white and treated them well, Rosy Dawn was widely regarded as a honky name worthy of ridicule, especially by kids who relished the opportunity to give back to whites the hard time they got from them. Hoppy was her defender and jumped quickly into fighting mode whenever she was harassed. He took risks so often that it became habitual. His attraction to action also made Hoppy attractive to young women who had yet to discover that dashing and dangerous don't pay the bills and may not be positive qualities in a father.

Growing up in the city, Hoppy loved western television shows and movies. He read Zane Grey in grade school and Louis L'Amour in high school. He also gobbled up nature programs and discovered he had an affinity for wild animals. He fed squirrels and pigeons in a park a block away from home and he knew where the raccoons who knocked over trash cans in the middle of the night denned by an abandoned railroad line. His parents took their kids camping on weekends, often accompanied by a half dozen of their city friends. He lived in the grimy fist of the city during the week but on weekends he learned by heart every trail in Muir Woods. Lately he lived on the road, taking in firsthand the best of the wonders he had imagined while living in Oakland. He visited national parks and other wild places he had read or heard about. He had just landed in Stony Mesa when he decided to join the Sea Ledges protest.

Hoppy brushed back a mop of sandy hair, quick-smoothed his beard, and walked over to the young woman who seemed to be as smart as she was pretty to ask her name and give her his. He'd been watching her for hours. He liked the way she moved so easily among those in the overcrowded lock-up, smiling, hugging, lighting up each person she encountered with her energy and charm. She could explain the chemistry of climate change to a fellow activist one minute and then engage in a heartfelt conversation about love and loss with that burned-out meth freak, Mona, the next. Her smile was radiant.

He stood near her and breathed in her aroma, an alluring mix of campfire, sage, and vanilla. Her clothes looked like a happy accident, maybe the best outfit that was ever pieced together from a free box. She even managed to make the orange jumpsuit that replaced her gypsy garb look stylish. She was small but athletic, and hot, very hot, in some way he couldn't explain. He just had to get to know her. Since he was new to this crowd, having arrived only the day before the protest, he knew no one who could introduce him to her. So he swallowed hard and approached.

"You're Luna, right?"

She turned to face him, smiled, and brushed a wayward tendril of hair from her eyes. Her gaze lingered and then she smiled, nodded yes.

"How did you get your name?" he asked Luna. "Is it your real name or did you make it up?"

"Waxwing is my mother's maiden name. I took it legally as soon as I could because I didn't want my father's name. He left us when I was two. My mom says he was home so seldom that it took me a few months before I realized he was gone. He paid for stuff—my braces, piano lessons, my tuition, stuff like that, but I never saw him."

Luna had secretly watched Hoppy from a distance, too, and now that he was in front of her she was so nervous that she couldn't stop talking. Her explanation wasn't going where Hoppy expected it to go but he did not interrupt her because he liked watching her talk, the way her brows danced above her eyes, the lilt of her voice, that beautiful loose curl of hair that would not behave.

She paused to brush the wayward lock away from her eyes and continued. "Well, I saw my dad once after he left us. He took me to

Disneyland but I threw up on one of the rides and then he got in an ugly spat with some guy who was there from Utah with a dozen kids when my father cut in line. I cried and wanted to go home. For days after I awoke with nightmares about hydrocephalic mice. The next time my father wanted to take me somewhere I broke out in hives and my mother put an end to that. She said that he was her mistake and there was no reason I should have to pay for it."

Luna's heart raced and she was running out of oxygen. Stop talking, she told herself, but she couldn't slow down. Words were the only defense she had against the urge to throw herself into his arms and melt. There was something about him that seemed so right. There was something she could almost smell or taste.

Hoppy primed the conversational pump again. "Where did he go when he left you and your mom?"

"On to the next wife and then another and another. He has a trophy wife now who raises Chihuahuas and has a line of little dog clothing and jewelry that she sells online. She calls it Bow Wow Wow! She has fake boobs and spends a fortune getting her nails done but she looks tan and fit on his yacht and stays out of his business. I guess she's lower maintenance than the others who ended up in rehab. Low maintenance is important to my father because he has more important things on his mind than the wife and kids. And the ironic thing is that he gives oodles of money to political candidates who proclaim family values and the importance of marriage. The man is a total asshole and I want nothing to do with him."

Hoppy nodded and furrowed his brow in sympathy. This chick was a trip. He could listen to her all day. "That's all very interesting but I didn't mean your last name. I meant Luna. Is that your real name?"

"No, my real name is Elizabeth—Elizabeth Suzanne Waxwing. My dad called me Betty Sue and my mom called me Liz. I decided I preferred Luna, after the redwood tree that Julia Butterfly Hill, the famous tree-sitter, saved. And it refers to the moon, which was worshipped by women and pagans before the patriarchs took over and burned midwives and crones at the stake for communing with nature and healing with herbs."

Hoppy was impressed. "Sounds like you're a student of history."

"Not really. I'm just trying to figure out how this world we have inherited is such a mess."

"So when did you do it? Ya know, change from Betty or Liz to Luna?"

She told him about the two seasons with the Pathway Wilderness School where she was sent after that unfortunate misunderstanding with the patrol car. She backpacked hundreds of miles with four counselors and a dozen fellow miscreants, aka troubled teens.

She arrived with a snoot full of resentment that she soon had no time or energy to feel because she was so busy just surviving. She had never backpacked before and it was grueling. Not only was the pack heavy, you had to find and filter your drinking water, make all the meals together, gather firewood, and wash yourself under a sloppy solar shower that was always too hot or too cool. Every day was a series of chores and struggles. At night she worked on staying warm. On days when they were not hiking they talked and talked and talked. The counselors were trained to rappel off cliffs and provide wilderness first aid but also to lead discussions about the emotional wreckage in the lives of their surly charges.

At night, the counselors took her shoes so she couldn't run away. She wouldn't have known where to run if she had the chance. Boon County included a thousand square miles of rugged wilderness. Although it was safer than any nighttime landscape she had ever known, with no cars to run you over and no lurking criminals, moving about at night was scary. Not a week into her first hike, she heard coyotes yip and a mountain lion scream in the pitch dark. There was no light but the moon and stars so it was easy to trip over uneven ground studded with sharp rocks. One must stay put at night.

Hoppy couldn't get enough of Luna and was afraid she might stop. He told her he hiked through several national parks and wilderness areas but he was unfamiliar with Southwest canyon country. "You must know this land here very well after so much time on it. What can you tell me about the Colorado Plateau?"

She told him how they hiked across forested mountains cut by deep ravines that descended into redrock canyons with fifty-foot spillovers. She learned to rappel. Some canyons narrowed into slots that were scoured by flash floods. She learned to fit herself into them and climb with her back to one wall and her feet on the opposite wall—chimneying, they called it. They humped their packs up and over giant mounds of soft turquoise ash from prehistoric volcanoes long dormant. They camped in pinyon islands that covered the tops of buttes they had to climb with ropes. There was one gallery of old trees she named "the bonsai forest" for the twisted intensity of its venerable junipers. They drank from puddles in sandstone rills and from potholes that captured rain water running over open stone. There was nowhere to go but right here where you walked, no time but right now. This moment, no other.

Far away from the ubiquitous thrum, buzz, honk, and chatter of the city, she discovered a soundscape free of the collective tinnitus that is the murmur of civilization. It opened her. Eventually the noise in her head, all that blabber remembered and wished, the fragments of music, television, texts, tweets, and ads that cluttered her inner narrative, faded to silence. Sounds that had been masked or absent from her life returned to her. She began hearing the wind rattling delicate aspen leaves above her as a music more peaceful than music, something like it but without pretense or conception. She saw how the wind pulsed and whorled across an open horizon of rice grass and sand, leaving a signature that was the same rippled pattern she saw on the sandy bottoms of the stream beds they crossed. She heard ravens comment on her passing and watched the slow, effortless spiral of hawks so far above her that they appeared as dark specs in an azure realm.

She listened to her own breath. The rhythm of her footsteps crunching across the earth held her attention for hours. In the end, she learned to take pleasure in simple things like clean socks, shade when hot, sunshine when cold, laughter, an unexpected kindness, honey in her tea. For the first time in her life gratitude and grace bore forgiveness.

It was at night when she got it. She was lying in her sleeping bag looking up. She had never seen so many stars. The Milky Way. Shooting stars! She gazed into eternity and found it beautiful beyond words. And then she realized it was all beautiful. And good. And right. Enough. All of it: the steep ravines, the dragonflies, the trees, the fragrant meadows, the stink of sweat, the rose-lit cliffs at dawn, cold showers, and the crackling fire at night. All of it was good and so was she. For the first time in her life she belonged to a place that made perfect sense.

"It's all connected!" she blurted out in the dark. "It goes round and round. Forever! And we are this momentary synthesis of sunlight, soil, and rain, seeing and feeling it all. That's our gift, to see the beauty! The beauty of all of it!"

"Shut up, Liz!" said a counselor.

"Yeah, Liz, plug your hole!" added Junior Crenshaw, who was busted for secretly filming the girls' locker room at his school and then uploading it to YouTube.

"From now on, call me Luna," she replied.

And then she lay back on the bundle of clothing that served as a pillow and watched her breath rise and drift away on a current of air that had been flowing forever and would never end, joining together her and a billion other breathing creatures, human and wild, into one luminous, dancing, shared river of life.

A year later, Liz Waxwing, now Luna, was home. She made peace with her mother, Virginia Waxwing. Back from the wilderness, Luna discovered that her mom was actually warm and smart and it was not that hard living within the boundaries her mom set for her. She made new friends and finished high school near the top of her class. The day after graduation her mother told her that unconditional love goes on forever but devotion has phases. After eighteen years of putting her own life on hold while raising a shimmering smart daughter, she was leaving with a friend to ride horses in Spain, sail to Bora Bora, and climb mountains in Patagonia.

She did all that and more and Luna watched from a continent away, always a continent away. Luna's mom was a moving target that was hard to contact. Although Luna loved her mom and wished her well, living independently was harder than she thought it would be. She admired her mom and was pleased for her but she wished she was near. She missed the bond with her mother, the security of that. She didn't appreciate how much she needed her until she was absent.

Luna accepted her independence. When she looked into a mirror she saw her mother's high cheek bones and the subtle cleft of her chin and she realized that as the years passed she would acquire the same laugh lines framing the same wide eyes. She would realize that as she lost her mother, she also became her.

Luna left for college on a handsome scholarship and support from the man she considered her ex-dad. Because the land healed her and made her whole she intended to return the favor. She majored in wildlife biology and became active in a community garden near her campus. She spent her vacations climbing through slot canyons in Utah and Arizona. After graduation, she did a brief internship with a professor doing research on the relationship between voles and soil moisture. Then she joined the Seafold Ledges Tar Sands Alliance and devoted herself to setting up their website and organizing demonstrations.

"My love of the land is like that," she told Hip Hop Hopi. "It's not just likeable land that needs nurturing. A pretty place like a national park will always have its defenders. The Sea Ledges has no fans. It's the stray dog of the American West."

"Sounds like you want to take it home and give it a bath," Hoppy responded. They both laughed. She asked him why he was there.

"I'm just tired of rich guys fucking up the atmosphere. This is where it starts."

Chapter 3

Bo Hineyman's ranch hand, LaVerl Woody, found the body. It was flopped across a smashed glass table that held a diorama of a trout in a brook underneath a shimmering surface of blue-green glass. Bo bought it for ten thousand dollars in an art gallery in Santa Fe. The stuffed trout, suddenly free from its glass enclosure, stared blankly at Hineyman's finely-tooled lizard skin cowboy boot, which was pointed at its face.

The heads of a dozen dead beasts, including antelope, elk, cougars, deer, moose, and bison stared down from the wall at what was surely a classic crime scene. Bo Hineyman himself simply stared at the ceiling. His face was purple but there were no wounds on his body to indicate a struggle. But the overturned chairs, tipped lamps, and paintings tilted at odd angles testified to a violent struggle. The sheriff concluded Hineyman had been strangled but sent the body off to be autopsied just to be certain.

The list of Bo's potential enemies included just about anyone who worked for him or had encountered him, even briefly. The sheriff had two deputies and a dozen volunteers, mostly men with four-wheel-drive trucks who could help search for and rescue tourists who got lost on the county's hundreds of miles of dirt roads. Sheriff Dunk Taylor had never investigated a murder but knew it would be more demanding than his small and inexperienced team could handle.

The sheriff rarely ventured far from the pillar of his own perspective. He looked around and concluded there were good people and bad. Bad people rarely turned good but good people sometimes turned bad. Either way, people who commit crimes do so foolishly and recklessly. They make mistakes. Find the mistakes and you catch them. But fine-tuned forensic work and lab costs were more than Boon County could afford. It was easier to look first at motives so he could cut to the chase and avoid all that painstaking and expensive analysis. Sometimes it just wasn't needed.

Otis was the obvious suspect. Everyone knew he hated Bo. Otis was a nice guy but ever since he made a solemn vow to his mother to give up drinking, the man could be pretty ornery. Maybe he just lost control. The sheriff had seen otherwise good people do regrettable things when they lost their tempers. Or when they were drunk.

An hour after he was notified of Hineyman's demise and given a rundown on the crashed-up condition of the Hineyman house, Sheriff Taylor knocked on Otis's front door. He wasted no time in case Otis had indeed gone nuts and was still a danger to the community that included his very own family, friends, and neighbors. As a precaution he asked his deputies, Eldon Pratt and Lamar Hanks, to stand behind him with their hands on their holstered weapons. "Don't draw it unless I say so," he told them. He was worried they might accidentally shoot him in the back and regretted his refusal to send them to the police training academy. The budget wouldn't support that, and besides, the kind of crimes that happened in Boon County were pretty minor and didn't require expensive training that Eldon and Lamar probably couldn't pass anyhow. The job of deputy in Boon County was an entry level position. If you were good, you left for some place where they paid higher wages and had a better benefit package. It was no use investing in a guy who might leave as soon as he upgraded his resume.

The sheriff knocked and knocked. Otis finally appeared, his comb-over undone in wisps above a week's worth of whiskers. Otis wore stained sweat pants and a sleeveless t-shirt. He looked awful and didn't smell much better. Dunk Taylor was greatly relieved to see he was non-frothing, even docile. Temporarily anyway.

"Otis, where were you last night?" the sheriff asked.

"Camping."

"Where?"

"Spider Woman Mesa."

"When did you get back?"

"I don't know, what time is it? Maybe four hours ago. I was asleep when you knocked."

"Who was with you?"

"'I was by myself, why?"

"What were you doing out there alone?"

"I was screwing my horse and finding a cure for cancer. What the fuck, Dunk? Is there a problem?"

"When was the last time you saw Bo Hineyman?"

"I try not to see that bastard. It's bad for my blood pressure. When was the last time you saw him, Dunk?"

"This morning at his ranch. He was sprawled out on a coffee table in his living room staring at the ceiling. He's dead, Otis. Dead."

Otis paused while he tried to process what the sheriff was saying. Then it dawned on him. "Oh shit, Dunk! You don't think that I . . . oh shit!"

It was soon clear that the mayor had no alibi. The company he kept on his camping trip was Jim Beam and Johnny Walker. He'd spent the previous two days falling off the wagon in an epic way. He was not the kind to drink alone but he had promised his mom, Ida May Dooley, to stop drinking after he ran over her favorite cat with his ATV, plowed through her flower bed, and passed out just as three members of the church choir arrived at Ida May's for practice. Otis did not want anyone to know he was getting smashed, especially Ida May. The Fourth of July business with Bo had pushed him over the edge.

On his way back from Spider Woman Mesa he promised himself that was the last time. He had worried that his lapse would have some bad consequence and now here it was.

"Shit!"

Chapter 4

Orin Bender was the CEO of Superior Pipes Corporation, a multi-billion dollar enterprise that laid gas, water, and oil pipelines throughout the American West. Superior was often the low bidder because Orin had many well-placed cronies who let him know what other companies bid before Superior issued their bids. This was not legal, of course, but it was lucrative. So lucrative that Orin spent much of his day on the phone managing the placement of pipes, the deployment of personnel, and the exchange of favors across his sordid empire.

Orin was talking on his cell phone to a foreman on a new project near the Sea Ledges. Although Bender was not in charge of the strip-mining operation, he did have a contract to lay pipe. The place was remote and would require a lot of pipe. Gif Hanford, the foreman, was upset and Orin accepted his interpretation of the Sea Ledges situation which was, according to Gif, dire.

"Okay, Gif, I got it. I'll see what I can do. I gotta go. I'm in a meeting of all my regional managers and sales reps here at the Regency Suites and I'm about to get called to the podium. Just sit tight now. If I need to talk to you about this again, I'll call you. Got it?"

"Mr. Bender, they're ready for you."

Orin Bender straightened his silk tie, pulled on the sleeves of his suit to straighten the wrinkles, and ran his left hand lightly over his silver mane to smooth any wayward strands of hair before walking up to the front of the stage. His managers applauded wildly, each one checking out the others to be sure he would not be outdone or stop clapping a moment too soon. Orin smiled briefly and nodded to acknowledge their adulation. As he scanned the audience in the Regency ballroom he remembered that he had meant to hire more women and people of color. This bunch was very white and male. His clients were also white and male. They wouldn't buy pipe from a woman unless she had some sexual favor to trade and he didn't want that kind of woman in the company. He thought of Superior as a decidedly Christian outfit. And black people? Well, they just made his clients uncomfortable.

The applause faded all at once when his employees, like a swarm of starlings, picked up some subtle cue from one another and quit. He began: "They are as fundamental as fire. Forget the plough, ships, the internal combustion engine, electricity, refrigeration, trains, planes, and automobiles. All the hallmarks of civilization cannot compare."

A suspenseful pause. "Pipes! That's what I'm talking about. We take them for granted but you couldn't live the way you do without them. You'd have no water in your home. Without pipes you'd be living in your own shit—pardon me." Nervous laughter. "Do you think we are healthy today because of modern medicine? Well, what would your health be without pipes to bring you potable water and carry away your waste? The wires for all those appliances you have that make life convenient and entertaining run through pipes. The fuel that runs your car runs through pipes. The heat that makes your office and home warm—pipes!

"So next time some granola-crunching, self-righteous know-it-all tells you you're in the wrong business, that you're just salesmen and managers, you tell them that you're what keeps civilization civilized. Tell them you make and lay the keystone in the architecture of our modern world. Our economy without pipes would be like a human body with no arteries or veins. Dead! So, say I'm proud because my business is pipes!"

The audience went wild. The old man was an inspiration, all right. No wonder he'd built Superior Pipes into such a successful enterprise, they told one another. He acknowledged their hysterical applause with a brief salute and then turned and left the room. Smiling and nodding, he made his way through a gaggle of wannabe winners vying for his attention, spinning in his wake and babbling to themselves. He had no time for them. He experienced an annoying moment of guilt. He'd read in an airline magazine about CEOs who make themselves available to their employees. He shrugged off the feeling of guilt quickly. Winning, he told himself, is not about playing Mr. Nice.

Orin Bender left the Regency and climbed into the back seat of his company SUV, a silver monster big enough to house a small bar, a laptop station, and a flat screen television. He reached into his valise for a cell phone he only used on special projects. He speed-dialed a number and shut the divider between him and his driver so he could speak in privacy.

"Nole, is that you? Orin here. I have an assignment for you."

Chapter 5

Elias Buchman was surprised to see Otis Dooley at his door. The two were friends long ago when they were boatmen for a river-guiding outfit in Utah. River rats. Three seasons a year for three years they took tourists on week-long adventures down the Green and Colorado. Then Otis applied to vocational school to get his plumber's license and Elias left for graduate school in journalism. Otis had worked with his dad who was a plumber and figured he was already halfway there. And you could move anywhere and find work because plumbing was ubiquitous and could be counted on to rust, clog, and leak. Elias took the academic route because he hoped that if he could explain a crazy world to others, he might understand it himself.

Otis moved to Stony Mesa twenty years before Elias arrived. They hadn't seen or heard from each other longer than that. Although they had renewed their friendship after Elias and his wife Grace retired to Stony Mesa, they were not close. Otis thought Elias had changed and was not so easy to be around, but he thought highly of Grace, who had retired from a career as a nurse to become a massage therapist. Grace laughed easily and Otis felt calm in her presence. She could teach yoga, ride a horse, and was a gourmet cook. She was lean and looked much younger than her years. Otis thought Elias was the luckiest dog on the planet. He was even a bit jealous. Otis had almost married twice after long courtships that ended when both women decided that although Otis was both likeable and good, they could do better. When asked why he was still alone in his middle age he just shrugged and said he wasn't the marrying kind.

Elias didn't drink. It wasn't a moral thing but a health thing. The wine he once loved now split his head, even one glass of red. Beer could give him dizzy spells the next day. He'd never had much of a taste for hard liquor but in the last few years it made him feel like he was poisoned. It was hard to conduct a social relationship with his old river-running buddy Otis if drinking wasn't your thing, because drinking was

Otis's thing. Nevertheless he thought highly of Otis and admired him for stepping up and being the mayor.

Elias noticed that the mayor had lost weight and hair. His pallor was anemic. Although not formally charged with murder, everyone knew he was in the crosshairs of the law. The people who knew him best couldn't believe he would actually kill anyone. Otis may growl like a bear but they knew his soft-hearted side, too. He wasn't violent, but still, who else hated Bo Hineyman more? Otis had a temper and he drank too much.

"Otis, how are you? You don't look well."

"Damn right, I'm a wreck. You know why. I need your help."

"My help? Why me?"

"Because you were a private eye."

"No I wasn't, I was an investigative journalist."

"Same thing."

"No it isn't. Private investigators hide their identity and sneak around. Investigative journalists state plainly who they are and then say publicly what they find. We don't solve crimes, we expose them."

Otis grew pale. "But you have those skills, man. I don't have an alibi and everyone knows I had a motive. The only way I can get out of this for sure is to find the one who did it. Find the guy who killed Hineyman and I'm free. You gotta help me. I'm begging you."

Elias Buchman had left his career as an investigative journalist five years earlier. He'd exposed polluters, cheaters, scammers, hypocrites, and a wide range of greedy businessmen and corrupt politicians. His friends and family wondered how he had the intestinal fortitude to keep uncovering the sleazy underbelly of the American economy scandal after scandal, year after year.

"It doesn't bother me, really. I detach," he would tell them. "I just do my job and have faith that in the end the truth prevails and the bad guys can't hide forever."

But in his last story, the one he didn't complete, he learned that sometimes it's hard to distinguish the good guys from the bad and the bad guys do get away and the truth is suppressed. He'd investigated the shooting deaths by police of homeless men. Not just homeless. There were many people who are temporarily homeless while trying desperately to land on their feet, but the people who had been killed were chronically homeless. They are the ones we point to, the ones who live on the streets, sleep in parks and alleys, spend their days reading in public libraries, and sometimes rant on sidewalks, piss in the courthouse shrubs, and scream in the subway when visited by their inner demons. They're the ones who cry with joy in fast food lines when angels appear above the condiment bar.

America, Buchman realized, had kicked the mentally ill out into the streets and then punished them for expressing the symptoms of untreated illness. Often, way too often, the ranters and screamers who didn't or couldn't respond to the police when confronted were coldly executed. In case after case, an order was given once and given again. If the raging didn't stop, a cop would calmly and deliberately take aim to kill and then fire. These incidents had a cold and calculated aspect and they were becoming almost routine, like removing pests from a garden, bullets instead of bug spray.

There was no outrage. Internal police investigations routinely favored the cops over the crazies. Mentally ill street people were isolated from their communities and often from their families. Nobody sues if nobody is watching. Everyone, it seemed to Elias, was averting their eyes but him. But the worst part was this: the cops shoot to kill, he was told, because a wounded man is alive to sue and some opportunistic lawyer might take his case and hope to pocket a worthwhile settlement. And a wounded bum, a cop he befriended told him confidentially, could collect disability benefits. From the taxpayer's point of view, the cop said, dead was better than wounded if nobody was looking, which was almost always the case. The cop's attitude was that he was doing society a favor.

That was the story that broke him. His editor suppressed it. Too risky, he said, not enough proof. Buchman took a leave of absence. He couldn't sleep and lost interest in the wonderful meals Grace cooked.

She tried in vain to cheer him up, distract him. Nothing worked. He paced and mumbled, cried and shouted. Weeks went by and then he quit.

He took early retirement and they moved from the city to the quiet, far away canyons of Stony Mesa where he had camped with his dad when he was a kid. He and Grace told each other that they would reinvent themselves, or rather become the people they had always wanted to be before the detours that came with kids and careers. Grace painted and taught yoga. She was glad to get Elias out of that gut-wrenching career of his and start over. The kids were grown and they deserved some peace of mind.

Stony Mesa seemed a likely place to find it. The nearby national park was a tonic. They had visited the park on vacations with the kids as they were raising them. Their kids loved the park. If Grace had one wish for her retirement years it was to be close to her son and daughter. Her daughter spent a junior year abroad in Rome and fell in love with a handsome man there. After graduation she headed back to Rome. That relationship didn't last but she fell in love with an American who worked at the embassy. He was set on a diplomatic career and Grace realized her daughter would always be moving. Their son also had wanderlust and traveled the world as an assistant to a man who starred in a television travel series. Grace figured that if she couldn't chase them around the planet, at least Stony Mesa and the nearby national parks would serve as a magnet that would draw her wandering kids to her on annual visits.

Grace had doubts about Stony Mesa's culture and lack of diversity. As a nurse dealing with all sorts of people, Grace learned to tolerate differences and appreciate variety. She knew that social life in Stony Mesa was dominated by the One True Church because most of the town's residents were members. She was concerned that Elias was an odd fit for a local culture dominated by gun racks and mud flaps. Elias didn't hunt or fish, drove a Prius, and preferred classic rock to country and western, which he described as codependency put to music. He didn't visit the Fox News bubble. But she knew there were many so-called move-ins and locals who befriended one another despite their differences.

They made many friends and their social calendar had never been so full. They hiked and rafted, started a garden, and canned apples in the fall. Their grown kids visited and wanted to come back soon. Elias was sleeping through the night and eating enthusiastically. Laughter returned to their days.

"Look, Otis, I don't know who you think I am but your problem is too big for me. I can't go around interviewing people on my own. I would need credentials."

"Sally at the Boon County Weekly will give you a press card if I ask her. She owes me. But you don't have to interview anyone. There's the Internet. You can find out lots of stuff on that. You've done it before."

"I once had the skills of a veteran librarian but I haven't done research for years. The technology keeps changing and I haven't kept up. I don't even do Facebook. I don't tweet. I have maybe four apps on my phone."

Otis looked miserable. The two men stood in silence. Otis stifled a sob and turned away. Elias caved. "Okay Otis, I'll do what I can."

"Thanks, Elias. I swear I'm innocent, man. Please believe me."

Elias turned back into the house as Grace entered the back door from the garden. "Who was that?" she asked. "I heard a truck."

"Otis Dooley. He claims he's innocent and wants me to find Bo Hineyman's killer."

"Maybe you could do something about global warming while you're at it," she joked. "And then there's always peace in the Middle East."

"I know, I know. I tried to tell him. The poor man is desperate. Where is my laptop?"

Chapter 6

Nolan Mikesel often boasted that he was a fourth-generation rancher. Four generations are about as far back as white people went in his corner of the American West and if you didn't understand that he would tell you his great grandfather was a pioneer. Nolan knew that when he characterized himself that way it smacked of deep roots in local history, the stamp of venerable tradition, and the authority of long experience. It conferred a dignity and respect that he often didn't get when changing tires at the Exxon station at the junction. There, he was better known for the gobs of gooey chewing tobacco he spit out on the floor and his penchant for using variations of the word "fuck" to supply the adjectives and adverbs he would have loaded into every single sentence he spoke if he knew any adverbs or adjectives.

Nole could have been considered ruggedly handsome if unrelenting anger had not twisted his face into a permanent scowl. A front tooth went missing after a bar fight and there was a scar over his left brow from the time his father clubbed him with a beer bottle after he caught Nole stealing a bottle of Jack Daniels from his dad's stash. His father considered Jack Daniels an upscale choice in the days before he was reduced to drinking mouthwash if nothing else was attainable. Nole was twelve and had already acquired the family habit of killing brain cells whenever the opportunity arose.

His arms and torso were covered with tattoos of screaming skulls, dripping daggers, cobras, and tits with nipple rings. An American flag was tattooed across his shoulders and back. Underneath the flag in an unknown font invented by a fellow inmate during one of his frequent trips to the county jail were the words "American Patriat." Yes, an a instead of an o. Neither the tattooer nor the tattooee caught the mistake. His cellmate Carlos, after all, just did tattoos on the side. His main gig was selling coke to bikers at the motorcycle shop he owned. Nole admired him for his entrepreneurial skills and all the cool biker stuff he owned.

The local cops knew Nole for hitting his wife, crashing his motorcycle, losing his kid, fistfighting on Saturday nights, and the memorable incident when he rode his horse into Foodtown and upchucked onto the cantaloupes before falling off his horse and crashing through the bakery case. When spring came and Nolan left his garage job to ride the range for Bunny Cleaver, every cop in three counties breathed a sigh of relief.

Bunny Cleaver had disputes going with every federal agency that touched his life. He let his cattle into areas on public land where his permit had been revoked because his allotment was so thrashed and cow-burnt. The precious springs on that allotment had been reduced to open sewers as time and again he put many more cows on public land than his permit allowed. He failed to pay fines. He used up water that wasn't his and issued threats when challenged. His defense of every self-serving violation of the law and public policy was masked by an ideological mix that was by his own math-challenged account, "half libertarian, half God-fearing Christian, and half cowboy common sense."

Nobody in those federal agencies would go after him because he kept a large arsenal and lived in a compound with several of his sixteen grown children and their spouses and kids. Bunny's clan held to an incoherent ideology that was a disparate collage culled from the Fox News bubble they lived in, a handful of conspiracy theories they picked up on the Internet, a literal interpretation of cherry-picked Bible passages, their own selective and peculiar interpretation of the U.S. Constitution, and old posse comitatus pamphlets that their patriarch passed to them as soon as they could read. The ranch had Waco written all over it. Bunny Cleaver was the perfect employer for Nolan Mikesel.

Like Bunny himself, Nolan believed that God had put man in charge and the world was here for our benefit. He fancied himself a "real man," in contrast to, as he put it, "those wolf-loving eco-pussies." He relished the company of other real men like Bunny Cleaver and his boys. While riding with his cowboy homies, Nolan could shuck his reputation for failure as the inevitable result of his oppression by the evil federal government. He was not a loser, he was a victim. A noble victim. A righteous martyr.

Beyond the hall of mirrors that was the Bunny Cleaver ranch, what was real about Nolan Mikesel was open to question. Even Nolan's noble pioneer genealogy didn't hold up under scrutiny. Yes, his great-great granddad was a fine man who fled debt and servitude in a mill town in New England and took a big chance on a better life. He came to the desert and made something out of nothing. His ranch was modest by today's standards but back then it was viable, sometimes prosperous. It afforded independence and opportunity that his great-great grandfather couldn't achieve in the class-bound industrial mills of his day. As far as the record shows, he never killed an Indian though no doubt his neighbors did with his approval.

That original Mikesel rancher had three sons that lived. They divided the ranch up; their parcels were hardly big enough to make a living individually so the Mikesel boys took up trades. One was remembered as a skilled carpenter and another could doctor sick cows and horses better than anyone in those parts. Nolan's great-grandfather was known for his ability to brand cows and cut off their testicles. Rocky Mountain oysters, they're called. He was a good man to help you on that aspect of ranching when it had to be done. He went by the nickname Nuts.

Nuts Mikesel had four sons. The one who was Nolan's grand-father lived through the Depression and went to war along with his Mikesel brothers. He valiantly fought the Japanese in the South Pacific. The Depression made him hungry and mean; combat hardened him. After he returned he often suffered depression and couldn't sleep. He drank too much and gambled. He lived just long enough to sire Nolan's dad and uncle before he fell off his horse and broke his neck.

Nolan's uncle got out of ranching early, earned a degree at the state college, and built a prosperous life in cities in California and Texas. Nolan's father stayed behind because he dropped out of high school and, like his own dad, he had a drinking problem. Even after he gave up the bottle he could never get his act together. He tried his hand at sales of this and that, did construction jobs when they were available, and collected unemployment over and over from a government he professed to hate. He got food stamps, too. He reconciled this conflict between his behavior and his beliefs by calling it "bleeding the beast." No, it wasn't welfare, it was revenge.

Nolan likened himself to John Wayne or Clint Eastwood and his other independent cowboy heroes. Mention welfare and he became defensive in an offensive way. Racism was always lurking in the background, ready for him to use when his dependence on the government was exposed or even suggested. According to Nole, it's those lazy black bastards and their slut mommas that are a burden on America. That and wetbacks. He knew it was a deflection that usually worked well because, apparently, it was grounded in widely shared beliefs.

Like the generation before them, Nolan had brothers and sisters who left for college and became successful in careers far away from the ranch where they were raised. As his family's lowest denominator dynamic played its last hand, Nolan became the sole heir of the Mikesel Ranch, which by then was composed of a hundred acres of dried-up pasture, two house trailers, a half-dozen dilapidated outbuildings, four abandoned trucks, and a rusty refrigerator that stood doorless next to a pile of broken bottles and squashed cans. There was a corral with one emaciated horse but no other signs of ranching activity. A large pit bull on a chain stood guard over the forlorn remains of the Mikesel legacy.

The loss of the dignity he believed he deserved made him angry. In his mind's eye he was a manly bull rider like the ones he watched on television, even though his most personal experience with cattle was more libidinous than brave. He'd spent most of seventh grade worrying that a calf would be born that looked just like him. No, he was a man, the real deal. That bitch who didn't understand him and the kid, they were what held him down. He complained that he was wronged by teachers, employers, and neighbors his whole damn life. He fumed when the guy at the unemployment office wrote "unskilled" on those papers he was filing.

But Nolan did hone a unique skill and found the means to make it pay. Nolan could kill anything. And would. He grew up hunting deer and elk out of season. Poaching taught him how to stalk and cover his tracks. He was practiced in the art of lethal stealth. He learned how to kill and get away.

A few years back, a construction supervisor who recognized Nolan's lethal potential introduced him to his boss, a real-estate developer who had a problem. A prairie dog colony was in the way of a housing development he wanted to build. Nolan took out thirty-seven dogs and pups in a single night. He used a laser beam on a rifle with a sound compressor and night scope. The little animals would be drawn to the light by curiosity and then paralyzed by the beam when it hit their eyes. Nobody in the nearby neighborhood heard a sound. After that, Nolan's reputation for "wildernessfixing," as he called it, was secure.

Another job required him to destroy an ancient kiva on land slated to become a golf course for a gated resort community. The ruin was un-listed and was discovered by a surveyor who had been paid to keep his mouth shut. Nolan used dynamite. Sometimes his job was more fun than challenging.

Nolan's bosses on such jobs paid cash. He could live well enough and never pay taxes. And his formally declared income was so low he qualified for an assistance grant for his so-called ranch. Changing tires was a cover. Riding for Bunny Cleaver was his first love. He could play cowboy with real guns and feel like a patriot to boot but extermination was his bread and butter.

The best thing about Nolan, according to those who hired him, was that he could keep his destructive adventures secret. It wasn't that hard to do since he'd run out of friends several fistfights and betrayals ago. So it was not characteristic when he stopped at the Lazy-O bar, ordered a beer, and told the bartender that he stunk because he'd spent the whole damn weekend hunting beavers.

"Aren't you supposed to trap them?" said the bartender. "I thought they were protected or something."

"Was nobody protecting them little fuckers yesterday," Nolan boasted and then laughed a little too loud. He lowered his hat closer to his eyes, chugged the rest of his beer, and muttered, "If it ain't legal to shoot them fuckin' water rats then you can take it up with the fuckin' irrigation company that fuckin' paid me. I just do whatever the fuck I get paid for."

He chugged one more for the road and walked to his truck. His cell phone was ringing. It said the caller ID was unavailable but he recognized the numbers. Orin Bender hadn't called him since that last job when some damn tortoise got in the way of a pipeline that Bender's company was laying.

He listened and his face tightened and his lips pursed. "I don't know, Mr. Bender, I don't do people. I mean I haven't done anything like that before. Animals in the way, sure, but a person?"

He stared at the ground in front of the truck tire, spit, and pushed his hat up. "How much?"

He whistled and took his hat off.

Chapter 7

Upon their release from jail, Hip Hop Hopi and Luna Waxwing retreated to a favorite campsite in Cistern Canyon to find out if they were sexually compatible. They tried every position their small tent would allow and then ventured outside for more athletic congress. They discovered that moss was a wonderful platform for lust but sand was irritating and tended to go into places that were hard to reach later on. Sandstone was definitely out as it left an abrasive rash on knees and rumps. They tried balancing in a cottonwood tree but that was too tricky and disturbed the squirrels. So, back to the tent. After two days the results were unanimous—yes, they clicked.

Hoppy had vagabonded around the West since he was expelled from a small liberal arts college in Colorado after the entire Young Republican Club was admitted to the emergency room complaining of giant wasps, women with scissors, and "invisible negroes." At a fundraising party for a candidate who opposed legalizing marijuana, Hoppy had infiltrated the group and spiked their bourbon with LSD. He and Luna had that in common: dramatic acid turning points.

After that, Hoppy made a pilgrimage to Portland, then San Francisco, Patagonia, and finally an ashram in Canada. It was in Canada that he saw what tar sands mining meant, a vast and wild landscape sacrificed for a fuel that was choking the planet. Two years later he was busing tables in a saloon in Stony Mesa and sleeping in his truck when he heard about the tar sands mine in Boon County and its ragtag band of ardent resisters. He left in the middle of his shift and didn't look back.

Hoppy had never met anyone like Luna. She amazed him. Smart, beautiful, warm, both serious and funny . . . she was the ideal woman he thought didn't really exist. He fell for everything about her: her voice, her laugh, her walk, the way her eyebrows danced along her brow when she was telling a story, even the smallest gesture like the way she brushed away that stray lock of hair that kept falling across her face.

Luna's attraction to Hoppy was harder for her to define. This wasn't a casual fling. There was no mistaking the chemistry. When he held her she swam in a pheremonal tide she could not resist. But the rest of him? He was not what she had imagined her dream mate would be and she was puzzled by her attraction to him. She questioned her feelings. Is this a revelation or an ambush?

After their second night together Hoppy had to leave because he had signed up to help transport beavers to a creek on the far side of Sleeping Maiden Mountain. Luna was supposed to be back at the office that served as a headquarters for the Sea Ledges Tar Sands Alliance, a converted shed behind the home of one of the members. She planned to consult the lawyer who had volunteered to represent them. There were press releases to write and she was asked by the others who had gone to jail to conduct a postmortem on the demonstration and get back to them. She wanted to review media coverage and the legal issues raised by their lawyer. In her head, she had already started to compose a summary to communicate to a large following on a Facebook page and the Sea Ledges blog.

She was eager to get to work but was also reluctant to leave. The bond between her and Hoppy was powerful and the project with the beavers sounded fascinating. Beavers had lived all over the southwest but were mostly trapped out decades ago. Unlike the millions of beavers that were killed across the continent for their pelts to make warm hats and coats for humans, the beaver colonies on Sleeping Maiden Mountain were removed by settlers who considered them pests. Cattlemen had dammed and drained every water source they could find on what the locals still called Sleeping Squaw Mountain several years after the official name had been changed to make it less offensive. Beavers clogged irrigation ditches and disrupted the plans of the irrigation company's engineers by building their own dams where they saw fit. Beavers, or dumb fucking rodents as they were called by irrigation maintenance workers, were messy and unpredictable so they had to go.

Years later, the Forest Service understood that the land suffered their absence and decided to reintroduce them on Sleeping Maiden Mountain where only a single remnant colony remained. Luna decided she could take care of most of the Alliance business that evening and the following morning, leaving just enough time to make the drive to the trailhead where the beavers would be carried to their new home.

It wasn't much of a trailhead. If it hadn't been for the Forest Service trucks parked on the side of the gravel road, she would have missed it. She jumped into the truck with Hoppy, who had arrived a few minutes earlier. Together they waited for the buck-toothed guests of honor to arrive in a separate truck that was specially equipped to be a safe water-rodent taxi.

"Okay," Hoppy said to Luna, "what do you know about beavers? You studied that, right?"

"Well, I studied wildlife and ecology generally and voles in particular. I never did fieldwork with beavers."

"So, tell me what you know about beavers."

She tilted her head back, arched her brows, brushed a loose lock of hair from her eyes, and smiled demurely. "Uh, that's slang for . . ."

"I meant the mammals."

She brushed herself off and straightened her posture. She was a student giving a report in front of a one-man class. "Alright, this is what I know. Beavers are like the original geo-engineers. They were once everywhere, at least a hundred million of them, across North America where they shaped the land. Then we trapped them out for pelts and they almost disappeared entirely. Now we are putting them back because the forests are dry. Burning up. The stick and mud dams that beavers build slow mountain runoff in the spring and recharge aquifers underground. Runoff water lasts longer when beavers are doing their thing. The ponds and wetlands they make eventually silt up and become rich meadows. In the meanwhile, they're habitat for fish, frogs, salamanders, and for all sorts of insects, like dragonflies. Birds are drawn to beaver-made wetlands for food. They enable water-dependent trees like willows that are food for elk. So add it all up and a landscape shaped by beaver colonies is more biologically diverse than land where they have been exterminated. A beaver-maintained watershed is healthier and more resilient, too . . . oh, and they're vegetarians."

Her performance over, she mock curtsied, grinned, and winked. Hoppy stared at her in disbelief, then laughed. He was attracted to smart women but this one was unique blend of intelligence and sass. Luna, he was discovering, was an erotic geek in gypsy rags.

"Bravo! You nailed it. You know more about this than I do. You are one smart woman, Luna Waxwing, and I am very impressed."

Luna smiled and arched her brows again. "And that's what I know about the mammal. We might save the lesson about the other kind of beaver for later."

The path up the side of the mountain was easy to follow as far as horses could go. In fact, horse dumplings littered the path. Luna was reminded of the story of Hansel and Gretel, who left bread crumbs on their path through the dark woods so they could find their way back to their home. Were horse dumplings like those bread crumbs if you were lost? She remembered when she was doing her turn at the hoods-in-the-woods program, how exciting and reassuring it was to come upon fresh horse turds because they were a sure sign she was near to some kind of civilization, even if it was the modest version offered in Boon County's little towns. Today she was eager to go in the other direction, as far away from the noise and contention of the manmade world as she could get.

They spelled each other carrying the box of beavers, two people on each side of the box. The terrain was uneven and it was hard to balance the load. Sometimes the path was so narrow that they had to squeeze sideways to avoid rock walls and tight trees. Where the trail was intersected by ravines and loose talus, it became faint. It was apparent that the route was not favored by hikers and had not been maintained. Thick moss on north-facing rocks was lush and unbroken by heel or hoof.

Off the south shore of a still pond they saw a long-abandoned beaver hut of chewed and stripped branches that looked like no more than a random catch of brambles. A closer examination showed its thin-boned architecture was bleached and dry. A ghost hut. There it is, they whispered, as if the beavers were already living there and shouldn't be alarmed.

Beavers, Hoppy and Luna realized, are not as cute up close as they are in photos. A beaver is a wet rodent that smells like its mud hut. They have big sharp teeth. You don't cuddle them, you treat them carefully with respect.

There were four beavers, youngsters both male and female. They were caged in specially designed crates to let in air but not enough light to agitate them. In the dark, they were calm. A beaver spends much of her life in a mud lodge covered with gnawed sticks and mud that is spread and patted in place with a broad, flat tail. To a beaver, darkness is familiar and comforting.

The crates were heavy and had to be carried from the Forest Service truck to a place deemed to be likely habitat by the conservation biologist assigned to the project. That's why Hoppy was along. The Forest Service relied on volunteers like him to help when extra hands and strong backs were required. The Forest Service crew was pleased that Luna was as strong or even stronger than most of the men among them. Luna tried hard not to show off.

To be sure that the beavers would build where they were placed, a small weatherproof speaker would be mounted at the base of a tree. It would play the sound of gurgling water day and night. The biologist explained that the beavers responded to the sound of water and would build where they heard it. The recording system was in a box with brackets and a hood to keep rain and snow off. There was a small solar unit to keep it charged. All of that equipment had to be ferried up the mountain on steep forest trails. By the time they arrived at their destination, they needed to sit, rehydrate, eat, stretch, and catch their collective breath.

The release itself was not dramatic. At first the beavers clung to their dark crates. The bright sunlight that hit them when the carriers were opened was startling and they were paralyzed by it. When they recovered, they left as fast as they could scramble away. They crossed a small creek and found a pool of water where they stopped and turned back. Soon they were carrying sticks to the small trickle of gurgle-enhanced water.

The trip down the mountain was quick compared to their ascent. With no heavy cargo to haul, they felt so light they practically flew down the trail. Hoppy and Luna removed their gloves and shook hands with the Forest Service staff at the trailhead. Cell numbers were exchanged. The conservation biologist who was in charge was impressed enough with their help that she offered to extend their adventure.

"There's a remnant colony up on the other side of Sleeping Maiden that I want to visit tomorrow. If you can stay another day, I'd be glad to take you with me." Mary Handy was a wildlife biologist with the Forest Service. She'd spent a lot of time arguing with her fellow rangers over the wisdom of reintroducing a species that ranchers hated. Many of her colleagues lived in town and went to church with the ranchers they regulated. Beavers were an especially tough sell in a community that regarded science as one more liberal ideology. Beavers, according to one prominent county commissioner, were an "environmentalist plot." It was affirming for Mary to have two smart young people along who understood her and embraced her mission.

Hoppy and Luna jumped at the chance to see the remnant colony farther along the mountain. Plans were made to meet the following morning. They drove away into the rose light of the evening that was spreading across the horizon. Hoppy and Luna were close to euphoric.

In their mid-twenties, they belonged to a generation that was raised with the specter of environmental catastrophe. The many ways human behavior destroys the living world were underlined constantly. Our discarded plastic fills the ocean and sea birds choke on it. Automobile exhaust warms the planet and sets off dangerous storms and droughts. The coal that fires our lights and television screens fills mountain lakes with mercury. An exploding human population eats up habitat and endangers hundreds of species—elephants, tigers, rhinos, frogs, birds, an ark's worth of unique and beautiful creatures. Hoppy and Luna grew up with the depressing awareness that almost everything they did somehow contributed to the destruction of the living world they cherished.

The upside of their ecological literacy was wonder and gratitude, the restoration of awe grounded in knowledge. The downside was that they saw nature's wounds and understood their own complicity. The simple question asked by grocery checkers, "paper or plastic?" translated to them as, "kill a tree or choke a seal?"

So the afternoon with the beavers was different. For once they were on the right side of life, contributing instead of taking away. The hard work hauling the crates with their wild contents was cleansing, redeeming in a way they had never felt before. It was validating and humbling at once, both visceral and cerebral, even spiritual.

The next day was unseasonably cold and wet, not rain so much as a fine and steady drizzle. The hike to the remnant colony was slick with mud. They grabbed ahold of shrubs to pull themselves up the steep slopes, then scrambled over ledges of loose rocks. Hoppy stopped twice to catch his breath. They were close to nine thousand feet elevation and the air felt light and non-nourishing as he sucked it into his aching lungs. As they got closer to the colony, the land grew moist and verdant. They saw abundant birds and critters flitting through the undergrowth. The beavers on Doe Creek under the south escarpment of Sleeping Maiden Mountain had only survived because they were so far up above the drainage that people with traps and guns couldn't reach them easily. The colony was impossible to reach by horseback and all-terrain vehicles were not allowed.

Luna slipped, hitting her knee on a rock. It bled but wasn't serious. Hoppy twisted his ankle on an exposed root. It was also not a serious injury, but he was followed up and down the mountain by a nagging pain.

They would later conclude it was one of the hardest days of their young lives, not so much because of the demanding hike to the remnant colony and the lousy weather but because of what they found there.

Chapter 8

Elias Buchman and Otis agreed to meet at the Desert Rose for coffee. Otis was nervous and was on his second cup before Elias got there. He had never been in trouble aside from a few drunken encounters with things that were not there, like the time he braked for a phantom cow, spilled beer all over himself, and was rear-ended by Dunk Taylor's patrol car. But those were the exceptions. He was once an eagle scout, a lifeguard, and he broke onto Stony Mesa's political scene as the chief of the volunteer fire department. Heck, he didn't even read mystery novels and preferred PBS science shows to the popular crime dramas. Being accused of a murder he did not commit was like landing in a foreign country where he didn't speak the language and didn't know the terrain.

Buchman carried a manila file folder under his arm when he arrived at the café. Otis focused on it and prayed that his salvation lay within.

"So, what did you find out?"

"Sorry, Otis, but not much that will help you out of the jam you're in. Bo didn't have any real enemies. He wasn't particularly liked but I couldn't find anyone who would want to murder him."

"What's in the folder? You must've learned something."

"I did." He pushed the cream and sugar jars away and laid the documents in the folder across the table. Out of habit, he subtly peered over each shoulder and scanned the café for suspicious-looking people who might be spying but only found the usual mix of hungry tourists in walking shoes and ranchers with dirt on their boots. One boomer-aged couple in floppy hats and sunglasses wandered by in that semi-zombie state of tourists that sometimes follows serial over-gawking. A cowboy in the corner watched them with a bemused smirk hiding behind an unkempt handlebar mustache. Elias continued.

"For one thing, did you know that the name Bo is from Boris? His grandfather . . ."

"Cut to the chase, Elias, gimme the dirt. Someone out there had it in for him. Who?"

"Bo's business lobbies and does consulting work on various management problems for various financial outfits—high rollers mostly, from back east."

"Yeah, I know that. I looked him up, too. He's written a bunch of corporate management guides that are used for training. How to lobby, how to negotiate and all that stuff."

Elias thumbed through the pile of papers in front of him and pulled one page out and passed it to Otis. "That's right. Here is what is not apparent. The real money is made by one division of his business that he never publicized. You might say he did his best to hide it. That operation is hired by corporations when they downsize or close an unprofitable business. Firing a bunch of people at once is risky and hard to do. There's always the chance for hysteria, confrontations, or even sabotage. So the termination management consultants—that's what they call themselves—go into a workplace or office and take care of the dirty work. The people who are being laid off are notified at their workstations individually by these hired guns. Their keys and computers are confiscated and they are escorted to a room where counselors stand by. Papers are presented that explain why they are losing their jobs, the terms of their being let go, resources that will be made available to them to deal with the crisis . . . they have all these brochures with titles like 'Job transition as an opportunity for growth.' If anyone freaks or becomes violent, these termination consultants are trained to deal with that. When the building is cleared, they change the locks and then secure all the computer files. Bo Hineyman found a way to profit from misery. After the financial meltdown in 2008 he couldn't keep up with all the business that came his way."

Otis was hopeful. "Well, if that's the case, Bo Hineyman had lots of enemies, lots of serious enemies, I'd guess."

"Not really. Bo never appeared at those places. He sat in his office in Washington and went to lunch with lobbyists and other venal cretins. The people who were fired never even saw his name."

Otis's face drooped. "What about his family? Maybe he has a crazy nephew, or a sibling or ex-wife who's jealous. Something!"

"If that's the case, I failed to find anyone. I'm sorry, Otis, but it's not looking good. If I had access to his personal communication I might pick up on something but I don't have that kind of power. But I did talk to one of Dunk Taylor's deputies. The guy has a business on the side installing rain gutters and was over at my place two days ago. He's not supposed to say anything but I buddied him up and after a second bottle of beer he became talkative. He said they went in and scoured Bo's place and didn't find a single incriminating fingerprint, a hair, a piece of fabric, footprint, nothing."

"No shit, they won't find my prints in there. I've never been in that log mansion he calls a cabin. Never."

"They don't have a case against you, Otis. It's all very circumstantial. We just have to sit tight and hope that something else shows up."

The two men stared at the table, not knowing what to do next. Buchman gathered his research and put it into the folder. "If I find anything else, I'll let you know."

"Thanks, Elias. I appreciate your effort on this. It feels good to just have someone on my side."

"Grace made a casserole for you. She's concerned about your health. She wants you to come over and get a massage, too. You gotta keep yourself well, Otis, despite the stress. Walk me out to the car and I'll give you that casserole."

Otis smiled. "Grace. What would we do without Grace?"

Chapter 9

Crazy Kitty heard about it at the post office. Bo Hineyman was murdered and Mayor Otis Dooley was the prime suspect. She knew it! Hadn't she told everyone that Mayor Dooley worshipped Satan? Hadn't she warned them? "What do you think he's doing under your houses all day? Plumbing, right? Well, you can go on believing that but I know better. He drinks three six-packs a day. Get it, 666? And he takes pictures of birds with that huge lens he lugs around. Hangs out with those radicals who turned the Wheeler place into a bird sanctuary. You can find all about their kind on the Internet. No-people zones, that's what they're after. One of these days the buses will come—black ones—and then you'll find out too late. They're building secret prison camps in the mountains. Underground with UN guards at the gate, Kenyans and Muslims mostly."

Kitty frowned and squinted as she muttered to herself. It was a loud simmering mutter that could easily escalate to a full-boil rant. Those waiting in line at the post office counter pretended they didn't hear her and hoped she wouldn't become even more agitated. The Stony Mesa post office was small enough without Kitty in it.

"Once they take all the guns away from us we don't stand a chance! That's why I keep mine in this big purse. People think I'm just carrying around my precious little pug, Hoover, but there's a loaded 45 in there, too. One of those Satan lovers like Dooley tries any of that hocus-pocus bird stuff on me he better watch out!"

Right on cue, Hoover the pug barked twice and concluded his cameo with a low growl. Like his mistress, he would snap at you if you ventured too close. Perhaps riding in a bag with a loaded gun made him a tad nervous.

Elias Buchman tried to avoid Kitty, especially on days when some current event or imagined slight set off a mumbling rant, but this morning there was no avoiding her. He needed stamps and was waiting for a package to be weighed when she cornered him in the glorified closet that served as the Stony Mesa post office. As he walked out, she walked in and blocked his path. Known for her creative attire, Kitty was wearing a man's suit jacket, a ruffled blouse, and a bow tie. A stained pair of gray sweat pants and red sneakers completed her ensemble.

"Excuse me, Kitty," he said as politely as he could, "but I have to get going."

"Oh sure," she responded, "you're one of those."

"One of those what?"

She shook her head, smiled smugly and cast a disdainful look directly at his eyes. "Liberals!"

Elias had a theory. Pollution was a kind of information. Smog, acid rain, toxins in drinking water, pesticides on fruit, all spoke volumes about the way we regard life, the way we grow food and make things, our priorities, our mistakes, who has power and who is powerless. In an age of digital information overload where we are saturated with multiple stimulations, distractions, and feedback during all of our waking hours, noise had become the new pollution and paranoia was the new cancer.

"Turn off the Rush Limbaugh, Kitty, you'll feel better."

Elias was there to mail a jar of jam that Grace had made from plums she grew in their backyard. It was a birthday present for their daughter, who lived in Europe. It cost a fortune to send jam across the sea by mail but you couldn't put a price on Grace's jam.

Sheriff Dunk Taylor pulled up in his patrol car just as Elias escaped from Kitty through the post office door. He rolled down his window and leaned out.

"Elias, I hear you're looking into the Hineyman thing. Is that so?"

"Otis is an old friend, Sheriff, and I'd like to help him. I can't believe he did it."

Although Dunk Taylor was a friendly neighbor, Elias had learned that most cops appreciated a respectful tone. The disrespect they got from car thieves, shoplifters, truants, assorted punks, wife-beaters, drunk drivers and their lawyers took its toll. Most cops imagined themselves as their favorite television characters and were deflated when they ended up writing speeding tickets to pregnant soccer moms.

So Elias massaged Dunk's battered self-image by calling him "Sheriff" often.

"I'd appreciate it if you share anything you learn. My guys are all tied up with that bass tournament at Jumpcut Reservoir this weekend and then the Boy Scout bike-a-thon comes through here on Wednesday. I'm so busy filling in gaps I don't have time to do some background work on this Hineyman business."

Good grief, thought Elias, that name is a problem. Doesn't go well with anything.

"Sure, Sheriff. Is Otis still your only suspect?"

"Unless you convince me otherwise."

"Just what I need," muttered Elias to himself, "more pressure." He remembered well how it used to be when he was working a story. Lots of dead ends and frustration, always deadlines looming. But if you keep following leads and stay on it, eventually there's a break. A door opens.

Kitty came out the post office door and was onto both of them. "And what are you two up to all secret like, huh?"

Dunk waved goodbye and pulled out with tires spewing gravel. Elias turned toward Kitty, raised both hands in a gesture of surrender, and walked backwards away from her and toward his car.

"Have a nice day, Kitty."

As he slid into his car and looked back at her he wondered if she hid a tinfoil hat in that handbag with the ugly dog and the handsome gun.

Chapter 10

Luna and Hoppy returned to their campsite distraught and exhausted. Neither felt like eating or talking so they crawled into their sleeping bags and tried to sleep. Luna couldn't get the images of carnage out of her mind, the torn fur and knots of clotted blood in the grass. She remembered the sodden bodies of two beavers floating in the pond and the others strewn in gun-blasted pieces along the bank. An hour after she lay down, the dam holding back her rage and grief burst and she turned to Hoppy and sobbed uncontrollably. He could find no words to comfort her, so he just held her until she fell into a fitful sleep.

She awoke and he was gone. She pulled her warmest fleece on and called to him. Nothing. His truck was gone. She made a pot of coffee and cooked oatmeal from a packet over an open fire. She thought she should tell others about the slaughtered beaver colony on Sleeping Maiden Mountain but she was at a loss for words.

All morning she waited for him to reappear. She questioned how he left in his truck without waking her. She was not so worried about his absence as mystified. She came up with a half dozen plausible reasons; all of them had benign outcomes. She focused on the best ones.

A day of nagging worry passed. That evening she needed to be back at the Tar Sands headquarters but couldn't leave while Hoppy was still missing. She walked around the campsite and tried to get a signal on her phone but it was no use. She could receive text messages intermittently but could not send. She cooked some lentil soup for dinner and waited. She watched rock walls light up as they caught the last rays of the setting sun. Their rosy glow contrasted with the dark pools of shadow spreading under the cottonwoods below. I am like that, she thought. I am lit up but standing on the edge of darkness.

Just after seven o'clock she received so many urgent text messages that her phone chimed continually. She couldn't keep up. Tar Sands Alliance members who had caught the evening news learned that Drexxel was reporting sabotage at their Sea Ledges site. Sand had been poured into the gas tanks of heavy equipment and the bulldozer that was so threatening just days before had been driven over a cliff.

The security guard at the site was interviewed and claimed that the man who did all the damage was wearing a hard hat with a Drexxel logo and claimed he was doing maintenance on the machines. The guard failed to mention that he spent the day playing Angry Birds on his phone, talking to his girlfriend, and downloading porn. He didn't hear the low rumble of the dozer or the crunch of gravel beneath its treads because he was wearing ear buds and listening to a sad country tune about the loss of love and the subsequent over-consumption of alcohol mixed with self-pity. He didn't look up until he heard the crash of the bulldozer as it rolled down the ridge. While he ran over to see what was happening, the mysterious worker in the hard hat set fire to the main house-trailer and then disappeared.

Luna's friends related these events frantically and waited for her to text back and make sense of it for them but she was too dumbstruck to reply even if she had been able to do so. Luna's stomach knew before she did—Hip Hop Hopi was the saboteur. Damn him! She tried again and again to get a message out but although she could receive she still could not send at all. She considered climbing the ridge above her campsite and hoping for a better signal at the top but she was too shaken to risk climbing over broken terrain with bone-breaking exposures. She was in for another sleepless night as the twin shocks of the past two days mixed into a bitter stew of grief and fear. She lit a lantern after sunset and meditated, prayed, and cried some more. She wanted to run out and find him but wasn't sure where to start. She wasn't sure what to think, what to feel, what to do. The first rule when you are lost is "stay put." So she stayed and waited.

The world was present while she waited. Birds flew homeward at dusk. Bat wings in moonlight swept the air and crickets chanted. She listened to the rasping branches and the shuffling of dry leaves caught in a whorl of wind crossing the canyon floor. The night was all snap and buzz, whispers, and the music of mad croaking. She tried to will into existence the sound of him approaching. Nothing.

As darkness fell she drifted into sleep for just a moment. She dreamed about a goshawk with brilliant eyes and a terrible beak. It was beautiful and she wanted to touch it but was afraid. She awoke to Hoppy standing there above her, backlit by the firelight with an incongruous halo of dim stars adorning his unkempt hair. When Hoppy was missing she calmed herself by breathing slowly and picturing anything but dead beavers, strip mines, and monkey-wrenched machinery. She found his sudden presence jarring.

"Where did you go?" she asked. "And how come you didn't wake me?"

"I didn't want you involved. This was my deal." He looked down and away. He could tell she knew where he had gone and what he had done and he knew she did not approve. He had risked everything, including a promising relationship with her. On the way back to the campsite he had second-guessed his actions. He reviewed what happened at the mining site and worried that he had left incriminating evidence. One small mistake could lead not only to whatever punishment they could impose on him but could also mean separation from Luna. That consequence frightened him the most. Now that he was standing in her presence he was steeped in regret.

Luna pulled herself from her sleeping bag and stood up. "Are you crazy?" she scolded. "Do you understand what you just did? We were so careful to keep it all by the book. Civil disobedience means you accept responsibility, you make a principled stand, and you do it publicly. Destroying their equipment also destroys our credibility and makes us the bad guys instead of them!"

"Sorry, Luna, but seeing those dead beavers . . . I just can't take it anymore. The people who are wrecking the planet write the rules. They own the system. They get away with murder and they have to be stopped. Resisting isn't enough anymore, it's time to stop them in their tracks. Now!"

"Oh so you're stopping them, huh? You alone, Hip Hop Hopi the superhero to the rescue! Well now you're a fugitive and I'm probably a fugitive, too. We're screwed, Hoppy, screwed!"

Minutes passed as they stared silently at the coals from Luna's campfire, winking in the dark. Finally, he reached over and took her hand. She tried to pull away but he held on. "I'm sorry. I should have told you. I knew you'd talk me out of it so I didn't. If I'm caught I will take the blame and if I have to I'll go to jail, whatever. You don't have to worry. I'll keep you and everyone else out of it. It's all on me. Okay?"

Why, she asked herself, am I so deeply attracted to a man who is so flawed? A voice in her mind said "move on." But he was so good and so right in so many other ways. There was something about him that seemed fundamental and necessary like the desire for salt or the need for air. And here I am, she thought, for better or worse in the middle of a very big mess with him on my hands. What else can I do?

She replied softly, "We'll figure it out. No more crazy stuff, though, or I'm outta here. Understand?"

"Yes, I swear."

The words were barely out when the campfire exploded. They jumped, she screamed. Embers rained down through a mist of ash as the exploded campfire settled to earth.

"What was that!"

Then the lantern hung just above their heads exploded. A moment later they heard the report of a distant rifle.

"Holy shit! Somebody's shooting at us!"

Their first instinct was to drop everything and run. They headed for her truck and jumped in. She turned to him and asked what they should do next, where they should go. He said he didn't know. That's when the rearview mirror exploded.

"Drive! Get outta here!"

The backroads were dark and twisted. Luna drove as fast as she could without losing control on sharp turns. They knew that hidden in darkness just off the side of the road were unforgiving shoulders of loose gravel above steep ravines. There were no guardrails or street lamps to guide their way. Hoppy watched out the back window for signs of a vehicle following. They drove desperately for several miles and when there was no sign that they were being followed Luna slowed the truck to a safe speed. An hour later they were thirty miles from their campsite and in the safety of a well-lit town.

"Where are we?" he asked as he opened the glove box and looked for a map. They left their smartphones behind when they fled.

"It's a back road to Stony Mesa. I've been here before. Jeez, look at that ball of light on the horizon. What the heck is that?"

"That must be that giant neon monstrosity in front of the new saloon in town."

They drove closer and saw an enormous pulsing neon sign in front of a saloon that was also too big for such a pastoral setting. It hurt their eyes to look straight ahead at the neon giant so they pulled across the street into a motel parking lot and reviewed their options. There weren't any good ones. They could go to the police and Hoppy could turn himself in. But Hoppy wasn't ready for that. He was willing to confess and express remorse to Luna but surrendering to cops was a bridge too far. And who was shooting at them? Maybe that was the cops. They had friends who would take them in but neither of them wanted to endanger their friends. To make it more difficult, they had no money or gear. Their backpacks were in the campsite they had fled. Hoppy's truck was back there. No phones, no Internet. They had the clothes on their backs. Her truck. Loose change. Not much.

They hashed and rehashed the bad news and then fell silent. Two long minutes passed. The interior of the truck was washed with pulsing lights from the sign across the street. Luna tried to slow her heart with long deep breaths. Her fingers clutched the steering wheel tightly. Above them moths batted a street light and flew in dizzying circles. She watched a family unload suitcases from a van and unstrap a toddler from her car seat. The family disappeared into the motel lobby.

"There may be one more option," Luna confessed.

"What's that?"

"My father, the one I don't have anything to do with, has a ranch near here. I visited it once a few years ago on one of my occasional attempts to reconnect. I know where the keys are to the guest cabin. We could stay there tonight. If I can figure out how to get into the main cabin we can find food and probably some cash stashed somewhere."

Hoppy was incredulous. "Why didn't you tell me that?"

"Why bother? Seemed irrelevant until tonight."

"And your father, will he be there?"

"No. I doubt it. He's probably off making money, selling what's left of his soul."

He was there when they pulled in. He saw their headlights from a distance and walked out on the deck to see who was coming down his private road into the ranch. Twin beams of light fluttered through the cottonwoods that lined the long drive. When the truck rounded the corner and drove straight toward him he was blinded by the headlights. He didn't recognize the truck. A man and a woman stepped out of the truck cab and he saw her under the dim yard light. It would be hard to decide who was more surprised, Luna or her dad, Bo Hineyman.

Luna managed a weak smile and small wave. "Hi Dad. Surprise!" Hoppy tried to smile, too, but he looked more like he'd just smelled a wet dog.

"Betty, is that you?"

"She calls herself Luna now." Hoppy was trying to be helpful but Bo stared at him like he had just discovered Hoppy had one eye in the middle of his forehead.

Bo ushered them inside. Hoppy entered and looked around. This so-called cabin was nicer than the home he grew up in. Navajo rugs on the walls, track lighting throughout. It looked like a professional decorating job. Who shot all these animals whose eyes stared down at them blankly from disembodied heads along the wall? The coffee table looked like a river of plastic trout.

The ensuing visit was awkward. Luna tapped her toe nervously on the floor and Hoppy was jumpy. She made up a story about how they were robbed while camping. Why not go to the police, he asked? Because the guy who robbed us was an off-duty cop, she lied. We didn't know what to do and you were nearby. She hoped she might awake some long-dormant parental instinct in him.

They were hungry so he fed them. Bo didn't do much cooking himself but his fridge was full of food he had taken home from the Bull and Stallion. He had just pulled out a big juicy bison steak as they pulled up to the house. He divided it in three and served that. A halting conversation followed. He told them he was alone because wife number four, or was it five, was attending a doggy jewelry show in Miami with her favorite poodle, Miss Desiree. She rarely visited the ranch anyway because she was allergic to sagebrush, juniper, snakeweed, pinyon, rabbit brush, and prickly pear cactus, which was pretty much the whole damn ranch. They did tests, he said. Bo did not mention that on his wife's last visit to the ranch Miss Desiree, who despite her rhinestone collar and weekly trips to a grooming salon, was a dog, ate a horse turd she found. She puked it out on the front seat of his wife's Mercedes. It was hard for Luna and Hoppy to feign interest or sympathy since they had their own challenges at the moment.

Hoppy told Bo he was a freelance photographer for National Geographic. Luna could barely conceal her astonishment but when it was her turn she swallowed hard and said she was waiting to hear from graduate schools, a lie she thought was at least close to the truth since she had considered that option. She decided this was not the optimum time to discuss controversial life choices and grad school was probably an acceptable and plausible direction compared to chaining herself to mining site gates. Uh oh, Bo thought, more tuition.

Bo wasn't happy about his daughter's situation. She has nothing to do with him for years at a time and then she shows up dirty, broke, and with some hippy loser at her side. They look like they slept too close to their campfire, their hair coated with ash. They look addled, he thought, as well as disheveled and he wondered if she was back on drugs. Damn, he didn't need another hefty bill for rehab. What was it with all the women in his life that made them swallow pills? But I'm her dad, he concluded, so I have to help. He gave them fresh towels and the key to the guest house. When they left him he turned back to clear the dishes.

Hoppy's plate was clean but Luna barely touched her bison steak. Probably doesn't approve, he guessed. And because he was a man with a big appetite, he picked up Luna's steak and ripped off a large chunk and stuffed it in his mouth. He felt juice running down his chin and he turned to pick up a dish towel and catch the drip before it stained his two-hundred-dollar western shirt. That was when he looked up and saw the man with the gun.

Chapter 11

The headquarters of the Sea Ledges Tar Sands Alliance was in chaos. Reporters called every other minute and nothing they were told satisfied them. The resisters who were bailed out of jail just days before coalesced back at the Sea Ledges hub. The storage shed where they had planned their civil disobedience was easily swamped by the influx of members, allies, and reporters wanting answers in the aftermath of the attack on the mining site. A member of the Alliance, an elderly woman named Brenda, stepped up and offered an empty apartment she owned in a duplex near the bus station and the crowd migrated there.

Brenda Savitt was the widow of a downwinder, the name given to those hapless misinformed citizens who lived too near to an atomic test site, or the betrayed soldiers and sailors who were guinea pigs at the advent of the nuclear age, or the naïve uranium miners and weapons makers who were unwittingly exposed, or . . . well, it was eventually clear that most Americans were downwind in that era but some more so than others. Brenda was a child then. She remembered playing in a storm of hot ash after one atomic bomb test. Nobody told her that leaping and twirling through the whirlwind was dangerous. Her future husband, Dwayne, was a boy herding sheep with his dad. They saw the mushroom cloud way in the distance and felt a blast of hot wind minutes later. He remembered how the sheep lost their wool in patches and a lamb that was born later that year had two heads and its heart outside its chest.

Like so many others caught downwind, cancer followed. During her husband's long-suffering years of cancer and a grim menu of other chronic illnesses, he was transformed from the Marlboro Man, that iconic cowboy with a cigarette, into a frail and helpless wreck breathing through tubes and eating whatever they put into his arm. Brenda Savitt's assumptions about how the world worked and who is right and who is wrong underwent a slow tectonic shift. She learned the hard way that humans embody their environments. Blood, bone, teeth, brain, skin, thyroid, lung, ovaries, testicles, pancreas, stomach, liver, and kidneys translate the physical realm into the health and daily experiences of the body's sole occupant, who is not shielded from reckless and unchecked behavior. Brenda had a visceral understanding of what she called ecological citizenship.

The scene at the new apartment headquarters could have been mistaken for a nail-chewing convention. The Alliance's designated and most effective spokesperson was missing. Worse, she was missing with that new guy, Happy Hippie or whatever he calls himself, who was the one person most of them thought was capable of sabotage. What does she see in him? they asked each other. Sure he was handsome and buff and, yes, he could be very funny but he had this reckless and dangerous air about him. Most of the Sea Ledges protestors had thought long and hard about their commitment to keep tar sands in the ground. They had read and researched, debated and discussed their way to that bold act of disobedience. They had the feeling that Hoppy took a shorter route. As Luna herself described him, "He is more animal than academic. We need both kinds."

If only Luna were here. Where was she? They milled around the room and bumped into one another as they stared down at phone screens and tablets, their thumbs twitching frantically, brows bent downward, lips pursed. She was simply out of range and unable to communicate, they reassured each other, but why? One scenario was an accident while hiking. She was last seen with that reckless Hoppy. Maybe they fell and needed help. Or maybe that old truck of hers broke down. And everyone wondered, though nobody would say it aloud, maybe she is with him and they did it.

"No, we didn't do it. No, we don't know who did it." They said it over and over but nobody believed them. The press was relentless. The Sea Ledges protest generated some media attention but they struggled to get noticed. The sabotage of the mining site, however, set off a feeding frenzy they couldn't tame.

The Alliance's pro-bono lawyer was distraught. Tony Baciagalupe had volunteered to represent the members who chose civil disobedience but sabotage was more than he signed up for. He sat on the arm of a blue velvet sofa and addressed those who gathered to hear how this might affect their own cases.

"Look," he said, "I'm two years out of law school and I need clients. Do you know how hard it is to get clients in this county with my last name? If I get associated with that kind of vandalism I'm going to be one lonely lawyer. I got a wife, a baby on the way, and a hundred grand in tuition debt. I don't do sabotage for free and you don't have any money."

They had a court hearing in less than two weeks and if Tony abandoned them they would be at the mercy of the prosecutor who looked at them during the arraignment like a lion regards fresh meat. Tony was right, the group could barely muster the change for the banner they held at the protest. A paid lawyer was out of the question.

If Tony was distraught, the Boon County prosecuting attorney was ecstatic. Lawton Hatch could barely suppress his glee at the news of the monkeywrenching at the Drexxel strip mine. It would be easy enough to fix the blame on the ones already arrested at the demonstration and call it good. The publicity in the case could establish his career.

He'd had a setback a year ago when some dumb-ass gearheads got drunk and carved the outline of a large penis on an ancient Indian petroglyph panel. Unfortunately, one of the four-wheeling idiots was Lawton's cousin. They were spotted doing the deed by a forest service ranger who was eye-glassing three teenage girls skinny-dipping in a hot spring just a hundred yards away from the vandalized panel. When the girls dressed, the ranger walked back to his truck and called for backup. Three hours later when the motor-heads passed out while cooking bratwursts over a campfire, rangers moved in and surrounded them. One of the boys had fallen asleep with his right foot too close to the campfire and his boot had caught on fire. He was driven to the local clinic and treated for third-degree burns.

Lawton Hatch let those vandals plea bargain and they got off with light fines and community service. Several of the recent move-ins from the Stony Mesa retirement community objected and wrote scathing letters in the local paper, even papered the state capitol with complaints. They accused Lawton of giving the defendants preferable treatment because one of them was his cousin. He replied that half the county was related one way or the other and that was just the way it is in Boon County. He reminded his critics that he'd been tough on a niece cranked up on meth who was caught stealing packages off porch steps over the holidays, but the damage to his reputation was already done. He reasoned that a big win over that bunch of tree-hugging weirdos could erase the damage. Your average voter, he thought, had the attention span of a gerbil and the memory of a melon.

Maybe he could launch a political career right after he sent them all away to prison. He imagined bumper stickers: Lawton Hatch is tough on crime. He wondered if maybe he could run for the state legislature. If you were careful, you could make a lot of money as a state legislator. People would come to you for favors and do favors in return. That's how it went: pay for play. Everybody knows that. He'd always wanted a sleek sports car—a babe magnet, though he was married and had six kids under the age of eight. He closed his eyes and could almost smell the leather upholstery and a slim whiff of perfume.

Lucas Hozho, a Navajo kid who had been arrested at the protest, knew they were all in deep trouble. Nobody else stepped forward to substitute for Luna as spokesperson so Lucas volunteered. He was calm, and the others decided that they should not appear strident. His face was almost cherubic. Lucas had watched a lot of TV while growing up on a remote part of the reservation. They owned a satellite dish and he and his siblings were transfixed by a faraway world that did not resemble their own. There were cars instead of sheep, skyscrapers instead of adobe huts, noise instead of silence, and very little hint of a sky anywhere on the TV shows. Outside their humble hogan, the sky was everywhere. "Where is the moon?" Lucas's baby sister once asked while staring at the flickering screen. "They hide it behind bright lights and pollution," Lucas told her. His answer baffled her and she was sorry for the moon that it gave its beautiful light to people who were so rude and thankless.

Lucas studied white people on TV. He knew that car and furniture salesmen in the ads he saw raised their eyebrows as high as they could to look open and innocent. That might also make their credibility suspect since most people understood that's how they lie. But if you furrowed your brow downward you came across as too serious, even scary. There was a middle way for white people's eyebrows that conveyed non-threatening credibility and as he faced the local TV reporters and their cameras, he would try to find that sweet spot. "Don't worry," Brenda Savitt reassured him. "You look like you are incapable of telling a lie. You'll do well, trust yourself."

The Alliance was a difficult group to coordinate under ideal circumstances and this was far from that. Many of the members were anarchic by nature. And bright white people, Lucas knew, often held several opinions at once and were prone to explain them all in great detail. It took someone of Luna's charisma to corral them. They needed a plan. If only they knew if she was on her way. Lucas reassured their nervous lawyer and sounded an upbeat note.

"Hang in there, Tony. I know Luna like a sister. She would never abandon us. I am sure there's an explanation and she is on her way here right now."

But she wasn't on her way there. She was too busy running for her life.

Chapter 12

Nolan never missed. Until that night. "I can't believe I fuckin' missed!" he muttered over and over.

Stalking her in the dark solved a big problem: how to kill her without also killing that curly-haired boyfriend of hers. This job wouldn't allow a witness. When he saw them sitting together by the campfire, perfectly lit and visible, he couldn't believe his luck. It would be easy to shoot her alone and flee under cover of darkness. The hippie boyfriend wouldn't chase him or see him. He'd be too busy wondering if he was next and trying to do first aid on her. But then he missed, not once but three times.

"Damn, I can't believe I fuckin' missed!"

They ran to their truck and he followed. He gave them just enough distance to feel secure, to think they had lost him, but he was not far behind. He tracked lots of prey over the years and knew how far back to stay, when to move without being noticed. Deer, elk, humans— all animals, after all. Maybe those eco-pussies were right, he thought. Didn't they claim that humans were just another animal, nothing special, no more worthy than a snail or frog? It amused him that he would prove them right in a way they never dreamed could happen.

The fugitives reached town and he pulled into the parking lot on the far side of the road. He slid down in his seat just enough to hide while keeping them in his view. He departed right after they did though he didn't know where they were going. Follow, he told himself. Be patient. Wait until the right moment. That's how it's done. But when they got to the ranch in Stony Mesa he had to cut his lights and pull over. The rest of the hunt would have to be on foot. Fine with him, he felt right at home.

He took his time approaching the lit window and the door framed in lamplight. They think they are safe, he figured. They're not going anywhere right away. I could wait until they're asleep. But nevertheless he was anxious. Killing turtles and beavers was to Nolan's mind just cheating. But killing a human, that was the real deal. He wanted to get it over and get away. Do it!

The lights were on in the main cabin and he heard voices. The two of them talking he guessed. He tiptoed closer. They sounded nervous. He heard the click of knives and forks on plates. A large cat was suddenly at his side, rubbed his leg, and let out a plaintive yowl for food or affection, whatever a cat expects to get from a stranger who hates cats.

Nolan had done awful things to cats as an adolescent. He taped a fire-cracker to one and used strays near the town dump for target practice when he was learning how to shoot with a bow and arrow. The beatings he suffered at the hands of his drunken father dug a hellhole of anger in him that he tried to fill with hateful acts against creatures even more helpless than himself. Seconds after she yowled, Skeeter the ranch cat was quiet, her neck broken. Nolan set her soft body down on the ground and retreated into the shadow of a propane tank next to the cabin.

He heard them come outside and then a door shut. He crouched behind the propane tank and waited for them to pass by on their way to their truck. He shoved the dead cat out of sight with his boot. He waited. Nothing appeared. A door slammed again and he stood to look. The lights to the main cabin were still on. He saw a shadow flicker against the lit window. They went back in there, he told himself, and now is the time to get it over with. He had resigned himself to taking them both down. The hippie boy was in the way. Sorry, pal, bad timing for you.

Their truck was the only one parked by the door. Bo's vehicles were in a garage beyond the cabin and since Nolan had never set foot there before that evening he was unaware the ranch might have other occupants. In fact, he figured the ranch belonged to the young couple. Rich little bastards, probably trust-funders. The notion fueled his rage.

He darted through the crescent of the porch light and slipped quietly to the door. One. Two. Three! But instead of finding his prey on the other side of the door, there was a pear-shaped man, bulging mouth full of something, holding a small stack of dirty dishes. Nolan noticed the expensive western shirt and turquoise bolo tie. Nice boots. Who the fuck is this guy?

Nolan had parsed the moral dilemma earlier. He agreed to kill the pretty slut, the leader of the eco-freaks. Yeah, he knew killing is wrong but people do it all the time and it's okay. He saw that movie about the sniper and what a hero he was. Lots of guys came home after killing hundreds of people in the oil wars over there in raghead land and they were decorated. What about those guys that sit somewhere in a military base in Nevada and watch a screen from a camera mounted on a drone that's armed with missiles? They push a button and blow up the bad guys along with a whole wedding party, families, kids, whatever and nobody condemns them for what they do. As pretty as she is, the eco-freak queen is a kind of terrorist, too, right? And the world will be better off without that slut and her pussy boyfriend in it. Yeah, I'm the hero here but as usual nobody gets it. I'm the real victim. Fuck.

Nolan was up on the news, mostly from Fox Radio. He knew there was a war at home, too. Like Bunny Cleaver said, it's the decent folks like us, the real Americans and patriots, against the niggers, queers, Mexicans, hippies, feminists, and feds. Liberals, too. Tree-huggers and the U.N. The Government. So the eco-queen of the eco-pussies is the enemy and her boyfriend is collateral damage like the people riding behind the Muslim terrorist who are hit with a missile not intended for them. And now this fat dork looking like Nashville on a Saturday night is just more collateral damage.

For all his killing, Nolan had never killed a human and he wondered how it was going to feel. He had wondered for many years, actually. It started out as curiosity but had lately become something more. Something like the taste you get before the food actually reaches your mouth, a kind of static when hunger approaches satisfaction. The animals he killed, especially the elk and deer, struggled to die, even the head-shot ones. It could take minutes for a body to shut down. The last gasp, the last gas, the quivering of a nervous system cut loose from blood and brain. How long, he wondered, would it take a human before the tremors cease and the final rasp of air is heard?

And the most important question of all: could he do it, pull the trigger, slip the knife? Under all his testosterone-fueled bravado, doubt lingered.

Bo Hineyman's demise was a complete surprise. Who would think it was that easy? You look at your victim and he stares back, his eyes bulge, he turns red and then thrashes across the room like a drunken acrobat. He grows purple as he goes. One last chubby pirouette and he crashes onto his back in the middle of a fancy coffee table filled with fake fish. A couple of gurgles and he was gone. Just like that. All Nolan had to do was watch the show and duck flying glass.

Could I really do that? Kill with a look? Like a fuckin' superhero? Too crazy, man. No time to think about it. Where are those two kids?

A search of the house turned up nothing. He picked up a blue and red vase in the hallway and wondered what it looked like in pieces. He smashed it against the tile floor. The tiles were from Mexico. Bo saw them on a trip to Cancun and had them shipped. Nolan thought the art he saw throughout the house might be valuable and considered taking something small like a sculpted ballerina standing on a bookshelf or a colorful glass ball on an end table, but where would he sell it? There wasn't a market for rich peoples' doodads in his neck of the woods. Redneck neck of the woods, he thought and it made him angry. We scrape by and they have so much they can fill their homes with art from the foreign trips they can also afford. Artsy-fartsy bling is for the rich. My yacht is a rowboat I haul to the reservoir and all I ever brung back was a fuckin' hangover.

It felt good smashing things and it was also the perfect cover for the dead bozo in the fake-fish pond. Make it look like a robbery. He pulled open drawers and dumped them, cleared an entire bookshelf with one swipe. "Where is it!" he cried aloud and then laughed at his own joke.

Breathless and spent, surrounded by debris, he stepped outside and looked toward the guest house. He saw them. They were running into the dark. He checked his gun and followed.

Chapter 13

Bo Hineyman had never felt so light. He was floating now, rising up. All the tension that had anchored him was unknotting. All the questions like who am I and what is my worth evaporated. Shame, doubt, worry gone. Oddly, fear, too. All that striving on earth seemed meaningless now, even silly. He felt the deepest sigh he had ever imagined possible. He looked down on a featureless plain all lavender and green. Sparks as bright as the arc of a welder's torch fell like soft rain. The sweetest music he had ever heard filled him, except there was no longer anything to fill or to hear, just currents of energy swirling into circles and waves. There was no need for words, nothing left to say.

Below him he saw a radiant being. Still capable of curiosity, he moved closer. It was Grace Buchman. She was bent over another figure, kneading his shoulders. She was working on his old nemesis, Otis Dooley. He felt no anger now, only this lightness, this blessed release. So this is what forgiveness is, he thought, but then there was no thinking at all. He rose suddenly upward, was gathered by the wind and dispersed.

Somewhere on earth, a mother raven felt a tremor beneath her. She stepped back and saw the egg she was tending tremble. A crack appeared and then a beak emerged. Then a head, eyes blinking, and finally a featherless wing, all appetite and longing.

Chapter 14

Nolan Mikesel held his flashlight close to the ground. It was easy to read their tracks. They were fleeing through pinyon and juniper trees, threading their way uphill to the top of a ridge above the ranch. Just like tracking deer. Same thing, follow until they are tired and turn, until they wait for you.

He could tell they were running from the way their footprints were gouged into the sandy soil, the depth and the wreckage of dirt around their tracks, the length of their strides. Hooves do that, too. Nolan Mikesel was familiar with the calligraphy of fear.

They ran bent and low, hoping the gunman couldn't see them behind dark bushes and moonlit trees. The slope was a maze of gnarly old juniper trees, half alive after a century of giving up limbs to droughts, insects, and other assaults that caused them to concentrate their life-giving sap into whichever branches were most viable. Ghostly gray limbs twisted through resilient green. The trees grew amazingly long roots across the hard soil that weaved in and out of the earth like thick serpents swimming through an ochre sea. The trees were survivors, only rooted instead of running like the fleeing couple. Enormous boulders that were spit from volcanoes eons ago then broken and polished by glacial ice loomed in the moonlight, watching the frantic human race with an unblinking indifference.

Just over the ridge, Hoppy and Luna hid behind some rocks and tried to catch their breaths and slow their racing hearts. Nolan let them. He preferred to wait until dawn and get a daylight shot. The memory of missing them in the dark was still fresh. At first light, Luna and Hoppy ran down a slope, crouched behind sage and serviceberry bushes, and made their way to the mouth of Rope Canyon. They were not aware of his exact location but they knew Nolan Mikesel was not far behind them. They had run from Bo's guest house when they saw him step into the yard light next to the main house.

He didn't have a clear shot though the scrubby brush and he knew that sooner or later they would cross open ground. Nolan saw them clearly as they entered the canyon. "Stupid move," he said to himself. "No way out. So stupid, queenie."

But it was deliberate and not so dumb after all. Yes, the canyon dead-ended at a huge pour-over about a mile up its serpentine wash. But Luna knew a route they could climb out and gambled that their pursuer did not. She had explored and climbed Rope Canyon years ago as a teenager sentenced to a year of camping. She strained to remember the hidden passage they took to the top. Once they were on the rim above him, he wouldn't have a shot at them—if they took just two steps back from the rim they would be out of sight.

Nolan stalked them slowly, confident they had nowhere to go. He looked up at the tall redrock walls on either side of the wash. Tourists loved those walls for the play of sunlight on texture, the abstract patterns made by stains and erosion, and the magnificence of bare stone soaring hundreds of feet above them. That's why Nolan hated those walls. They made him feel small, ant-like. He'd had enough humbling experiences in his life and didn't need any reminders of how puny human life can be. He preferred roughing up roads in his four-wheel drive truck so he could feel the motorized thrust and power of himself against the unfriendly landscape. Hiking was for sissies. Backpacking was for birdwatching suckers. Real men rev engines, kick up dust, and proclaim their presence loudly.

Luna and Hoppy raced ahead through the morning's first light. She knew they had to get to the route she remembered before the crazed man with the gun caught up to them. The first section going up that route rose along a thin ledge where they would be very exposed and he'd have a clear shot at them. Once they were about sixty feet from the floor of the canyon they could slip into a crevasse that was dark and obstructed from view. It was easier to climb with ropes and gear for safety but they could free climb it easily enough. The last part would also entail some exposure but by then they'd be two hundred feet above the shooter and coming in and out of his view. None of this could be discussed because they were too busy running. Luna told Hoppy she knew a way out and he trusted her and followed.

They reached the route Luna remembered and she signaled to Hoppy by pointing up. He nodded and she led the ascent. Hoppy tripped on the first section of the steep and broken path and planted his hand flat onto a prickly pear cactus. There was no time to pull the spines from his hand or complain. He grimaced, swore, and kept moving. Up. Up. Panting and scared, they clawed at shallow hand-holds in the rock wall with desperate concentration.

When they reached the crevasse they looked back and saw Nolan coming around the last bend in the canyon before their escape route. He held the rifle in front of him with both hands, barrel pointing forward, ready to raise the stock to his shoulder and shoot quickly. He saw them, too, swung his rifle upwards and fired twice, both shots clattering into the slope of rocks they had just climbed. They fit themselves into the cool, dark slot and climbed as fast as they could, grunting with the effort, scraping knees and elbows recklessly against the narrow walls. In one long passage they put their backs to the wall, pressed their feet against the opposite wall, and shimmied up to a ledge they could reach. If the gunman caught up to them while they were in that narrow chimney he would have an easy shot—they would be the proverbial fish in a barrel—but if they were too hasty in their climb they could slip and fall and surely that would mean broken bones, game over.

Nolan realized he was about to be out of firing range. He needed to get up there before they could exit the narrow passage. He could point his rifle straight up under them and shoot them down. He saw it in his mind's eye. She would scream, maybe plead. He felt himself getting hard.

Up he went, the rifle in one hand and his other grabbing at every handhold he could find. About fifty feet up from the floor there was a short traverse over a thin ledge. He took it too quickly and lost his balance. He reached out and grabbed ahold of a hank of rice grass to steady himself and regain his footing. The rice grass held him for a second before it tore loose. He spun hard and dropped about ten feet onto a boulder. There was a sickening snap and a pain shot from his ankle up to his hip.

He paused to assess the damage. A sprain, he thought, just a sprain. But when he stood up and took a step, his leg buckled and he tripped forward, pitched over a dead juniper log, rolled twice downhill and was airborne. He hit the canyon floor feet first and his knee was driven up into his chin. He lost consciousness briefly. When he regained it he was spitting blood. He brought a finger to his mouth and discovered a massive tear in his tongue and the jagged edge of a broken tooth. He gurgled blood and spat. When he looked down he noticed that the toe of his boot was pointed to where his heel should be. He reached down and felt a raw bone protruding underneath his denim pant leg.

When the earth's atmosphere became overloaded with the CO_2 and methane emitted by a carbon-based civilization, its oceans overheated and pushed the river of air flowing above them into wildly oscillating waves. The atmospheric currents that had regulated the benign flow of seasons and weather for thousands of years were overwhelmed. Whiplash waves drove Arctic air due south where it collided with warmer southern currents, spawning clusters of tornadoes and monster storms. Whole landscapes caught fire or were underwater from one season to the next. Droughts here, hurricanes there, it seemed like extreme weather was the new norm on an unpredictable helter-skelter planet. A clustering of consequences was at hand.

The southwest had always had a monsoon season marked by dramatic thunder and lightning shows that Luna referred to as "our daily cloud opera." But now the thunderheads rose even higher and faster until they collapsed in pounding rainstorms that the landscape could not contain. The morning that found Luna and Hoppy running for cover was like most other hot summer days, hardly a cloud in the sky. In just a couple hours the sun sucked moisture into the sky and clouds like a herd of fluffy white bison grazed across the blue. Their bulk became so great that they pulled on one another, coalesced into an anvil-shaped monster cloud that became so thick it turned a bruise-colored purple at its core.

Nolan looked up from the sandy wash where he lay broken and twisted. He saw a darkening sky. Thunder boomed and rolled away into the distance. Rain started slowly, big wet drops splattered down and polka-dotted the ground. There was a brief pause and then all hell broke loose. Rain came down in sheets so thick he couldn't see twenty feet away and so hard that the sand where Nolan lay was bouncing. Water poured down every slick surface of redrock. Rills and rivulets of rain braided together as they swept downward across bare stone and poured over canyon rims, making a universe of waterfalls.

Nolan tried to pull himself up above the canyon floor before the flash flood that was surely building arrived. He tried to stand but his bent leg would not hold him. He crawled but any effort he could make to get above the wash was too slow, too painful, too late. I'm pathetic, he thought. A fucking loser.

Rocks thudding underwater and the shush of dry leaves and dead twigs pushed forward by the flood's advancing tongue told him it was coming closer. He read a faint change in the air pressure close to the ground and then he smelled its moist breath. Flood! It looked so odd coming toward him, a dry wall of sticks and branches, dead grass and leafy detritus, rolling almost lazily. The flash flood was pushing the debris it had scoured from the canyon floor ahead of itself. The wall roiling toward him was neither dry nor slow despite appearances. Behind the debris was a wet fury he would not survive.

His last words before it swallowed him were, "Oh fuck!"

Chapter 15

The new security guard at the Sea Ledges tar sands mine saw the gathering clouds. They built up into a towering mass above the mine site. The topmost layer of the massive cloud was etched in silver but the dense bottom was a dark and ominous grey. The guard was not alarmed. Monsoon season was like this. Usually the storms passed or dissipated. You could see storms on the horizon all day long and never get wet. The desert is big and thunder storms are a hit-or-miss affair.

This one was different. Darker and bigger than most, it rumbled and growled for close to an hour. The guard went into the shed where they kept equipment and broke out a rain poncho. He lit a cigarette and leaned back on a plastic lawn chair under a sheet-metal eve. "Bring it on," he said aloud. "Start the show."

A couple of days before, an eco-terrorist set fire to a house trailer and drove a bulldozer over a cliff. The site was strewn with yellow police tape because the detectives who were supposed to examine the crime scene were on another case and getting to the Sea Ledges site was a long and difficult trip. Construction was temporarily halted. The guard who was on the site when the sabotage occurred was fired and everyone who worked at the site was tense. But the young man on duty that morning reasoned that monkey-wrenchers don't work in the rain and they don't hit the same place twice in a week. He wanted to relax and the storm offered welcome entertainment.

In the first minute after the rain began to pour down it was clear this was no ordinary thunder bumper. It was as if someone turned on a fire hose. Rain came down in pillars of gray and silver. A trillion fists pounded the ground. The storm cloud pulsed with lightning and cracked with thunder so loud he felt it in his teeth. His hair lifted from his head and crackled with static electricity.

The dry washes filled with rivers of water and every low spot became a pond. The metal shed behind him buckled under the weight of the wet onslaught. He heard a groaning sound and realized that the company Hummer he rode in on was moving, lifted by rising water and headed slowly downhill, wagging back and forth as it moved like it was happy to be swimming away on its own. He scrambled to a ledge above the mine site and watched the carnage unfold. Machinery slid this way and that, shed roofs caved in, cement pads snapped as the soil beneath them disappeared into the maelstrom. Debris tangled in downed power lines made a temporary dam across the wash below him. Eventually the pressure of the mass of water trapped behind it snapped the lines and unleashed a small tsunami of mud and metal.

He tried to call his supervisor but the phones didn't work. He crouched under a rock ledge and watched the amazing fury all around him. It stopped as suddenly as it had begun. He stood in a moist and eerie silence, broken only by the soft swish and gurgle of the receding waters. He walked the sloppy remains of the gravel road to where he could get a signal. The site was wrecked. The storm had swallowed the place and spit it out.

"It's over," he said to himself, and wondered if there would be severance pay when the owners saw the damage and fired the crew. He reviewed the bills he had to pay and calculated how long he could be unemployed before he, too, would be underwater.

The Drexxel managers flew over the site the next day in a helicopter. They concluded that the destruction from the storm was serious but could be repaired in time.

"I don't think so," said Orin Bender, who had come along for the ride with his Drexxel partners. "The price of oil is too low and dropping further. At a hundred dollars per barrel you can make a profit off tar sands, but not at fifty. It doesn't make much sense to start over now. Maybe down the road, but this . . ."

He swept his hand across the view of the half-buried mine site below, where scattered and tilted debris was cemented into the drying ground, and he shook his head and looked away.

Chapter 16

Elias Buchman was sitting in Dunk Taylor's office when they got the autopsy report on the late Bo Hineyman. Dunk was telling Elias about the body that had washed up at the mouth of Rope Canyon. One of his deputies identified him as some creep who lived over near Myersvale. They had no idea why he was in the canyon but the popular guess was that he had been poaching when caught by a flash flood. The man was well known to local game wardens who suspected he was killing elk out of season but they never caught him red-handed. A rifle was buried in the mud a hundred yards farther down the wash. Eldon Pratt sat in an adjoining room cleaning it up so they could read the serial number.

Elias was prone to peppering others with questions until he got everything they knew. Sheriff Taylor put it all out there at once to short-circuit the inevitable interrogation. "His name was Nolan Mikesel. I think he pushed cattle for Bunny Cleaver. He was a handful, always in trouble. Ask anybody who had to deal with him—a real dick."

The sheriff's secretary burst through the door, slapped the autopsy report from the coroner on Dunk Taylor's desk, and stood in the doorway to hear the results. Sheriff Taylor abruptly cut his conversation with Elias. He popped on his reading glasses and began to read the report to himself. Elias and the secretary looked at each other and then studied Sheriff Taylor. Neither of them said a word. They waited impatiently until the sheriff smiled slightly, let out a sigh of relief, and pushed the envelope and its contents toward Elias.

"I got a meeting this morning. You go tell Otis the news."

Ten minutes later Elias skidded up Otis's drive and jumped out. A black and white cat sunning on the hood of Otis's jeep jumped three feet in the air and then disappeared, as Otis would say, like a fart in a hurricane. A blur of two more cats followed at ground level.

"Otis! Hey Otis!"

Otis came around the side of the house carrying a pail full of freshly pulled beets from the garden. "Jesus, Buchman, you scared the cats. What's going on?"

"The autopsy report. Bo Hineyman choked to death on a knot of bison gristle. You're clear."

Otis set the pail of beets on the ground. "But what about all that mess in his house? Who tipped over the furniture and knocked that painting loose? Why was he found sitting in a pile of plastic fish?"

"Who knows. He must have thrashed around pretty hard when he started choking. Don't question it, buddy. I was just over with Dunk. You're off the hook."

Chapter 17

They heard the gunman fall and saw him crumpled and crawling on the canyon floor. They reached the top of the canyon rim before the rain started. Once the deluge was in full force visibility was poor but they could hear the flash flood knocking and scraping its way down the canyon. In their last glimpse of the gunman he was crawling, crawling. They could read his pain and panic even from such a great distance blurred by rain. After the flood passed and the sky cleared they looked down and saw nothing but a landscape of scoured stone and sand. They couldn't move for an hour. They huddled under a sandstone alcove and held each other.

It's okay now, he told her. It's over. They waited for the adrenalin flood generated by the chase to subside. Although they knew they were no longer the gunman's prey, the residue of terror stayed with them, pressed on his shoulders, tightened her temples, accelerated their hearts. Breathe, they told each other. Breathe deep and slow.

Eventually, they walked back to her father's ranch. Luna opened the front door and called "Dad!" several times but there was no answer. They debated whether to go in and decided against it. Luna had no energy for another awkward encounter with her father. They wanted to retrieve the camping gear they had abandoned when the gunman chased them away from their campsite the night before. Hoppy's truck was still back at the campsite and it was unlocked as far as he could remember. They weren't sure where they had left their phones. Exhausted and still shaky, they just wanted to get in her truck and get out. They climbed into the truck quickly and drove away. Luna turned and glanced back briefly at the ranch house receding from her view. They agreed they would never go back there again.

They drove to Sojourner Draw because it was remote, beautiful, and safe. They set up a tent in the shade of a cottonwood stand about twenty feet from a large pothole that was rimmed each night by croaking frogs and singing crickets. That incessant primordial beat soothed them and released their stressed-out bodies to healing sleep. They were hungry but rationed the food they had so they could stay out of town longer. They needed time to process what happened and decide what to do next. They made camp and were quiet for a very long while.

Eventually they argued, made up, and argued again. Luna told Hoppy that the traumatic chase they had endured was what you get when you give in to violence, like when he trashed the tar sands site. Hoppy contended that violence against property is okay. The corporations like Drexxel are the violent ones, he claimed, just look at what they do to the planet, to lungs, to life. Their violence is systemic and our violence is resistance to their more pervasive destruction. Violence against the land and water, the air, the natural systems that support life, sometimes requires a kind of creative violence in return. What you get in return, she told him, is the madness you just experienced firsthand.

On the second day of the debate they agreed to disagree but Hoppy was remorseful and promised to respect her way. She forgave him. They needed each other. They recovered well together. Despite any lingering differences of opinion they were attentive and careful with each other. The shaking stopped and confidence returned.

They drove to a nearby hill where they could get a signal and called the members of the Sea Ledges Alliance with carefully rehearsed excuses for where they had been and why they didn't contact anyone. They concocted a story about the truck breaking down and how Hoppy was able to fix it but it took him three days. They couldn't get a signal in the canyon and the batteries in their phones went dead while they tried in vain to call or text. It wasn't much of an alibi but it was all they had. They agreed they would apologize frequently. Thank goodness you called, Brenda Savitt told them, because we were about to report you as missing persons. Brenda breathlessly related the news about the Drexxel mining site's destruction. Yes, Luna said, we heard that. No, we haven't a clue who did it.

They ran out of food and decided to venture into town and find out what had happened while they were hiding in Sojourner Draw. The gravel pass to Boon County was dry. A fine powder was lifted in the truck's wake. The trip into town took an hour. Hoppy tried not to imagine police waiting to arrest him for sabotaging Drexxel's mining site and Luna tried not to think about how awkward it was to explain why she was missing when the Seafold Ledges resisters needed her most. Halfway there he pulled over and they both left the truck and peed behind a tall stand of yucca just off the road. When they climbed back in the cab of the truck they confessed to each other.

Luna first. "I'm scared."

"Me, too."

"Hoppy, I keep going over it. Was the man who drowned in the flood hired to kill us? I mean did he come after us for his own reasons or did someone put him up to it? Maybe he was a miner who was angry because he thought we threatened his job but he was so determined to get us that I feel he was hired. Shouldn't we find out? What if another assassin is hired to finish the job? Shouldn't we go to the police and find out what they know?"

"And how do you think you're going to do that? Excuse me, officer, but we have reason to believe that man you found dead in Rope Canyon was really after my boyfriend, the saboteur."

"I don't think he was after you. He couldn't know that you trashed the Drexxel site. He was after me because I've been so visible as the spokesperson for the Sea Ledges Alliance."

"It doesn't matter. Anything that draws cops to our door is bad news for me. They might find out more than you want them to know. I'd just as soon we avoid scrutiny, okay? We can go to the police if we're sure we're in danger but we're not sure now. Don't panic. Not yet."

He had never seen her so unsure, so tentative. "You look pale, Luna, are you alright?"

"I don't like this. This isn't me."

He looked straight ahead and for several minutes the hiss and pop of the tires rolling over loose gravel filled the cab. The wind whispered through her partially opened window. "I'm sorry," he said. "I never wanted to mess up your life like this. I was . . . I was . . ."

"Never mind that now. Let's be a team on this next part, okay?"

Luna and Hoppy learned that the storm that saved them from the gunman also swept across the desert and crushed the Drexxel site. They could not look at each other for fear of revealing astonishment and joy. They understood immediately that if the police couldn't retrieve fingerprints, footprints, traces of DNA, and surveillance pictures, pinning the destruction on Hoppy would be near impossible. They had not only escaped murder but fate gave Hoppy a do-over.

Luna was forthright about why. "It's karma. You defended Mother Nature and she returned the favor."

"Really? I think Mother Nature is feral and indifferent."

"No, she's not! She's reciprocal, responsive, generous, abundant!"

He paused. "Yeah, you're right, it's karma. Feels good." He agreed because he didn't really care why it happened, he was just glad it happened, period.

Their good cheer was soon crushed. Luna asked what else had happened while they were gone. She said it casually, not anticipating anything. Her friends told her a rich guy over in Stony Mesa was found murdered in his cabin. Strangled. And some dirt bag from Myersvale was drowned in a flash flood through Rope Canyon. They had no way of knowing that the murdered rich man was Luna's estranged dad. She was frank with friends about the reasons for her emotional distance from her father but the question of his physical distance never came up and she never volunteered that information. Why tell someone he has a place just over the hill in Stony Mesa when that place might as well be a million miles away?

As soon as the tide of fear retreated from her veins, a flood of remorse took its place. Luna and Hoppy looked quickly at one another and then tried not to let their faces betray Luna's secret. They departed from their friends as soon as they could and found a quiet bench in a nearby park where she could sit down. Luna was sure that the gunman who had chased them to her father's door was the murderer.

"I brought this on, Hoppy. I never should have gone there. He'd be alive if I hadn't run to him."

"You didn't run to him, Luna, you ran to his guest house, remember? He wasn't supposed to be there. How could you know that?"

Luna went to bed and stayed there. Hoppy stayed close and held her hand, dried her tears, handed her Kleenex, and tried to convince her she was not to blame. Luna understood she wasn't exactly a ray of sunshine, so she appreciated Hoppy's attentive devotion. Obviously, she thought, there is more to our relationship than acrobatic lust. He fed her chicken soup because he'd heard somewhere it was good for the soul and he read Mary Oliver poems aloud because Mary Oliver was her favorite poet. He saw an ad for free puppies and considered getting one because the joyful play of puppies is irresistibly lifting but he picked a bouquet of wildflowers instead.

Hoppy wrestled with feelings of guilt and remorse, unknown to him so far in his young life. He was sure the gunman who chased them up Rope Canyon was after Luna because she was a known leader of the resistance to the tar sands mine. And how would anyone know he had attacked the Sea Ledges site so soon? Even so, he suspected his law-breaking spree was a kind of karmic trigger. His heart ached to think he had contributed to Luna's unrelenting sadness.

The hardest part for Luna was talking to her mom over the phone. Hoppy's monkey-wrenching and the subsequent chase by the gunman were now bound together and consigned to secrecy forever. She was unable to tell her mother why she was devastated that a man she barely remembered was dead, that she felt responsible for drawing his killer to his door. Her mom chalked up Luna's grief to the regret she must feel for the hole in her life that was never filled by a father. The death of her biological father just triggered those feelings. Her mother was on an island in Greece and the reception was terrible. Luna concluded that she would have to face her feelings of guilt alone.

Had the couple known that Mayor Otis Dooley was suspected of killing Bo Hineyman, they would have faced another moral dilemma. They had knowledge that could clear Otis and they might have come forward and told their story about leading the gunman to Bo's ranch house. But they were not members of the Stony Mesa community and did not know Otis or his dilemma. They retreated to a cabin owned by a friend who was away visiting her mom in Cincinnati. There, Luna could grieve without inviting scrutiny they could not afford.

A week passed. They did not hear the news about Bo Hineyman's autopsy because of their self-imposed seclusion. Luna could only be coaxed out of bed for warm baths. The crying subsided. Hoppy convinced her she needed to go out, feel sunlight, hear birds, breathe fresh air. They would meet friends from the Alliance and hike over Star Pass to Spring Lake, a peaceful pond set among slim aspens and delicate willows that were sure to heal Luna's damaged heart. She pulled herself together slowly, moving her limbs that were heavy and reluctant to do her bidding.

They drove through Stony Mesa to get to the trailhead and passed her dad's saloon. The Bull and Stallion reminded her of her father's permanent absence and her complicity in his death. It was closed and the empty parking lot signified loss. She choked back a sob and held her breath until she regained control.

Hoppy tried to distract her. He pointed to the massive neon beast in front of the saloon. "Gee, when you see that thing in the daylight it looks so innocent. You wouldn't guess how much it sucks at night."

She quickly wiped away a tear that had rolled halfway down her cheek and managed a small smile. "Yeah, who knew light could be that loud?"

The tires of the truck rattled over a washboarded section of the road. He waited for the noise to subside and then turned to her. "I love you, Luna."

"I know you do, Hoppy. I love you, too."

"It's going to be alright. My mom used to say that it will all turn out to be good in the end, and if it is not good yet, then it is not the end."

Their friends were waiting when they reached the trailhead, adjusting gear and checking their backpacks to be sure they had what they needed. Hoppy greeted them enthusiastically, glad to have allies in his campaign to restore Luna's peace of mind even if they were temporary. Luna took a deep breath, smiled, and told herself to act normal.

Halfway up the trail to Star Pass Brenda Savitt volunteered the latest news on that man that was found dead at his ranch in Stony Mesa. It was not murder, after all, she explained. They did an autopsy. He choked to death on bison meat, according to the report from the coroner.

Not her fault. Hoppy and Luna looked at each other and she began to cry softly and then broke down and sobbed. Brenda and the others were alarmed at her sudden emotional response to news they considered to be merely by the way.

Hoppy drew her to him and lied. "Uh, it's okay. Her best friend in college choked to death. She gets upset when she hears about anyone choking."

"I'm so sorry, Luna, I didn't know . . ."

"It's okay, Brenda, you couldn't have known."

The Sea Ledges Tar Sands Alliance disbanded. The mining site they opposed was ruined by the storm and the word was that it would not be rebuilt. Not anytime soon, anyway. Eventually the wind and rain would clean the remaining scars from the desert floor and the debris left behind would be considered mere artifacts rather than the instruments of ecological folly. There would be more mine pits and pipelines to resist but this campaign was over.

The Sea Ledges Tar Sands Alliance denied any involvement in the monkey-wrenching of the mining site while the state's crusading attorney general, elected years ago on a platform of preventing gay couples from marrying, vowed to bring the perpetrators to justice. But he had barely begun his plan to demonize the activists and heroically put them away when a confluence of flash floods wiped out the site and made the controversy moot. Flood water cleaned out all the clues. The security cameras that were not washed away showed only blurred images in the dark. Unless the vandal boasted recklessly or stepped forward and confessed, the investigation would go nowhere. Drexxel suspended operations until the price of oil recovered. It never did.

The Sea Ledges Thirteen, as the protestors came to be known, had all charges dropped when the prosecuting attorney, Lawton Hatch, failed to appear and present the case against them that he hoped would launch his political career. The prosecutor, they found out later, had been trading sexual favors for lighter sentences. He was in a motel with a meth addict named Mona an hour before the trial started. He was stranded there, naked and alone, when the woman he assumed was going to give him a thrill stole his clothes instead. She ran across the motel parking lot gleefully waving his underpants over her head. When apprehended, Mona grinned and declared, "Luna, this one's for you sweetie!"

The resisters went back to their lives or drifted off toward other causes. Lucas Hozho went home to visit his grandmother on the reservation and Brenda Savitt flew to San Diego to welcome her daughter's newborn baby into the world. Luna took Hoppy to meet her mother, who was now living in Italy but flew to Denver for a visit. They enjoyed a week together and when the couple returned they had no place to stay. They camped, hiked every day, and slept in. She gathered applications to graduate school and Hoppy re-read *The Monkey Wrench Gang*. Both of them wondered what comes next.

Bo Hineyman's last will and testament came next. Luna could barely hear her phone buried in the pocket of her daypack in the tent. She dashed over and unscrambled the contents of the pack to find her phone in the nick of time and answered without thinking. Had the phone been more conveniently placed, she would have had the time to see it was an unfamiliar number and ignored it.

"Ms. Waxwing, I am Bo Hineyman's attorney."

Those were the last words she remembered clearly. By the time he finished, she felt so light headed she wondered if she would faint. Wouldn't that be melodramatic? She listened to her breath and stayed on her feet. When the conversation was over, she turned to Hoppy, who had noticed the look of surprise on Luna's face and heard her identify herself as Elizabeth Waxwing. What now, he thought. Maybe her globe-trotting mom fell off the planet and she's being notified. He wasn't normally so morose but their recent adventures as fleeing prey and the sudden death of Luna's father had dimmed his usual sunny disposition.

"What? What?"

She took a deep breath, counted to three, and explained. She felt like she was explaining it to herself, too. Her biological father, Richard Boris Hineyman, left the Bull and Stallion Saloon and his ranch in Stony Mesa to his daughter Elizabeth, aka Liz, Betty, and Luna. The rest of his estate was divided among wives who had no interest in running a ranch and cowboy bar and grill in the middle of nowhere.

The following weeks were the most creative of their lives. It was as if they had a MacArthur Grant from the Grim Reaper. Luna changed the name of the Bull and Stallion to the Desert Rose. The waitresses were told to dress nice and just be themselves. The sequined cowgirl outfits were tossed in the free box in front of the general store. For many years afterward they would reappear in annual Halloween parties.

Luna redesigned the menu to eliminate most of the meat and include fresh salads and vegetables that they could grow on the ranch after they removed all those cows and put in organic gardens. They called up friends from the Tar Sands Alliance and asked them to come help them build a greenhouse. They met local folks who could help, too, and invited them to share in what became a community project. There was even talk of planting an orchard on the ranch. They read books on bees and drip irrigation. The ranch became a magnet for ideas about how to live sustainably while making a livable income. They cleaned out the old bunkhouse and opened it to visitors who wanted to stay and help. Luna, of course, charmed them all by turning sweet, ethereal, corny, naughty, inspiring, or brilliant according to the circumstances and audience. As Hoppy observed, she always let others have her way.

Hoppy looked over his shoulder for many months, expecting that any day now his monkey-wrenching spree would be revealed and he would be held accountable. He plunged into the reshaping of the Desert Rose enterprise, especially the organic farm they began at the former Bo Hineyman ranch, just up the road from the café. Putting his hands into soil was therapeutic. In his quest to smooth his troubled aura, he even took up meditation. Although it never resulted in blissful experiences, it did relax him and make him aware of where his thoughts and feelings were coming from. He learned how to step back from the impulses that made him charge forward when staying still and listening might be a better choice.

Otis was re-elected mayor and quit drinking for good. Cleared of all suspicions, he felt reborn. The clarity he gained through sobriety made him confident and creative. He told "the new kids," as he referred to them, that he would look for grants to start a culinary high school at the Desert Rose. Otis though that becoming a chef was a smart alternative to moving sprinkler pipes, fixing busted fences, and waitressing for Stony Mesa kids who couldn't afford to go away to college.

Grace Buchman did what she always did. She listened to all of them attentively, praised and encouraged them. She might add a word of wisdom now and then but she was careful to respect their choices. She was sure everything would turn out well.

For his part, Elias Buchman promised to write it all down and tell the whole story from beginning to end. He had a hunch that the new kids who took over the Hineyman ranch (what were their names, Lana and Happy?) would add a much needed dose of positive energy to the community. And maybe some drama, he thought. We'll see.

There would still be battles of course. The predatory dynamic of America's economy was still a destructive force to be resisted. Orin Bender would sign another contract somewhere else and slip cash to another twisted thug to thwart any law that got in his way. Bunny Cleaver still rode the range, or what was left of it after his bovine locusts chewed it to the nubs. Drexxel had to keep turning a profit to keep its Wall Street investors in yachts and mansions. But for now Luna and Hoppy and their new friends in Stony Mesa had this abiding need to build something positive. The defense of life in the maw of the voracious culture they had inherited begged resistance but arks were needed, too. They'd make a space where people like themselves could commune with their better angels and work together.

Luna Waxwing and Hip Hop Hopi felt liberated and empowered. There were so many wonderful possibilities, so much opportunity, so much to be done. Luna and Hoppy couldn't wait to get at it. But they both agreed that the first thing on their list was clear: get rid of that damn neon sign.

TRICKSTER'S

BOOK TWO
(the present)

BONES

P r o l o g u e

Bones, human bones. Hyrum Allred stared at the pile of dirt he had just dumped while his backhoe engine idled. He could make out a curved rib and a long femur that could be animal bones but there was no mistaking a child's small skull. It looked up at the sun, grinning through a patina of amber dust.

"Holy shit," he whispered and then looked from side to side and over each shoulder to check that he was alone. He turned the switch to kill the engine and hopped down for a closer look. Brushing aside the sandy soil, he immediately found a tooth and a finger bone.

He walked to his truck and retrieved a shovel, which he used to gingerly remove more of the top layer of dirt that his backhoe had pushed aside. An hour later he had unearthed a dozen more skulls amid a nest of tangled ribs. He found a whole pelvis and pieces of others, more arm and leg bones, an entire hand, and a hundred other small bones from vertebrae to knuckles.

At first he thought he had uncovered an Indian burial ground but these skeletons were too crowded and haphazard for ceremonial burials. It looked like a mass grave.

Hyrum took off his hat and wiped sweat from his forehead. He stood for several minutes, unable to process the scene before him. He tried to imagine why the bones were there but couldn't come up with one good reason. Whatever happened, he concluded, it wasn't pretty.

Chapter 1

It wasn't fair. Stony Mesa already had a designated town crank, Kitty Fontaine, and was too small a village to handle more than one. And yet, there was Olene Miller standing up in the middle of a public hearing and becoming seriously incoherent. The meeting was called to unveil plans for a proposed gated development that would include a golf course and grand vacation houses. The development would cover the Jango Ranch, a swath of green alfalfa dotted by black cattle and framed by redrock cliffs on the south side of town. The notion that the familiar river valley would be transformed to attract rich outsiders was upsetting to most of the town's permanent denizens.

The frontier was long gone but the circle-the-wagons mentality remained. The old-timers disliked change and were suspicious of outsiders, especially wary of their citified penchant for rules and regulations. The "move-ins" already living among them were hard enough to accept because they did not belong to the One True Church, but at least they were friendly and respected tradition.

Newcomers like the Buchmans, for example, liked Stony Mesa just the way it was. But what about the move-ins who objected to junky yards with abandoned cars that locals kept for spare parts? If local folk couldn't ride their all-terrain vehicles through the Jango Ranch they'd lose access to hunting grounds. Hunting was no mere hobby but a source of precious deer and elk meat. Rich people would expect services like garbage pick-up, snow removal, and animal control, maybe even recycling that the town could not afford.

The vision of a gated community was downright threatening to the status quo, patriarchs mostly, who pushed cows and wore the names of their pioneer ancestors like a badge. They remembered their experience with that Bo Hineyman who owned the Bull and Stallion before his daughter and her partner transformed it into the Desert Rose.

Rich guys like that Hineyman jerk played "my lawyer is bigger than your lawyer" whenever they didn't get their way. Worse, the people who inhabited the Highlife Holiday Estates or whatever they were calling it might not be around much but they could still be snobbish bullies when their interests conflicted with locals who had fewer resources to fight back. The rich would probably look down on people like them, people with dirty boots and raw knuckles. In the recesses of their minds the good ol' boys and their extended families understood that the trip from pioneer stock to white trash could be a short ride once their clannish hold on the county was broken.

So much was on the line: familiarity, control, dignity, respect, and morality itself, according to the elders of the One True Church. Their hearts raced as they took their seats and waited. The meeting commenced and the crowd of locals peppered the spokesperson for the developers, Highlife Holiday Estates, with the usual questions. They mostly wanted to know about water rights and tax impacts. Olene's critique, however, was unique.

"On a vibrational level," she explained to the crowd of a hundred worried citizens, "golf turf is even more out of alignment than alfalfa. There is a tipping point, you know. Put that new development in the middle of the already troubled wave lines emanating from there and you're just begging for a major psychic disruption."

The assembled citizenry leaned forward on creaky folding chairs, listened with cupped ears, cast side glances at each other, tried to make sense. Olene was well-known and well liked. Eccentric, yes, but nothing like this.

A pause. Olene felt herself falling through the well of her baffled neighbors' ensuing silence and she became alarmed. Instead of backing off she doubled down. "This is important! We have to learn to read the signals! Look around you! We have knocked the climate gimbal askew and extreme gyration is the new norm. It's no longer about buy and sell, me and mine in a static world. That story is a fiction because the real world is fluid. We're all in it together and we have to read the signals."

Utter failure was apparent. As if she were explaining algebra to cows. Panic now. "I mean I'm talking about saturation and flux . . . flux!"

Almost directly behind her, Crazy Kitty Fontaine sat transfixed. If she sensed any threat of competition for the title of village idiot, she didn't show it. Olene finished and sat down abruptly among neighbors who avoided eye contact with her. Kitty looked about and smiled almost gleefully. As her sparkling eyes darted from one awkward fellow citizen to another, her smile grew as they avoided eye contact with her, too.

She broke the pregnant silence that followed Olene Miller's incomprehensible speech by blurting out for all to hear, "Makes perfect sense to me!"

And that's when laughter muscled its way through the inner bouncer at the door of civility and several in the audience snickered and chuckled. A couple of loud snorts signaled failed efforts to suppress guffaws. If Olene was off the tracks, that was upsetting, but Crazy Kitty's endorsement of Olene's incoherent outburst and her assumption of her own credibility, now that's funny.

Elias Buchman wondered if Kitty was aware of the way her neighbors regarded her and was deliberately making a joke, maybe even providing a bit of comic relief to break up the awkwardness and confusion that had settled over the school auditorium like a sour syrup. Or was she, as everyone else assumed, simply clueless.

Elias had spent hundreds of hours interviewing so-called street people back in the city where he had made his career as a reporter. He investigated the killing by police of homeless people who were undeniably mentally ill. He haunted homeless shelters and piss-stained alleys, sat cross-legged on damp stairways and park lawns while listening to stories about how bad luck and untreated mental illness became prescriptions for tragedy. It was his job at the end of a long career to tell their stories, or at least he thought it was his job even though his editor, his colleagues at the newspaper, and even his best friends told him otherwise. Let go, they said. Enough. Move on.

Maybe so, he thought. I was obsessed. I just felt so compelled. But he'd learned this much while listening to the untreated ravers and ranters on the streets of the big city: Sometimes street-corner crackpots are hallucinating and sometimes we are the ones who are blind. Sometimes the individual fears and fantasies of the mentally unhinged express a collective truth we do not wish to acknowledge. Their radar is imperfect to say the least, but occasionally there is a nugget among the noise.

Later, he would be the only one to approach Olene and tell her he found her remarks interesting and would like to know more. Stony Mesa's other citizens had come to the public meeting to learn about the sale of the old Jango Ranch to a developer who planned to use water currently spread across alfalfa fields to grow a golf course. The golf green would be surrounded by second-home mansions of the infamous one percent who favored redrock scenery with eighteen holes in it. For those townfolk who came to voice concerns about a sea-change in the history of sleepy Stony Mesa, Olene's outburst was only a humorous distraction. They focused instead on who would pay for water infrastructure and road maintenance and how their home values might be affected. The only flux that mattered to them was a change in their property taxes. Saturation and tipping points were not an issue. Elias alone thought otherwise.

Elias Buchman was an ex-reporter who no longer followed the news. He knew firsthand how it gets chopped up by editors and publishers intent on attracting advertising and making more money. Reporters learned soon enough two unspoken rules: first, do not piss off the rich and powerful, especially a corporation that advertises in your business; second, avoid stepping on the toes of higher-ups who sign your paychecks and decide promotions. His fellow reporters competed to get their stories in front of the other guy's piece so they could add such minor triumphs to their resumes. Sensationalizing your piece made it more competitive but often distorted the truth, whatever that was. Elias disregarded any political message, right or left, that was designed to induce fear, which was most of the signals out there. Despite all their shortcomings, he still believed in the power of journalists to inform, inspire, and empower their fellow citizens. But again, you had to separate the nuggets from the noise.

He was wary of ubiquitous chatter, the hype and rant of pervasive media, the scrape of information traffic across the membrane of one's consciousness. At the end of his working life he grew too sensitive to all that noise, imagined or real. Beyond the rude growl of trucks, cars, and planes, he could sense the collective drone of a million various machines, a constant cacophony of voices, and a zillion signals that saturated the city from building basements to rooftops. They made a deep but almost imperceptible humming that only those who have known true silence notice.

In Stony Mesa, he found that silence. His wife Grace taught him to feed on that, to breathe deeply. They recaptured their middle-aged bodies with lots of hiking in the nearby national park. They skied cross-country in winter, did yoga in the morning. Clean food, clean air, and drinking water from snow-fed springs in the mountain above their home completed the healing process. And beauty. The redrock cliffs that towered above Stony Mesa from the sage green valley to the big blue sky provided abundant beauty. The tall walls of fractured and stained sandstone, the pastel hills of ash, stunning vistas . . . visitors would gaze at the horizon and say there's something about the light here. Many had never peered through air so pristine that one could see individual trees etched across a mountain peak twenty miles away, never witnessed the Milky Way or seen a shooting star.

Grace painted and he took photos. They made friends easily. They planted a garden. For the first time in his life he felt he had enough time to read. My god, he even napped some afternoons. Life in Stony Mesa was positively medicinal for the Buchmans. In a few years he had forgotten the stressful hustle of his previous life as an investigative reporter. His blood pressure dropped. No more headaches.

"Odd," he thought aloud, "how I spent so much time and energy in my life trying to bring about change, hoping for change, and now I feel threatened by the prospect of change here in this peaceful valley. Maybe I'm just getting old."

"Oh nonsense," said Grace. "You've always been cranky. And stubborn. Relax."

She was probably right. It was all just talk so far. Just a lot of dog n' pony until now. What's the harm in talking?

Kayla Burnside held her stomach and rocked slightly back and forth in a folding metal chair near the front of the over-packed school gym. Her anxiety was apparent to those around her and they struggled not to stare at her. Many of them had watched her grow up. They rooted for her when she rode her horse around barrels at Saturday night rodeos and they applauded her when she danced and sang at the annual high school talent night. They remembered the controversial cut of her prom dress and how, when Principal Pate asked her if she thought her dress was appropriate, she broke out in a hardy grin, punched him playfully on his shoulder, and replied, "More like bodacious, dude!" That gal is a real pistol, they said, and often added: She's the best thing that ever happened in the entire history of the Burnside family. It hurt to see how hard she was taking it. Her distress spoke to their own misgivings.

Like Elias and Grace, Kayla loved the peace and quiet in Stony Mesa. She spent summers on her grandfather's Jango Ranch far from the city where her father sold hardware and plumbing products to chain stores while her mom managed a boutique. The household she was born into was far from peaceful. The constant struggle between her parents provided their only child with an environment often described by concerned family friends as "toxic." But summers at the Jango Ranch were wholesome and quiet and when her parents finally split and she was old enough to choose, she chose neither, opting instead to live with her grandparents while she finished school. Her grandmother was warm and attentive and her grandfather was well known and admired. She took her identity from them and from their Jango Ranch. She loved the village of Stony Mesa, too, and she was proud to call it her home town.

The Jango was paradise for a teenager who loved horses and needed room to grow. A jewel set among river stones strewn by a thousand floods, the Jango featured long swales of cottonwoods and willows that enclosed bright green fields of alfalfa and pasture. The ranch was rich with water that spread from irrigation ditches into pastures in crooked ribbons that reflected the sky, blue and silver by day and blood orange as the sun set or rose. Contented cows meandered along winding banks of grass. And all around were redrock vistas equal to any postcard a tourist could purchase at the local Desert Rose Café.

As a little girl, Kayla built huts in the brush that were connected by tunnels she wove through supple willow branches. She could nest there under a halo of soft green light and hide from the confusion of adults and confess her secret fears and dreams to Cassidy, her favorite doll. After she left her warring parents and moved in with her grandparents full time, Kayla rode horses, went rockhounding with her cousins, and did chores that she enjoyed, like feeding animals. When she was twelve, her grandfather trusted her to drive the tractor through rows of cut hay while he and his hired hands lifted the bales onto the trailer behind her. Wearing her cowboy hat, jeans, and boots, she looked like any of the other kids who attended Boon County High and nobody was aware that she was the only child of two unhappy adults who were so intent on tearing each other down that they were blind to the suffering of their daughter.

The ranch became the wellspring of her dreams where yellow marmots talked to her and the rough complaints of badgers and jays interrupted the soothing quiet of her friends the deer. In one ecstatic dream, flocks of sparrows and finches lifted her into the cool summer clouds as the setting sun lit tree tops above the darkening meadows. In slumber she flew in a spiraling gyre far above the green fields and ragged cliffs below. Until Highlife Holiday Estates threatened to eat it whole, Kayla hadn't realized how the Jango Ranch was not only the source of her peace and security, but also where her imagination took root.

She listened to the man in the crisp gray suit explain the images he clicked through on the screen at the front of the gym. Her identity took a major hit. The notion that the old ranch house, pastures, and corrals would be scraped clear for a golf course and 7,000-square-foot mini-mansions overwhelmed her. The land where she and her loved ones made a life would be erased so some rich people could vacation behind walls.

Generations had taken their turns living there. Indian inscriptions of bighorn sheep carved into the canyon wall behind the bunkhouse were a thousand years old. There was a hand-lettered sign by her great-grandfather, Jango Burnside, that hung on the wall of the screened-in porch, "Jango Ranch" printed on one line, "hay and cattle" beneath in an elegant cursive script that schools no longer teach. And now, instead, these shiny brochures handed out to the Stony Mesa audience and the bright images flashing across the screen before their wide eyes. The artist's version of a luxurious gated development with a golf course, tennis courts, a pool, and a clubhouse restaurant and bar was so bright it hurt her eyes.

"From animals to amenities," she whispered to herself. It's almost funny. From chisel to digital, the path of progress.

"But your grandfather will be rich," her friends told her. "They'll pay millions for the Jango. You'll be rich, too," they said.

"No, I won't," said Kayla. "I'll be lost."

A seat was reserved up front for Jango Burnside Jr. but he declined. JR or Junior, as everyone called him, stood in the back of the school's gym, the only option for many of the town's citizens who arrived late at the meeting place that held barely a hundred seats. JR scanned the audience and read their body language. He carried mixed feelings about his choice to give up the hard life and sell the ranch that had been home for generations of his family. His grandfather invented the name Jango for himself when he settled the ranch and then passed the name and the ranch to his son, who passed the ranch and the name to JR. The ranch and his very identity were fused together. He never thought it would end this way. If a ranch had been in the family for generations, the heirs were supposed to keep it going and pass it on. His decision to sell and move on defied convention and was tainted with a whiff of shame.

His neighbors and friends were upset. His potential buyer was a corporation nobody in town had heard of because it was invented to do this deal, to build a gated subdivision of rich vacation homes. A resort on JR's prime valley property would change the character of Stony Mesa. JR felt guilty, but then that's the way we do it here in America, he reasoned. Everyone is on his own and the top dog gets the bone. Go for the gold, right?

JR owned a new slate-gray suit because he attended church faithfully and wanted to appear respectful and successful within his church community. Otherwise, it was mostly coveralls. You can't pull a calf out of its mother or grease a truck axel without the kind of sturdy work clothes he bought at the local feed store. He wore out a dozen pairs of gloves a year. Tonight he decided to split the difference between his Sunday wardrobe and his work-week attire. He wore new blue jeans, a white dress shirt with a turquoise bolo tie, a shiny leather jacket, and finely tooled cowboy boots that looked like they were fresh from the store. He wore his immaculate dress Stetson, not white but cream. His other hats were sweat stained and frayed but he kept the Stetson in a hat box in his closet. He reached for the box that evening and saw a jewelry case that belonged to his beloved wife. He paused and whispered, "I'm sorry, honey. My life here just don't make sense now that you're not by my side."

People coming into the school gym for the meeting nodded cordially and some shook his hand. Their hands were gnarly and some were missing fingers. Some of his neighbors avoided eye contact altogether. Conversations hushed as they passed by him. He noted their responses. He had separated himself from them by selling what was familiar and respected so he could leave them. It wasn't just the upsetting surprise that the Jango Ranch was up for sale that his neighbors had to process but the implicit rejection of a way of life by one of their own who personified that way.

The developer's techy assistant busily sorted plugs and wires so he could connect a laptop into some sort of projector. Junior watched the kid. This is one more sign that my days are over, he thought. He could weld and plumb, break a horse, and make a field of alfalfa glow green but all this power point stuff was beyond him. And smartphones? Cars that drive themselves? Drones? Good Lord, his inner voice muttered, the world has changed. Science fiction is no longer fiction. His kids moved away rather than herd and brand. They had seen him get kicked and burned, his knuckles scraped and busted, his back bent into a permanent hunch. Ranchers may express pride in a traditional way of life based on hard work and tenacity, but it is hard for their kids to accept that gloss on why ranching is worth the struggle. Why be chained day in and day out, they asked, to a long list of hard chores for little pay and no benefits?

Ranching was a life of constant uncertainty. The weather was against you half the time and you couldn't tell from one year to the next what your needs would cost or if there'd be a market for your alfalfa or beef. JR knew that people like to glorify cowboy living in songs and stories but the actual doing of it is tough. He was now old and his bones ached. Damn, on winter mornings he even needed help getting up on his horse. Did John Wayne need a step ladder?

It was one thing when his wife of fifty years worked the ranch with him, always sharing the workload with her cheerful and optimistic spirit, but when she succumbed to cancer, he lost heart. It was too hard to do alone. All of the daily activities that once sustained him no longer made sense. Kayla went off to college and he was lonely.

This is the only way, he told himself. It makes me and my kids secure. I can pay off my debts and maybe even pay my grandkids' tuition or help them with a downpayment on a house. I'll take my family to Disneyland or maybe on one of those cruise ships. People in town will get over it. Stony Mesa can't stay the same forever. Funny how these newcomers changed the place when they moved here but now they don't want the next wave of newcomers to come in and change it some more. Just the way it is.

But it was more than that. There was something embarrassing, maybe even shameful, about it. JR and his ranching neighbors were caught in the riptide of their favorite myth, that a cowboy with grit never quits, and JR had decided not to drown. To reduce a proud way of life to market value, income, medical bills, and so on seemed to demean them and expose the hollow glory that justified their sacrifices and let them think they were exceptional.

Old Zeb Holleran hobbled up. "Junior, it's your property and I hold property to be sacred. A man has a right to do what he pleases on his own land. But seeing the Jango go for this . . ." He waved his arm toward the smiling suits sitting center stage in front of shiny posters of log and stone mansions. "Well, it's a damn shame is all. I hate to see you go and I don't like the way you're going."

"I understand, Zeb. I'm not happy with it myself. But it's time for me to find a way out. Look at us, Zeb. We're old and you're so bow-legged and stoop-shouldered ya look like a pretzel with whiskers. What are you going to do? Work your whole life until you drop dead fixing a fence for the thousandth time?"

"Yeah, I guess so, Junior. Guess I'll live 'til I die and I'll die doing what I know."

JR shook his head. "Well not me. Look around, my friend. Poverty has been nipping at your heels your whole life. Get ahead, go broke, get ahead, go broke. And when you reach our age it's your body that's broke. If you own your own place, you are on your own if you get sick or hurt. But if your ranch is owned by some car dealer or investment banker and you're just tending it until they build on it or sell it then you got coverage."

"I never took a dime from that car dealer who owns my old ranch and you know it."

"No, but your sons did and still do. They're on the payroll because the ranch is a tax write-off for Midas Auto Mall. Doesn't matter if you and your boys turn a profit or not because you're just placeholders until the owners of Midas cash out. We're all taking what we can get, aren't we? Your boys made a deal with Midas Auto so you and them could stay on and keep ranching. I'm making a deal so I can get out and stop ranching. I've been kicked enough, Zeb."

"I'm not blaming you, JR. I'm just saying it's a damn shame."

"I agree. A damn shame."

Macon Wilson surveyed the crowd watching his presentation. He was the point man for Highlife Holiday Estates and had done presentations like this on many occasions. He'd worked for several days with his staff to make sure the images he projected showed the proposed subdivision in the best possible light.

"Clean, well-built homes is what I want," he told them. "Always call them homes, sounds better than vacation house. You can save that for the sales brochures. Make 'em look more modest than we plan. I want kids in the pictures playing, smiling parents. Most of our buyers will be older people who have made their fortunes and some will be retired. Those buyers don't really want noisy kids in their neighborhood, but remember that these brochures are for distributing in Stony Mesa. We have to anticipate the local audience."

He stopped and lit a cigarette. "Oh yeah, draw in mature trees—the way they will look twenty years after we plant. And no walls, no gates. I know they are in the blueprints but take them out of the show. This audience will think the walls are there to exclude them. I want to emphasize the jobs this could bring, so I want a couple of pictures of construction workers. Happy ones. Understand?"

They assured him they did.

"Oh, one other thing. It goes without saying but I'll say it anyhow. Just white people. I expect this audience is lily white except for their red necks."

His staff laughed nervously.

"I'm not kiddin'. Boon County hasn't any—how shall I say it—diversity. But I'm pretty sure the customers for this project will be just as pink and ivory as the locals, so there's no need to pander to political correctness. The locals I've met so far are real gomers, get it?"

His remarks might have been considered offensive in other settings and the awkward response of some on his staff was a sign that they at least knew he was politically incorrect, but Macon Wilson was safe among his own. His sales crew were free-market believers who mistook their selfishness for righteousness. In their cosmos, wealth was a reward for the virtuous individual who succeeded in accumulating more than his competitors. To such egocentric hustlers, redneck rubes struggling to stay afloat through a flood of debt were losers who were morally expendable in the holy pursuit of glorified treasure.

Now, looking out on his audience, he could see that it wasn't altogether true that Stony Mesa was a hillbilly haven. There was no shortage of cowboy hats and boots and he noted that the young men still wore their baseball hats with the visor forward, another sign that the natives were white and rural. But there were others sprinkled among the audience that looked like typical yuppies on vacation with their zip-off cargo pants, Teva sandals, and designer sunglasses pushed up and resting on shaggy gray manes.

Retirees. Damn boomers. They had time on their hands and were an opinionated bunch. They could be trouble. Generally, though, this community would be easy to overcome. When that woman who looked like she might've been a college professor at one time stood up and blathered on about vibrations, he smiled within. No problem dealing with New Age kooks like her, he told himself. He'd roll right over them. He'd done it before.

After his presentation he invited people to come up and talk more but most of the crowd shuffled out of the school gym. They seemed to be afraid to even look his way. No confidence, he concluded. Another good sign.

Chapter 2

Suski's children were starving. It had finally come to that. When Suski was a child, hunger was rare. They grew squash, corn, and beans in the valley. They hunted deer, elk, antelope, bighorns, and rabbits. They fished. There were pine nuts and berries in season. There were lean times but they always had enough to share and get by. Then the white people came and took over the valleys where they grew their gardens. They killed the game—everything, even wolves and cougars, which they skinned and stuffed to look alive or laid them on the floor of their houses and walked on them. It was shocking how little awareness they had about the power of animals. He could not imagine such disrespect. Suski wondered how lonely and hard his life would be with no animals to guide and teach him. He mourned the loss of a world that was imbued by the spirits of animals and ancestors.

The white people had the cow. Maybe that was their spirit animal but if so they didn't treat the cows with the respect and caution one would show toward a powerful ally. He had to admit that what he had seen of cows did not impress him. They were dumb and slow. He had never known a wild beast that was like them. But even though their flesh was not as red as elk or bear, it was succulent. Better than rabbit. Better than the insects he had fed his family yesterday and again today when there was no game, no fish, no corn, not even an edible root, nothing.

Suski and his family, thirteen in all, lived by a canyon spring that was cut off on both sides by hundred-foot pour-overs. Their band had become so impoverished it had lost the last horse they had. They retreated to the canyons where the white man's horse could not climb. The men they called cow worshippers did not dare go on foot. Whites were clumsy and poor climbers. They wore the cow skins on their feet but made them too stiff to grasp thin toe holds on the faces of the canyon walls. Suski's family sheltered in an old stone ruin that had been a hunting camp built by ancestors. It was never meant for permanent habitation but Suski could protect his children there. He knew how to take cover there and defend himself.

Suski paced back and forth across the camp while he unknotted his troubled heart. What good is safety if you are starving? There is a point when you are so hungry you cannot feed yourself because you are too tired to go out and hunt or even check snares, too exhausted to even sit in the hot sun and pick pine nuts. He looked at his wife and remembered how her matted dry hair was once lustrous. Her once-resplendent blanket was tattered and stained. He did not understand how the white people could be so cruel. They take away your food and then when you are too tired to do anything but sit, too tired to wash, they call you dirty and lazy.

Not long ago there were many people of his tribe living nearby but they were marched at gunpoint to a land far away. Suski's band hid and ran. They had waited many seasons to come out of the deep canyons to try to live again in the valleys where their ancestors lived. They were wary of the ones who called themselves Christian and it was difficult keeping peace with them because they were strange and could not be trusted. It was a lonely way to live, just one single band hiding with no dances, no trade, no medicine, no help. Where did the others who were marched away go? Were they alive? Did they suffer like his family suffered?

He watched the bellies of his children distend as they grew listless, the light in their eyes fading with each foodless day. Enough, he said to the others, I will do what I must. The white men killed our animals and I will kill one of their animals. Just one, enough to feed my wife and children, my brothers and their wives and children, my sister and her family. We are so hungry and there are many cows.

Jango Burnside was born poor in England where he faced a future of cold winters, hard labor, endless debt, and joyless struggle in the mills of a soot-stained city. He watched his father struggle as he was cheated and exhausted by fat men with top hats in fine carriages. He watched as the lords of England's new industries addressed their employees from carriage doors and windows because they did not want to soil their boots in the grimy yards of the factories they commanded. Jango was alternately angry and despondent as he watched his father worn down to a bent figure, too soon gray in hair and spirit. His old man died broken and bitter.

Jango's real name was John, he supposed, because he remembered being called Jack as a boy. He didn't remember nor care about his birth name. When the missionary came to his home and promised a better life in a land of milk and honey where you could cast aside the grim fate generated by a humble origin and start over, young Jack jumped at his chance to escape a life he despised and a future he dreaded. Yes, he told himself, I can be who I want to be, and he chose Jango over Jack to signify and affirm his leap of faith into a new world. It was a musical and free-spirited name that spoke to his dream of an open and harmonious future. He was sixteen when he said goodbye to family and friends and left England knowing full well he would never set eyes on them again. His sadness was tempered by hope and ambition.

He was deceived. It was not a land of milk and honey. He arrived in the valley that would one day hold Stony Mesa after ten years of struggling in the new land of America. He worked long hours of hard labor on a farm and slept in a mildewed barn to pay off his passage and then he went westward to cut timber and build roads. He worked beside men who had become angry and mean during their struggle to survive and compete. Many were Civil War veterans who learned to kill without remorse, and desperate men who were stalked by hunger and haunted by past traumas. When he finally had the chance to homestead, he took it.

It was a hard land. The growing season was short and the weather included hail storms, dust devils, flash floods, and searing heat, sometimes all in the same day. The soil was sandy and didn't hold water. And there wasn't much water. There were days he looked upon the stony mesa that rose above the river bottom he had chosen for his ranch and imagined he was looking upon a slim ribbon of green winding through the mountains of the moon.

The first winter a bear broke into the root cellar and wiped out precious provisions. Coyotes took his chickens. A late frost took his fruit. And then the Indians stole his chickens. He dealt with them the same way he dealt with the wolves he killed and hung on his fence. The corpse of the Indian he hunted down after he stole a chicken hung by its neck from a tree for a few days until it disappeared one night, carried off, no doubt, by other Indians.

Since that ugly incident, ten years had passed and so far his relationship with the few remaining Indians was wary but polite. He traded with them but allowed no trespass. They were naked, shameless heathens while he was a Christian. The Bible was clear: God gave dominion to man. And not just any man, but Christians like himself. He knew two or three Indians who had been baptized and lived among Christians, dressed like them, spoke English. He accepted those Indians as examples of God's power to redeem even the most hopeless sinners, but the rest of the Indians he regarded as wild animals who only resembled human beings.

Jango Burnside put on his hat and picked up his rifle. At the door he turned to his wife. "I'm going to ride the northeast corner and see if any of those cows have calved. I will be back before sunset."

Suski gathered the adults who had the strength to listen and talk. He explained his plan to them. The cow was big like an elk. He would need some strong people to carry the meat back to the canyon. They would have to hang back and hide, wait for his signal that he had found a cow and killed it. The white people were strange and unpredictable but he guessed they would be unhappy. He conveyed the seriousness of what might happen if they were caught by reminding them of how his sister's husband was caught stealing a chicken one winter long ago and the white demon chopped off his fingers and hung him from a tree.

They muttered agreement and fell quiet while thinking of the dangers that might lie ahead.

His sister broke the silence. "We will need a basket for the heart and liver."

Chapter 3

Elias wondered out loud about how to approach Olene and ask her what she meant when she went public about flux and disruption at the meeting about the sale of the Jango Ranch. As usual, Grace knew what to do.

"Do you need an excuse to talk to a neighbor? Why not just go over?"

"It would feel less awkward if I had a reason." Elias was less confident than Grace, or maybe he understood his motive was not so pure as hers. Grace would approach Olene selflessly and with compassion for a friend in need; Elias's intent was more about his own curiosity. He was once paid to satisfy his curiosity in a professional manner but now it was just a habit, more compulsion than compassion.

"Bring her some of my strawberry jam," Grace suggested. "She stepped away from the community last night and I guess she has some anxiety about that. Maybe a gesture is needed. Bring her jam and tell her how much we appreciate her courage. Most people don't speak up. That was brave."

He arrived, jam in hand, the following morning. He had visited Olene before to learn about birds. Olene could spot birds as well as anyone and identify unseen birds by their songs. She harbored an owl in the eave of an abandoned hayloft in her barn and she fed ravens, whom she named. A favorite was an aggressive trickster she named Bo. Olene was retired from a career in some university lab far away that she never discussed. She made soap and candles that she sold at the farmer's market. She kept chickens and had a goat named Esther. She played flute in the community orchestra. It seemed everyone recognized Olene and liked her but nobody really knew her well.

She stood on her porch trimming a wisteria vine that had wrapped itself around the railing and was climbing toward the sunlight falling on a banister above them. She wiped her hands on her work apron and shook his hand, untied the apron, and invited him to sit at a kitchen table covered with art projects and cook books. A counter next to the stove was crowded with small jars of seeds she had collected and a pile of envelopes she had started to fill and label. She had recently taken up weaving and there were books on the table about that, too. There were scissors and a flute case, sheets of music, a paint box, two laptops, and a half-dozen books stacked under a reading lamp. The stack of books leaned precariously and threatened to knock the lamp over.

Olene pulled off the bandana that tied her hair back and a silver avalanche followed. She was not one to cut her hair short just because she was older now and gray. She had remained trim and taut-skinned into her late middle age. Her complexion that morning was rosy from a little too much sun the day before. Elias noticed a bandage on the side of her neck and she explained that the dermatologist had just removed a suspicious mole. Such bandages from minor skin surgery were common among the sun-worshipping retirees in Stony Mesa who had learned too late about the sun's ability to scramble skin cells after years of boating, beaches, hiking, swimming, gardening, tennis, golf, and deliberately frying themselves to accrue those latte tones genetics had denied them.

Pleasantries over, Elias got to the point.

"Olene, I admire you for speaking up and I want to honor your courage by learning more. Honestly, I didn't get it. Please tell me again because I want to understand."

She turned toward the stove and put on a tea kettle. He couldn't read her reaction and suddenly wondered if he was stirring a pot that was better left alone. He tried to think of something reassuring to say.

She turned back, set the kettle on the table, and sat across from him, leaning forward. "Well, Elias, I should probably quit before I make a bigger fool of myself. Believe me, I wish I had kept quiet. But I guess if there's one person in Stony Mesa who I trust to give me a fair hearing it's you. Where do you want to start?"

"I think I need some context, Olene. Like I'm not sure what you mean by vibrations and waves and flux. Honestly, it sounded kinda spacey."

She sighed, sipped her tea, and waited to compose her story. Elias understood she was careful and serious so he waited patiently. She began. "I started out in science and math. I learned to identify the verifiable components and measure things. That means of perception works well, just look at what our mastery of chemistry has done for us. There's medicine and all the amazing technology we have. Humans are skilled at breaking things down into their parts and then reassembling them. That's how a barrel of crude oil becomes jet fuel or a pesticide or a lawn chair. But you can't reduce everything in the world to parts. What do you know about a bird by examining its feather? Or if you only look at an individual bird you miss the wonders of seasonal migration. Look at one lone bee and you miss the life of the hive."

She paused, lost in thought. "What I eventually learned is how often the parts interact and change, how behavior emerges, how surprise happens. So, for example, there are what scientists call complex adaptive systems. Like your brain, your immune system, fetal development, ecosystems, and the climate, where the whole is greater than the sum of its parts. Those are all non-linear systems so you can't just look for those clear sequences of cause and effect as if you are looking at chemicals in a lab or planning a trip to the moon. Complex non-linear systems are not so predictable. There are basins of attraction, thresholds, and all sorts of surprising phase changes."

She checked his face to see if he was following her. "And the same reduction and fragmentation that we apply to nature is what we do to each other and we even do it to ourselves. It's what makes us think we are these disembodied egos separated from nature and each other. But really we are all connected because we eat, drink, breathe. We embody our watersheds and soil. The salt of the sea is tasted in a teardrop."

Elias nodded affirmatively. He covered the aftermath of an industrial accident that contaminated nearby wells. He interviewed families devastated by cancer and chronic illness who learned the hard way how we embody our environments. "I know what you're saying, Olene. Every one of us now has synthetic chemicals like dioxins and traces of fire retardant in our blood. Our modern world is saturated with chemicals."

"That's right, Elias, and our precious skin does not keep it out. The boundaries we think are there are temporary, arbitrary, or just plain imaginary. We are all downstream and downwind and borders are ridiculous constructs to keep us divided. Look how we divide ourselves from animals and the suffering that causes. Even the boundary between the living and the so-called dead is not what we think it is. Another delusion."

Elias hesitated. "You mean there are spirits and ghosts?"

"No, I mean stone becomes soil, soil becomes food, food becomes you, and we sit here with our great big brains and think how special and separate we are from the rest of our fellow creatures and especially the cold dead stones beneath our feet. We pronounce the world dead and it becomes a self-fulfilling prophecy. And then we lose those deep feelings of kinship and gratitude that might lead to restraint, even reverence."

She paused and waited for Elias to respond. He did not.

"I'm sorry, Elias, this is all too much. You can see my problem if this makes no sense to you."

"No, I get it. You're saying just what Grace tells me and it's all very holistic but I still don't understand what you were trying to say at the meeting. What was your message about the Jango Ranch, specifically?"

She poured another cup of tea and swept some crumbs from the table into her palm. She turned to brush the crumbs into a waste basket and he could see she was choosing her words carefully.

"Okay, Elias, I'm going to trust you. Let's just keep this between you and me, okay? I don't think what I am going to tell you will go over well in the rest of Stony Mesa, so I'd rather not have it out there. It's not Facebook material, okay?"

"Agreed. And I don't do Facebook."

She got up and washed her cup under the sink, dried her hands on a kitchen towel, and then returned to her chair by the table. She looked into his eyes and studied him intently as if waiting for a sign that she could trust him. He let her look, had nothing to hide.

"I left my research and teaching career after the accident."

"What accident?"

"I was in a bad car crash. I was knocked unconscious and they tell me my heart stopped. They did CPR on me until the ambulance got to the emergency room and there they used paddles to shock my heart alive. I came back."

Another pause. "I'm sorry, Olene, but you're still not clear."

"I saw angels, Elias. Demons, too. Not the kind with wings or horns but spirals and bursts of light and shadows so deep that they had a kind of gravity. I watched how these powerful surges of energy swirled and formed, broke apart and then reconfigured. I watched synapses of energy snap and curl through my own brain and then radiate out through my fingertips and tongue. My skin tingled and my fingers crackled with energy while all around me roared life that flooded through me. There were no boundaries. I was not separated. I was blessed."

A breeze lifted the curtain and they both turned toward the window. Olene smiled. "When I was released from the hospital I quit my job at the university. I traveled, read, and explored my own intuitive powers that had been dormant until the accident. And when I was so thoroughly loose from all the perceptions and assumptions I had carried for so many years I became this incoherent person who stood up and made a holy fool of myself before the entire town. And that's a shame because I moved to Stony Mesa to live a quiet life, a private life, and until this week that's what I had here."

"Then why do it? Why try to explain something others are unlikely to understand?"

"I believe we are driving off a cliff."

"We? Who is we, Olene?"

"Civilization, as if that is one big thing that can crash. More like a troubled hive, I suppose, or a sickness in the hive that is dying by degree. One way or another, though, ignorance will bear tragic consequences. A reckoning is at hand and I foolishly thought I could wake them up."

Elias admired Olene for being so articulate. As a reporter he had interviewed thousands of people and his standard for what made a person articulate had been lowered by the hundreds who habitually scrambled grammar and saturated their responses with ya knows, uhhs, and other inane fillers. Some grunted and barked and some were so verbally constipated they could only squeeze out yes and no. And then there was that annoying uptick tonal inflection used by young people that turned every statement into a question. Olene was a joy to listen to. Like the meticulous reporter he once was, Elias had to dig deeper.

"Olene, that's a pretty big picture you're working on there. What does any of it have to do with the development of the Jango Ranch?"

"Because the day before the public hearing I walked over to the Jango Ranch on a full moon night. I sat quietly and watched and listened for hours. And then that feeling returned. I swam through the air while standing fast. I heard voices and shapes moving under the ground. I felt a powerful malevolent energy trapped there and waiting to erupt. That ground was not always covered by alfalfa, you know. It's alive and sensitive. It talks to me, Elias."

He held her gaze. He wanted to acknowledge her but also owed her an honest response. "I don't hear it, Olene."

"Of course not," she replied, "because you refuse to listen."

Chapter 4

Less than an hour's ride from his cabin, Jango saw ravens bouncing up and down around a large vulture who was crouched over a glistening red pile. One raven grabbed a piece of meat out from under the vulture's feet and flew away quickly, trailing a burgundy ribbon of flesh while the vulture hissed and snapped at the other ravens. Jango turned his horse toward the commotion and trotted over. The birds flew off protesting loudly.

Cow guts. Mostly intestines, the head. The grass was speckled with blood. Everything else gone.

Animals don't do that. Even cougars leave a half-eaten carcass. They drag it into some brushy hiding place and roll it up for future meals. The carcass was too clean and incomplete to tell a tale of animal predation. No, he thought, humans did this and I know who.

He rode past his cabin and up the long lone road to town. He stopped at the feed and grain yard of the general store where he found three men loading lumber into a wagon. He told them and the word spread: tomorrow morning at his place and bring a gun. Nobody had to be told that last bit because they knew full well what Jango's intentions were. They didn't want to leave their chores to children and women while they were gone, but when an Indian goes bad it was everybody's business. Best to nip it in the bud.

Shortly after sunrise the next day there were ten of them, their demeanors somber. They were impatient with snickering horses as they adjusted bedrolls and bags of food they hoped they wouldn't need. Some no doubt relished the hunt and were excited by the prospect of violence and danger. Most, Jango suspected, were like him. He wished this nonsense wasn't necessary. Why, they asked themselves, couldn't Indians act right and stop their thieving ways? Why couldn't they learn and improve themselves? To Jango and most of his neighbors, putting wild Indians under control was not an adventure but a distasteful obligation and necessity. He sensed the group was ready so he spit on the ground, pushed his hat down hard on his brow, and wheeled his horse westward to the maze of canyons where the heathens were surely hiding.

"Let's do it." Ten men followed Jango on horseback. Rabbits scattered before the approaching storm of hoof beats and pale clouds of dust curled in its wake.

They had to leave their horses at the mouth of each canyon they searched. They stumbled through washes strewn with boulders, quicksand, and snags. The glare of unmediated sun on sandstone walls made their heads ache as they squinted to see tracks and movement. When cornered, the Indians climbed out. The posse might get close enough to their prey to see flashes of hair or skin as their Indian prey scrambled above them but they never got a clear shot. There was nothing the Indians couldn't climb and the posse riders began referring to them as "those monkey bastards."

The hunt had lasted three days when they decided it was time to turn back and resume the farm work they'd left to their wives and children. They'd had enough of climbing through steep slopes of loose talus to find abandoned camps. One canyon after another the same damn thing: too late, gone. At one point Suski stood high above them on a canyon rim they had no chance of climbing and shook his fist and yelled something in his tribal tongue that none of them could understand. They drew pistols and fired but he was too far away and the sun was in their eyes.

Suski's family could scamper over steep cliffs because they knew where there were toe-holds carved by ancestors into the canyon walls. They knew which slot canyons offered passage and which ended abruptly in rock falls and pour-overs. They knew secret routes to seeps and potholes for drinking water and to caves and alcoves for sleeping. Again and again they escaped through narrow labyrinths of stone where horses were useless.

The hunting party pursued their prey on foot until their legs ached and their feet were bruised and blistered. Zeke Tandy slipped off a ledge and busted up his foot so badly that it became too swollen to squeeze his boot on. Others were scratched and bleeding from pushing themselves through scrub brush and tripping over broken rocks. The knees on their pants were torn. Hal Bundy couldn't stop sneezing; because they had no knowledge about allergies in those days, the others wondered if the red devils were capable of some kind of evil magic. At night they worried about being ambushed and they awoke with every little sound. They were out of coffee and down to dry biscuits that just increased their constant thirst. Stew Young relieved himself too close to a nest of poisonous nettles and now scratched ferociously at hives that girdled his loins. His fellow vigilantes worried that he would fall off his horse as he rode along with both hands down his pants at once.

Frustration made them murderous. "That son of a bitch is gonna die, you wait," said Jango. "If it's the last thing I do."

Damn right, chimed the others. If they get away with killing your cattle, what's next? Your woman or your children? They have no sense of property, no sense of right and wrong, the law means nothing to them. But after a couple of minutes of angry venting there was silence. They knew they were beaten, for now anyway.

Arlo Doyle spoke for the others. "I'm sorry, Jango, but it's time to turn back. You ain't gonna get him this way. You best keep your eye sharp and we can take turns riding the far range and helping you look out. Could be one of our cows next. First man that sees him shoots him. He'll be back, you wait'n see. We'll get him eventually. Just a matter of time."

"Thanks, Arlo. Thanks to all of you. But I got a plan."

"What's that?"

"Remember years ago when that wolf pack was taking calves right and left? We got rid of them, didn't we? How did we do that?"

"We baited them."

"That's right, we baited them. Poison instead of bullets."

"What do ya have in mind, Jango?"

"I'm thinking I got an old mossyback cow I could part with if it meant no more thieving Indians."

Chapter 5

Elias ran into Hip Hop Hopi while buying eggs at the Desert Rose Farm. Hoppy and his partner Luna Waxwing ran a bar and restaurant that was supported by their organic farm just down the road. People came from all over to see the landmark artwork that stood in front of the former saloon. Luna and Hoppy created the art with the help of several friends and Stony Mesa residents eager to mask the obnoxious structure beneath, a garish neon monster that the star-gazing citizens of Stony Mesa detested. Hoppy and Luna described their project as a "colossal collective folk-art creation" to anyone who pointed at the strange textile tower and asked, "What in the heck is that?"

That was a thirty-foot tower of diverse pastel parachutes that had been sewn together and draped over the sign. This loose quilt of lavender, pink, yellow, and blue folds of parachute silk cascaded down through a web of red climbing ropes. The silken folds were also crisscrossed by strings of hundreds, perhaps thousands, of brightly colored Tibetan prayer flags. A banner announcing the Desert Rose Café and Market was wrapped around the odd beast at about two thirds of its height. A rope line that ran along the skirts at the bottom of the sculpture was hung with dozens of baby shoes but nobody could explain how or why the tradition of tying baby shoes there began.

Word got out on the Internet and tourists stopped to see it. Lately, young couples could be found posing for pictures in their wedding clothes in front of it. It had a gazillion likes on Facebook. It was weirdly beautiful and, like the canyon walls of Stony Mesa, it changed with the weather. On windy days its prayer flags fluttered and a symphony of whispers from a thousand delicate wings filled the air. On sunny days it was all about shimmer and shadow. When soaked with rain it expressed a sodden sadness that filled the café's bar with hushed bikers slowly sipping beer.

The Desert Rose was formerly a saloon for upscale bikers, not the gang-bent bikers who spit, stab, and smell bad, but the kind that ride shiny Harleys on weekends after too many hours litigating or doing root canals. The original saloon was called the Bull and Stallion and was despised by most of Stony Mesa's residents, who regarded it as a cheesy parody of the mythic Wild West performed on a stage that was out of scale and in their faces. They welcomed the part-time jobs the saloon required but the former managers were generally regarded as toxic control freaks with entitlement issues, accomplices of the rich owner who nickel-and-dimed the help. The glaring monster sign next to it looked like it was straight out of Vegas. When the saloon's owner passed away suddenly, his daughter, Luna Waxwing, inherited both the bar and her old man's ranch just down the road from the saloon.

Luna and her partner Hoppy were working hard to transform the ranch from a cow-growing business to a small farm growing organic vegetables and heritage fruit that they sold at the Desert Rose. They had converted the saloon and restaurant into a multi-purpose destination where you could buy fresh kale or homemade salsa, eat a grass-fed burger or wok vegetables, drink a beer or a smoothie, meet your neighbors or talk to a tourist. Most recently they tried turning goat milk into specialty cheeses and raw apple juice into hard cider.

Down the road at the Desert Rose Farm they converted a bunkhouse into a greenhouse and raised two more hoop-house nurseries with the help of an itinerant crew of dreadlocked drifters and vegan vagabonds who stopped in to work for a few days or a few months. They built a goat barn and a composting pit. As Luna and Hoppy struggled to find a niche, the ranch's old holding pens and corrals were replaced by raised bed gardens, a cheese cellar, and a platform for ten beehives. Luna understood that the agricultural marketplace was designed to favor factory farms, monoculture, genetically altered seeds, and other tools for volume and efficiency, so making a small farm viable would be a tough challenge.

The transformation of the former Bull and Stallion Saloon into the Desert Rose Café, however, was an unqualified success. When Luna took over from her deceased father she eliminated all the displays on the walls that she regarded as "implements of torture." First to go was the barbed wire collection and the old six-shooter above the bar. Then braided whips, spurs, branding irons, and lassoes were taken down from the walls. She considered putting them up on eBay but then decided the world would be better off without such violent gear in it. The wall next to the restroom featured a colorful antique quilt crowned by a busted old banjo and surrounded by a halo of horseshoes. Several rusted farm implements completed the folksy chaos. She kept the photos of Hopalong Cassidy, Gene Autry, and Roy Rogers, who seemed benign, even corny.

John Wayne's life-size portrait, however, was too much to tolerate. Wayne had been an avid supporter of the Vietnam War and was otherwise a macho Republican moron, according to Luna. The Duke's portrait went into the men's restroom next to a quote by William Irwin Thompson, one of her favorite authors. A cartoon voice-cloud came out of John Wayne's mouth with the quote within, so that it looked like the Duke was saying, "The mental habit of the West is one in which being is posited as a being and called god; in which process is arrested in substance and called material reality; and in which mind is made into an organism without an environment and called the self." Luna thought irony was more effective than censorship when promoting one's beliefs.

A bar still stood at one end of the large building but it only served local micro-brews and regionally produced wine. In the restaurant portion of the building a customer could still order a bison steak but could now also select from a wide range of vegetarian dishes prepared by an old Mexican chef named Lobos Zapata and a small crew of young aspiring cooks who had migrated from Seattle and Santa Fe. There was nowhere else to get a spicy curry within a hundred miles. A side room with a counter and patio seating bustled with drive-by tourists looking for coffee, sandwiches, and salads. They learned from their smartphones that all but the java was grown right down the road at the Desert Rose's own family farm.

The Desert Rose Café and its farm got such enthusiastic reviews on social media that it was soon known as a food oasis for travelers weary of interstate pit stops where bogus burgers and big gulps are the only choices. To your average French, Italian, or Chinese tourist, eating

American fast food was the equivalent of drinking out of a toilet bowl. Local cuisine wasn't much of an alternative. Too many mom n' pop cafes served comforting assortments of fried food and sugary desserts that should have included a coupon toward double bypass surgery or a first insulin shot. The Desert Rose Café was definitely off the four-lane beaten path, but many tourists thought it was worth a detour.

Hoppy wiped his hands across his apron and slipped a large pair of scissors into a leather slipcase. "Elias, I missed that meeting," Hoppy called to him. "What happened?"

Elias walked over to Hoppy, who was washing a fresh harvest of spinach in a porcelain sink behind the counter where produce and baked goods were sold. Clots of soil speckled the floor beneath him. Elias looked up to see the carved wooden ravens that Luna had affixed to the wall where a bison head and a stuffed cougar had once reposed. Like real ravens, they were shiny black with flashes of blue as the light from the Desert Rose window played on their wings. They seemed to be listening.

Elias tried hard to concentrate. "What did you hear?" he asked Hoppy.

"That the suits were slick and everyone was dazzled by the show. That we're gonna get a bunch of rich people behind a gate. That Olene stood up and talked crazy. That Kitty cracked a joke and everyone laughed. And that I better learn how to caddie golf and clean pools so I can be of use to the rich people who live behind the gate."

"Well, that's as good a summary as I've heard so far, Hoppy. I'm not sure about the golf part though."

"So what are the chances that this is really gonna happen?"

"Hard to say. Looks like they've just about got a price negotiated with Jango Junior. They've already made an impressive investment in the plans they drew up and the presentation they put on. I hear they're doing tests on soil out there, which is a first step before you site your roads and buildings. They got lawyers working on converting alfalfa water to golf course water. So yeah, they're moving forward."

Elias put his hand up and said, "Time out. Let me go back to my car. Only take a minute." He returned in two with a handful of brochures and pamphlets. He brushed away beet stems and spread the glossy advertisements across the counter for Hoppy to inspect. "Look at these brochures. They only give these to prospective buyers and there aren't any in Stony Mesa so you probably wouldn't see them otherwise. You can choose the style of your vacation getaway house."

He handed Hoppy a brochure. "This one is a southwest adobe model called the Cliff House that comes with a home theater in the shape of a kiva. Sits thirty. Look at the giant flatscreen. And here you see a fireplace straight outta old Santa Fe. Rich interiors, rugs, blankets, and such."

Hoppy shook his head in disbelief and Elias handed him another advertisement. "Or choose a log motif. This one is called the Sweetwater Cabin because it's only five thousand square feet. That's modest I guess, by their standards. Comes with a massive stone hearth. Turn the page, antlers everywhere. Rustic charm on a massive scale. Look at the woodwork in this picture. Or go for stone. Here's a model with a ripple rock exterior. Look above the mantel. That's an amazing display of fossils."

"Do they come with their own fossils?"

"No, you have to buy your own art and antiquities."

Hoppy did not hide his disgust. He wiped his hands on his apron and lifted it over his head, hung it on a stool, and tugged gently at his beard. "How about costumes, do they throw in an appropriate costume?"

"No, you have to buy that separately. Hey, you oughta know. Luna's dad, the late Bo Hineyman, sold fancy cowboy shirts and hats when the Desert Rose was still the Bull and Stallion. I guess we should've seen it coming when Bo moved to town and put up that damn sign. We dodged the bullet then, but rich people were bound to come sniffing around eventually. We've got two things they like to acquire: scenery and water. So they flock to places they haven't wrecked yet and play their old game of 'my lawyer is smarter than your lawyer.'"

Hoppy shook his head again and sighed. "I hate to see something so out of character with the town. It doesn't fit. Who are these people, anyway?"

Elias reached into his jacket pocket and pulled out a small flip pad. He had a stash of them leftover from his years at the newspaper. He flipped over a few pages, flipped back two, and looked down at his notes. "Well, I looked into it. The Highlife Holiday Estates Corporation is basically three individual investors. One is a man named Orin Bender who has made a fortune laying pipe. He's got contracts all over, everything from municipal water and sewer lines to building pipe systems for oil and gas fields. He made so much money during the fracking boom that he is looking for a place to invest it. He came through here and he says he 'discovered' Stony Mesa while visiting the Sea Ledges tar sands project before it got wiped out by that flood a few years back."

Elias flipped a few more pages and paused. "Okay, here it is. Bender brought in an old friend named Les Huntley. Huntley worked with Bender at Beksell Construction. They started at Beksell after getting degrees in engineering and they worked their way up through management. When they started out, Beksell was building nuclear plants overseas, dams here and in South America. Then they built ports for tanker ships in the Middle East. Orin Bender left and started his own pipe business but Les Huntley climbed to the top rung in Beksell. His golden parachute was in the order of fifty million dollars and he's also hungry to invest."

He flipped more pages and then back again. The cover of the notepad was worn at the edges from its frequent trips in and out of Elias's pocket. The suit jackets in his closet were frayed at the pockets from the same career-induced notebook traffic. Grace tried to replace them but the material never matched. She accepted the damage as the unavoidable consequence of his profession, like ink-stained fingers and constant questions.

Elias was on a roll. "The third partner is unlike the other two. He's a hedge fund guy, younger, Ivy League college, MBA from Wharton, an office on Wall Street, stylish, carries two cell phones and has a cellar full of fine French wine. His name is Warren Smithfield. I wondered how he fit in and then found out his daughter married Orin's son. Despite their differences, Orin and Smithfield like each other, and from what I can glean the young couple are nice kids and the parents are proud. Plus Smithfield had ten million to throw into the pot."

He closed his notebook and stuffed it into his pocket. "But this is a side show for these guys. They get to build another nice vacation home for themselves in a beautiful place and make some money, too. That or avoid taxes. You know how that goes."

Hoppy looked downcast. "So can we get in front of it and stop it?"

"Unlikely. The law favors them and so does public policy. This is what America is all about—build and grow, buy and sell. The country is driven by a belief that making more, always more, is the main goal. The developers make the rules so guys like you and me don't get in their way."

"So that's it, it's hopeless?"

"No! I didn't say it was hopeless, I said it will be difficult."

Hoppy felt impatient. Sometimes, he thought, Elias parses his case a little too much. He tried to get him back on track. "What do we do first, Elias?"

"Sit back and watch for now, but get ready. This thing is still in the bullshit and pretty pictures stage. They're testing the waters. But now is the time to raise awareness and get your circle of friends and neighbors talking. Make a list of who might be willing to resist, note their skills and useful connections. Watch how they interact. Get ready to put together a meeting at some point. That's where your group decides goals, targets, tools. The name is usually the hardest part. Create a means of communicating, definitely a Facebook page and maybe a website. We would have to hire a lawyer so that means pooling our resources or fundraising. If we're lucky, there will be some angel with deep pockets."

Hoppy was hard pressed to break in. "Elias, wait. I said what was the first thing? Talk it up and scope the community, is that what I heard you say?"

"Yes, no need to get ahead of ourselves."

Hoppy had been listening to people who came to the Desert Rose to buy the eggs and greens that were grown at the Rose's farm. Everyone hoped that there would be a way to block the developers from taking over Stony Mesa and "Aspenizing" it. Hoppy said, "But if this is just a side venture, maybe they don't care that much; if we put up enough resistance, will they give up?"

Elias, as usual, was realistic. "Or maybe it's a pet project and they'll fight tooth and nail to defend it. I don't know. That's how it goes with an outfit like Holiday Highlife, they only tell you what they want you to hear, only show you what they want you to see. You have to get behind their curtain to understand their motives and resources."

Hoppy laughed. "Something tells me you've peeked behind quite a few of those curtains, Elias. I wish we all had those skills."

Elias smiled sadly. "I wish we didn't need them."

Chapter 6

JR slumped forward on a kitchen chair, an elbow resting on his knee, his head resting in his palm, a black phone held to his ear. He listened quietly for minutes and interjected only short affirmations while his granddaughter delivered her cracked-voice testimony about the irreplaceable value of the Jango Ranch. "It's the only home I ever had."

"I know, honey, I know," JR assured her. "That piece of ground means more to me than I can say. I don't cry out loud like you do, Kayla, but I have shed tears in privacy."

"Then why sell? There must be a way to keep it."

"Kayla, facts are facts. And the fact is that when your grandma got so sick we had some major medical bills pile up. Stuff Medicare don't cover. We haven't had a good year on the Jango for a long while and I'm too old to squeeze another drop out of it. Since Grandma died I lost heart. That ranch is something your grandma and I did together. We held each other up and we kept at it even when it made no sense to go on. Nobody else in this family wants to do that kind of work anymore. Look at you, you're gonna be a veterinarian and I'm very proud of that."

She sniffled loudly. "Could you give it away?"

He paused and smiled slightly. This reality check was hard and she just didn't get it. "Well, darlin', if I drop dead tomorrow and leave it to you, the hospitals will want to be paid from my estate and you'd have to sell the ranch to do that anyhow. Besides, if I can't punch cows anymore what am I gonna live on? They don't give old cowboys pensions. But I can do just fine on what I make on the sale. I can pay off the bills and even spread what's left over around a bit. I'm lucky because not every ranch like mine has a buyer. People aren't going into ranching like that anymore and you're lucky if some big fish like Highlife Holiday Estates comes along. It's an opportunity for us all to move on."

He could hear her crying softly.

"Look, why don't you come down and visit? Nothing is happening on this right away. Look at your calendar and see when you have your next vacation day. We'll go riding. We can talk more then."

"Okay."

"It's gonna be alright, Kayla."

"Okay, Grampa."

He hung up and sighed so deeply that his chest ached. He walked to the back porch, swatted away a moth that was attacking the light above the door, and reached for the porch railing. He clutched it with both hands and leaned over, looked up briefly at the night sky and then stared down into the dark yard. He had to be the strong one for Kayla even though he felt crushed and broken. Stiff upper lip the British called it. He would put the best face on his defeat. Accentuate the positive, he thought, wasn't that a song?

He searched his brain for the tune he vaguely remembered, a light and sweet melody that would be a balm to his troubled mind, when the plaintive yelp of a coyote punctured his consciousness. Again, a crazed yip yip yee!

He stepped out from the porch light and scanned the dark horizon. Another high-pitched howl and a minute later another. It was pitch black. The beasts, he thought, always have that on their side. The darkness. And men's weak eyes.

Chapter 7

Lucas Hozho heard it, too. He smiled. His Navajo grandmother always called coyotes "God's dogs." Indigenous lore has many stories about coyotes who play the role of clever tricksters who are killed and then somehow return to life. His own tribe admired coyotes for their adaptability, their stealth, and their resilience. A people who struggled to survive on an unforgiving desert landscape could appreciate a creature that was the ultimate survivor.

"Did you hear that?" Lucas asked Luna and Hoppy.

"Sure did. Listen, there he goes again."

They walked out onto the porch and listened without speaking. Like most nights in Stony Mesa, there was little ambient noise to compete with the cry of a coyote. The village's isolation from traffic and industry was so complete that it could have been designated as a refuge for silence seekers. Noise in Stony Mesa was not a general mix of sounds as in a city or suburb. You could pick out the hoot of an owl, cats fighting in yards, a crazy rooster doing his job way too early. The six ears gathered on the porch strained to hear more but only heard the sound of moths batting their wings against the porch light. When they were sure the coyote show was over they walked back in.

Luna spoke first. "I read that officials in Chicago estimate that there are two thousand coyotes living within the city limits. They're in every big city, Boston and Los Angeles, coast to coast, everywhere. They'll eat anything from dumpster food to pets, fruit, anything. A few years ago they caught one in Central Park in the middle of Manhattan. It either crossed a bridge or hitched a ride on a truck."

Lucas knew what it is like to be a misunderstood underdog. Like those urban coyotes, he learned how to slip stealthily between worlds and how to adapt to new habitat in order to survive. Lucas understood how challenging that can be. He believed that the difference between the Anglo worldview and his own native worldview was revealed in the way each regarded coyotes. Whites thought coyotes were varmints to be killed on sight.

"Indian people," Lucas explained, "call them 'tricksters.' Coyote gets in trouble and causes chaos but the mess he makes is often creative. Like the story of how he was given a blanket full of stars to hang in the night sky. He was directed to set them in orderly and even rows like rows of corn or the stars on the flag but he got bored and flipped the blanket into the sky, scattering the stars into the beautiful patterns you see today. But mostly Coyote is all about appetite and opportunity. He will always adapt if there's a meal in it for him. Or sex—in the stories I've heard, Coyote is a lusty character. He survives because he's so clever and resilient."

"Yeah," said Hoppy, "but my neighbors kill them on sight. Some towns even hold contests to see who can kill the most. Coyotes are hated by ranchers. Seems odd since most of them like and own dogs."

"But coyotes are dogs that don't serve or obey," Luna interrupted. "They won't sit, stay, roll over, beg. They don't fetch or cuddle. Instead they steal and kill. They once inhabited the edges of civilization and haunted the night but now they are everywhere. Maybe there are no edges left. After the coyotes are gone my ranching neighbors will complain about all the marauding foxes and skunks that are no longer held in check by the coyotes. We're the bosses of nature and we can't stop tampering."

Lucas laughed lightly and shook his head, issued a quiet smack of disgust, and rendered his verdict. "Don't worry, because coyotes will always prevail."

He swept his arm across the horizon of Stony Mesa. "Long after this town is gone, coyotes will be waiting to inhabit the ruins. I'm pretty sure Indian people will still be here, too."

"Don't be too sure," Hoppy warned him. "In the world to come, Lucas, coyotes will be wiped out by drones with DNA-seeking missiles that inject genes into them that turn them into bovine-like dogs called cowyotes. Cowyotes will be especially tasty in tacos because of their beefy texture and peppery aftertaste."

Lucas and Luna cracked up laughing and Lucas replied, "No, Hoppy, in the world to come my ancestors walk on the bones of people whose arrogance makes them reckless. And in this world now I'm guessing some people smoke pot."

Luna: "In my world to come we all cum."

Lucas: "You win. I can't beat that."

Luna: "Did you say beat that?"

They laughed again, not because her response was so funny but because they enjoyed laughing together and didn't want to give that up. Although humor may be spontaneous, the response can be almost ceremonial, a way to affirm friendship and good intention.

Luna asked Lucas if he wanted some tea. Luna and Hoppy had met Lucas Hozho at a protest at the proposed Sea Ledges tar sands mine a few years before. "What are you up to these days and why visit Stony Mesa?"

"My grandmother, Nanny Hozho, is a hundred years old. She's still pretty lucid and I have been interviewing her and recording her stories. She's the end of an era in my family. Nobody lives today like she did back then. My sister married a white guy and they live in San Diego where she cleans teeth. My brother and I went to college. He's a pharmacist and makes good money in Tucson. My cousins all left the rez and work in cities, too. I want to capture her life story before she dies."

Luna poured three cups of tea and set a small pot of thick honey on the table. Lucas continued. "You know, we've always been an oral culture that passes down the stories and history of our people by word of mouth. Hey, if you've ever spent nights in a Navajo hogan you realize there isn't much else to do for entertainment. And now we have the means to record it all and so that's what I'm trying to do. Sort of a high-tech way for me to try to reconnect to a very old oral tradition that is disappearing. If you heard me speak in my native tongue, you would think I am fluent. But my grandmother and her sisters would not agree. If I have kids, their first language will be English. So I want to look through the window before it closes."

Luna and Hoppy encouraged him and expressed interest in hearing what he had recorded. He promised he would try to put together an

English transcript of the highlights of his interviews, which were conducted in Navajo. He asked them to think of other ways he might share his project when it was completed and they promised to come up with suggestions. Luna said she would get on her laptop that evening and explore crowd-sourcing options.

"But what brings you here?"

"My grandmother told me she had an aunt who told her that she was born somewhere near here. She told my grandmother that they hunted and farmed and gathered pine nuts and herbs in a land they called Many Rocks. She remembers geese and ducks sheltering along a river and meadows teeming with rabbits. Elk came down to drink by the river's edge. Stony Mesa fits that description, or maybe you could say it fit that at one time.

"Her aunt told granny that the people were starving and the white people were cruel so they retreated farther into the canyons. Her family split off from people who stayed behind, including cousins she loved. Eventually they settled where my grandmother lives today. She never saw the people who stayed behind at Many Rocks again. They disappeared, she said, we never saw them again."

Luna winced. "What happened to her?"

"She was still a child when she was captured and sent to a boarding school for Indians, one of those places where Indian kids were taught to be like white Christians and punished if they spoke their native tongue and didn't measure up to Anglo expectations. Years later she tried to find the place she had last seen her cousins who vanished. She told my grandmother that it was now called Shanegoat. When we were traveling back and forth to the Sea Ledges tar sands protests, I came through here and noticed a sign for the Jango Ranch. I know it's a stretch but I thought there might be a connection."

Luna sliced some homemade bread and put it on the table with a jar of Grace Buchman's homemade jam. "The Jango is going to be sold and turned into a fancy gated community with a golf course. You probably heard that, because everyone in town is talking. They're worried that it will change Stony Mesa and that it will attract more of the same."

"Yes, I heard that. I tried to talk to Mr. Burnside, whose grandfather was the original Jango. They call him Junior or JR. He still owns the place but at first he was too busy getting ready for some kind of hearing and now he just can't be bothered. I talked to his granddaughter who was visiting for the hearing, but she was upset and had no idea what I was saying. Must be some other Jango, she told me, because she was very familiar with her family's history and never heard anything at all about Indians."

Hoppy scoffed and gave Lucas the local account. "The old-timers here claim that there weren't any Indians here when their ancestors arrived. There were petroglyphs and granaries, potsherds and arrowheads from hundreds of years ago but nothing recent. I read the local history collection at the county library and they mention that Indian hunting parties came through. Supposedly they traded and got on fairly well with the few Indians they saw. It was a fairly common practice to take in Indian orphans. From what I know about that, the kids were treated more like domestic servants than adopted children, but the settler families were proud of their own generosity and liked to point out how they had 'civilized' those wild children."

Lucas smiled. "Well, that's an old story, isn't it? White settlers always claim they were fair and friendly. Hey, no problem here, they say, must've been somewhere else that all that killing happened. And where did they think those orphans came from, anyway?"

"What do you do next?" asked Luna. She offered him a second cup. "I mean, you know, to find out what happened."

"Nothing, I guess. I don't have time to be a detective. I just thought I might get lucky and there'd be a connection between the Jango Ranch and Shanegoat in the old woman's memory."

Hoppy said that after his grandmother died he thought of many questions he wished he'd asked her. "When I was a child I thought she would live forever and I didn't know what to ask. Now I wonder about how she grew up, why she made the choices she made, where she met my grandfather, that kind of thing. When a generation dies we lose the personal histories and all the stories that might tell us where we came from and who we are. There are funny stories, scary stories, stories that warn us or have a moral lesson. We manage to hang on to fragments. We might forget the stories but what happened in them was real and still resonates through the next generations."

Luna picked a napkin from the floor where it had fallen. She turned to Hoppy and said, "Elaborate. How does the family's past resonate?"

Hoppy had expected her to challenge him with a question and he was ready. "So for example, a person might be afraid of dogs because his great grandfather was bitten in the butt by the neighbor's dog and he passed his fear to his kids and then they gave it to their kids. You know how that goes: watch out! Don't trust the dangerous doggie, honey. Stand back! Maybe they all learned to clench when in the presence of dogs and the body language itself is imprinted and passed on from one generation to the next."

Luna's eyes suddenly welled with tears. "I never knew my father, never wanted to. But here I am living on his ranch and running a business he started. I took the shell of his life and I'm making it my own. I don't know why he came here and made this place for me but I don't have to know. It's mine now and I can make it what I choose to make it. I hated him all my life, but I never knew him and now I get this amazing gift. So now I wish I knew more, because now it matters."

Lucas leaned over and brushed her hand gently with his fingertips. "We all do that. We take what is passed along and try to make something out of it even though the past is hidden. We build on top of the mystery of it. And what you have made from the ruins of your father's life is beautiful and good, Luna."

She took a handkerchief from Hoppy's breast pocket and blew her nose so loudly that they all laughed. She wanted to move away from the sad place where she had fallen. "Lucas, did you know that Hoppy is part Hopi?"

"Well, one eighth," Hoppy added. "I grew up in Oakland with parents who were part of the sixties thing, so I am more hippie than Hopi but mostly glad to just be Hoppy." They laughed together again, this time more subdued.

"Where are you staying?" Luna asked Lucas. "You are welcome to stay here. There's a guest room at our place."

"Thanks but I'm leaving tonight. It's hard to be a stranger here. Everyone stares. I think I make the people here nervous. I'm going home."

Hoppy wagged a scolding finger at Lucas and offered his analysis. "You don't look like a tourist, that's why. Lots of strangers go unnoticed but they're wearing shorts or yoga pants. Maybe you should trade that ball cap for one of those wide-brim floppy hats from REI and a daypack with a North Face logo. Carry a camera and wear a tee shirt with the name of a national park on it. How about a vest with pockets for sun-screen and bug juice. Or you could go the other way and dress cowboy. You know, boots and tight jeans, big hat, spit a lot."

Lucas laughed softly and nodded. "Maybe next time I'll wear different skin."

Chapter 8

Hyrum Allred took his hat off and made sure his boots were scraped clean before he knocked on Jango Junior's door. He waited on the porch for JR to answer. Wisteria and honeysuckle climbed a trellis and the scent of iris was in the air, but the other flower beds around the ranch house were barren since JR's wife, Annie May, passed on. Hyrum noticed a hummingbird feeder that hung empty from the porch ceiling. A hummingbird attracted to its bright red color zoomed in and hovered beside the vacant feeder, buzzing in place and then darting nervously toward the red glass and then back. When it concluded that this red flower had nothing to offer, the bird shot away so quickly that it made a ripping sound. Hyrum knocked again, waited, then rang the doorbell.

Junior didn't hear the knock on the door or the doorbell because he was on the phone and had his hearing aids off. But he noticed Hyrum's truck in the driveway and greeted him just as he was giving up and turning to go.

"Hyrum, what's up my friend? Did you finish digging that ditch for the soils test?"

"That's what I came to talk to you about, JR. There's a problem."

"Good lord, what now?" JR objected to having any soil tested and told the developers that his ranch house, a substantial barn, and several outbuildings had been on that ground for more than a hundred years and did just fine so testing the soil was not necessary. It seemed to him that life today had too many permits, licenses, contracts, tests, fees, reports, files, and applications. Annie May handled that end of the ranch business while he was out doing a man's work, so he didn't know if it had always been that way or just lately. He accepted that Annie's sickness and treatment resulted in endless paperwork, but in the old days the sale of a ranch was done eye to eye and ended with a handshake. These Holiday Estates people excreted paper.

"I think you better come to the truck and see for yourself."

JR slipped on some shoes and followed Hyrum outside. Hyrum opened the passenger-side door of his truck, lifted a round object wrapped in a yellow kerchief from the floor, and laid it carefully on the seat. It looked at first to be a huge egg wrapped in tissue, maybe from an ostrich or emu. Hyrum unwrapped the object carefully to reveal a human skull.

"Jumpin' Jehova! Where did you find that?"

"In the hole I dug. Or maybe it wasn't even a hole. I just scraped the top layer clear and there they were."

"They?"

"I have thirteen skulls and lots of other bones that went with them."

JR insisted that they hop into the truck and go over to the bone-yard so he could assess the scene for himself.

At the site, the two men were silent as they moved about, crouching or stooping occasionally to pick up bones and turn them in their hands, weighing them, returning them gently to the sand. JR stood, ran his fingers through his silver mane, and shook his head softly from side to side. He looked at Hyrum and said, "This is a complete surprise. I'm baffled. What do you make of it?"

"I have no idea." Hyrum turned and walked several paces away from the ruptured soil and the bones as if he didn't want them in earshot while he and JR talked. His voice dropped to a whisper.

"So what do we do about it?"

"It's my land. I own what's on my property don't I?"

Hyrum hesitated and then offered, "I guess so, but I'm not sure about archaeological stuff. And these are human remains."

"I know this. I got Highlife Holiday Estates chewing on my hook and half the town riding my back. If this deal gets complicated it could fall through. I can't stand much more of this pressure. It's best for me to get this done and I don't want those old bones in my way."

JR waited but Hyrum did not reply.

"I think the best thing to do, Hyrum, is put them back where they were and cover them over. Let them rest where they are for now and we can deal with the rest of it later. You can do your test dig somewhere else. I'll pay you very well."

He waited. No reply.

"I'm asking you as a friend, Hyrum."

Hyrum Allred agreed and finished the job by nightfall. He did it all by hand. The erupted graves were filled and smoothed over with a rake he kept in his truck. All bones laid to rest but one. Tucked tenderly in a jacket behind the driver's seat of his truck was one small, delicate skull. Hyrum was sure his cousin Lou Jean could make it talk.

Chapter 9

When in the presence of wild beauty, Elias Buchman lived in the moment and in those moments he was at peace. He believed in the healing power of awe. Bathed in the buttery light of sandstone cathedrals he felt washed clean of the hyped-up chatter that had been his trade. Elias was a paid thinker in recovery.

It was easy to recover—he just followed Grace, who seemed to live apart from the hurry, worry, and fear that saturated the lives of those around her. She had become immune to anger, both the personal kind generated by jealousy, regret, rivalry, and all the other landmines in the path of one's life journey, but also immune to the collective anger that lubricates violence on a vast scale. On her car's back bumper was a sticker that read "War is Never the Answer."

When they first moved to Stony Mesa, Elias was so wary of the rightwing reputation of his new neighbors that he covered that message with duct tape. Grace never mentioned it. Maybe she never noticed, but it is more likely that she extended to Elias the same pacifist approach she expressed on her bumper sticker. She turned the other cheek. He was anxious to fit in and worried that socially they could be round pegs that wouldn't fit into Stony Mesa's square hole. She understood that and saw no need to aggravate his anxiety.

Thankfully, the town proved to be more open-minded, tolerant, and creative than Elias expected. There were now two art galleries, a few small restaurants, a handful of bed-and-breakfast homes, three RV camps, a scattering of rental cabins, four motels, one gas station, two burger joints, one pizza parlor, one general store, and a half-dozen outfits offering guide services on horseback. Most of the tourist trade was owned and operated by "move-ins," a label applied to those who had migrated to Stony Mesa over the past fifty years by those who had grandparents and great-grandparents sleeping under stone in the cemetery behind the town's One True Church.

The gulf between the old corps of cattle keepers and the new wave of outsiders from places far away and unfamiliar to the natives rarely led to confrontation. Differences between the two groups were largely unspoken, though each tribe was sure the other one was critical and judgmental behind closed doors. In a village as small as Stony Mesa, residents were bound to encounter one another continually at the post office, the school, sports events, community fairs, the grocery store, church, the playground, anywhere two people can share space. Civility made life smoother.

Still, there were areas of mutual exclusion. Few if any of the move-ins had attended a rodeo or the annual demolition derby and the cowboys didn't attend the annual plein-air painting contest for artists or the vermiculture workshops at the Desert Rose Farm. Grace always looked for a reason to reach across this division and connect with the cowboy culture. Elias, as usual, worried about it.

On this morning he spent an hour pacing and muttering softly while spilling small drops of coffee from the mug he was holding while he gestured dramatically in some imaginary conversation. Grace hoped he could pull out of it by himself but after an hour she distracted him with a piece of pie and a request to take a bowl of apple peels out to the mulch bin. All day his brow was furrowed. She decided to drive him to the Desert Rose for a take-out dinner and picnic.

As they pulled into the parking lot, he turned to her and with gravity in his voice asked, "Grace, why are we here?"

"Exhale, Elias. Breathe deep. Enjoy the ride."

"That's it, that's why we are here?"

"No, it's what I thought you should do right now. I thought you were experiencing a bit of that cosmic anxiety you've been wrestling today. No?"

"No. I meant are we here to pick up avocados to go home and make our own dinner tonight or are we going to get burritos and take them down to the river? What did we decide?"

"Burritos and the river," she said as she rolled up her window and grabbed the keys.

Elias liked the feeling he got when he walked through the Desert Rose but he found it hard to think in there. The walls of the Desert Rose were covered with hanging plants, maps, notice boards, racks of back-packing and climbing gear, paintings by local artists, broken guitars, photos of people flying over rapids on the back of rafts, racks for herbs and oils, shelves of books on gardening, canning, drying, and fermenting foods, more books on biking and hiking, used books that mixed astrology uncomfortably close to books by Noam Chomsky, and even more shelves with local honey and homemade salsas and jams. A display case held lip balm and sunscreen next to a bin of garlic. Luna had installed a wide rainbow-striped awning over the south-facing windows. When the sun filtered through the awnings the interior light was at once soothing and enchanting. On a sign above the door, Luna printed a quote from the British philosopher and sixties icon Alan Watts: "You and I are as continuous with the universe as a wave is continuous with the ocean." It was an insight she received on an acid trip in her teens and it came to her just moments before her arrest.

Locals shopped at the vegetable stand open to the parking lot if they favored fresh greens and clean vegetables. Luna's hens laid eggs with blood-orange yolks that were almost neon in their intensity. Elias ordered burritos and Grace picked up a dozen of those eggs and a bundle of Swiss chard. She stopped along the way to talk to neighbors. The Desert Rose was a welcome source of part-time jobs. Most working-age residents held seasonal positions with the national park or tourist amenities and combined that work with one or two part-time jobs to make ends meet.

Grace gently squeezed an avocado to determine freshness and noticed Kayla Burnside in an animated conversation with her cousin Junie Gay. Kayla wore tight blue jeans with a heart-shaped rhinestone pattern on each cheek of her butt. Elias wondered if rhinestone-butted jeans left scratch marks on wooden chairs when they sat on them. "I don't get it," he told Grace.

"You're trying too hard," Grace replied.

Kayla mostly avoided Junie Gay, who led a reckless life that whirled broken hearts and misdemeanors in its wake but she loved her self-described "crazy-cuz." Kayla enjoyed hearing about Junie Gay's latest misadventure and Junie Gay enjoyed telling on herself and often interrupted the telling with bouts of snorting laughter. She was unconcerned about who overheard her.

This time Junie Gay was telling a story about how her Chihuahua climbed into the clothes dryer and nestled under a pile of warm towels just before Junie Gay closed the door and set the machine for another ten minutes. By the time she opened the door and discovered her little dog, its bulging eyes were dry and opaque and the pupils darted about spasmodically with no apparent symmetry. They eventually calmed down and cleared, but for a week afterward the little dog's farts and belches carried the sweet aroma of fabric softener. He soon recovered and the only lasting effect was that he drooled uncontrollably whenever he heard the dryer on. His original name was Tico but after that everyone called him Smoky.

Junie Gay punctuated the end of the story with a series of exclamatory snorts. The cousins hugged; Kayla turned and came into the presence of Grace. Kayla and Grace knew each other in passing but were on opposite sides of that unspoken but nevertheless observed settler/move-in division. Grace could see that Kayla was nervous and hesitant. She smiled and asked if she was feeling okay.

"Grace, can I ask a question?"

"Why certainly, dear, what is it?"

"A friend told me that Elias might know a lot about business and the law because he was a reporter in the city before you two moved here."

"Well, Elias knows a lot about many things because he has a restless and curious mind, but I don't know that business and law are among them. Do you need advice?"

"Yes. I am trying to figure out how I could buy my grandfather's ranch and keep it from being developed."

"I see." She invited Kayla to join them by the river park for a take-out meal and she could explain her concerns then. Kayla turned Grace down twice but when Grace insisted and bought another salad and an additional burrito, Kayla agreed to follow them down to the river and break beans with them.

They parked their cars by a footbridge next to a picnic table and bench. There was some careful small talk while they became accustomed to each other's presence. Elias, always impatient, asked Kayla to express her concerns before they had finished eating. Grace cast a frustrated glance his way. She would have let them finish their meal and become more relaxed but she realized Elias was conditioned by years of deadlines. Get to the story fast was his way, no three cups of tea for him. Kayla told them she wanted to buy her grandfather's ranch and keep the Jango running.

Unfortunately, Elias couldn't encourage her. She was about to graduate from veterinary school and like many students in her generation was beginning her professional life with a mountain of student loan debt that precluded buying a bungalow, let alone a working ranch. With no income until she established a practice, there would be no loan. He supposed she could work out a contract of some kind with her grandfather but he had obviously taken another option. It was impossible to see her competing with the deep pockets of the Highlife Holiday Estates investors. "I'm sorry," he said, "but those are the hard facts."

Grace consoled her and talked about the stages of grief and how to get through them. The sun set and they shared stories about Stony Mesa and nearby places of wonder they had experienced. Kayla told them that while Elias and Grace hiked into places like Pastel Paradise, Agate Draw, and Broken Bow Arch, she rode her horse into those places. Horses were a passion that bonded her to her grandfather and his rancher buddies who shared her equine love.

"I became a vet because I love horses. Always have. Most little girls have a thing for horses but they outgrow it. I never did. Most ranchers here have had a lifetime love of horses, too. They may call themselves cowboys but cows are just the means to an end and the end is a horse."

Grace nodded. "I love horses, too."

"Yeah, but they don't define you."

Elias asked, "How so? How do horses define you?"

Kayla leaned back on her chair and looked up at moonlit clouds. Elias let her have a moment to think. She looked at him and leaned forward. "Imagine your iconic Western scene. There are two cowboys in a mountain meadow leaning against bed rolls with a campfire going next to them. It's evening. Two horses are tied to a tree limb and browse grass by their feet. Cattle lowing in the background. Maybe one of the men strums a guitar. Got it?"

"Okay, that's easy to picture."

"Now take the horses out of that picture and what's left—two peasants by a campfire. Horses make heroes of herders."

They left the impromptu picnic to depart for their respective homes. Grace and Kayla hugged. It was clear to Elias that they had created a strong connection. Grace could do that, pull people toward her quickly. Elias was more of an acquired taste. He was impressed with Kayla's ability to articulate herself and her insights.

On the drive home he turned to Grace and said, "What a surprise. And before today I thought she was just another local rodeo princess."

Grace laughed. "Yeah? Well, don't let the rhinestones fool ya."

Chapter 10

"Hells bells!"

JR discovered three dead hens in the yard beside the barn and looked up to see a coyote running away with another hen in his teeth. The bird was orange and still alive, wings twitching violently in the coyote's sharp teeth and strong jaws.

JR shook his head and kicked the dirt. He was looking forward to fresh eggs and bacon and instead this. The man had been harassed by wild creatures all his life. Though wolves were long gone by the time he took over the Jango Ranch, the occasional cougar still stalked through the valley. He lost two calves one year and three the next. After the cougar was hunted down, coyotes moved in. When he killed them, foxes and skunks took their turns eating his chickens. One year a bear killed a cow and returned a few days later to eat his chickens. He ate the bear.

The conflicts were never ending. A badger once tried to chew on his leg and ruined a brand new boot. He'd been bit by a cow dog, thrown by a horse, kicked by a goat, and butted more than once by sheep. Cows stepped on his feet. He'd killed rattlesnakes by his back door and under his front porch steps. Every spring gnats left itchy welts across his forehead and scalp. More than once he shook scorpions out of his boots. He was allergic to beestings.

If they're not after you directly, he thought, they want what you got. His cats weren't pets, they were there to kill the mice that invaded the house each winter. Mice gnawed the corners off cereal boxes and soiled cabinets with their urine. They pulled threads from the seat cover of his truck and made nests from them in the air filter. The cats that killed the mice were sometimes killed by owls and hawks. Deer ate his alfalfa. Heck, rabbits consumed even more of his crop than deer and multiplied faster than he could shoot them. Marmots dug a hole under the hay shed and raided his melon patch. Ten years ago a plague of grasshoppers devastated his fields. They ate old gray fence posts down to the raw blonde wood underneath. He had to leave a broom by the front door to sweep them away before he entered or he'd have hoppers inside the house where they launched themselves into cereal bowls, smacked into windows, and perched on the back of the sofa and stared at him.

A single red ant was the worst offender. JR was standing before his congregation and offering a blessing to a newborn who was being welcomed into the One True Church when a tiny red devil climbed over his shoe and crawled up his pant leg until it found the tender white flesh that his tiny ant brain told him was the most vulnerable. JR had just cupped his hand over the baby's head and solemnly proclaimed, "In the name of our Lord," when the ant bit him. He clasped both hands over his crotch, jumped in the air, knocked over a pitcher of baptismal water, yelped once, and shouted, "Jesus Christ!" Although he finished the sentence he had begun with the right words, he used the wrong inflection. The pain was soon gone but the humiliation still stung years later.

The coyote with the chicken in his teeth was just the latest thief but he felt more like it was the last straw, the final insult. In JR's mind, that damn coyote bore the sins of fifty years of troublesome untamed creatures. JR ground his teeth, his nostrils flared, his fingers curled tightly into a fist. The veins on the back of his hand rose and turned blue.

He tried to quench his anger with a deep breath and he told himself no more of that. When the ranch is sold I'll find some place to live where the only animals are poodles and bluebirds. But still the image of that devil-dog trotting away with orange wings poking out on each side of his mouth enraged him. It was as if the frustration that had been building for fifty years as he ran his cows through the claws of a voracious wilderness was coming to a head.

He made a vow. One last varmint. He'd kill that damn coyote and nail its hide to the front gate for all to see. That hide nailed to the gate would stand for the birthing, branding, butchering, and all the other bloody chores that were necessary to keep cattle alive until he turned them into money. That hide would stand for every wound he'd suffered at the hands of a feral, capricious, indifferent wilderness. It would be the last word in an argument he'd been having with wild creatures for more than fifty years, ever since he inherited the Jango Ranch from his father and grandfather, the original Jango Burnside. It would punctuate a life of struggle, one last act of naked aggression that would be a fitting conclusion to a life of raw assertion.

He skipped dinner and cleaned his deer rifle and scope instead. He did it slowly, mindfully, like a ritual. He banished from his mind the coyote running away with its stolen goods. Instead he imagined his knife entering the coyote's skin. He imagined the tip of his knife piercing the hide and the resistance as he ran the blade from throat to dick. He, JR Burnside, would let loose a mighty long-buried howl and be free of all the pain nature had inflicted on him during half a century of a hard life. He would make that thieving coyote pay. The beast was no match for him.

"God's dog, my ass."

Chapter 11

Juniper was gone. It was not unusual for her to disappear for an hour here or there because like most dogs she liked to chase rabbits, hunt lizards, and follow her nose. But dogs like Juniper stay close to their owners because they are pack animals and Luna and Hoppy were Juniper's pack. She thrived on their affection and reassurance. So where was she all day and all night?

Luna woke in the morning, wrapped a quilt around her shoulders, and walked barefoot onto the porch. She pictured Juniper lying outside the door waiting, her tail thumping against the floor when she saw Luna. No dog. She called and whistled while scanning the horizon. She prayed her prodigal dog would return and tried to quiet the alarm building around her heart.

After silent minutes with no sighting or response, Luna turned and went inside.

Hoppy was up and pulling on his clothes. "Any sign?"

"No, nothing."

She made herself a mug of yerba mate and headed for the bedroom. "I'm going to get dressed and go look for her."

"I want to go with you but I'm supposed to work on the Cramer's water line with Otis. They've been without water for three days now. I also have a meeting with the new vendor for the fish. It's at 2 o'clock. I could help Otis and then cancel the vendor."

"Don't do that yet. Maybe I'll find her soon and that won't be necessary."

She tucked on a fleece jacket and wool cap. Stony Mesa lay more than a mile above sea level and mornings were cool even in summer. She tied her hair back and tried not to think of all the negative possibilities. There were at least three sightings of mountain lions near town so far that year.

She paused on the porch steps and wondered where to start. She took three deep breaths followed by a simple question: Juniper, where are you? She held the dog's image in her mind and cupped her hand lightly over her breast so she could feel the rhythm of her heart and pick up on any subtle fluctuations that might guide her. Through her fingertips, her pendulum heart might whisper, You are getting warmer, or the trail is growing cold, go left, go right, yes, no.

"Where?" she asked. "Show me."

Her legs carried her down a winding dirt road into the Jango Ranch. She whistled and called, whistled and called. Suddenly anxiety turned to dread that spread through her heart like a dark stain. But this feeling wasn't about Juniper's fate. It came from some place she couldn't identify or locate. She was puzzled and wondered if she had encountered some toxic chemical. Maybe the Jango Ranch carried a residue of pesticides and herbicides that had built up over decades. She turned around slowly and studied the land for a poisonous source of her discomfort. Nothing stood out.

She asked herself if it were evil. No, too simple. More like horror distilled into dread. Something is held here. Something that can't let go.

The road to the Jango was lined by willows and open fields. The sweet smell of tamarisk and Russian olive trees infused the air. She walked past a clutch of young willows that encased an abandoned pickup truck used to anchor a fence row. The steering wheel was woven with vines and daisies crowded the bumper. In the near corner of a meadow she saw raw dirt that had been upturned recently and then smoothed over. She saw nothing that could off-gas a cloud of poison but a feeling that burned like ice wrapped around her shoulders and grabbed at her neck. Her stomach ached and her breathing became labored.

She stopped and froze still. An unfamiliar current raced through her veins. She took a breath and pressed her palm to her heart. One, two, three beats and then it jumped. It spoke an unmistakable "no" so she retreated down the road toward the river.

Several paces closer to the thick brush that crowded the river bank, she heard a low whimper in the sagebrush. She called and Juniper answered hoarsely with a forlorn moan. She called again and Juniper yipped frantically. A moment later Luna found her. Juniper thumped her tail on the matted grass and shivered with relief.

Juniper's paw was clamped in the jaws of a trap set for a coyote. The tall grass around her was flattened during her struggle to pull herself free. The trap caught only the end of two toes but that was enough to hold her. Her trapped foot was wet and raw all around her toes. Luna guessed she had tried to gnaw her toes free. She'd heard stories of coyotes and wolves actually gnawing off paws and now she knew it could happen.

Luna wanted to scream and puke at the same time but she remained calm for Juniper's sake and even tried to sound soothing and reassuring. She was unfamiliar with traps and it took her several minutes to figure out how to release the dog's crushed toes. She wondered if she had the strength to carry Juniper home but when she lifted her it was surprisingly manageable. She cradled her tightly and Juniper licked the salty tears Luna could not contain from Luna's trembling chin.

At home she laid the dog on her bed and called Hoppy, who dropped everything he had planned and raced home. They made a bed in the truck for Juniper and Luna talked softly to her as they drove forty miles to the only veterinarian available that day. Hoppy drove and stared straight ahead.

It was a hard reality check. He reminded himself that this is Boon County where people trap coyotes for a fifty-dollar bounty. He had met young men who trapped to earn money for Christmas or to buy their first truck or give their girlfriend a ring. It is a dangerous place for a dog, he admitted, especially a pampered canine like Juniper who may be way more sociable than a wild coyote but is not nearly as wily. And that's just the way it is here. They want to get the wild creatures out of the way so more of their animals can be raised, sold, and slaughtered. In this business of growing and butchering generation after generation of cows, horses are broken and then ridden to help their masters do the gruesome work. And dogs are trained to herd other animals like sheep that will eventually be eaten. And here we are in the middle of this . . . this . . . this Cowschwitz!

Hoppy was well aware he lived in two worlds. There was Luna, the Desert Rose, and a large circle of friends. The food they ate, the books they read, the films they watched, the music they listened to, the way they dressed marked them as different from the people who lived around them. The rest of the West was still at war with nature. Juniper was just collateral damage. He was not sure if there were more of them than us but he knew they had power they didn't want to share. Look at governors, legislators, commissioners, mayors, judges, police, even the clerks at the bottom of the governing pyramid, and you find the same mind-set, same assumptions, same habits and behaviors. He wondered if and how that would change some day.

He broke the silence in the car. "We're opposite sides of the same coin."

"What?"

"Never mind. Just thinking."

Luna was alarmed. "You and me are opposite sides of the same coin?"

"No! Not us! You know, people like us and people like them. In Stony Mesa."

"Huh?"

"I mean there's one land and . . . uh . . ."

She offered him a weak smile and her best pleading eyes. "Please, Hoppy, I don't feel well. I need you to stay clear-headed. Okay? Stay on track. Please?"

"Sure, sure."

"And no more weed, okay?"

"Yeah, good idea."

"I need you, Hoppy."

"I know you do. I'm here for you. A hundred percent. I promise."

Juniper lost the ends of two toes. Dogs are resilient, the vet told them, and he described two dogs he knew about in Boon County that ran around amazingly well on just three remaining legs after losing one whole leg. Farm machinery and traps, ya know. Yeah, they said, we know.

By the time they returned to their cabin, Luna was shivering and crying softly. Hoppy held her close and told her everything was going to be okay now. We're home now and safe, he told her. Juniper will get better.

"It's not just about Juniper. Right before I found her something stopped me cold. Something entered me. I feel sick."

"You mean like poison or some kind of pollution? A virus? Maybe you walked through herbicide or . . ."

She cut him off. "No, something else. Something dark and old. Something like grief or despair but more powerful. A turbulence."

Chapter 12

Lou Jean left Stony Mesa when she went to college and never returned. She and her horse won medals for her barrel racing and she won straight A's in school but never wore a tiara, never was asked to bump and grind with the cheerleaders. Years later a friend from college observed, "Lou Jean, you look like the girl in the marching band who carries the tuba."

She was that girl. Exactly. And she couldn't wait to escape Stony Mesa and its claustrophobic culture. She graduated high school with scholarships in hand. She left and didn't look back. In college she studied archaeology because as a girl growing up in the canyons she had encountered the scattered clues left by ancient people. After windstorms raked plowed fields, she would set out on foot looking for the arrowheads that might be exposed and waiting for her to find them. She would rub them in her fingers as she traced their finely cupped edges and delicate notches. There was a granary she would hike to where slim cobs of desiccated corn were mixed into sand littered with mouse turds. She had a collection of potsherds she'd found on trips to remote cliff dwellings.

In her junior year she saw a television program on crime scene investigators who solved mysteries in labs with the tools of modern forensics. She realized that it was the mysteries that archaeology tried to solve that drew her to it and she changed her major to forensic pathology. She reasoned that jobs for archaeologists were rare because few people really cared how people lived thousands of years ago, but crime, on the other hand, was widespread, constant, and compelling.

Now, just a few years out of grad school, she spent her days in a white smock in a basement lab, bent over a microscope looking at bones for clues. No autopsies were conducted in her office because her specialty was skeletal remains. There were more of those to examine than one might imagine. Hunting season was especially busy because that's when hunters found the bones of the missing in ravines where they had fallen, jumped, or were dumped.

Lou Jean looked up and saw her cousin Hyrum standing in the doorway. At first, she didn't recognize him. It wasn't that he looked any different from the last time she saw him but he was out of place. He never visited her, not at her home and certainly not at work. As far as Lou Jean could determine, Hyrum Allred had never left Stony Mesa in his entire life. And yet, here he is. Holy shit!

She broke for lunch and they went to a taco wagon one block away. Hyrum said he didn't feel hungry but when she insisted and offered to pay, he agreed and walked away with a beef burrito. They found a bench in a park and sat down. Lou Jean looked at Hyrum. "This is surreal."

Hyrum looked down at his burrito with a worried stare. "Cereal? I thought it was beef."

"No, no, that's not what I meant. Nevermind." She offered him a smile and asked how he was. He smiled back, said fine, and then looked away.

Lou Jean was dying to know why her seldom-seen cousin was visiting her. "Okay, Hyrum, what is this about?"

"You need to keep this quiet, okay?"

"Keep what quiet?"

"This." He reached into a knapsack and removed a brown paper bag. It was worn soft and the edges were as supple as cloth. He had cupped it in his hands and held it to his chest for many long hours, evening and dawn, wondering what to do. The bag grew soft under his pondering hands. Over and over he asked it, "What do you want me to do?" Eventually it came to him. It was simple: take me home. "But who are you," he replied, "and where is home?"

He reached into the bag and carefully retrieved a small skull. It was delicate, especially on the crown where it had been exposed to rain seeping down through a quilt of root-hair and ant-works that covered it. The topmost surface was as fragile as an egg shell.

She jumped in her seat. "Jesus Christ, Hyrum, what are you doing?"

"I'm showing you what I found. I need to know how this child died. I want to know anything you can find out."

"Where did you get that?"

"I can't say."

"Bullshit, Hyrum, you MUST say! What do you think I do for a living, handle skulls under the table? For cash maybe? I could lose my job if I don't report this. You had to know that, right? Tell me you live in the real world, Hyrum."

"Hold on, calm down. I got it all figured out."

"Oh, this should be good. Go ahead."

Hyrum carefully slipped the small skull into its brown paper nest and cradled it in his arms. He looked over his shoulders for eaves-droppers and lowered his voice. "You tell them the bag was left on the seat of your car and you don't know who put it there. Then you find out what you can. When I know that much then I'll come forward and tell you I'm the one who left the bag and I show you where I got it. Okay?"

She started to reply but then paused. He jumped in to plead his case. "Look, Lou Jean, it's complicated."

"Complicated to who, Hyrum," she interrupted. She was not buying it, period.

He pleaded. "I just need some time. If I get the timing wrong it could affect this big deal that's going down in Stony Mesa and I'm not sure if wrecking that would be a good thing or bad. I need time to think and pray on it."

"Emphasis on the thinking part, please." Lou Jean did not suffer fools, even fools who were also cousins. She folded her arms across her chest and her frown did not budge.

Hyrum wiped burrito from his chin and rose slowly to go. "I don't have to give this to you."

"You DO TOO have to give it to me!"

She reached to grab it but he pulled away and she missed. Hyrum turned and faced her, arms crossed and covering his delicate treasure. He stuck his chin out defiantly, a rare posture for him. "Oh yeah, what if I just walk away with it? What will you do, call the cops? You think you're in control here Lou Jean, but I'm the one giving you your choices and they are: go along with my plan or make it even worse between you and me and it all goes God knows where. My way it all turns out in the end."

He had her. He had possession of the little skull and, no, she wouldn't have him pursued by the cops. She agreed.

They walked to her car and he gave it to her and said goodbye.

"I don't like this one bit, Hyrum," she said as they parted.

"Oh my heck, Lou Jean, have a little faith."

Chapter 13

Hoppy wanted to call a doctor but Luna said no, she wasn't sick that way. "Then what? How do I help you?" he implored.

"I don't know! I don't know how to get rid of this . . . this cold, sad feeling." She tightened the tie-dyed blanket around her shoulders. Strands of loose hair obscured her face. Her breath smelled rotten and tasted bitter. Hoppy imagined that Luna's once bright aura was tattered by distress.

Distress reminded him of Olene Miller's famous rant at the public meeting about the sale of the Jango Ranch. Olene Miller might be helpful. Someone told him that Olene could see auras. She kept essential oils and did massage. Luna told him that Olene had taken courses at the Esalen Institute in Big Sur and learned polarity massage in Santa Cruz. She was someone Luna trusted and liked. Maybe she could figure out what was pulling Luna, his positive and cheerful soul mate, into a tearful torpor. He called her.

Olene was surprised to hear Luna was ill and came over to the house immediately. She laid her hand across Luna's brow and checked her vitals. All the signals she checked seemed normal. She anointed Luna's feet with lavender and massaged them.

"Describe how you feel."

"I feel bad. I don't know, like something bad entered me."

"Bad as in a threat to your physical health or morally bad as in evil or violent?"

Luna hesitated. "Both. I mean what's the difference, really?"

Olene smiled softly. "Of course, you're right about that."

She massaged Luna's hands next and stroked her hair slowly and gently until Luna fell into a restless sleep. Hoppy left them alone but was waiting when Olene quietly tiptoed out of the bedroom.

"So what do you think is wrong?" he asked her. "What can I do to help her get better?"

She didn't answer. He could see she was thinking and waited for her to go over it and get it right before she spoke. She gathered her herbs and massage creams and prepared to leave. At the door she turned to him.

"You have a friend. Lucas Hozho?"

He was surprised. "Do you know Lucas?"

"Yes, several years ago I taught biology at the high school at Navajo Mountain. Lucas was my student. I was quite impressed with him, his whole family really. I helped him get financial aid for college."

"What has Lucas got to do with this, Olene?"

"His grandmother is a healer. In the old way of her tribe, that is. I wouldn't trust her to remove a tumor from a brain but if the illness is spiritual in nature, there is no one better."

Olene paused and shook her head slightly as if she had missed something and was annoyed with herself. She smiled at Hoppy and added, "I'm pretty sure that Grandmother Hozho would tell us that a tumor is, in fact, a spiritual illness, too, but you know what I mean."

"Okay, how do I get Luna and the old woman together?"

"Call Lucas and ask if she is willing to see Luna. Luna isn't too sick to travel. If I were you I'd get her there as soon as you can."

"Would you go with us, Olene?"

"Yes, of course I would."

Hoppy called Lucas Hozho, who offered to meet them at an intersection along the highway on its way through the reservation and then guide them to his grandmother. He warned Hoppy to come in a truck with four-wheel drive. His grandmother's hogan was remote and the roads across the reservation wound through washes that could be muddy and deeply rutted. If it were dry there would be sand drifting across the road. "And make sure you have plenty of gas and water," he added.

"What can I bring to offer her thanks?" Hoppy asked.

"Hmmm, let me take care of that. I'll bring her a load of firewood, maybe a big bag of flour. Her needs are pretty simple. Well, there is one thing she really craves and doesn't get much."

"What's that?"

"Chocolate. Not that dark stuff that's so good for you but milk chocolate, the sweeter the better."

They made a bed for Luna in the back of Hoppy's truck from camp mats, yoga mats, pillows, and a thick comforter. Hoppy asked Luna if it was too much cover in the hot weather they were experiencing but when she tucked herself in she looked like she was in a cocoon and she fell asleep immediately. Hoppy had never seen her so drained. Luna had more energy than any man or woman Hoppy knew. Her somnolent state was alarming.

They drove for five hours to reach the intersection where Lucas was waiting. He led them to the hogan across miles of washboarded roads that wound in and out of dry washes. They lucked out; mud ruts and sand drifts did not impede their passage. An hour later they pulled up in front of a modest hogan, a round adobe home surrounded by corrals made of dry brush. Sheep and goats ran to the truck and surrounded them. Like curious fans they crowded their bony faces into the window. Hoppy had to push firmly on a billy goat's chest. They came face to face and Hoppy sniffed once and winced.

"Whoa, dude! Try flossing!"

Hoppy broke free from the clutch of goats and a large yellow chicken pecked at his feet while she tried to catch his shoelace. He pushed her aside with his foot and walked to the back of the truck and opened it. Luna was covered in a thin layer of talcum-like dust. She sat up and looked puzzled.

"Where are we? Why am I in the back of your truck?"

"It's okay," Olene told her. "We're here to see Lucas Hozho's grandmother."

"But I don't feel up to visiting right now. I have a headache and I'm too sleepy."

"I know," said Hoppy. "Hopefully, Lucas's grandma can help with that."

They carried her to the door of the hogan and introductions were made. Hoppy offered a box of chocolates and the old woman, Alice Hozho, brightened. She wore her white hair in a long braid that complemented a black blouse. Four strands of turquoise and silver hung from her neck and shone against her black shirt like moonlight against a night sky. The old woman directed them to bring Luna in and lay her on a blanket by the hearth. She then scooted them out the door and closed it. Navajo healing, apparently, was not a spectator sport.

Hoppy and Olene looked around but there wasn't much to see. The goats climbed up on the hood of his truck to get a better look at the strange visitors. Hoppy chased them off twice and then gave up. He had hoped the setting would be more like Monument Valley with its magnificent buttes and spires but this was just a wide horizon of sand and sage broken by low outcroppings of ragged stone.

Lucas sensed Hoppy's disappointment. "Most of my family was living on the Hopi reservation years ago when they developed the strip mine on Black Mesa. They'd been there forever and got along just fine with their Hopi neighbors. They traded mutton for corn and squash. But then the politicians in Washington, Barry Goldwater was a leader of them, concocted this big conflict and said the Navajo had to get off the land. Thousands of them were forced to move. But it was really about the coal that they lived on top of. They were in the way."

He laughed. "We have a long history of being in the way. My grandmother was lucky in a sense that she lived out here and wasn't near anything valuable. They didn't give the prime real estate to Navajos."

Hoppy shook his head in disbelief. "Seems like there is a lot of coal that is easier to get to."

"Yeah but it's not that simple. There was a huge electrical generating plant built near the coal. They go together." The people Lucas met off the reservation rarely knew the history of Black Mesa and he was accustomed to telling the story.

Hoppy was clueless. "But why build either out in the middle of the desert?"

Olene took a turn. She worked on the reservation and knew the story of Black Mesa well. "It's all about water. They put in the massive Hoover Dam and impounded the water running down the Colorado River. That's Lake Mead except it isn't a lake, it's a reservoir. A massive one and all that water goes to Las Vegas nearby and then to cities far away like Phoenix and Los Angeles. There are pumping stations along the way and they require a lot of energy to move so much water. That requires a power plant, the power plant requires coal. And so it goes."

After the history lesson, hours passed. Hoppy got tired of the chicken working at his cuffs. He took his boot off and tossed it a few feet away. The chicken chased it and clucked excitedly. "Knock yourself out," Hoppy said.

Olene napped in the shade of a pinyon tree. Hoppy tried to get a signal with his phone but there was nothing. They could smell the pungent aroma of burning sage and could hear muffled chanting but since it was in Navajo Hoppy wouldn't know what was said even if he could hear it clearly. He turned to Lucas. "What are they doing in there?"

"I can't explain it," said Lucas. "If Luna came here with a rash or cough she'd probably be treating her with herbs or plants she grew or collected. But this is different, more like illuminating a shadow."

"Come again?"

Lucas studied Hoppy and tried to get a better sense of him. It was always the same questions for Lucas, who navigated between two very different cultures. How much will this person before me understand? How do I explain? Can he be trusted? Is his curiosity sincere? He took a deep breath and plunged forward.

"In college I learned that if you can't describe something in words and break it apart with reason and logic, then it doesn't exist. My grandmother doesn't know that. In her world, everything is alive. Even stones have spirits. And if that sounds trite or corny it's because I'm borrowing your English words. Spirit is just another word that tries to capture something that won't be contained. Nanny Hozho feels rivers of energy that connect us in ways I can't explain. And time for her is not a line but more like a spiral. Again, it's not easy to explain in plain English, not easy to reduce it or define it or to make it familiar. To understand her way of looking at life on earth you have to pretty much throw out everything you think you know and start from scratch. And it would help a lot if you spoke Navajo."

Olene heard them talking and woke up. She too listened near the hogan door and tried to make out the words to the chants and mutterings coming from inside. "Prayers I guess."

"That's it, prayers?" Hoppy was disappointed.

Lucas explained as best he could. "My grandmother leads a very prayerful life but not the kind of prayers you hear in church. When I was stepping away from my Navajo culture—you know, going to college and succeeding according to Anglo standards and beliefs—I would visit her and find her way of life annoying. I'd ask Grandmother, why do you spend so much time praying? You're wasting time you could spend helping yourself."

Lucas stared at something in the distance as he searched his memory for that time. He turned back to them and spoke in a hush that expressed the reverence in his grandmother's words. "She told me her grandmother taught her the power of prayer. The most powerful prayers don't beg, she said, but thank. Gratitude is never a waste of time. When you show gratitude for a gift it will return again and again. In the city, she told me, you cannot pray so easily. Do you thank the chicken for her eggs if you buy them in a box? The lamb whose wool is in the sweater you took off a rack? What about the lamb you buy all cut and wrapped behind a counter—do you thank that lamb, the grass that fed it, the rain that nourished the grass? Do you thank that lamb's mother? Then she made a clicking sound with her tongue to show her disgust and she scolded me. You watch out, she warned, or you'll become one of those take n' grab white men."

Hoppy was confused. "So what kind of prayers is she offering for Luna? Something to do with gratitude?"

Lucas smiled and shook his head. "No, that was just an example. I mean to say that my grandmother sees a world where everything touches everything else. It's . . . well, you might use the English word reciprocal. In the old way of thinking, gifts are not free. Again, it's difficult to explain in English because words like obligation, responsibility, or duty don't quite fit her concept of why she perceives life on earth as a gift that compels her to return her own gifts to it. To her it's just the way the world works and giving back is a way to be what you might call a cosmic participant."

He smiled and rolled his eyes. "Cosmic participant. You can tell I went to college. More simply, it's a way to celebrate her kinship with . . . all of life, I guess. Or maybe even less complicated than that, my grandmother feels that the earth loves her and, like anyone who is loved, she loves back."

Lucas let that sink in and then claimed again that he had only a passing knowledge of his native culture and shouldn't speak at all for his grandmother.

"I understand that," Hoppy replied, "but please don't stop. The most important person in my world is inside that small stone hut with a woman I never met before today. I just need to know who she is and what she might be doing in there. What about those prayers?"

Lucas nodded. "She has prayers to thank the plants and animals that sustain her life, prayers for the rain, of course, and corn, bees, many things. It locates her. She acknowledges her dependence and shows respect like from one species to another." Lucas laughed. "No, really, it's a humbling place to start from."

"But," Hoppy protested, "she has gifts for healing that are so powerful that she's known in her community for them."

"Yes," Lucas agreed, "but her power is not arrogant power. She's not some sorcerer or wizard. Arrogant power imposes, intuitive power invites."

"Luna is so giving and careful. She's not religious but she counts her blessings every day. I don't get it."

"Well, she's also pretty intuitive and sensitive. That might make her vulnerable. But it's not about Luna alone. We're all in this life together and our energies mix in ways that we struggle to understand. Nanny Hozho is spiritual in the old way—and 'spiritual' is another word that doesn't quite fit—so her perception of the energetic realm is hard for those of us who are not familiar with that realm to understand. That's why she's in there with Luna and we are out here getting bit by gnats while chickens pluck our shoelaces."

Hoppy smiled and rubbed his furrowed brow smooth. He stood and stretched his arms above his head, arched his back, rolled his shoulders. "I guess I'll just have to believe she knows what she's doing."

Lucas stood and put a hand on Hoppy's shoulder. "Honestly, Hoppy, I can't explain it. You're talking to a guy with one foot in two worlds and I often find one world as mysterious and hard to reckon as the other one. I don't really know what is going on in there, so I can't say."

"Can't say or won't say?"

He laughed. "A little of both."

Dusk settled upon the desert and gradually erased the horizon. Luna and Alice Hozho emerged from the small round building. Luna looked tired but smiled weakly. Her eyes were bright again but her face and limbs sagged with exhaustion. The old woman spoke first and Lucas translated. "Nanny Hozho says Luna is restored."

Hoppy wanted more than that. "What happened to her? What is this all about?"

Lucas conferred with his grandmother and turned to the others. "She won't say. Luna stumbled into some troubled spirits that entered her and Grandma expelled them and cleansed her. She won't go into specifics."

Luna looked at Hoppy. "I'm tired. Take me home, please."

Hoppy and Olene thanked the old woman profusely and packed Luna into her makeshift bed in the back of the truck. Lucas leaned in and Luna sat up and put her arms around his neck. "Please tell your grandmother thanks again. I cannot tell you how grateful I am. You are so lucky to have her in your life, Lucas."

They stopped at the intersection on the way home and said goodbye to Lucas again. Luna was asleep. For the next hundred miles Olene and Hoppy drove on in silence. Worry and waiting under the hot sun had drained them. They stopped at a truck stop halfway home to pee and get coffee. Luna did not wake. Hoppy turned the truck onto the interstate and asked Olene, "What does a scientist say about what we just experienced, Olene?"

She took her time to choose her words. "I think that on the other side of silence, life roars. There are voices, cries, and calls from the top of the trees to the bottom of the seas. A billion wings carve currents of air, hearts beat, insects click under bark. The huff of lungs and the scurrying of feet never stop. Waves crash and rivers rush over stone. The wind howls or whispers. If we could take all that in at once it would overwhelm us. And so there are boundaries on what we can perceive. There are ranges and limitations. We take what's left and we box and label it."

"Now you sound more like a poet than a scientist." Hoppy reached for a water bottle under the truck seat and tucked it under his arm while he unscrewed the lid with one hand, the other hand on the wheel. He offered her a drink and she said no thanks. He knew she wasn't through. "Go ahead, Olene. I'm still listening."

She took off her sunglasses and wiped clean a smudge on one lens. She put the glasses back on and adjusted them. "Science helps us get beyond our limitations. It shows us microbes and galaxies, fossils and x-rays. Science gives us a method for knowing what works and what doesn't."

When she was teaching in a classroom, Olene knew she was supposed to keep talking. In the lab, quiet was the rule. Outside of those environments with their clear codes and boundaries, she often stumbled between talking too much or not at all. Her filter was unreliable. She was energized at Nanny Hozho's hogan and she brimmed with thoughts she struggled to contain and direct. She kept these thoughts to herself and let Hoppy alone. Another long stretch of highway passed without conversation. Olene looked out the passenger-side window as sagebrush blurred by and a gray range of bare stone crept across the horizon. They passed through a rain shower. There was a sudden drumming on the roof, splatters on the windshield, the soft clip-clop of wipers clearing the rain.

Olene turned to him. She needed to complete her thoughts. It was ingrained in her and she knew Hoppy would forgive her if she talked too much. "Okay then, enough. But let me say one last thing. Indigenous explanations of life are based on thousands of years of local observation and experience. I respect that knowledge, too. Look at what Native Americans did with irrigation and astronomy, or how about horticultural achievements like corn. Science also tells me to pay attention and keep an open mind."

There, she was done. She let out a deep sigh. The soft rain was steady now. The moon broke through the overhanging mist and turned raindrops into globes of silver light that raced from the heavens into the earth beneath them. Olene smiled as she looked out the window and remembered how Lucas describe Granny Hozho's way of healing. "Illuminate the shadows."

Hoppy thought it over. "I'm just glad I have Luna back."

He struggled to hold back tears but they rolled down his cheeks as he stared straight ahead at the highway. Olene reached over and squeezed his arm. "Me too, Hoppy. Me too."

They carried her to bed and closed the curtains tight. She slept for twelve hours straight. Juniper curled against her chest and slept too. The dog's paws twitched as she chased a phantom rabbit through a dream and Luna's lips softly whispered words of praise and gratitude that could not be heard.

Chapter 14

"Hyrum, it's me, Lou Jean."

"Lou Jean, hi."

"The lab work is back on your little friend. We examined her carefully."

"Her. You can tell it was a girl?"

"Yes, here is what we know for sure. She was a child of maybe five or six when she died. Native American, for sure."

"How did she die, can you tell?"

"Yes, we found traces of strychnine in her teeth. She was poisoned."

"Makes sense. I mean there were no bullet holes, no busted-in skulls."

"Skulls? How many skulls, Hyrum?"

"Thirteen."

"Okay, this is where the game you're playing with me ends, cousin. You come here or I go to you but one way or another I want a full account of where, when, and all the rest. No more bullshit, Hyrum, this is it. You come clean and let me take this over, understand?"

"I understand, Lou Jean. I'll meet you first thing day after tomorrow . . ."

She cut him off. "No, Hyrum, not the day after tomorrow, TOMORROW!"

"Hey, I have work to do. I promised I'd bring my backhoe over to—"

"Tomorrow, Hyrum, tomorrow! Got it?"

"Jeez, Lou Jean, calm down. Okay, I'll make a phone call and see if I can change my schedule."

"Tomorrow, Hyrum."

"Okay! I get it. Tomorrow. I promise I'll give you the whole story tomorrow."

She hung up. He was ready to tell what he knew. He had trouble sleeping and couldn't stop thinking of that small smooth head of a child, a girl as he had suspected, who must have laughed and sang, dreamed, loved, been loved. Lately he had started to talk to her. "Don't worry," he whispered to her. "I will take you home."

JR Burnside would forgive him for telling or not, it didn't matter now. The news would mess up the deal JR had with Highlife Holiday Estates or not, it wasn't up to him.

"Home." He said it aloud. "She's going home."

Chapter 15

After she had recovered her strength, Luna rode her bike out to the Jango Ranch to directly confront JR or Jango Junior or whatever he called himself. She dressed in her newest casual clothes, tied her hair into a loose bun, and put on her most sensible shoes. She arrived at his doorstep and got off the bike, rolled her shoulders, breathed deeply, and set her jaw. He was cordial as he met her at the door and clearly puzzled about why that pretty little hippie gal wanted to talk to him.

She described how her dog had been caught in a trap set for coyotes on his property. She tried her best to be diplomatic but it was clear she was offended and angry. A couple of times her voice cracked and she struggled to remain composed. It wasn't just Juniper's missing toes she mourned. It seemed to her that the incident was the latest sign that she and her friends lived at odds with so much they found here.

"What was your dog doing here?" he asked her.

"Just being a dog. They roam and chase things. They follow their noses."

"Well, sis, I guess I'm a rancher who is just being a rancher. This is still my land and I have a coyote killing my chickens. It could kill calves if I let it get that far. How about them animals? Do you have pity in your heart for them, too, or just your dog? Do chickens count?"

She tried to reply and he interrupted her. "Look here, it's simple. If you don't want your dog to get caught in my traps, keep your dog home and off my land."

He didn't expect her to cry. Neither did she. She held her breath for a moment and tried to gain composure while cursing herself for this unplanned show of emotion. *I must be weak from that episode of illness. I should have waited until I was stronger, until I recovered fully.*

She brushed back tears and his heart softened. She made one last attempt to connect. "I don't know why it has to be this way. You call us move-ins and after twenty years we are still referred to as the new people. It's like no matter how hard we try to get along and see eye to eye we're still like second-class citizens. What is this that divides us? Don't we love the same blue sky and the same beautiful land?"

"You're naïve, sis. I love the smell of cattle. I like the squeak of my saddle when I tighten it onto my horse's back. Heck, I love my horse most of all and you don't have a horse, do you?"

"I do have a horse. I have three horses and I still have cows, too."

He chuckled softly. "You still have cows? You mean you have the cows your dad left you because you haven't got rid of them yet. Look, you and I cherish this land but for different reasons. You look at the land and see the birds and the bees and I see the clay that made me."

"You don't find this land beautiful? What do you mean? It's just a place to raise cows and ride your horse?"

"Now hold on, I didn't say that. Sure, I see beauty but there's a difference. You and I can look out on the same mountain meadow and you see the glorious face of Mother Nature and I see the Kingdom of God. He made the fruits of the earth and sea for man and gave us dominion. It's a gift, a sign of His love. But you think Mother Nature is perfect so don't touch it. We can only spoil it, right? But my God says be fruitful and multiply. Use it! I think my God trusts me and your God or whatever you call it doesn't trust you."

"So that's it, we're on opposite sides of some spiritual fence?"

"Oh no, darlin', that's just me talking. I'm a minority in my own community. I love the land but most folks I know are here because they were born here and can't figure out how to leave. A lot of them are as mean and selfish as people are anywhere. They're out for a buck and don't give a damn whether you approve of them or not."

"Is that what you're doing? Making a buck? Escaping?"

He shook his head no and sighed. He ran a set of gnarly fingers though a full head of silver hair. His voice dropped to a rough whisper. "No, sister, I'm not escaping. Surrender and retreat are more like it. I've struggled long and hard at ranching and it grieves me somethin' awful to walk away. But I'm done. What do they say, take the money and run? Know when to fold 'em?"

She expected him to be angry. She even nurtured her own anger like a banked fire so she would have the courage to walk up to his front door and confront him. But this conversation was not about accusing or defending. She was trying to understand him and he wanted her to see him clearly.

He wore a painful smile. "Well, it isn't just me. We reached the end of the line, darlin'. It was a fine ride but it is over. There are limits." He laughed quietly and shook his head. "Never thought I'd say that. We played it out and we done that all across the country. We won and lost in the same grab. Well, the big question is where next, but there ain't anywhere left to run to."

"Or what next?"

"Pardon?"

"If not where next then what next. There must be another way to make a life here," she answered.

"If there is, I ain't up to it. Maybe you youngsters can invent a better way. Good luck on that."

A long minute passed. They stared out different windows. She watched a robin pulling worms out of a small patch of lawn. He watched shadows moving across the hay shed wall, a cat stalking a mouse in the tall grass beside the pump house.

"Let me tell you a secret, sis. Most of us ranchers are on the dole. We get grants and subsidies. Uncle Sam signs the checks. We graze our cattle on public land for almost nothing. Without help from the feds we wouldn't have reservoirs, pipelines, roads, schools, clinics, fire stations, you name it. We say we're so darn independent here and don't need nobody or nothin' but that's a lie."

"I know that. Most people understand that." Luna was respectful but her honesty matched his.

"But you don't know what it does to us. We have this picture of ourselves that we got from a hundred Hollywood westerns and dime novels before that. Zane Grey, Louis L'Amour, John Wayne, and a slew of others telling us we're the real Americans. We don't need nobody telling us what to do because we can take care of ourselves. But that's a lie. We work hard and still can't make it alone. So we take what is offered from the same government we curse and that feels shameful."

Somehow it felt safe to tell her what he had never said aloud. Who else could he confess to? Certainly not his neighbors. Why not tell this radiant young woman, this stranger.

"We live a lie. We tell it to each other until we believe it. We think we're ol' Clint Eastwood but we probably have more in common with them welfare queens in the city, except they take the help they get shamelessly and don't work hard for it like we do. But there's no doubt in my mind that we are just as dependent. Well, I'm done with it. I'm through acting like the dang Marlboro Man but wondering what I'll do if Uncle Sam cuts me off. Well, sis, when I leave here I don't ever want to put my hand out for help again."

Luna had never talked to Jango Junior other than to say hi at the post office or general store. She didn't attend his church and he didn't drop by the Desert Rose to pick up organic arugula for a dinner salad. This conversation was a breakthrough.

She had intended to confront him with the consequences of his war on coyotes, namely her dog's toes. She understood that the law, tradition, and habit were on his side but a motherly instinct that so far was only applied to a dog named Juniper with different-colored eyes overcame her doubt and hesitation. She empowered herself to speak up. Because she was not given to confrontation, this was not easy. Walking up the steps to the ranch house Luna steeled herself for battle, tightened her core, braced her legs, and curled her fingers against her palms. But now in the presence of his honest and revealing response she softened. In her experience, old cowboys didn't have Oprah moments and if they did, they did not share them. You are as likely to hear a good ol' boy discuss his feelings as you are to encounter a dog teaching French. She had not expected him to open a window onto his soul and was unprepared to respond.

She wanted to acknowledge his problem but show him "sis" had a brain. "I'm sorry you feel trapped. That must be hard on you. I think they call your dilemma cognitive dissonance."

"Yeah? Well, you can label it as you please but every one of us is born and everyone dies. In between you have to make sense of the world around you. We all do that. My church has been my steadfast guide. I'm sorry you don't have that. Must be hard on you."

Their conversation was a balancing act by two tightrope walkers trying to meet in the middle. Each step on the wire of their words sent a wave of vibrations toward the other walker; the trick was to send out pulses and not tsunamis as they sought the sweet spot between risk and trust. They were exhausted.

He stood and the conversation was over. He walked her to the door.

"I'm sorry about your dog." He held the door open for her.

"I'm sorry you have to leave this way. I mean . . ."

"Don't be sorry for me. My family and I had a good life here and I don't regret a minute of it. I'll land on my feet. Always do."

Chapter 16

Otis Dooley shifted his truck into four-wheel drive for the final ascent up Dizzy Dog Mesa. The road across the windswept plain beneath the mesa had narrowed and become so eroded that it was more like a ravine than a road. Otis and Elias were tossed from side to side as he navigated exposed boulders and twisted roots that were all that was left of the old mining road.

Otis raised his voice above the straining engine. "There's an old prospecting camp near a spring. We can stop and camp there. Have you ever been this way before, Elias?"

"No, but I heard about it. It's been on my list of places I want to explore. How about you?"

"Oh yeah, several times. I used to come up here with my telescope and look at stars. There isn't a light for twenty miles in any direction. Wait 'til you see. The night sky is so awesome."

His mood shifted downward instantly. "I also came here with Dunk Taylor after those two kids disappeared down the old mining shaft. The bodies had just been retrieved and Dunk was pretty shaken up. He didn't know the kids but one of them bore a striking resemblance to a favorite nephew of his. He was determined to seal that damn hole up as soon as he could. I welded the gate we installed."

"There must be a hundred of those abandoned mine shafts out here." Elias cupped his hand over the top of his head to protect it from hitting the ceiling when the truck bounced over boulders and ruts.

"More like a thousand. And most are open and dangerous. I've seen shafts that go straight down into the earth a hundred feet or more. A few years back a kid rode up a pile of tailings with his motorcycle, ya know to catch some air on the other side. Well, the air he caught was a black hole straight down on the other side of the tailings pile."

Elias frowned. He had a white-knuckle grip on a strap above the door and he tightened his core against the truck's violent rocking. "Aren't the mining companies required to close them up, make them safe?"

Otis laughed and shook his head in exaggerated disbelief. "Elias, how could you be so naïve after all you've seen? Good luck finding anyone who will own up to an abandoned mine that has no profit left in it. This plateau is riddled with old mines and heaps of radioactive waste blowing in the wind. Back then there was a uranium boom and there either were no rules or if there were any they were never enforced. We were racing to build a nuclear arsenal and that was the priority. They didn't know or didn't care that breathing unvented uranium dust all day was hazardous. There are a lot of dead miners who could have used protective rules but there weren't any. It was a free-for-all out here and nobody wants to clean it up. There's no money in that, is there?"

Elias braced his hand on the dashboard as the truck bucked and swayed. "Yeah, what was I thinking? That's the American West—a free-for-all. Goes back all the way to the conquistadors I suppose, then land scalpers, miners, dam-building good ol' boys, and today it's drill baby drill. Fuck it up and walk away. Let the taxpayer clean it up."

Otis nodded. "And now we have hedge fund guys and other corporate types buying the scenery that's left unmarred, too. Nothing is spared. Build a tram to the sacred kiva! Everything has a price."

"Can't you do something about Highlife Holiday Estates, Otis? I mean, you're still the mayor."

"Nope. The Jango Ranch is just outside the town limits—unincorporated county over there. Boon County commissioners decide what goes in at the Jango and they like revenue. They'll tell you it's for schools and roads but that's bullshit. The state and feds subsidize most of what we need but local revenue pays for county jobs. If Monette Windy wants a raise next year the revenue pot has to grow. She'll let anything into town as long as it pays her salary. She's the one who approved that neon sign we all hated,remember?"

Monette Windy was over the Boon County economic development office. Hers was one of the few jobs in Boon County with generous benefits. Most of Boon County's citizens suspected that the only reason she got the job was because her uncle was the commission chair. Nepotism rules didn't apply in Boon County because it had fewer than three thousand residents. Besides, almost everyone outside of those newcomer move-ins in Stony Mesa was related. Jobs were scarce and they weren't handed out to strangers, whom the county commissioners figured were probably over-qualified anyway. Employees who were smarter than them made them nervous and defensive. The commissioners kept within their tribe.

"But there must be something you can do."

"Like what, Elias? All the laws and policies were created to encourage development, not stop it. I don't like the sale of the Jango to those rich assholes either, but money talks and guys like you walk. And that, Elias, is what we are here to do. You need a hike. You can dissect the workings of American capitalism on your own back in Stony Mesa. We are here to relax and forget for a while, okay?"

Elias Buchman and Otis Dooley were friends long ago. They lost contact for several years but were reunited after Otis was wrongly accused of a murder that Elias tried to solve. Otis was in love with Grace Buchman, as were half the men in town. It wasn't a lusty attraction but more platonic. Grace was serene and wise and Elias was widely considered to be lucky to have such a calm presence in his life since he was anything but calm himself. Lately he was more agitated and distracted than usual. Grace worried. She asked Otis to take him camping and get his mind onto something besides the situation in Stony Mesa with its profound implications, at least according to Elias, for the health and well-being of the entire planet itself.

They made camp under the shade of an old cottonwood, close enough to the spring that they had fresh water but a stone's throw from the old mining camp. The spring was small but rich with lilies, wild irises, catspaws, yarrow, and asters. Daisies embroidered its borders. A slick of mud that rimmed the spring showed deer prints and the tracks of a dozen lesser animals. Sparse water is a magnet for wildlife and they decided to camp far enough away to give nighttime visitors their space. Otis once slept too close to a desert pothole and awoke at dawn to find a cougar crouched by his side lapping up a drink. Despite his surprise he managed to stay very still while making promises to God he knew he would never keep. The cougar drank its fill and walked away. Otis's hands shook so hard that morning that he spilled hot coffee in his lap and had to go to the clinic and get a salve for a burn on his thigh. As the story was passed around town and distilled to its most amusing elements, it became the story of how a cougar burned Otis's prick.

The prospector's cabin was reduced by time and looters to scattered junk. Otis found a porcelain wash basin laced with tiny holes from a shotgun blast, a broken pick-axe, the springs from a mattress, oil cans, and broken whiskey bottles. Elias built a fire using the wood from a dead pinyon tree that was loaded with pitch. It sputtered and snapped as blue flames fed on thick sap. A frog down by the spring serenaded them with a rough and rhythmic chant that was as primal as it was rare. As Otis promised, the starlit sky was amazing.

In the morning they put on packs and headed down a side canyon that wound for several miles through white sandstone domes that were ribbed with splashes of pale violet, yellow, and red. Otis named it Wine Stain Canyon. It wasn't named on any map. Elias stopped several time to take photos. He decided to call it Painted Paradise, and he had a hard time fitting its expansive beauty into his meager camera.

"Don't call it that, Elias, or word will get out and everyone will want to visit. It'll be all over the Internet, Facebook, Twitter, and whatever else they got out there now to eliminate every last secret and stitch of privacy from our lives. Keep it the way it is and nobody will be curious about Dizzy Dog Mesa."

The derivation of the mesa's name was uncertain. The mesa rose within the last area of the continental United States to be officially mapped. The first explorers, surveyors, and cartographers named the prominent mountains and other geographic features after their sponsors back in Washington D.C. Other features were given anglicized or Spanish names, depending on who got there first. If there were indigenous names they were forgotten, ignored, or unpronounceable. Dizzy Dog may have been the strangled pronunciation of an indigenous name, however it was more likely that it was named the way most geographic points were named. Something happened there that was memorable and the story stuck.

Otis explained to Elias that in this instance, the mesa may have been named for a dog named Diz owned by a renowned canyoneer. Diz was scrambling ahead of his owner on a fragile traverse when the thin ledge broke under him and he fell two hundred feet but survived. "Another version says a cowboy, sent to look for strays, got drunk and passed out with an open jug of beer by his side. His blue heeler finished the jug and the cowpoke awoke to find his dog staggering around the campsite and bumping into rocks and trees. Like most place names in the American West, the narratives are unclear or conflict."

There was no trail, just a meandering canyon bottom that narrowed and opened, narrowed and opened. Sometimes the wash was blocked by rockfalls and they scrambled over broken ledges thick with serviceberry and sage. They focused on their footing and balance across uneven ground, so conversation ceased. The bottom of the wash was lush from the flash floods that pulsed seasonally through the narrow canyon. A grove of willows was busy with small birds and they startled two deer and a few rabbits. If cows had ever grazed there, it was long ago. Grasses were rich and diverse. There were patches of cactus but it was not epidemic as it is in cow-thrashed meadows. Even in the heart of the American West it is hard to find uncut, ungrazed, ungraded, unmined, self-willed land, and this was it. The scope and grace of bare stone scattered across wide horizons humbled them. They were ants crawling through the cracks of an enchanted land. Each turn revealed another gallery of scuffed stains on looming walls.

It was hot so they aimed themselves through the shadows that clung to the canyon walls. They reached a pocket oasis of willows and cottonwoods and settled under their shade to eat a late lunch. They had not spoken for hours by then and were reluctant to break the spell.

Otis leaned back on his pack and waved his arm across the horizon before them. "Well, Elias, what do you think?"

Elias chewed and swallowed, brushed crumbs from his shirt, and took a drink of water from a stainless steel bottle. "I'm not sure what to call it. Eden? Oasis? The land that shaped our national character? Wilderness?"

Otis laughed quietly. "I would have called it 'good' and stopped right there, but then I'm not a writer." He stood and stretched, lifted his pack, slipped one shoulder through a strap, and then adjusted his hat. "Thank God I didn't get that curse," he muttered as he turned away from Elias, who called after him.

"Otis, how long have you lived in Stony Mesa? Twenty years? Twenty-five?"

"Twenty-four coming right up."

"So are you still considered a move-in?"

Otis sat on a fallen log and pulled his foot out of his boot, grabbed his toes and worked them back and forth. He shrugged. "I guess that depends on who you are talking to. The newest move-ins regard me as a local but the old-timers think of me as a move-in."

Elias screwed the cap onto an empty water bottle and gently brushed a small wild bee away from his ear. "I think it's a matter of scale. To the Native Americans the cowboys are the move-ins. At one time the Hopi saw the Navajos as move-ins. Migration is written in our bones. The term move-in says less about the nature of the person described and more about the perspective of the person using it."

Otis stared at Elias in disbelief. He pulled off his hat and slapped it against his knee. "Shit, Elias! You're supposed to be letting go out here! Be in the moment, ya know, but there goes that overactive brain again. I think you've been hanging out with Olene too much. I'll bet you two like to swing around on each other's mental monkey bars. Reel it in, pard."

They had to hustle to get back to camp before dark. Too tired to make dinner, they feasted on the guacamole Grace made for them. They had placed the cooler under the truck to secure some additional shade but the food in it had warmed in the desert sun.

After dinner they sat on a ledge with a wide view of the canyons stretching out to the horizon. The light was softening now and shadows were pooling around the curves and swells of bare rock below. The underbellies of the day's last clouds were stained pink from the light reflected off of the redrock landscape. The bushes lining the crevices darkened.

"Do you find this landscape erotic?" asked Elias.

"You mean because of all the smooth hips and naked breasts of stone? Because of the flesh tones and nipples? Because of all those erect spires and pink caves? Do I find that erotic?" Otis paused for effect and shrugged as if the notion had never occurred to him. "Why no, not at all."

They laughed together. Elias concluded, "It is a landscape of lingams and yonis."

"Stop trying to sound like a cowboy, Elias."

That night as Elias lay on his back in his sleeping bag and stared at the wheel of stars above, just before he nodded out for the night, a meteor as bright as any he had ever seen slid across the blackness and disappeared.

"I am blessed," he said and slept soundly through the night. Otis snored peacefully beside him.

They were awakened by a helicopter. It was so loud that the sharp chop of its blades registered in their shoulders and hurt their ears. Swirling dust covered the dawn light. Tall grass around them was pressed flat while a whirlwind of ash was sucked from their firepan and thrown into their faces.

"What the fuck!" Otis was up and covering his head with his hand. Elias sought cover deeper in his sleeping bag. After the helicopter set down, the engine was cut, the noise faded, and the dust settled. Elias emerged from his protective cocoon to see a man jump out of the chopper. They were so surprised and disoriented that neither could come up with an appropriate question or comment. They stared at the apparition-like figure walking toward them through a dim haze of roiling pollen and dust.

The apparition spoke. His name was Bob. "Holy shit!" he said. "I'm sorry. I've never seen anybody out here before now. What are you two doing?"

Otis and Elias turned toward each other and tried to pick up a sign but both were too incredulous to respond. They looked back at the inquisitive stranger from the sky and Otis at long last found his voice. "We are camping here. What does it look like, dude? And who the hell are you and what are you doing here?"

Bob explained he was from an outfit named the Geologic Assessment and Production Access Corporation, GASPAC for short he said. Their business was exploring for gas, oil, and even coal although lately the market for that had collapsed. GASPAC would soon have a team on the ground on Dizzy Dog Mesa and Bob was scouting for a base camp. Seismic measuring equipment would need to be airlifted in and a team to operate it needed a camp. He explained that their drinking water would be dropped in by helicopter too but it would be great to have some additional water handy so they could clean up and wash tools, that kind of thing. Bob had his eye on the nearby spring and had the helicopter set down so he could get a better look.

Elias and Otis were speechless. It was all too surreal. Here they were in the middle of some of the last wild places left and in comes a helicopter with no warning. And now this guy, talking so matter of fact like he was merely talking about going shopping or planning a picnic.

"But isn't this public land? BLM?" Otis inquired sheepishly, intimidated by the steel blades of the helicopter still rotating slowly above his head. He stood on top of his rumpled sleeping bag in his underwear. His bladder was full and his breath tasted like kerosene. His hair was startled to attention by the helicopter-induced vortex and had not yet succumbed to gravity. Bob, on the other hand, was so neat, handsome, and sure of himself that he might have stepped out of one of those television commercials for white teeth or payday loans.

"Yes, it's Bureau of Land Management ground," he said cheerily. "They're leasing it and we have the contract to . . . how did you guys get in here?"

Otis pointed to his truck.

"Wow!" Bob proclaimed happily. "That's good to know. If we can get vehicles in here we'll save a lot of money and the job goes quicker, too."

Otis and Elias looked at each other with regret, as if they had let slip the magic password to the clubhouse.

By the time they pulled on their pants and combed the dead bugs out of their hair, Bob was waving goodbye and headed for the chopper.

"Wait!" Otis yelled. "Aren't you going to stay longer? You just got here." He hoped to get more information that might help him make sense of the bizarre scene that had unfolded so unexpectedly.

"No," Bob called. "I gotta get on to the next site." He waved a clipboard in the air. "I have a list."

A deafening roar followed as the helicopter revved its engine, lifted through another storm of dirt, and ascended out of sight.

Otis and Elias stood watching an empty sky and listening to the fading chop-chop-chop of the mechanical beast. They were too dumbfounded to make sense and communicate with each other.

Finally, "What was that? Did that just happen?"

They stood there, baffled.

"There is no place untouched, is there?" said Elias. "No corner left alone. Nothing sacred."

Otis picked up his hat and fixed it over a mop of unruly hair. "Let's go home. I could use some peace and quiet."

Chapter 17

It was a clean shot and the damn thing dropped cold where it stood. A hole in the head, no doubt.

"Got ya!"

Jango Junior Burnside felt a thrill unlike anything he'd experienced in many sad and lonely months. A deep satisfaction lit him up. He straightened his spine and stood taller. He was not just invigorated but righteous!

He had planned for this moment carefully. First he baited the back corral with two chickens tied to stakes. He mounted a spotlight on the corral fence and rolled out a long extension cord to a blind he built from hay bales a hundred feet away from the bait. His rifle ready and the spotlight switch at his side, Jango Junior sat silently for several hours in a plastic lawn chair he'd bought on sale at Walmart two weeks before. He'd neglected to remove the sticker that listed the chemical make-up and manufacturing biography of the chair. He assumed that like every other cheap thing he owned it was made in China. The laminated tag was bright white and it gleamed like a badge in the moonlight. He tore it off and stuffed it in his coat pocket. Junior placed a cushion on the chair for comfort and a thermos of hot coffee stood like a sentry at the foot of the chair. It was likely to be a long night so he wore a back brace the chiropractor gave him after he tore a low back muscle while pitching bales of alfalfa onto his trailer.

He nodded off twice and admonished himself. Snoring did not normally attract coyotes, after all. He figured that varmint was too smart to walk into a trap but it had by then acquired an appreciation of fresh chicken and JR was gambling that the palate was more powerful than precaution.

At four a.m. the gamble paid off. The staked birds clucked and fluttered and then squawked loudly. Through the moonlight he saw a sleek shadow moving in a circle around the tethered fowl. He raised the gun and set it against his shoulder, then dropped one hand to his side, found the switch at the end of the extension cord, and flipped it. The spotlight flooded the target area. Surprised and blinded by the bright beam, the coyote braced its feet and hunched reflexively. She froze for only a second. A sharp crack of the rifle and she spun halfway around with the impact and then dropped dead.

"I may be old but there's nothing wrong with my aim." He said it aloud. And then, "That's the end of you, ya damn thief. Yeah, no more chickens for you. You're off my property for good now."

It was heavy. An old female. Death had not robbed her of her supple animal body and as JR lifted her he struggled to balance her limp corpse. He dragged her across the farmyard and hung her by her back legs from the limb of a cottonwood by the back door. It was all he could do to lift her and he had to sit and recover his breath afterward. He meant to get the hide off and salt it the next day but he had meetings with the Holiday Estates lawyer who went over a checklist of particulars that had to be settled before the deal was final. He questioned whether nailing a hide to the gate post was a good idea. Those corporate types from the city seemed a bit sensitive to him and the sight of a fresh hide nailed to a gate post might turn them off. It would be the first thing they saw as they drove into his ranch. Squeamish bunch, those corporate guys. Three days later he decided to do it as he had planned. It's still my ranch, he told himself, and I can still do what I damn well please. I'm tired of tiptoeing around these city slickers with my hat in my hands.

The next morning he cut the hide free and tossed the body in the flesh pit he kept a hundred yards from the house. The coyote's red body, reduced to raw ropes of muscle, bounced off a bloated calf and landed on a maggot-covered pile of pig entrails. A cloud of flies rose above the corpse and then settled down on the fresh feast. JR had prepared cow hides as a kid and then skinned and prepared a deer hide. An elk was next but it was too big and hard to handle. He stuffed a badger and a couple of bobcats and helped a friend stuff a cougar. All but the cougar he shot himself. He never prepared a coyote hide, however, because they were not worth it. Nobody wants a stuffed coyote or a coyote rug or coyote-skin gloves. He did his work quickly.

JR wanted to nail the hide to the post that afternoon but tended a sick cow instead. It was nearly dark by the time he got back to the hide. Just as well, he thought. I don't want some faint-hearted move-in like that pretty gal Luna to see me do it. It was unlikely anyone would be near the gate of the Jango Ranch at that hour but even so he was cautious.

He drove down to the gate and parked a few feet away. The gate consisted of two upright posts hewn from large Douglas firs. Spanning the two upright posts was a third log that held a hand-carved sign announcing the Jango Ranch, the words framed by carvings of a rearing horse on each side. JR slid out of the cab and opened the camper shell on the back of the truck. He took the fresh hide in one hand and held a nail gun in the other. He carried a cartridge of hefty nails in his right pocket.

He dropped the hide by the gate post and hooked the nail gun to a hose attached to a generator in the bed of the truck. He returned to the post and picked up the hide. It was heavy and he tried to lift it up to the place where he wanted to mount it but he couldn't do it with his left hand. His left shoulder joint hurt too much and his left wrist was weak from the time he was thrown from his horse and broke it. He put the nail gun on the ground and grabbed the hide by its neck with his stronger right hand. He picked up the nail gun with his left hand, pressed the hide against the post with his right, and put the nose of the nail gun against the hide. He pulled the trigger, pumped the nose of the gun against the hide, and braced himself for the sharp bang that he expected would follow. Click, click. Nothing. The nail gun didn't fire.

It was now dark and hard to see by the light of the single solar-powered bulb that illuminated the sign above. He thought he saw something wrong with the nose of the gun, so he held the hide in place with the back of his right hand, lifted the heavy gun with his left hand to where he could reach the nose of the gun with the fingers of his right hand. The tool trembled in his weak left hand while the fingers of his right hand explored the gun for a defect. The hide slipped to the ground and he looked away for just a moment.

Bang! The sound of the nail gun firing sent a wave of adrenalin rolling through his veins. The force of the nail exploding out the front of the tool so startled him that he dropped the nail gun. He bent over to pick it up and was pulled back by his taut right arm. He tried to pull his arm toward himself but it wouldn't budge. What the . . .

He stared at his hand in disbelief. A couple of tugs confirmed what his eyes perceived—he was nailed tight to the gate post. The shiny head of the nail sat in the center of his unnaturally dimpled palm. He gathered his wits and was surprised that he felt no pain. No blood either. He figured that when the initial shock wore off the pain would be fierce. More worrisome was his predicament. Night had fallen and he was alone.

He touched the nail head with his free hand and found that it was so tight against the skin of his palm that he would have to dig through his own hand to get a grip on it. The pain that succeeded shock would not allow him to tear his hand free. He remembered a movie he saw about a hiker whose hand was accidentally pinned between a large boulder and a slot canyon wall. The young man cut off his hand to free himself. He knew he would not be able to do that. He once found a trap with a fox paw in it and realized that the fox had chewed it off to get free. No, he would not gnaw his own hand off but for the first time he felt the creature's desperation. His situation was not unlike the hippie gal's dog that was caught in a coyote trap he set. This was beyond embarrassing—humiliating was more like it.

He scanned the options. He could yell for help but who would hear at this hour? The Jango Ranch was too far from town, too far from his nearest neighbor. Eventually, he would cry for help at the end of an interminably long night but by then his voice was weak with fatigue and his lips numb from the chilly night air. He pulled his thin coat across his chest and tried to zip it with his good hand. It was hard to clasp the zippers together at the bottom, normally a two-handed operation. The warm bank of heat that had gathered around the sun-baked shoulders of the canyon walls had lifted in the evening breeze and dissipated. He was cold, so very cold.

A flashlight and tools that might be useful were in the truck but he couldn't reach them while nailed to the gatepost. He was stuck, both physically and mentally. Pain began to register in his punctured hand, and it was too hard to think of much else beside the terrible strange ache that traveled up his arm and into his heart. It became so sharp that he wondered if it were his heart and not his hand that was spiked.

I'll just have to stick it out tonight and wait for morning. Surely someone would be by to rescue me then. Hyrum will be over to finish cleaning up an abandoned corral and the remnants of old wood piles before the next visit by the Highlife Holiday Estates people. An assessor was supposed to come by soon. Maybe he'd be here tomorrow morning. I'm a tough old coot, everyone says so, and I can endure this. I am not just tough as nails, I am tougher than this nail.

The high desert steppes are hot by day but can be surprisingly cold at night. JR was shivering hard. He looked down and saw that he dropped the coyote hide on the ground when he accidentally nailed himself to the gate post. He hooked his foot under it and lifted it until he could reach it with his free hand. He draped it over his shoulders. The skin was still damp but the fur was thick and would hold his heat in and the cold out. He told himself that he would survive by wearing the skin of his enemy.

Later, in the twilight of dawn, when he understood he would die before he could be saved, he was surprised by the mix of emotions he felt. He did not feel fear or panic as he supposed he might. Instead he was surprised, emotionally hurt, very embarrassed, and then angry with himself for walking into this trap he should have seen coming. He felt the way he did when practical jokes were played on him. He had never considered that death might be the ultimate practical joke. You round a corner and the bucket of water drops on your head, the rubber-masked monster pops out and scares you, or you are fastened by a wild nail to a log from a tree you cut yourself and raised into place, stuck fast to the earth like that tree before you cut it down.

JR Burnside was a religious man who adhered to a doctrine of salvation that promised an ever-lasting afterlife to those who believed and obeyed. His wife would be waiting there for him and others from his One True Church who had kept the rules and followed them to the letter. His body, he believed, would be restored and clothed in the light of his Lord. But if this were the portal to that kingdom, it was adorned with agony and doubt.

He was drifting downward into darkness when awakened by a delicate flutter of wings that brushed his cheek gently. He looked up expecting to see an angel but it was only a hawkmoth in the moonlight searching for flowers to probe for nectar. Hawkmoths are large enough to be mistaken for hummingbirds and pollinate at twilight, but this one had lingered under a full moon. Like its kin, it had begun as a bright green caterpillar with a voracious appetite. JR had hunted for them in his tomato plants and had plucked and pinched hundreds of them in his lifetime. The moth fluttered before his face and seemed to mock him, as if to say, Now you are the worm fastened to the vine. This time you pinched yourself, old man.

"Go away!" he shouted hoarsely and swatted at it with his good hand, but when it disappeared he was utterly lonely. "I'm sorry," he whimpered. "Come back."

Another joke, this wanting comfort from an insignificant bug he mistook for an angel. He looked up and exhaled under the slow wheel and winking presence of a billion distant suns.

Chapter 18

Three SUVs descended the road toward the river in a cloud of yellow dust. The dust rose into the slanted sunlight of the early morning and then dispersed in a lazy breeze. Birds no bigger than a child's fist burst into the air ahead of the caravan and scattered seeds and pale droppings that splattered the windshield of the lead vehicle. In the turbulent wake of the passing vehicles a hawkmoth tumbled in flight and was pushed to the ground where it was pounced on and plucked up by a vigilant raven. The raven followed the modest caravan from twenty feet above the rolling dust like a black flag, flapping and squawking. If the passengers in the SUVs heard the raven they said nothing but instinctively looked up and saw only an upholstered ceiling.

In the first car was Sheriff Dunk Taylor, who was there to lead the others down to the Jango Ranch and then stand by, his presence mostly honored protocol. The sheriff was accompanied by his best deputy, Jace Kingman, who had so far not screwed up like the other two. A job as a deputy in Boon County was an entry-level position in a law enforcement career and there was a lot of turnover as the new hires succeeded and moved on to better pay and more benefits or failed out altogether. Sheriff Taylor often said that keeping the law in Boon County required him to continually conduct auditions.

The second car carried an investigator from the state police department, who had organized this trip and was in charge. Kent Medal had worked his way up from street cop to motorcycle cop to captain of a special tactical assault squad when he slipped on a patch of ice in his backyard and busted four vertebrae. It was very embarrassing, since he had made the patch of ice himself. He took his dog out one sub-zero evening to do its business and he decided to relieve himself as well. A minute later he slipped on his own frozen puddle of pee. He was found unconscious with his head resting in a halo of icy piss. His injury halted his macho-cop trajectory and he found himself training police recruits in Taser techniques, a job he so detested that he wept when alone at night. Finally his pleas to his fellow state policemen were answered and he landed the investigator job. It was a big step up for Kent Medal and he intended to make the most of it.

Officer Medal was accompanied by a woman from the state pathology lab who was considered an expert on skeletal remains. She was pleased to be away from the lab for a couple of days and see some beautiful country. She'd camped with her family near Stony Mesa a few years ago and had fond memories of chasing her little boy around the majestic cottonwood trees in the national park campground. There were horses nudging grass under apricot trees in bloom. The deer seemed almost tame. Chuckers and quail ran through the picnic area and they had to brake for wild turkeys.

The state archaeologist rode in the last car with a representative from the state's Bureau of Indian Affairs. All but the sheriff and his deputy stayed at a motel the night before and they were sipping coffee and trying to wake up. There was no suspense about this field trip other than not notifying the ranch owner, a Mr. Jango Burnside Jr., whom the state people did not know. The state police investigator told them he would rather not announce his visit in case Mr. Burnside, so alerted, would tamper with the burial site. Kent Medal was taking no chances.

Dunk Taylor wrestled with his distress. "You don't have to worry about Junior Burnside because he's as honest a man as you'll ever meet. Why not just a phone call first? What kind of damage can an old man do in the next half hour before we get there?" Sheriff Dunk Taylor had known Junior all his life and like most of the residents of Stony Mesa he held him in high regard. He was not comfortable going over there without warning. Seems unnecessarily rude, he told the others when they met at the motel restaurant.

Medal was unconvinced. "If he's so honest, Sheriff Taylor, why didn't he disclose the grave when his hired hand discovered it?"

Dunk fell silent. There was really no use arguing. He would go along this morning and make his apologies to Junior later. And now, as he descended the last stretch of the Jango Ranch road before the Burnside house fell into view, he was agitated, unlike the others who were still drinking coffee out of paper cups and making small talk about sports and celebrities. They expected Dunk to deal with the old man while they set about a long day of pulling bones up from the dust and recording where they lay. They didn't know Mr. Burnside and, honestly, couldn't care less whether he liked them there or not. The warrants they needed were in order and that was sufficient reason to intrude.

They rounded the last bend before the ranch gate and Dunk slammed on his brakes and skidded to a stop. The drivers in the two cars behind him hit their brakes hard too so they wouldn't smash into the back of Dunk's patrol vehicle. The others were so focused on the sudden near collision that they did not see what stopped Sheriff Taylor short.

"What the heck, did he hit a dog? Was it a deer? A cow?" they asked each other.

Their eyes scanned the scene before them to find clues. They saw something at the gate that was so odd and unrecognizable that several seconds passed before they understood what Sheriff Taylor saw first. A human body was slumped forward, bent at the knees and hanging by one outstretched arm that was affixed to the gate's raw pine pillar. Its head was bowed beneath what looked like a blanket or rug that was draped across its shoulders. A closer look revealed it was an animal hide, probably a coyote, though the hide was very large for a coyote. The unfamiliar hunched beast with a burnished silver mane and a single flannel arm was a warped amalgam of human and animal. With one hand aloft behind him and the other resting on the ground, with knees bent and head bowed forward, the creature was performing a rag doll curtsy.

They found it hard to process the grim genuflection before them but Officer Medal jumped immediately to thoughts of cults and Satanists or maybe those animal rights freaks. His experience told him that the scene was too weird and grotesque to be an accident. Maybe the perpetrators were about to nail the victim's other hand to the gate and they were interrupted. That would explain the half-assed crucifixion. Or maybe the murderer staged the scene to look cultish in hope of throwing off the investigation, when their real motives were the usual mundane mix of greed, jealousy, hate, and anger. The strain from sorting so many possibilities hurt his brain.

The passengers bailed out of their vehicles for a closer look. Kent Medal's hand moved instinctively toward his firearm in case whatever it was lunged forward. Dunk's deputy was the first to recognized Junior Burnside. "My God," he whispered so quietly the others barely heard him. "It's JR." His voice cracked when he asked, "Why? What?"

Sheriff Taylor reached to take the ghastly robe from Junior's shoulders. "Don't touch!" yelled Officer Medal. "Treat this like a crime scene! Tape it up and don't touch anything! We need lots of photos right away."

Dunk Taylor winced when he realized that photos of the awful scene before his eyes would soon exist. And as long as they existed they might be seen by Junior's family, friends, neighbors. Worse, strangers. It was at times like these that Dunk Taylor wanted to take his badge and chuck it off a cliff, go home, sleep twenty hours, and forget.

The woman with skeletal expertise was allowed to step into the mess and check the limp body for vital signs. She reported, "He's not only dead, he's cold."

Under the loud orders of Officer Kent Medal, the "crime" scene was secured, the coroner was called, and two-hundred photos were taken, mostly by Medal himself. A CSI team was dispatched from the state police crime lab three hours away, a long while to be stuck next to a corpse in a bizarre posture. A tarp was propped over it to mask the macabre scene and provide shade for the body that was beginning to bloat under the waxing sun.

JR was Dunk's fellow church elder but he couldn't remember if or how they might also be distant cousins. Tracing his genealogy distracted him from the grim job at hand. To make the situation worse, Officer Medal decided to get a jump on the investigation by interviewing Dunk.

After the obvious "who would do this?" questions resulted in a long recitation by the sheriff of all the reasons JR Burnside was a beloved and respected member of the community, Medal asked about the sale of the Jango Ranch to Highlife Holiday Estates.

"People are upset, sure," argued Dunk, "but not enough to do this."

"What about that group that hangs around the Desert Rose?"

"Why them?"

"Oh, don't be stupid, man, we know for sure that some of the people who visit and work there were involved in that tar sands protest a few years ago. In fact, the woman who owns it was a leader."

"Ever convicted, ever tried?" Sheriff Taylor had been slouched in remorse but now he pulled himself up a good three inches and leaned over the smaller state policeman.

"No, but . . ."

"Then innocent! Look, officer, this is a pretty tight little community. Live here and you see the same folks over and over—church, school events, basketball games, the store, the gas station, community celebrations, you name it. We only have a few places to eat out so if you take the wife out to dinner chances are your neighbors are at the next table. We see each other and we don't have to listen too hard to hear about each other. My heck, before there was Facebook there was gossip. If you think those kids down at the Desert Rose haven't been looked over long and hard, then . . . well, you're not thinkin' straight."

Medal gave Dunk the look he reserved for pitiable idiots. Dunk spoke louder. "I'm not wild about their appearance, mind you, and I don't have much in common, but in all my encounters with them they been friendly and honest. They worked hard to change that place around and done a fine job of it, too. People who work for them like them because they're fair and generous."

Medal smirked. "See any vegans there? Animal rights types?"

"They serve bison steaks and burgers there. They got beef on the menu, too. Grass-fed and local. And chicken, they got chicken on the menu, too."

"Organic, no doubt."

"I suppose so. Don't make much difference to a dead chicken though does it? Look, Officer Medal, if they were animal rights nuts they wouldn't be serving meat. And Luna still has cows. And chickens!"

"Right, chickens, got it." He snapped his notebook closed and walked away.

The CSI team arrived earlier than expected and went over the crime scene and took samples. JR's body was released to the coroner and the CSI team moved through the house. No signs of violence or theft, no messages, nothing out of place, no clues or leads. Officer Medal decided it was time to call in Kayla, the granddaughter who was close to Mr. Burnside and visited him often. Dunk Taylor watched helplessly as the strangers snooped about and Medal fired orders. Medal opened drawers and took out a notebook he found and started turning pages. Dunk stood over him and tapped him on the shoulder.

"What is it, Sheriff?"

"You don't have a search warrant."

"I'm looking through this address book for Kayla Burnside's phone number. I can't get a signal here so I'll use the landline. I'm going to notify her."

Dunk's misgivings about the way Medal was handling the situation reached a tipping point. It was one thing that he had to put up with that pushy rat-faced know-it-all but the thought of him breaking the news to Kayla and then interrogating her was too much. He slipped out the back door and stood under an arbor of honeysuckle. His brain was in overdrive. What can I do? He called Elias Buchman.

"Elias, it's Dunk Taylor. I need some help."

"Sure, Sheriff, what can I do?"

"Ya gotta keep this under your hat, understand? Junior Burnside is dead. The state police cop that's down here with me is a horse's ass and he's making this into a big mess. Next he's gonna pull Kayla into this and I've had enough. He came down here to look into another matter altogether and just stumbled into this. I think it's my jurisdiction and I want to take over but I'm not sure if I can. Can you look into that for me?"

"Gosh, Dunk, I'm not a lawyer . . ."

"I know you're not but you can look stuff up faster than anyone I know. Just get on the Internet and let me know what you find out."

Elias called back in twenty minutes. In the meanwhile, Officer Medal left a message for Kayla to call back but she hadn't responded. When his phone buzzed, Dunk Taylor snapped it to his ear and held his breath.

"Dunk," said Elias, "there's no clear answer but I think you can stand your ground and take over. That would be defensible, anyhow."

Less than a minute later, Sheriff Dunk Taylor approached Officer Medal, who had just downloaded photos from his phone onto a laptop he carried into the house from his car. He used a printer he found in Jango Junior's office to pop out eight-by-tens of the grisly scene at the ranch gate.

"What the hell are you doing?" asked Dunk. "This is a crime scene."

He looked down to see the photos and turned a color of red that bordered on purple. Medal looked at him and grinned with amusement. "You look like you're tryin' to swallow a baseball, Sheriff."

Dunk grabbed the rest of the photos and crumpled them in his fist.

"Hey! What do you think you're doing?" yelled Medal.

"If you show Kayla Burnside these photos of her grandfather, or show them to anyone else for that matter, I will shove that dang phone so far up your ass you can dial it with your nose." This was not what Sheriff Taylor had planned to say and he was not sure now what to say next. But as he began to sputter it was very clear he had reached full boil.

"Whoa there big guy, take it easy! If you so much as touch me I will have your badge."

"You fuck this up and hurt that girl and my badge is the first thing going up that ass of yours, understand?"

Medal retreated. He was soon calling his office to ask about help since the local sheriff was "off the rails."

An hour later Kayla drove down to her grandparents' ranch, a route that was normally familiar and comforting, but now she struggled to still her racing heart and hold in the tears brimming her eyes. Fits of sadness competed with feelings of dread and panic. Her tears were the trailer for a god-awful film that would soon play night and day with Kayla Burnside captured in the lead role, but for now disbelief and poisonous suspense ruled her.

The yellow police tape was removed from the gate before she arrived—Dunk Taylor had ripped it down without permission—but there were police cars pulled up to the front of the porch. She stepped from her car as a dragonfly brighter than a jewel was caught in the sunlight and floated past her face. She could hear cattle lowing in the nearest pasture, a dog barking in the distance, doves cooing, ravens chattering as they chased their shadows across a canyon wall. Everything seemed so normal, so unchanged, and that seemed weird or wrong. She reproached herself for thinking the world would change because JR Burnside was no longer on the land. Just me now, she thought, just me.

Her grandfather's body was removed by the coroner before she arrived and the CSI team was packing to leave. Medal and Dunk agreed to interview Kayla together but Dunk made it clear that if he thought Officer Medal was in any way anything less than considerate and compassionate, Dunk would . . . well he wasn't sure what else he could threaten to shove up Medal's skinny butt, which was already reserved for a phone and a badge.

Kayla pulled up and saw Dunk. She started to weep. He stepped forward and took her into his arms. He was her basketball coach in eighth grade. Kayla was a classmate of his own daughter. She'd been to his home for sleepovers and birthday parties. When she broke her wrist while roping a steer, it was Dunk who drove her to the Boon County Clinic. He let her cry and then gave her a handkerchief to blow her nose.

Kayla walked through the house and saw nothing out of place or unusual. No, she knew of no enemies or threats. No, she could not imagine why anyone would do this. No, her grandfather wasn't suicidal. No, he didn't do drugs or drink. Asked by Medal about Junior's relationship with the "hippie element" at the Desert Rose, Kayla related how JR had talked to Luna Waxwing just a couple of weeks before. The talk ended on a congenial note. JR was impressed with the young woman and asked Kayla if she was acquainted with her. She saw no reason to think any of the Desert Rose people were involved.

Medal insisted she consider the possibility that the Desert Rose was a "hang-out" for nefarious radical types. "We have dossiers on Ms. Waxwing and her partner, the one they call Hopper. We suspect he was involved in the sabotage of some heavy equipment at a tar sands mine a couple of years ago."

Kayla was surprised to hear that. "I thought a flash flood took that mine out."

"It did, but that was after the fact." Medal was frustrated that he couldn't get her or the stupid excuse for a sheriff to feel alarm or suspicion.

"What does the tar sands thing have to do with this?" Dunk Taylor asked. He was as exasperated with Officer Medal as Medal was with him. "Look, I'm not happy about that bunch down there and there's not much we agree on, but they're not murderers."

As for the coyote hide draped across her grandfather's lifeless body, Kayla told them that her grandfather was trying to kill that coyote for weeks and finally succeeded. He showed her the coyote's body just a couple of days before when they Skyped. He told her he intended |to nail it to the gate. She thought she'd talked him out of it but wasn't surprised if he tried to follow through.

After an hour of what he thought was unnecessary and repetitive grilling by that obnoxious pipsqueak of a state cop, Dunk was convinced that Jango Junior Burnside had accidentally nailed his own hand to the gate post, that he probably pulled the hide over his shoulders because he was cold, and that the death was accidental. He told Medal and Kayla as much and added that, in his opinion, there was no need to rob JR Burnside of his dignity by prolonging an investigation into his death. Why publicize the freakish details for no good reason?

Officer Medal was frustrated by their naïve obstinacy and about to set them straight when the news helicopter from Channel 4 appeared on the horizon and approached the ranch. It hovered overhead and they saw a man attached to a harness leaning out over the churning air with a camera. The lens was the size of a cannon. Their voices were drowned out by the loud chopping noise made by the helicopter's blades. Dunk Taylor pushed Kayla Burnside into the shelter of her grandfather's house. Officer Medal swore and kicked the dirt.

The developers behind Highlife Holiday Estates became skittish even before bones were unearthed at the Jango Ranch and before JR Burnside crucified himself under the skin of a big coyote. Given their misgivings, they may have turned away from the deal even if no bones were discovered and if JR hadn't . . . what? Was it a murder? Suicide? Freak accident? It didn't matter. Once they saw the footage on the web of police cars and flashing lights, that iconic yellow police tape draped from shrub to shrub, the hints of violence and atrocity were too powerful to ignore. They scanned the videos taken from the Channel 4 chopper as they knew their potential buyers would and it was all bad. Their meticulous campaign to portray their development as a place above and away from the chaotic grind of daily life was replaced by images of body bags and bone fragments. From the vantage of each of their different perches a single conclusion emerged. The place was now contaminated in the public's consciousness. It was time to get out.

Orin Bender had enough on his plate without the Holiday Estates deal, which was now getting much too complicated. His next-to-last trophy wife, Kimberly, described on a video that went viral how Orin kept boxes of cash and stashes of gold and jewelry in a vault inside a secret mountain tunnel. She drew a map for the television reporter who interviewed her. She claimed there were also secret bank accounts in Switzerland and Panama. She asked her ex-husband why he stashed his wealth in hiding places. He joked, "Ya never know when you might have to escape." She then ran down a who's who of legislators Orin boasted he could bribe. He called them the RFMs which meant "ready for more."

Kimberly's television interview was a desperate attempt to attract attention. She knew she was easy on the eyes, after all that was how she landed Orin, but she wasn't getting any younger. In the coming months while Orin became a political pariah dogged by prosecutors, the woman he once affectionately called his "Little Kimmy Kitten" eagerly awaited an opening bid.

Unfortunately for Kimberly, she became the least of Orin Bender's worries. His attention was mostly focused on a woman neither of them had ever met named Della Sue Mikesel. Della Sue's husband, Nolan Mikesel, was a man known across Boon County as a violent and dangerous creep. Why she married him was one of the great local mysteries. Sure, she was knocked up and not out of high school, but marrying Nole was generally viewed as a case of compounding a problem. The town knew she was trapped because she rarely showed up in public and was more stooped and bruised when she did appear. Friends and neighbors were afraid to approach her until Nolan was killed by a flash flood. Then classmates who grew up with her but had not talked to her in years showed up at her door. Everyone wanted to help now that she was liberated and they didn't have to encounter Nolan when they visited her.

Della Sue rented out the single-wide trailer she shared with Nole and the two kids and moved in with her mother. The rent from the trailer provided her with an income until she got back on her feet. She got a job in the school lunch room, which was handy since Nole's son had what are politely labeled "issues" that required frequent trips to the principal's office to retrieve him and take him home. The child was angry and fought frequently with the other boys in his class. Della Sue told the school social worker that her boy witnessed beatings and drunkenness, constant screaming, harsh punishments, and foul language. He was given counseling, which seemed to help.

A few years after Nolan was killed, Della Sue resolved to clean out the storage shed behind the trailer and once and for all scrub the stain that was Nolan Mikesel out of her life. Clearing out Nole's junk felt more like an exorcism than housecleaning. She picked up the things she hated and held them gingerly as if they contained a poison that could spread if handled carelessly. She filled three garbage bags with magazines and DVDs of his favorite porn, the kind where the man grabs the woman by the hair or throat and thrusts maniacally like a psychopath in a stabbing frenzy. She tossed out his extensive literature on guns, knives, bows, traps, monster trucks, motorcycles, kick-boxing, and all-terrain vehicles. She could tell some were his favorites because the covers were greasy and the pages splattered with tobacco spit.

She opened a book that was on the top of a pile of knife catalogs titled How to Kill Predators for Profit. He had underlined certain passages with a yellow marker. She had never imagined that Nole could be so attentive to anything he read. It didn't fit Nole, who wore his ignorance proudly. He often proclaimed he had no need for science or reason like those pussy liberals he heard about on his favorite alt-right radio shows. She wondered if there were any more surprises.

She lifted the edge of a stack of magazines and discovered a notebook underneath. He never referred to it and she had never seen it before then. It looked like a diary and she hoped it might contain a personal account of his feelings and most private reflections. Maybe she could gain some insight into this monster she had invited into her life. The notebook held another account altogether, a strange tally of death and payment. It didn't take her long to realize that the mysterious income that had kept them one notch above poverty during those years of shouts and punches was generated by her husband's paid killing sprees. He was a secret exterminator and as she thumbed and studied the pages she realized he had progressed from killing prairie dogs to people. At the time of his death he was planning to kill someone he cryptically referred to as the Hippie Eco-Queen. Clearly written was this final passage: "Orin Bender agrees half now, half after in cash."

A phone number followed. For several days she held her secret tight and tirelessly mulled the possibilities. She decided to call the number. The phone on the other end rang twice and she hung up. A week later she tried again. She had examined her struggles and they all boiled down to one thing: money. She couldn't handle rent yet or even put down a deposit, couldn't pay the debt Nole left her, couldn't get her son new shoes to replace the tight ones he wore, couldn't afford the things they saw on television. She couldn't afford cable or an Internet connection. Her kid seemed to be the only one in school who didn't have a tablet or smartphone. There were holes in their teeth. They were falling behind everywhere at once. She tried the number again.

The voicemail came on but it did not identify who she was calling. She took a chance. "Is this Mr. Bender? If it is I want to talk to you. I am Nolan Mikesel's widow. I found a notebook I thought you might want to purchase." She left her number.

Two days later she tried again. The number had been disconnected. The next day she received a call from a man who claimed to be Orin Bender's attorney. He asked her to meet him for lunch in the city. It was a three hour drive and she worried about the cost of the gas and whether her beat up car could make it there and back but she agreed.

She hesitated at the restaurant door, breathed deep, and walked in. It was a high-end restaurant, not a chain, and she was self-conscious about her blouse and skirt, as if everyone there would know she got them on the discount rack at Walmart. A man in a dark gray suit and purple tie waved to her and she walked over to the table where he sat alone. She smiled and said hello. He didn't smile back at her. She sat down.

A waiter approached and the man waved away the menu and ordered a gin and tonic. He asked her what she wanted and she asked for water, no ice. He smiled at the waiter and said, "We won't stay long. Just drinks, thank you."

"I didn't get your name," she said.

"You don't need my name." He was all business. "Let me see what you have."

She took a plastic bag from her purse and pulled out the greasy notebook. She held open the notebook to a page where Nole had listed jobs done for "Mr. O. Bender." Amounts paid were in one column, dead animals in another.

She was cautious but felt a need to explain the circumstances that led to the discovery of the secret ledger. The man in the dark gray suit didn't want to hear it and cut her off.

"Here's how it's going to go, miss. You give me the notebook and keep your pretty mouth shut tight. Understand? You tell nobody. Nobody. You take the envelope I will give you and walk away. I never want to hear from you again, understand?"

"Okay, but how much . . ."

"More than you deserve and the most you're ever going to get. Consider yourself lucky. My client is sorry for your loss and he thinks you are capable of discretion. He is trusting that you will know better than to ever say another word to him or anyone else about this. Understand? My client does not like people who betray his trust. If you fuck this up, young lady, you will be very, very, very sorry. Understand?"

"Yes. Yes! I won't be back, I promise." She wanted to cry. She wanted to run. The man reached beside his chair and pulled a manila envelope from a briefcase. He tossed it across the table. The waiter appeared with two glasses on a tray. She grabbed the envelope, stood, turned, and walked abruptly out of the restaurant and into the street.

When she got to her car she sped toward home. The following week she didn't sleep. Every little noise made her jump. On Wednesday she suffered a migraine worse than anything since the time Nole cracked her front tooth with a hair brush and then choked her until she passed out. She feared for her kid. She put the ten thousand in the bank and although she desperately needed it for bills she was afraid to touch it. The following week she went to the police. By then she was a sobbing wreck.

Orin Bender called his old buddy Les Huntley whose friendship went back to their corporate careers at Beksell. Huntley was his main partner in the Highlife Holiday Estates deal and Orin knew he had to be the first to give Huntley the troubling news about the investigation generated by some crazy woman who tried to blackmail him. He assured Huntley that he had no idea who she was. And don't worry about all that nonsense Kimmy is spouting because he was about to settle with her and secure her silence.

His old friend listened quietly. He assured Orin it would all blow over and of course he'd stay in the Jango Ranch deal. "Just sit tight," he said. "We've been through worse, haven't we?" Huntley ended his call to his old pal and immediately called his lawyer. He told him to get right on it. He wanted out of the deal with as little liability and cost as possible. He was considering running for office now that he had time and lots of money. There was no way he could be associated with Orin Bender. "From now on," he told his lawyer, "it's Orin who? Got it? I can't afford to be associated with him anymore."

If Les Huntley was alarmed, Warren Smithfield, the third partner, was relieved that Orin's problems might kill the Highlife Holiday Estates deal. He had unexpected financial problems of his own. The development of a revolutionary nanobot deodorant that he had sunk a wad of money into was not going well. The first round of test subjects developed a rash and there were troubling signs that the nanobots didn't just eat perspiration but also mucous, saliva, ear wax, and any other fluid that reached the surface of the human anatomy. The human body is a community of fluids and the nanobots enjoyed wetter reaches. When they tapped out one human landscape they could migrate to another human. The spouses, lovers, masseuses, hair dressers, and other intimate associates of the test subjects also developed rashes and dry skin.

It was suggested that the product could be used instead as a decongestant but when tested on mice they died. In fact a small dose of nanobot deodorant could turn them into mouse jerky in less than a week. To make matters even worse, the deodorant was infused with an aromatic blend of cinnamon and hibiscus scents but after only a couple of days of use, test pits smelled more like a bait can that was left in a hot trunk for a week. The project was in disarray and needed even more investment.

On the home front, Smithfield had even more reason to back out. He took his wife to see the Jango Ranch and despite his best efforts to paint an attractive picture of what they would develop there—the golf course, the tennis courts, the pool with a wet bar, the stable full of thoroughbred horses—she was definitely opposed to the whole thing. He could still hear her.

"There are bugs, for chrissake! Everywhere! God knows what else is out there. Horses stink, did you think of that? And when was the last time you rode a horse? Ever? We are in the middle of nowhere.

Nowhere! Look, you do what you want. You want to play cowboy go ahead. But not me, I can find better places to be than in the middle of . . . of . . . nowhere!"

He waited for her to calm down and tried again. The house would be spacious and there would be a big Jacuzzi tub with a picture window. "You can stay inside and look out. Orin told me the last time he was here he saw an elk."

"Elk! They have ticks, don't they? Or lice! Ew!"

On the ride home a bobcat ran out into the road in front of them, and Warren braked so hard that his wife put her hand out and broke a fingernail on the dashboard. She acted like she had severed a limb.

"Monsters! There are monsters!"

"I think it was a bobcat."

"Don't tell me that wasn't a monster. And snakes, did you think about the snakes?" He knew it was no use. Her mind was made up. Nevertheless, he started to make his case once more before they went to bed.

"Stop! No more of that soft-headed postcard crap. Nature is nasty. Period. Where's my eye pillow?"

Success is heralded with trumpets but failure is a squeaky thing. It was several weeks before the good citizens of Stony Mesa caught on to the fact that the Highlife Holiday Estates project had come apart at the seams as all three principal investors tore for the exits. Whether glorious or profane, the prospect of a gated ghetto of mini-mansions was dead and gone, caput, adios, history. Just as quickly as the big deal appeared to trouble their minds, it went away. They were left to debate what was now moot. Some thought the town had missed a marvelous opportunity while most felt relieved that it was over. JR Burnside was dead and the Highlife Holiday Estates boys were nowhere to be seen.

The good citizens of Stony Mesa turned back to their lives as they had been doing for a hundred years. They raised their kids, fixed their trucks, brought in another crop of alfalfa, trucked their cows to market, cursed the weather, attended church, and blamed the government. Normal.

Chapter 20

They wore their best dark suits and somber dresses, black without relief throughout the grandest church in town. Shiny shoes and finely tooled cowboy boots scuffed and patted the tile floor. They held books of doctrine and hymns on their laps, faced forward in orderly church pew rows, whispered and wept softly. They waited for their pastor, who approached the pulpit and tapped the microphone twice, provoking a crackling distortion followed by a painful feedback moan. Those parishioners with hearing aids cupped their ears and winced.

Reverend Pettybone began. The service followed the order described in the programs that the congregation tucked into suit jackets and purses. They retrieved them every few minutes to check on what would come next and gauge how much longer JR's funeral service would last. They sang and prayed between tearful testimonies. The people of Stony Mesa were not likely to cry, especially in public, but in church they broke down regularly. Relating their memories of old JR was an especially wet and salty experience. Tears filled eyes, spilled down cheeks, and hung precariously from the tips of noses and chins. Speakers delivered halting eulogies with cracking voices. They stopped in mid-sentence to stifle sobs, their shoulders quivering slightly.

Like his father and grandfather before him, JR was a pillar of the little community and mourners were grieving not just the passage of a man seventy years familiar but the passing of an era. If any among the mourners hoped that Junior's passage meant the end of the upsetting Highlife Holiday Estates deal, they did not show it. That speculation was for another day. They were there to put Jango Junior Burnside in the ground.

The evening before, there was a viewing where, against the family's wishes, the casket was closed. Some vocal family members expected an open casket viewing as was the tradition in their church. Others in the extended family had fallen away from the church and didn't really care. But Kayla, who never accepted her church's preference for viewing and addressing the body of the deceased, was more than adamant, she was fierce. Outnumbered and, worse, outnumbered by men, Kayla threatened to close the casket herself if they opened it. She told them she did not want to remember him that way, waxen and still. But, they argued, it's the way of our church. She was resolute. "I shared him with the church while he was alive but they don't get to own his dead body, too."

Family members who were on the sidelines intervened. They pulled others aside and whispered, "You know, she just might close the casket herself." Please, they said, let's get through this without all the stress and drama. Let Kayla have her way.

The singing that accompanied the funeral service lurched out of tune here and there because Wanda Gussy hadn't time to rehearse the choir and their usual organist, Breanna Barney, was visiting her sister in Dallas. Otherwise it was all predictable until Kayla Burnside walked to the front of the church to bear her testimony.

Two days earlier another ceremony was held. The skeletons and scattered parts of thirteen human beings, individually wrapped in new body bags, were turned over to representatives of four regional tribes. There was no way of knowing which of the people whose skeletons were surrendered was funny, which one was wise, or brave, generous, beautiful, mean. They were bones with no stories. They generated no memories, no tears.

The Native Americans wore shirts of bright red, turquoise, purple, and blue. Bright sashes and silver jewelry completed their formal attire. The county commissioners were all a hundred miles away attending a workshop on wresting control of federal lands and turning them over to state government, a move that Elias described as a land grab plain and simple. The secretary to the county commission, Margene Kimble, who was also a cousin to two of the commissioners, was designated to greet the tribal reps and welcome them to Boon County. She called to ask them if they wanted the Boy Scouts to provide a color guard with a flag to lead the pledge of allegiance and they said definitely not. How about the local pastor to say a prayer? No thanks on that, too. Margene was baffled about what to do next or instead.

The old man from the Navajo tribal office assured her that they just wanted to retrieve the bones and be on their way. They would take care of any ceremonies at an undisclosed location on one of the reservations when the bodies were "repatriated." Margene googled that word and then decided to keep it simple. She called the county coroner to see if he could attend.

The release of the skeletal remains to the tribal representatives was unusually swift. Bones have lingered for decades on shelves in boxes because of jurisdictional disputes and the bones from the Jango Ranch were marked by a tragedy that begged an investigation, always a good reason in the minds of investigators to hold on to them for further study. But a protracted and public dispute over indigenous remains between a capitol city museum and the Shoshone tribe had just been settled and nobody in government wanted to revisit those issues. To top it off, a backcountry pot hunter had stumbled onto a cave with an unrecorded burial site. He dug up a woman and her infant. The baby was badly deteriorated so he discarded her and sold the cradle she was buried in. However, the woman, presumably the baby's mother, was a perfect mummy.

He carried her home in the back of his ATV and stored her in the basement where it was cool and dry. He sold baskets, pots, and other artifacts like knives, tools, and toys that he dug out of the graves he robbed, but never an entire body. He had no market for that. Soon she became a burden because it seemed she was always in the way. She rolled off a shelf and dove headfirst into a laundry bin next to the washing machine. She came up with a sock in her mouth. He tried keeping her in a broom closet but opening it up and seeing her there was spooky, like a scene in a cheap horror flick. There wasn't a convenient or logical place to store a corpse in his house and he even considered taking her back to the cave where he found her.

One night he had too much to drink and got the wild idea of taking his treasure to the bar with him. She would be his date. She rode in the passenger seat and at some point in what was reported to be a raucous night a cigarette was added to her lips. The party ended when a cop pulled the car over and, seeing a corpse of some kind in the passenger seat who was smoking a Marlboro and grinning inappropriately, asked the artifact poacher to step out of the car. He did so but when told to put his hands behind his back he spun around and jumped backward two steps away from the cop and into the road. He lifted his middle finger at the policeman and started to speak when he disappeared with a sickening thud beneath an oncoming tractor-trailer truck. The story of his shocking death went viral. The state bureaucrats agreed: let them have the bones.

The decision to repatriate the bones was unexpected and caught Kayla Burnside by surprise. She called around to find out where the transfer would take place. She was appalled when she learned it would happen at the Boon County Civic Center, a low brick building built with a federal grant and used for senior citizen lunches, blood drives, flu shots, Grace Buchman's yoga class, Cub Scout meetings, and the county quilters club. She offered the Jango Ranch as an alternative. The ceremony should take place where the skeletons rested all those years, she argued. Margene told her she didn't think the Indians wanted to go to much trouble and she gave her the phone number of the man who seemed to be making plans for the tribes. Kayla called it and found herself talking to a Hopi elder. She offered him her vision of what could take place.

"I want to put a fence around where they were buried. I'll plant grass there and a shade tree. When the tree is big enough to sit under I want to add a bench with a plaque commemorating them. I want to make this as right as I can."

The Hopi elder was silent and she could almost hear him wince. "What's wrong? I'm sorry, did I say something offensive? I only meant to . . ."

He cut her off. "No, I understand your intentions and they are very honorable. I appreciate your concern. But that is not the way my people do it. We bury our dead as quickly as we can and only a few see the body. The Hopi and Navajo don't want to be near the body and if you are near, you don't distract the dead one's spirit with emotions and crying. We accept death. It is part of life."

Kayla's eyebrows lifted. This was a surprise, so different from her own culture's practice. The man on the phone continued. "What concerns us is if the spirit of the dead one remains or returns. This is bad, very bad. We keep emotional outbursts to a minimum so the spirit does not become distracted. We bury in unmarked graves with a stick protruding from it so the spirit has a ladder to the sky. We pray for the dead one to have a swift journey. We are afraid of spirits that linger and attach. Sometimes we burn down a hogan where a death occurred. You would be wise to leave that ground alone. Avoid it, don't attract something bad."

Kayla was embarrassed. "I'm sorry, I had no idea. I should have known better, please forgive me. It's just that I feel responsible, I mean my great-grandfather might have . . ."

"That's in the past now," the old man replied before she finished.

"Is it?" she asked.

He chuckled. "No, nothing that happens is ever in the past. But you are not to blame. You seem like a good person. Take what you have learned, young lady, and move on. Speak the truths you find in your heart. Be brave."

The testimonies before the congregation painted an anecdotal portrait of JR Burnside as kind, generous, and clever. It seemed there wasn't much left to say. Kayla Burnside was last. She walked slowly to the pulpit, wiped a tear from her cheek, and cleared her throat. Her nose dripped and she caught it on her sleeve. She breathed one deep sigh, stole a quick glance at the sun beaming down through the south windows of the church, and began.

"My grandparents were my north star. They gave me love, security, and confidence. When I graduated high school and left for college, they were already old. Grandpa couldn't lift a saddle onto a horse by himself because he had a bad shoulder. He couldn't haul sprinkler pipe anymore. Grandma had trouble lifting all sorts of things and couldn't see to thread a needle after sundown. I was becoming their muscles and their eyes. It was clear they needed me but they insisted that college was my future. By the time I started veterinary school, Grandma had passed and Grandpa was starting to get pushed around by his cows. While loading a horse into a trailer he got knocked down and limped for months. Again I offered to stay and help but he would have none of that, my place was in school. He was very proud when I graduated. My love of horses came from him and most of what I know about horses I learned at his knee. I am who I am because they loved me and put me first. They were irreplaceable."

She reached into her pocket for a Kleenex and dabbed tears from her cheeks. Her hand trembled and she gripped the pulpit to steady it. "Others have described his good humor, his generosity, his plain-spoken intelligence. He was also known for speaking frankly and getting straight to the point. We can't bury him today beside his beloved wife Annie May without thinking of the terrible way he died."

The congregation began to twitch. They did not want to go there. She persisted. "You can call it a freak accident but I think hate took him. Maybe it's impolite to bring that up here but we should talk about this. You have also heard about the bones of Indian people, many of them women and children, that were found on Grandpa's ranch. Traces of strychnine were found in their bones."

She heard someone gasp softly and she looked up. "We know what that is, don't we? It's been with us since the beginning of our pioneer ancestors' days here in this land. There were wolves when they arrived but that first generation of our kin wiped them out. There were plenty of coyotes to take their place—still are. Maybe those whose bodies were buried at the Jango were the next nuisance we tried our poison on. Or maybe it was an accident. Maybe they harvested carrion that was laced with strychnine and meant for a coyote or a cougar. We will never know."

She had come this far and was determined to finish, to say it. "My grandfather had a history of killing whatever intrudes. For most of his seventy years he battled 'varmints' as he called them. There were mice in the cabinets and a messy owl in the barn who ate those mice and then excreted them onto his workbench. If it wasn't one creature it was another: chipmunks in the garden, marmots in the melons, and coyotes killing his birds. That got to him the most because eggs were a staple of his diet and the coyote who had the nerve to help herself to his chickens was the last straw. That animal stood for all the frustration he accumulated and carried for almost seventy years as he forced himself against the grain of this hard landscape and its hungry creatures. Weather, insects, and disease are acts of God, he told me, but the wolf and lion are the devil's work and so is the coyote. So slaughter is permitted. And yet it never ends, they keep coming back and that frustrated him to no end."

She was crying now. "Throughout a lifetime lived with dignity and kindness there was in him this one breach in the wall and hatred climbed in. Hatred made him hasty, hatred made him reckless." She paused so they leaned forward. "Hatred made a fool of him. Hatred killed him."

She stopped there and looked at the friends and neighbors assembled before her. They were upset and confused. And silent. You could hear the proverbial pin drop or, as Otis Dooley later told the story, you could hear a mosquito fart. She held them there for a long moment and then continued so softly that it seemed she was whispering the words to herself.

"We have to stop this war. Not the war far away but the one in our own backyard. Not because it is violent and futile, not because it is wrong. We must end it because it diminishes us. My grandfather was a wise and dignified man. Look what hatred did to him."

It was time to close. "I have no plan and I have no answers. I just know there has to be a better way than a life that requires endless strife with every creature on this wild landscape that has escaped our control. Please, if you loved my grandfather, help find a better way."

Chapter 21

Alone at the Jango Ranch, Kayla walked into the kitchen. It smelled like oatmeal and bacon. If she closed her eyes she could almost smell the aroma of her grandmother's fresh biscuits and cornbread. This is where Kayla was taught to cook and can, bake and butcher. At home in the suburbs with parents too busy to prepare food, she ate pizza, soda, burgers, fries, microwave fish sticks, bags of salty stuff that dyed her tongue orange, and oriental take-out dishes laced with MSG. Food there was a commodity that was mass produced, packaged, and marketed. In her grandmother's kitchen, food was made so close to its source that you could wait to pick the corn until the water was boiling. Meat was from animals that she had named. Eggs came with chicken feathers stuck to them. Carrots held dirt in crevices that must be scrubbed.

She picked up a teapot with delicate rose and blue petals painted around its rim. It was warm and smooth, curved perfectly to fit into her cupped hands. She looked out of the screen door to the backyard and saw fine tendrils of hops and silver leaf bobbing in a gentle breeze above a latticed arch that towered over the back steps. She thought about the way those tender new vines reach upward in search of a surface to envelop. Once it is gripped, the object is wound and knotted tight in cables of slender green. I am like that, she thought. I am sending out fingers of yearning into the light and hoping for a lattice, a frame, a solid limb to hold tight.

She suffered a familiar feeling that was widely shared among her friends and neighbors: she felt powerless. As much as she wished she could live off the grid and divorce herself from a world that seemed cold and unfair, she was tied to that world, one more tiny thread stitched by costs, debts, needs, expectations, and assumptions into an invisible societal fabric. It's hard for us little threads to see the whole cloth that holds us. She could see this much: her dreams for the Jango Ranch would slam head-on into bankers, lawyers, and the pervasive infrastructure of the make-a-buck world that awaited her.

"Lawyers and bankers and loaners, oh my!" she said aloud, remembering that scene in *The Wizard of Oz* when Dorothy sets out on the yellow brick road, arm in arm with her three improbable companions. "Where," she asked, "is my tin woodsman, my loveable scarecrow, my lion?"

When JR's lawyer told her that her grandfather left the ranch to her in his will, she was overwhelmed. She understood she couldn't just move in and live happily ever after. If she took over the Jango there would be bills to settle and she would have to figure out how to make the ranch pay. She called her parents who advised her to sell it for whatever she could get and consider herself ahead. She wrestled with that idea for a few days and then firmly rejected it. Somehow I'll do it, she told herself. But I need help.

Many ranchers who were friends of her grandfather would gladly advise her. They would tell her what her grandfather himself told her: don't do it, don't ranch the old way. It's too hard and doesn't pay, they would say. They might rant about the damn feds and how put-upon they felt because they had to acknowledge the government they depended on and they had to follow rules designed to save them from themselves. Failure often begs blame. Rant or not, they would tell her to forget about all the hats, horses, and hoopla, the romantic paraphernalia of the mythic cowboy way. You have options we never had, they would say, so take them. Subdivide and sell or just sell and move on.

But where do I move, she asked and they did not know because all they had ever known was this valley, this way of life. "Where do I go" is a familiar question in Boon County, asked by each new generation of high school graduates as they disperse to further an education or get a job. Some are glad to go and others feel like exiles and maybe always will feel that way because no place they go ever feels quite like the home they left behind. Few from America's rural diaspora were like Kayla and wanted to be back for more than holiday visits.

And if I find a way to stay here, how do I know this place I love will not change? Ten years from now will this be the same place, the same community that I choose to live in today? When she imagined the future it was easy to conjure either condos and gates or a landscape torn up and infested with gas pumps that spew bad air and taint the water. Why stay and witness heartbreaking ruination?

Her shoulders ached. She was tired of this puzzle. How, she asked, can I fit myself into this matrix of lawyers, bankers, and real estate agents who made the rules and direct the game? "Minions of the empire," she said to herself and then again and again. "Minions of empire, minions of empire." She was alarmed. What's with all the repeating! Has stress finally unhinged me? Am I losing my mind?

After a sleepless night interrupted by nightmares involving claustrophobic tedium, cigar-smoking kangaroos with chainsaws, and camels with Swedish accents, it came to her. She was rescued by a metaphor. Illumination is tricky: sometimes it's a steady low beam on the path ahead of you and sometimes it's a bolt of lightning.

I need a lifeboat, she thought to herself. Then she said it aloud. Then she said it louder. "Lifeboat, lifeboat." She smiled. Hmmm, maybe this repetition thing is going somewhere after all. But no, not a lifeboat, an ark! But an ark was more than she could do. Maybe that came later. Maybe an ark was several life boats hooked together. For now, just a lifeboat.

The next part was easy. She asked, who do I want in my lifeboat? She eliminated the cowboy caucus, her grandfather's ranching pals, because she already knew what they would say and she did not want to be hobbled by the notion that success is not failing for one more year. She did not want to see herself as a victim. Who, she asked, is right here on the ground in Stony Mesa who might offer insight or a hand?

Grace and Elias Buchman came immediately to mind. And then there's that couple over at the Desert Rose who seem to be making a living here despite the odds against them. The young woman inherited her dad's ranch so she and I share that experience. She's been where I am now. I think her name is Luna. She's the one Grandpa talked to about her dog. What have I got to lose by reaching out that I'm not already losing anyway?

She called Grace Buchman and asked if she and Elias could come over and talk about her new situation and the future of the Jango Ranch. Grace also thought of Hoppy and Luna and asked if they could be included because they were also trying to make an old ranch sustainable. "Sure," replied Kayla, "I need all the advice I can get." Later Grace called back to see if inviting Olene would be okay.

"You mean the woman who spoke at the public meeting about Grandpa's ranch and the Highlife Holiday development who didn't make much sense? I don't know her but she seemed a bit wacky to put it frankly." Grace assured her that Olene was misunderstood and actually very reasonable, even wise, if given half a chance.

On the day of the meeting Kayla stood by the window and waited. They arrived in quick order and as they closed the car doors behind them and stood on the walkway below the porch she felt a shiver of misgiving flash across her shoulders and up her neck where it dissipated like a shadow thrown across her brain. "I would have guessed," she whispered, "that the men in my lifeboat wore jeans, not cargo pants and shorts, that they'd have respectable cowboy hats, not shaggy heads of unkempt curls. And the women in my lifeboat . . . look at Luna, she's wearing coveralls and a lace shawl. Is that a nose ring? And even Grace and Olene look like gypsies who have been hiding in a Patagonia Outlet." She took a deep breath. "Well, here goes."

They made introductions and took seats around the kitchen table. Grace made coffee and tea. Kayla found some cookies in the cabinet above the stove. Luna took a loaf of sourdough bread she had baked that morning out of her backpack. Grace, of course, brought jam and they all oohed and ahhed when she pulled it out of her handbag. Kayla put butter on the table next to the bread and jam and sat down.

"I have some good news," Kayla said cheerfully.

"What's that? Tell us!" they chimed in at once.

"Doc Brown in Boon Township called. He saw me at my grandfather's funeral. I knew him when I was a kid and he didn't know I was graduating from veterinary school. He's getting old and he wants to back off his practice some. He asked me if I'd like to work there two days a week. It isn't much, but it helps. If he likes me and how I work, there could be more days. He might like to have me be on call when he's away, maybe even take over the practice someday."

Their congratulations were enthusiastic. Kayla reminded them that it wasn't an answer to her question about how to keep her grandfather's ranch but it was relief. "A part-time job won't pay the bills here. I still need your thoughts and ideas," she said, but she knew that what she really needed was their friendship.

They agreed to brainstorm options and then narrow them down to the ones that had a better chance of survival. Kayla wondered if the ranch might be turned into an animal refuge.

"What kind of animals?"

"I don't know. All kinds. There are old circus animals, animals that were used for research and are too old to be useful anymore. Animals whose owners have died. I'd be thrilled to care for old horses."

"Horse hospice!" Olene clapped her hands together, laughed, and nodded her approval.

"What about micro-farming?" asked Hoppy. "They call it heritage farming or niche farming. It's basically what Luna and I are trying."

"You wouldn't feel threatened if I did something like that, too?"

"No, not at all." Hoppy turned to Luna and she nodded. "I wouldn't mind a little company to talk things over, trade ideas and observations, maybe share tools, we might even find a way to market stuff together. I'm not sure what we are doing will work out even for us but I know that it's not like a business where you compete and it's not easier trying to do it alone."

Luna added, "We prefer synergy over competition. You could plant fruit trees, like a heritage strain, and we could build a cider mill together. Or maybe heritage grains and we build a bakery."

Olene was on the edge of her chair with excitement. "A bee ranch! You could do a bee ranch and sell the honey!"

Elias took a turn. "Grace and I stayed at a farm in Italy, in Tuscany actually. It was a family operation where they made cheese and wine but to make ends meet they had a house to put up tourists. They call them agro-tourismo farms and they do quite well. Or maybe you turn the Jango into a conference center. Maybe a fly-fishing retreat and conference center."

Grace lit up with an idea. "I wish every child in America had a garden! You can learn so much that's practical in a garden, so much science and even math can be taught there. A garden is like a living classroom that is wondrous. Inspiring! Maybe the local schools would like to start a program. You can learn so much about life and about yourself in a garden."

When the ideas stopped flowing Kayla summed it up. "Okay, what about an all-of-the-above approach? I could make the Jango into a horse hospice micro-farm bakery and fly-fishing conference center."

"Don't forget bee ranch!" called Olene, who had gone to the sink to refill a pitcher of water.

Kayla confessed that it all seemed a little overwhelming.

Olene sat down and poured water into empty glasses. "The impeded stream is the one that sings."

"What?" They looked at each other with the same silent questions: Is Olene having another episode of passionate incoherence? And if she is going off into some deep end, what do we do about it?

Olene smiled. "It's a quote from Wendell Berry. He's a poet and farmer. Kentucky, I think."

Sighs of relief were exhaled politely. "I mean to say," Olene continued, "that our challenges that are the hardest are the ones that lift us up and give us our voices."

Elias worried about the direction the conversation was going. Kayla needed ideas and information, options, pros and cons, numbers crunched, and blessed human reason applied, not three choruses of "Climb Every Mountain." He turned them back to the practical. "What about water, have you thought of that? You need to understand how that works, not just the plumbing and irrigation systems but your rights."

They drew up a list of possible options that might fit a reborn Jango Ranch and each of them volunteered to go home and do research. They agreed to send Kayla interesting articles and websites that might help her decide her next steps. Another session was scheduled a week hence. For the first time, Kayla felt confident. Her new friends would uncover hidden opportunities and feed her enthusiasm and confidence with their own energy and faith. They would empower her. "Thank you," she said, "thank you, thank you." Her gratitude, naturally, generated reassurance and commitment.

Elias was about to stand and make his departure when he saw a crinkle in Olene's eye accompanied by a quick quiver of her lips. "Olene, you look bemused. What's going on in there?"

Olene shook her head no but Elias grinned and insisted. "Come on, Olene, out with it."

"I was thinking about how we fit a very old and familiar pattern. We think we're so modern, I mean look at all our gear and devices like our magical phones with built-in GPS and a million apps but really we're just the latest wave."

The others in the circle exchanged that uh-oh look again. Hoppy volunteered. "Wave of what, Olene?"

"The people who painted canyon walls with strange spirit-beasts thousands of years ago were an early wave of migration. The Navajos came later. Pioneers and settlers next. Now us."

She paused for agreement or any signal they understood her. Or cared. The signals were unclear so she continued.

"Look at where we've been, travelers all. Hoppy, you once told me about British Columbia and Grace and Elias traveled widely and so did you, Luna. I've been all over the world. And now we are here just like the other migrants who came through here."

Elias was puzzled. Olene was stating the obvious. So what? Where's that characteristic nuance?

She wasn't finished. "A wave of migration goes on for generations. The first people had to find their way down through the ice. There were scary beasts and storms. They navigated a fickle shore. They were challenged to make sense of new habitats and survive. The later waves of migration had to deal with settlers from the first waves, just ask the Navajos about the resistance they encountered when they migrated down from the north. We all know about cowboys and Indians, of course. And now us. Like those before, we make sense of our habitat and experiment along the way. We struggle until we fit. We are no longer leaving because now we are coming home. We are sitting in this room right now doing that."

As was usual when Olene spoke at length, a silent mulling period followed. Brows humped up and down while fingers brushed chins. Grace broke it. "That was wonderful, Olene. Thank you."

Elias also enjoyed Olene's way of putting daily life into a grand context but he knew that right now Kayla needed to be grounded in the practical aspects of her situation. He started to speak but the others at the table pushed their chairs back and stood to leave. He turned toward Kayla and saw that Grace had enfolded her in her arms. Kayla was sniffling and her eyes were turning wet. Grace did that to people because she could not contain her affection and most people sucked that up. He was always thankful when they left the grocery store if Grace didn't hug the cashier and checkers for some reason or another, leaving him to stand with a load of groceries in his arms and no idea what to do next.

Kayla said goodbye to each one and thanked them. They were encouraging and offered help anytime. When the last one was through the door she walked to the parlor window and watched them leave. Luna's dog Juniper, who had been asleep on the doorstep only moments before, was alert now and joyfully exploring each bush for lizards and the aromatic mysteries known only to the canine realm. Kayla watched her guests hug each other at their cars as they departed. She wished she could take part in that. In time, she told herself, in time. We are all on the same path, moving together in fits and starts, navigating a fickle shore.

Chapter 22

Jango Burnside rode to the rim of the canyon and dismounted. He tied his horse to a tree and walked forward quietly to look over the ledge above the Indian encampment. He had made a "peace offering" to the heathen band a week before. Their leader, Suski, was confused and wary. White people were so hard to understand. One day they are trying to kill you and the next day they feed you. But meat is meat and he took what was offered and shared it with his starving clan. He hoped the whites had learned what his people knew from their ancestors and by observing their fellow creatures in this wild landscape they had always known. Suski did not know the English word reciprocal and English words like ecosystem did not yet exist, but his own language had many words to describe the dynamic synergy and balance that are the earth's green fuse. Perhaps, he thought, the "loud monsters," as his wife called them, had learned to become human. When you are hungry it is hard to be wary. The stomach says yes, please, yes.

Jango stood stone still and listened. Silence. He crept forward and peeked over the rim to the valley floor below. He steadied himself with one hand that gripped an exposed pinyon root while he shaded his eyes with the other hand. Nothing moving. He waited. Still nothing. It was an eerie scene. Instead of conversation, laughter, crying, singing, shouting, and all the other audible signals of human activity, a silence so deep it registered as cold. A raven squawked above two fellow ravens walking calmly among the stick huts below.

He climbed down the embankment of loose stones, half sliding and digging his heels in to arrest his descent. At the bottom he brushed off the red dust and looked around. Again, nothing. He called. No response.

He walked up the wash toward their camp on a bench by a spring. In the first hut woven from willows and covered with blankets was a family. And flies. He slapped the side of the hut and they swarmed off the corpses and buzzed madly about his head in a thick cloud. He got one in his mouth and spit it out, gagged and spit again.

He once saw a dead man mangled in a rail yard accident and another time a man who fell from a bridge he was working on whose head burst like a melon. Over years of hard labor before he settled in the valley he saw women and men who died of exhaustion and whatever illness was in season. He was no stranger to death but this was different. They died wrapped in tight bunches, some with knees curled up into their bellies like newborns. They embraced one another as they died. Children were comforted by parents who held each other's hands. He'd never seen anything like that.

He found a woman cradling a small child in her arms and then an old couple lying on their backs, arms at their sides, thin fingers woven together in a tight knot. The rest of them were scattered. Some were doubled up as if in pain, their arms hugging knees loosely now. He imagined the pain in their bellies. The corpses grimaced or looked surprised.

In the river of his veins a slow stain spread. His heart raced. He took off his hat and brushed a fly from his eyebrow. Suddenly his whole body was awash with a chilling tide. He sat and caught his breath, willed his beating heart to slow down. A heaviness succeeded agitation that came close to paralysis.

He forced himself to stand up, took a deep breath, swallowed. He pushed his hat back and brushed weed seeds from his beard. He began to build a shell. I'm a man, he told himself. I have a family to protect. I am a Christian and they were heathens. I did what I had to do. I didn't want it to end this way but they made me do it. Damn them for doing this to me.

He brought his horse down and gathered the bodies, one, two, and three at a time and laid them across the saddle. Hunger had made them light. He carried them back to his ranch and returned again and again, lifting them tenderly one by one and tying them down on the horse's back. The collective weight of them seemed impossible to lift and carry but he could not stop. He worked alone and did not ask for help from neighbors or friends. I did this, he said to himself, and I will carry them myself one by one. I will feel the weight of them now and remember it forever. Forever I will ache in the night and wake panting from the image of a loose hand flapping against a horse's side, the braid undone, the fingers knotted together that were too stiff to separate so that the pair had to be packed and buried together.

He dug a pit a hundred yards from his cabin and laid them in on top of one another. He covered them and said a prayer. When the last shovel full of earth was gently patted onto the grave, he wiped the dirt from his hands, picked up his lantern, and stumbled to his cabin under a starlit sky that witnessed but did not judge him. He collapsed on his bed and slept in his soiled clothes.

He awoke at first light and needed to see it with the light of day illuminating the grave. He pulled on his boots and walked toward the freshly turned soil. His wife was visiting her sister with the children. He was glad he could do this awful job while they were gone. There would be no need to tell anyone about this, even her. A couple of weeks later the raw dirt would sprout cheatgrass, snakeweed, and thistle. After a month a fresh sleeve of green would be pulled around the shoulders of the burial mounds that would slowly subside until the earth was level and plain and even the contours of the land would no longer remember them. Nobody would suspect what happened. No man would ask questions let alone hold him accountable. He would lock it up inside himself and go to his grave with his secret. It's over now, he said to himself. This is between me and my God.

From the rim of the canyon above him came a sudden deep-throated wail. He looked up and saw the most majestic coyote he had ever seen. She was bathed in the rays of the morning sun and her coat bristled and gleamed like thousands of tiny flames. He stalled in his tracks, transfixed by the radiant wayward angel on the cliff above him.

She stood with her forelegs on an altar-like rock as if she were addressing a congregation from a sandstone pulpit the color of dried blood. Coyote looked straight down at him, studying him intently. Her gaze seemed human to him and he could not look away. She was steadfast, not frightened. He decided she was not threatening, she was amused. He assured himself this is a mere animal, that's all, just an animal.

The coyote raised her head and let loose another plaintive howl so loud that it resonated in Jango's skull bones, teeth, and rib cage. He heard himself make an unfamiliar low moan followed by an unmistakable grunt of fear. He blinked and she disappeared from his view, only the echo of her lament fading in a cold gust of wind. He strained to listen. He thought he heard a woman singing and then a baby crying. No, he told himself, it's just a chorus of coyotes yipping. But their voices seemed so human to him. Like madmen laughing.

NAVIGATING

BOOK THREE
(the near future)

A FICKLE

SHORE

Chapter 1

Luna's breasts ached and her nipples were sore. She wondered if she had given birth to a baby remora. She wiped a thin film of milk from her baby's lips, lifted his warm body to her shoulder, and patted his back gently. His head lay sodden on her shoulder but then stirred and lifted as his bunched-up legs jerked twice. He burped, drooled, and surrendered to slumber.

Luna laid him in his crib and walked into the kitchen where Hoppy was leaning over the stove and preparing two bowls of oatmeal with raisins and bananas. Her silk robe was still undone and as Hoppy turned to greet her a swollen breast escaped its milk-stained enclosure and practically smiled at him. He smiled back, of course.

Seeing his lascivious look, Luna tucked the fugitive back into her robe. "Hold on there, pal, I can only handle you boys one at a time."

Hoppy was already running late but he needed to fortify himself with oatmeal, fruit, and Luna for the long day ahead of him. Together they had built a web of start-up enterprises that kept them and a dozen other young moms and pops whom they employed running all day long. Years before, Luna inherited a cheesy upscale saloon designed to lure tourists who had only a Hollywood image of the American West. She and her then boyfriend and now husband transformed the predictable saloon and nearby ranch into an ever-morphing incubator for new-old ways of living in place.

They changed the name of the saloon from the Bull and Stallion to the Desert Rose. They partnered with Stony Mesa's lone horse doctor, Kayla Burnside, who had also inherited a ranch that once set cows upon a fragile desert landscape but now sheltered a community garden. Kayla, too, was determined to apply science to old problems and aim for sustainable solutions. Kayla's specialty was coyote contraception. Together, the three partners were leading a local reformation of the failing ranch economy.

This morning that meant that Hoppy had to feed chickens, check bees, and water the orchard before installing solar panels on the local hardware store. A side business installing solar had grown rapidly in the last couple of years and he struggled to balance the new demands for his expertise and the commitments he had made to the Desert Rose Farm. Jay Paul Ziller, aka Hip Hop Hopi and now just plain Hoppy, wandered into Stony Mesa as a vagabond adventurer, one of a hoard of young people who wanted to climb cliffs, camp under the Milky Way, and get awestruck over and over again by the spectacular canyon landscapes of the Southwest. They were hooked on astonishment.

Before he stumbled into her path and met Luna, he had traveled extensively. During a previous trip through the Canadian West, Hoppy witnessed the devastation of tar sands mining in Alberta. The sight of that scarred and stained landscape stripped of soil, plant life, and wild creatures stayed with him, gnawed at him, sickened him. So when he heard about a looming protest against a strip mine for tar sands at the nearby Seafold Ledges, he joined in. It was there his chance encounter with Luna Waxwing changed his life. He had gone from a free spirit with the responsibilities and schedule of a feral dog to the tasks of deep devotion to wife, child, and community. Sometimes he paused in his busy life to reflect on the sea change he was living and he shook his head in disbelief and smiled. "I am blessed by my burdens," he whispered. "Thank you, thank you."

The management of the Desert Rose Café itself, the food and drink part of the business, was left to Luna, who could perform most of the tasks needed with a baby on her hip. Hoppy managed the market for local produce, especially the fruit and vegetables grown on the Desert Rose Farm just down the road. Luna also handled the local arts and crafts trade that discerning tourists favored.

She herself created something called a memory stick: a baked clay tube painted with pastel pink vistas of cliffs and the soft green of cactus. It looked like a phallic artifact on one end, perhaps a primitive dildo potted and shaped in an old pueblo village a thousand years ago.

The other end of the memory stick concluded with a vulva-like opening with a small button in the middle. Flick the button in the dark and a tiny LED bulb lit up inside the tube and shone through a thousand tiny holes in the surface of the memory stick, reminding one of the incomparable night sky over the wild canyons of Stony Mesa. If you turned on the memory stick in a darkened room, the walls and ceiling became a kaleidoscope of dancing rays and shadows. Like Luna, her art was at once erotic and sublime. She made them individually and sold them for a hundred bucks each.

Hoppy and Luna shared the duties of the organic farm that supplied the café and market until Luna was very pregnant. Lately most of the chores were done by Hoppy as Luna had her hands full and her breasts busy with their baby. He was on his own for a while when the solar business took off. The success of their solar business was a complete surprise and good news but bad timing. It began when he and Luna installed solar panels and water heaters at their own Desert Rose farm and café. Next he was hired by a neighbor to install panels on his barn and garage. Soon word was out that Hoppy knew how to do solar well and before long he couldn't keep up with the demand for his services.

In the face of episodic grid failures and the collapse of so many carbon-based utilities, the public understood that electricity was as vulnerable as it was vital and there was a desperate scramble to harness renewables, as they were called then. The price of solar kept falling and the quality improved. Batteries improved, software apps were added, and co-ops formed local grids as an alternative to the grids that were too big to succeed. It wasn't just the enviro-minded hybrid drivers who wanted to go solar. Even the leftover tea-hadi wingnuts wanted solar panels for the same reason they hoarded gold and guns. Everyone, it seemed, wanted to survive the turmoil that had gripped the nation for several years now. Hoppy served everyone equally and without judgment. The global transition from fossil fuels to wind and solar was urgent and he felt he was on the front line of the most daunting challenge humans had ever faced—themselves.

He was always running. His solar business had grown to the point where it would soon have to morph. Either he would have to partner with someone or employ someone, but one way or the other he needed relief. That was a surprise, too, because when he and Luna arrived in Stony Mesa they wondered if they could make a life in a land with so little opportunity. They wanted to do more than just pay bills. They wanted work that was meaningful and challenging. They asked themselves if they could fit in socially or find enough "culture" to fill their cups in a place as isolated and tradition-bound as little Stony Mesa. And now their cups overflowed. By opening the Desert Rose Farm to others who were experimenting with new-old ways to grow food and make energy locally and lightly, Hoppy and Luna created their own culture. Their table was crowded with friends and partners who enjoyed the anarchic synergy of the Desert Rose. They sat at the table drinking local wine and brew, eating homegrown food, and conversing about worms and bees, herbs and apples, raisin bread recipes and sourdough starters. There were artists at the table, painters and musicians mostly, and a surprising mix of ages as retired teachers and administrators played peekaboo with babies sitting on their mother's laps. Luna and Hoppy set out to make a living and made a life.

As Hoppy's truck pulled away, Luna changed the baby's diaper and packed a satchel with the paraphernalia he would need to survive an afternoon with her mother, who had agreed to babysit while Luna and her friends took a field trip to the Sleeping Maiden beaver colony. A local Forest Service biologist, Mary Handy, had arranged to take Luna, Olene Miller, Grace Buchman, and Kayla Burnside to see for themselves what the proverbial busy beavers had been up to since they were reintroduced several years earlier. It was difficult finding a date that would work because Kayla's schedule was so overloaded.

Luna was thankful to have her mother back in her life. Virginia Waxwing returned to America in time for the birth and stayed to help with the newborn. She had met Hoppy briefly during a previous visit and she was curious about this handsome young man who had won her daughter's love. She liked him immediately. He was polite, bright, and obviously devoted to Luna and now the baby. She was impressed with the life they had created in Stony Mesa and the creative energy that was drawn to the Desert Rose. She fell in love with the little town and the wild canyon landscape that surrounded it. There was something enchanting about the long lines of canyon walls with their hammered curves, the wind-cut spires, the stone galleries of burnished stains, the sharp edge between the dense land and open blue sky.

The kids seemed impossibly busy, their baby was beautiful, and they wanted her to stay on and help them. Why not? She was ready to give up the restless sojourn that had pulled her across the planet for several years. She rented a cabin just outside Stony Mesa proper near a stream that fed the river. Slim willows and thick cattails crowded the back yard. The cabin shared sun and shade in equal measure and there was a porch with a view of a sandstone butte peppered with juniper trees. She was careful not to intrude. Hoppy and Luna were a powerful force of nature that was anarchic and cluttered but somehow also self-sufficient and resilient. She offered help frequently but only offered an opinion when asked. Caring for Sage was her usual role. She was grateful that she had been there for his birth and when he was named.

Virginia had enough traveling during her years of robust wander-lust. As soon as Luna was packed off to college, Virginia kissed her farewell and took off on her own quest. A childless uncle who struck it rich selling pianos in the Midwest died and left her enough money to quit her job and travel modestly. Eighteen years of single-motherhood was enough. After that rough spell when she had to send Luna, or Liz as she was known then, to an outdoor rehabilitation program for troubled teens, her daughter turned her life around and became the capable person she was raised to be. The new Luna, in fact, couldn't wait to embrace life outside the familiar and safe boundaries of her childhood and adolescence. Virginia saw Luna's independence as a ticket to her own independence and flew away to see the world.

Luna missed her mother more than she had let on during those years when her mom was away but wished her well even so. She was indeed capable of taking care of herself. But when Luna was pregnant, that all changed. Luna wanted her mom close and Virginia wanted to be close, too. This morning was one of the many reasons why. She could give Luna a chance to get out and at the same time indulge in her love for her new grandson.

Hoppy pulled into the driveway and steered as close as he could to the roof where the solar panels were to be installed. The less distance he had to carry equipment the better. As he searched for the optimal spot his focus missed the man leaning against the wall, waiting. Hoppy stepped out of the truck and the young man approached. He pushed his sunglasses up until they rested over a curly mess of amber hair. He extended a hand and smiled easily.

"Are you Hoppy? I'm Skip Dunneman."

The two shook hands as Hoppy nodded.

"I'm camped over at the Settlers Pass campground. I'm moving from Florida to California and seeing the sights along the way, but I had some truck problems and now I'm broke. I was hoping I could pick up some temporary work until I have enough to move on. I asked down at the Desert Rose about possibilities and they sent me over here to talk to you."

Hoppy asked him about his skills and experience and heard that he had been a carpenter. He'd learned electrical skills during a stint in a machine shop and he also knew roofing. He was a perfect match. Hoppy was astonished by his good luck.

It was like Luna always told him: Jump and the net appears. Only he didn't even jump, just wished and wondered. Anyway, Skip Dunneman happened in his life at just the right time.

"When can you start?"

"How about now?"

"Great! Let's get to work."

C h a p t e r   2

Kayla shuttled between the Jango Ranch and a university lab three hours away via a winding two-lane blacktop. For three years she braved rain, snow, and suicidal deer so she could divide her life between the Stony Mesa ranch she inherited from her grandfather and the lab where she was designing a coyote contraceptive. She wanted to live at the ranch full time but had to make the place pay, especially after she quit raising cows, which require full-time maintenance that she could not provide. Growing alfalfa alone didn't generate enough bucks to settle bills against her grandfather's estate and pay the taxes, let alone the daily expenses like food, utilities, and the costs of maintaining a very old ranch. She raced to keep up with broken things like hinges that give up their screws, fence posts that rot, wires that twist and snap, bearings that start to grind, eroding pastures, and roofs that weep in the rain.

When staying at the ranch she was on call to back up a local veterinarian. What she earned by repairing cats and dogs who ventured too close to farm machinery or agitated animals with hard hooves was almost enough to live on. She and her lab colleagues at the university lived on modest grants that were also not quite enough. Combining the lab job with the veterinarian work on the side was enough to stay afloat and pay for the gas required to divide her week in half. She could not afford an electric car and Boon County was still awaiting a station that offered natural gas and plug-in bays so she made do with her old Corolla. It had two hundred thousand miles on it and had an almost repair-free history. Kayla knew its days were numbered and spoke encouraging words to it whenever she departed for the long trip between the Jango Ranch and the lab.

Kayla could have joined a veterinary clinic in the city that paid well but the lab work was a passion that made monetary sacrifice and the hours she was stuck in her car worthwhile. She and her colleagues at the state's agricultural college were developing a tasteless, odorless powder that when digested by female coyotes rendered them sterile. It was intended as a non-violent alternative to the serial slaughter of coyotes that had been going on since the first settler punctuated the narrative of Manifest Destiny with a rifle shot.

Unlike the indigenous people who originally lived on the land before it was declared a frontier for European settlers, coyotes did not die off, surrender, or retreat into remote reservations or alcohol. Resilient coyotes generated constant aggravation, anger, and violence as they mocked those who would control them. And as the two populations co-evolved, only the clever coyotes survived the human predator and succeeding coyote generations became stealthier. The habitual solution, killing them, made the problem worse. As Mayor Otis Dooley put it, "Kill one and two come to the funeral."

Kayla understood that her family had prospered by raising animals to kill them. The faded bumper sticker on her grandfather's truck said simply and directly, "EAT MEAT." Her Boon County neighbors also raised cattle with little success, hanging on year after year by poking their cows through a dry-shrub desert and then trucking them to the auction center where they were weighed, sold, and again loaded onto trucks headed for the great fajita in the sky.

It would be hard to modify a culture based on habitual slaughter but Kayla hoped the results of her research might at least take the violence down a notch by eliminating one constant inducement to killing. It was personal. Her grandpa died in a freak accident a few years earlier when he overreacted to a chicken-robbing coyote and ended up nailing himself to the ranch gate. Just as that coyote stood for more in her grandfather's mind than that one particularly clever varmint, the old man's death loomed larger than an individual tragedy in Kayla's perspective. Asked by a fellow lab worker about how her grandpa died, she replied, "a lethal habit backfired."

The odorless part of the contraceptive equation they were perfecting was the hardest. Coyotes, like their dog and wolf cousins, are blessed with an amazing sense of smell. Unlike the smooth twin holes of the human nose, the canine nose is spongy and loaded with scent receptors, glands and nerves that, taken together, are thousands of times more powerful than the human nose. A larger portion of the coyote brain is devoted to scent. They can detect pheromones in urine and feces or on fur or skin that humans have only recently been able to detect.

Scent tells them time, sex, mood, history, health, location, and so much more that humans understand visually. Kayla learned the hard way through trial and endless error that tricking the coyote's sense of smell was almost impossible. Eventually they gave up on the notion anything could ever be odorless to coyotes and aimed to develop a scent that would attract them. They brewed one pheremonal stew after another but most didn't work in the wild.

Although failure was frustrating, it was also humbling. She learned that the source of her failure was awesome. In her eyes, Coyote rose from a fallen beast, or damn varmint as her grandfather called them, to a powerful and wondrous creature. That insight led her straight into a religious crisis.

Kayla's family belonged to the One True Church, where her grandfather served as the leader of the Stony Mesa congregation. She was raised in a household where going to Sunday service was the rule, no questions allowed. As an independent adult, Kayla attended church intermittently and resisted suggestions that she take over as choir leader or become a leader of the young women's association. Her excuse was the crazy schedule she kept while constantly trying to be in two places at once but she knew it was more than that. She was falling away from her religion and the main reason for that was her immersion in science.

When she was a child she shuttled between volatile divorced parents before settling with her grandparents. Her mother and father fed her contradictory versions of what was going on in their lives and it was impossible to predict when the next blow-up would happen. She remembers lying in bed at night and staring at the shadows that played across the walls while she struggled to understand what was happening now and what would come next. She talked to her nighttime confessor, the moon, while she chewed her lace blankie until it was just a shredded rag that she wrapped around her tiny fist and held against her temple.

Occasionally she became constipated by the threads she swallowed, usually after her parents fought and threatened each other. Her encounter with her grandparents' religion gave her a certainty and security she had longed for all her short life. The One True Church and her grandparents, inseparable in her child's mind, were a life raft in a storm-tossed sea. She became an ardent believer.

It didn't hold her up for long. In her teens she was introduced to science by a teacher, Mr. Wyatt, who sensed in her a logical streak that contradicted the One True believer who thought Adam and Eve rode dinosaurs and that the world could be known through revelations and prophecy. Kayla was intensely curious and tenacious. Under Mr. Wyatt's tutelage, she learned to love the method of trial and error, objectivity and attention to results, the way every claim is subject to testing and peer review. She learned that it was hard to get to the facts and put them together in a credible way but once that was achieved, it was something she could lean on, something sure. To neighbors, childhood friends, and beloved cousins, this was embarrassing. How could she prefer science, another liberal ideology, over the One True Church?

Kayla was troubled by her loss of faith and confessed to Grace Buchman, who she saw at the Stony Mesa Farmers Market. Grace noticed Kayla's anxiety when she was approached by the local Church president, who dropped a cucumber and a couple of onions as he tried to juggle his armload of produce to shake her hand. Kayla picked up his cuke and handed it to him. He called her "Sister Burnside" when he thanked her.

As soon as his onions and his cucumber were safely in his hand, she aborted their conversation, wheeled on one heel, and disappeared behind a trailer loaded with heritage tomatoes, sweet corn, and buckets of sage honey. It was the Desert Rose's trailer and Grace Buchman was standing there, examining the pale kernels glistening under a squeaky green husk of corn. Grace looked up and watched the scene unfold. She concluded her purchase quickly and followed Kayla to her car.

She called after her. "Kayla, are you okay?"

Kayla started to reply and then choked back a sob and shook her head no. Grace invited her to share an impromptu picnic down by the river. She had done that once before when Kayla was troubled and the two women had a heartfelt and honest exchange. Grace wondered if the river could work its magic one more time.

It did. Two minutes after they found a comfortable place to sit beside a set of whispering riffles, Kayla softened and confessed. "The church has been so much a part of my life and I love the people I know there, but I just don't feel right. I think the folks at the One True Church would be shocked to hear me say that science, that working in a lab and all, has been a spiritual experience, but it has. It made me understand that animals and even fish and birds are intelligent in ways that are beyond the limits of our own human abilities to sense the world around us. But we miss all that because we assume intelligence outside our range doesn't exist or it's inferior. They have rich emotional lives, too."

Grace looked puzzled. "Kayla, I know what you mean but is it really so important? You can love people for who they are and still disagree." She smiled and took Kayla's hand. "I am married to a man I love deeply and we could not agree less about how the world turns. I see angels in the architecture and he sees . . . well, he's a lot like you maybe, he wants proof."

"But Grace, I'm a veterinarian. I work at what might be called the intersection where the human and animal worlds mix. Collide is more like it. We love our pets, sure, but wild animals are also God's wondrous creations and they are reduced to dumb beasts, mere fish, or bird brains in the hearts and minds of almost everyone I know. But in the lab we can see through the bubble of human arrogance and what we see beyond that is awesome and humbling. Bees read the sun and birds and fish can sense magnetic and electrical fields that humans don't perceive at all. Whales can call to one another through a hundred miles of sea water. There are infrared and ultra-violet light that insects see that we don't. There are oceans of pheromones humans can't detect but animals do. Bats have echo-location. Or look at migration. What ancient rhythms do animals, birds, and fish still move to that we have lost?"

Grace was surprised by Kayla's passion. She sounded like she was straight out of a PETA protest but Grace knew Kayla was raised by ranchers, ate meat, rode horses, and doctored sick cows. Her observations about the wonders of the animal world were a strange match for someone so embedded in the ranching economy. And what does any of that have to do with religion?

"Kayla, you have a wonderful way of describing all that. Is there something about animals and the One True Church that troubles you?"

Kayla shrugged and sighed. "I don't know, Grace, it is all so confusing. Their attitude toward animals is . . . maybe like a window. I mean, I know humans come first but there is so much amazing life out there. Animals are not just props or background. They matter. I don't know, it seems so narrow and selfish not to see that."

Grace turned Kayla's hand over and rubbed the back softly. "Kayla, I know what you mean. Why not share it? I'm sure the others in your church can appreciate that, too. They just don't know and you can help them understand. And as a veterinarian you have credibility, too."

"Oh no, I don't. I've tried. It comes across as some woman thing. Last week I was talking to an elder about light receptors in reptiles and he cut me off and patted me on the head. Really, it's like I live on a different planet that they can't see or don't see or won't see or something. And the part that really gets to me is how I feel when I walk into church and participate. It's like . . . willful estrangement. I have to disown who I am when I walk through those doors."

Grace suppressed laughter as she pictured the scene in her mind, Kayla explaining the wonders of evolution to a patriarch of a church that preached that dinosaurs and men cohabitated on a planet no more than six thousand years old. Kayla's earnestness in the face of such righteous ignorance endeared her to Grace.

"Well, Kayla, you said it—a different bubble. I guess it's fair to say that I am in my own bubble, but I still love people who are not in my bubble. You belong to such a solid community through your church and that is a powerful thing, a beautiful thing. Why not focus on that and leave the doctrine to others?"

"Oh you can't just ignore Church doctrine! Oh my gosh no! Grace, you must be Catholic."

Grace laughed. "No, honey, I'm what might be called a Buddhist-Quaker-Pagan."

"It's not as simple as rules in a book, Grace. Do you know that I am the only girl in my high school graduating class who is not married with kids? I'm not even thirty yet and they think I'm an old maid. My senior year I could've been voted Most Likely to Land a Hunk and now I'm the very last to be hitched. I don't even have a boyfriend!" She paused and flashed a bittersweet smile. "From hot to not."

A canyon wall lit up behind them as sunlight escaped a cloud. A blue jay landed on a trash can next to the parking lot and scolded a squirrel that was sniffing a wrapper on the ground. The ruckus erupted ten feet from their table. Grace turned around and faced them. She clapped loudly and the scavengers fled.

She turned back to Kayla. "Kayla, I wish I could help you but I have no answers to your questions. But I'm sure of this much. You're as smart as they come and you have great intuition. Everything you need to find your way, you already have. Trust yourself. Keep an open heart."

Kayla sighed. "Maybe I'm making too much of it. You're right and I do feel blessed for my life in the church. I'm just torn." She paused. "And I am lucky to have work I love. I mean I love to solve problems by finding the missing piece in a very complex puzzle and then fitting it in. But lately it's me that can't fit in. Wasn't this supposed to be over in seventh grade?"

They laughed and hugged. Grace had to leave to pick up Elias at the bookmobile that stopped every other week in the city park that adjoined the cemetery. She knew he didn't like to wait because it upset him to see children playing among the tombstones. Seems creepy, he told her. Not that creepy, she replied. Kayla walked her to her car and then returned to her truck. She had to be at the university first thing tomorrow and should have left an hour earlier. Running late as usual.

Chapter 3

Bunny Cleaver swallowed the sun. The brilliant light of the Lord Almighty split his head in two. The world was on fire all around him. Even the cows had auras. But unlike the migraines he had last winter, this invasive light came with a voice. God talked to him! It made him feel wonderful. He was invincible and right! God's chosen one!

But those who have divine conversations with the Lord know how hard it is to get others to believe that the chosen one hears what they cannot hear, sees what they cannot see. His family, of course, would never doubt him. His six sons and four daughters who still lived on his isolated ranch compound were raised by a man who went beyond mere fatherly assertion and proclaimed himself not just patriarch but prophet. In his domain, Bunny Cleaver was the top mansplainer for the ultimate man-in-the-sky, specifically called Heavenly Father. Being a prophet is the patriarch's favorite fantasy and Bunny Cleaver reveled in his self-proclaimed role.

Doubt was not allowed in the Cleaver household. He home-schooled his children and because they lived ten miles from the nearest neighboring ranch, twenty from town and school, there were no competing influences. The rusty gate that stood before the ranch house might as well have been a moat. His children believed in his powers and were proud to be the offspring of such a gifted man.

As they grew up and started families of their own, his children's spouses also professed their belief in the power of his prayers to reveal God's will. They knew that was the deal when you marry into the Bunny Cleaver clan. Their children, Bunny's grand-children, were raised with the same unquestioning belief in and obedience to the aging patriarch who showed them how to saddle and ride, rope and brand, cut nuts and read the Bible. Some of those kids were now in their teens. In fact, he was surrounded day in and day out by people who accepted him as a prophet who alone knew and communicated the Lord's plan. But that's as far as it went.

God told him that wasn't far enough. He needed to take His message to the multitudes. He needed a bigger stage. When the time was right, Heavenly Father would let him know so he could start the transformation to a society based on Christian principles, private property, and the divinely inspired Constitution. All the federally managed lands in the West would be turned over to those rightful owners who had been using them as they pleased for generations since the first whites took them from the indigenous tribes that did not share their concept of ownership and who had no cows anyway. The Indians just roamed the countryside like animals, explained Bunny, and ownership begins with those who improve the land. His great-grandfather built the first dams in the watershed, dug the irrigation ditches, plowed, and planted. He prayed in an adobe church he helped build with his own two hands.

The Cleaver compound was now home to twenty-two adults and thirty-seven minors clustered together under the single power line that reached the ranch from a transmission line running parallel to the interstate twenty miles away. Bunny and his sons struggled to make ends meet. Almost all the adults had seasonal or part-time jobs to supplement the family business but cows were the main event. More Cleavers required more cows. If he could expand his ranch across public land there would be room and cows enough for all of the faithful Cleavers and their progeny.

More cows required more land under his thumb and without interference from those damn feds. If the land he had been leasing from the federal Bureau of Land Management for decades was actually owned by him, he could cut timber and invite in a fracking corporation for a cut of what they make. And isn't that the way it is supposed to be? he asked. The land is God's gift to mankind. God will provide if we can get the naysayers, the tree-huggers, and the appeasers out of the road. The beautiful thing about Heavenly Father's plan, mused Bunny, is that it worked so well for him personally. He attributed that to blessed coincidence and not his own intent.

His ranch hands also believed in his powers or they wouldn't be working for him. They were local men who were raised under the roof of the One True Church that was founded on revelation. Conformity and obedience to authority was a way of life under the One True Church and authority came from revelation, so they accepted Bunny's visions as fundamental and deeply validating. Their lens on the world was undiluted by cultural diversity. They were a tribe, really, and tribes don't need rules, especially those written by those outside the tribe.

His followers were often broke and always angry. They saw themselves as righteous victims of an unholy federal beast that roped them away from success. There were many men like them across the country who were just waiting for a strong leader to emerge. They considered themselves fortunate to have found that strong leader in Bunny Cleaver.

Bunny's boys, not only his sons but also the disaffected ranch hands he drew into his defiant gang, believed their role in God's unfolding plan was to follow without questioning. Bunny had ignored grazing fees for years and got away with it, although the Forest Service and Bureau of Land Management said he would eventually be held accountable for the fortune he owed the taxpayers. Bunny ignored the limits they set for his cows, how many and where and when they could go. Bunny Cleaver was already a law unto himself and was proving that the big bad federal government was actually a big soft paper tiger.

Bunny's believers regarded the Constitution as a divine document that was misread by every cop, judge, jury, taxpayer, politician, journalist, lawyer, and government bureaucrat in America. They knew better than all those blind fools who thought they had the authority to tax, license, ticket, or otherwise hold accountable All-American cowboys like them. They carried miniature copies of the Constitution in their breast pockets and had enough firepower to take down a helicopter. They'd suffered pointy-headed fools long enough and they were ready to ride.

Bunny gathered them in a makeshift chapel he added on to the bunkhouse back when Heavenly Father first tapped his shoulder and spoke into his ear. Several ranchers from across the region whom Bunny knew shared his hostility to all things federal were invited. They pulled up in double-cab diesel pickups and shuffled into the chapel. Most wore side-arms, camo coats, riding boots, and jeans that were a kind of informal uniform, a style that marked them as militia-minded. They met on a Sunday evening after they had been to church and finished their chores. A glorious sunset shone through a west-facing window and conferred a holy touch to the meeting.

Bunny began. "The Constitution is hanging by a thread! The federal government has no right to the land. Article one, section eight, clause seventeen—look it up. The usurpers in Washington must be stopped!"

The men in the room nodded, set their jaws, and pushed their hats down squarely on their heads. They believed that America's corrupt federal government was controlled by immoral urbanites beholden to black people, Mexicans, Jews, feminists, environmentalists, queers, and liberals. And behind them all were Illuminati or secret Muslims or Jewish bankers or the Anti-Christ himself pulling the strings. An interlocking claptrap of conspiracies explained the world.

"We will no longer be an endangered species!" Bunny often played the victim card because it was so much easier on one's self-esteem to be an outraged victim of injustice rather than a cranky loser. "We've been locked out of our rightful heritage and destiny and the time has come to take back the land and use it like God almighty intended. It's time to cut the timber, mine the coal and uranium, build more dams, and open hunting season on any damn owl or liberal bureaucrat who gets in our way!"

The men in the room, normally a taciturn crew, cheered and stamped their boots. Spittle gathered at the corner of Bunny's mouth as it always did when he was in the midst of a sermon. His children learned early on to stand back when their dad was ranting or they might be sprayed by foaming saliva.

Bunny continued and the men assembled in the makeshift chapel nodded in agreement. They were not likely to jump up and down and shout amen, but their enthusiasm was evident. They were men common in the American West who mourned the passing of the unregulated frontier where "men could be men." That place and time were long gone if it ever existed at all but they denied it even though their daily lives contradicted that mythic era. They watched television, had e-mail accounts, and shopped at Walmart. They poked at smart-phones to read the weather and compute routes. They paid profession-als to find loopholes in their taxes. They vacationed in Vegas when they could afford to and hoped to send their kids to college. They depended on prescription drugs for aches and pains. They drove their cattle and alfalfa to market on federally funded highways and the feds also picked up the cost of the water infrastructure, medical clinics, schools, local civic centers, and fire stations that made life in the desert viable. When they got old they filed for Medicare and social security.

Nevertheless, the Old West lived on in their imaginations, fueled by the movies they played on their home entertainment systems and the western novels their spouses checked out at the public library. Their cherished delusion was reinforced by the immediate popularity of any product that was associated with iconic hats and horses, boots with spurs, and holsters filled with six-shooters. When the cognitive disso-nance became too much, they blamed others and retreated into ideologies that told them they were sovereign and righteous. They found like-minded people online and together they built a reassuring matrix that explained the conspiracies and injustices that kept them from being the heroes they conjured from a distant past.

It wasn't just the passing of the frontier that upset them but their own powerlessness. Some had worked in the coal mines before they closed and most had bounced from job to job in an economy that no longer afforded them dignity and respect. Some had endured bank-ruptcy, some were divorced and saddled with payments to wives and children that they struggled to pay and resented. The only young men present in Bunny's chapel were Cleaver kids and grandkids. The rest were middle aged and older, white men who felt they had lost their place in an ethnically and racially diverse nation bound to a global economy beyond their reach and understanding that was continually disrupted by technological innovation also beyond their understanding. In an increasingly diverse America, the last badge of their privilege and security—white skin—seemed to them devalued and, worse, disrespected. Feeling like a neglected artifact was bad enough but they were also challenged by a new generation of women whom they believed were out to emasculate them. Assault rifles restored their visibility and their allegiance to the Constitution made them patriots. When they lost their cherished and familiar place in the world they found each other.

Bunny was climaxing now. "The time has come to take back the land of our forefathers and restore ownership to its rightful heirs! It is time for the God-fearing people to restore the Constitution and seize what is rightfully ours! It is time to be the men God wants us to be! It is time to show the weakling liberals that they cannot take away our guns and we have the guts to face them down! I have heard the Lord speak! He has told me that the end of days is nigh! The wicked shall perish! Jehovah's hand is upon us and we cannot fail!"

It was inspiring to see such passion and confidence but they needed more than a fire and brimstone reprise, they needed a plan. Blaze Worthington, a rancher who had his cattle allotment reduced by Forest Service range managers, raised his hand. Range scientists concluded that drought had devastated the forage on Blaze's allotment and it would no longer support as large a herd as he was accustomed to grazing. Blaze agreed that putting too many cows on a drought-pounded land was unwise, but so was missing a mortgage payment.

The price of beef was controlled by a meat-packing monopoly that never let the little guys get ahead no matter how many cows they put out there, but the meat-packing monopoly was too abstract and distant for Blaze to fathom. He chose instead to blame his sorrows on local Forest Service personnel who further drew his resentment because they were among the few securely employed residents of his little hometown of Soda Gulch on the far edge of Boon County. Government employees had benefits, too. He called them "elitists" and he was ready to take them down.

Blaze dropped his hand as men in the room turned his way. "That's all well and good, Bunny, but could you be a little more specific?"

Bunny stretched himself to his full height and leaned over the pulpit to cast a baleful stare at Blaze. "You will know when the time has come and where we will strike when it is time to reveal that. Go home and oil and clean your guns." He promised to keep them up to speed through a Facebook account set up by a daughter-in-law and maintained by grandchildren, since Bunny regarded any technology invented on the "Left Coast" as suspicious. Cows he understood, computers not so much. But he recognized a useful tool when he saw it and in a rural landscape where people lived miles apart, the Internet was a godsend for efficient communication.

In fact, the Cleaver clan had a satellite dish and Wi-Fi. They mostly watched Fox News and religious channels because PBS and mainstream television shows were off limits. "Degenerates, race-mixers, heathens, and reprobates!" Bunny shouted whenever the subject of watching other programs came up. The mere presence of a person of color was enough to condemn a show and gay characters made him apoplectic. At the end of the programs he detested the credits would roll across the screen and he would point out every name that sounded Jewish to him and say them loudly with obvious contempt. Consequently, if the homeschooled Cleaver grandchildren saw an African American person while on an infrequent trip to town to buy supplies, they would stop and stare, both fascinated and frightened. When his daughter Felicity Jo was three he caught her sucking on a nickel she picked up off the floor of the Redi-Mart. He admonished her. "Don't do that, child, you have no idea where that came from. Some nigra or Mexican could have had that last and their germs are all over it."

So the Cleaver clan was of one mind and that mind belonged to Bunny, who shaped them according to his delusional whims and fears. They were his human fractals, mirrors, and confirmation. And now he had a dozen ranch hands, unemployed coal miners, and struggling ranchers who were zealous followers. They called themselves Cleaverites. The Lord was shining through him and it was just a matter of time.

Chapter 4

Mary Handy met them at the trailhead. She was the wildlife biologist who spearheaded the reintroduction of beavers into the Sleeping Maiden watershed and she agreed to take the women up the mountainside to show them the results of her work. Luna and Olene rode together and Grace drove with Kayla, who had carved out time for a recreational afternoon from her overloaded schedule.

Olene thought Luna seemed distracted on the ride to the trailhead. "Are you okay? You seem lost in thought."

"No, I'm fine," she said with a little too much conviction. "I'm just thinking about my mom and the baby, you know, wondering if I forgot anything. I might have left the binky in our bedroom and I hope my mom can find it if she needs it."

It was a cover. She couldn't tell Olene about her history with the beaver colonies on Sleeping Maiden Mountain, how she and Hoppy helped Mary release a pair of beavers there, how another colony they visited had been slaughtered, how the horror of that day triggered Hoppy's sabotage of the Sea Ledges mining site. She remained unsure of how all of that might be connected to the gunman who tried to kill them a couple of days later. The events of that week were all inseparably mixed together in her mind. She had locked away the who and why questions of that drama when she decided to keep the secret of Hoppy's monkey-wrenching. Those episodes in their past were a Pandora's box that Hoppy and Luna had agreed never to open. Luna wondered if there would be evil spirits along the trail, some lingering vapor from those troubled days long ago, a faint signal she could read.

She purposely arranged to ride with Olene because Olene was delightfully distracting. During the hour it took them to drive to the trailhead to meet the others, Olene told her about the time she was backpacking in Guatemala and stopped to volunteer at a Quaker school for indigenous kids. A civil war was going on and a terrible gunfight broke out in the neighborhood where she was staying. She crawled low along a wall covered in bougainvillea until she reached the river. She jumped into a canoe and untied it, lay down, and hid. She didn't look up until she was sure she was safe. An hour passed and she sat up to see she was floating down the middle of the river without a paddle.

She drifted downstream and deep into the jungle until a tribe camping along the river pulled her in. There was no way to communicate with the villagers because their Spanish was rudimentary and she didn't understand their native tongue, a version of Mayan, she supposed. The outside world was also cut off. She lived there for a month before she was discovered and rescued.

"Wow, Olene, that's amazing! Did you have any profound revelations from that?"

"Not really. Believe me, it wasn't some romantic adventure, it was tough. I ate lizards and the Indians fed me mushy stuff that made me gag, kinda like a bark and moss smoothie. I was bitten by bugs I couldn't identify. I kept waiting for the universe to reveal some big meaning through all my suffering but all I could think about is how much I missed clean water and toilet paper, pillows, ice, shower curtains, soap. Toothpaste! Oh my God, what I would have done for toothpaste!"

Luna laughed. "I had a similar experience when they yanked me out of my mom's house and stuck me in a wilderness program for troubled youth, as they called us back then."

"And what did you learn there, Luna?"

"Everything."

The last mile of the trail up the mountainside became lush and verdant. "Beavers do this," Mary explained. "Their dams catch water and spread it out. We've been measuring the aquifer down below us and since the beavers were put back onto the land above here, the aquifer is recharging quickly. A lot of our snowpack these days melts fast in the spring and rolls away too quickly to capture it, so putting that water back into the ground is a healthy development. Unfortunately, for the first couple of years the flow into the reservoirs below us at the bottom of the mountain was reduced but then it picked up and it is much more reliable today. But you know how it goes. You can't tell a rancher or farmer whose operation is marginal to begin with that he will have less water for a couple of years. He won't go for that even if he would have a better water source in the long run because he's afraid that even one more dry year will put him out of business. You can't get people to sacrifice for a future that doesn't include them in it."

Grace grabbed Olene's sleeve. "Watch out, don't step in that. It's bottomless."

Olene skipped over a glistening green pile of turd and turned. "I thought cows weren't allowed up here."

Mary shook her head in disgust. "There aren't supposed to be cows but rules are one thing and enforcement is another. Bunny Cleaver cuts the fence that's supposed to keep his cattle out of here. He does it every year."

Olene wanted to know what percentage of federal land allowed grazing in America. Mary answered, ninety percent. Olene was surprised. She wanted to say something more about the impact of cows on a high desert landscape that was baking in a warming climate but did not because she was aware that grazing on public lands was an uncomfortable issue for Kayla. As was often the case, Kayla was torn between her ties to the Stony Mesa ranching community and her respect for science. Science told her cows do damage to sunburnt land but her heart told her she loved the people who put the cows out there.

Luna stopped short. "I see one! Hush."

They crouched on the bank and watched two beavers swim from their stick-in-the-mud huts to a stand of willows on the far shore. Back and forth, over and over, dark heads and thin wakes one way, limbs in teeth on the return trip. They left a trail of sodden leaves across the pond. Each time they disappeared under water the women waited, craned their necks, and focused harder until one reappeared. A hawk settled on the bank of the pond and hopped down for a drink. The beavers looked over and saw the hawk leaning over the water. That spooked them and they slapped their flat tails hard on the surface of the pond before they dove under water. The loud crack made the women flinch. The hawk flew off and the pond became still. The women waited for the beavers to reappear. They willed them to gently nudge the surface with their noses first and then bob up full-bodied into the light. They did not emerge.

The show was over. The women stood and gathered their packs, munched their last apples, and re-applied sunscreen. Luna got up the courage to bring up the past.

"Isn't this the colony that got shot up several years ago?"

It was a question Mary expected. "Yes, it is. The poacher didn't kill them all and the surviving pair kept surviving. These beavers are offspring. If I remember right, Luna, you witnessed the aftermath of that slaughter."

"Yes, I did." The others stopped what they were doing to turn toward her and listen.

Mary's voice dropped. She abandoned the pitch and tone that was her ranger voice, the one she used when educating and guiding, for the voice her children knew. "I'm sorry you saw that, Luna. That was tough. Real tough."

Luna was silent but tipped her head forward so that her hair fell across her face and hid her expression.

Mary led them away from the sad place they stumbled into. "Beavers don't hold grudges and have no time for pity or regret. They don't keep score. They just keep doing what they do and look at what happened." Mary swept her arm across the horizon of the pond. "Stick by stick they weave a world. Look around. Beavers invite in birds, amphibians, reptiles, insects, all the layers of life woven together. And it all begins with sharp teeth and persistence."

Grace rose to her feet after tying her boot lace and groaned loudly with the effort. She looked at the others and pumped her fist in the air. "Resilience!" Laughter. Grace threw her pack over her shoulder. "Let's hear it for the resilient beavers! And now for resilient old broads who keep on hiking!"

They had begun their descent when a young man in a Forest Service shirt appeared on the trail. Mary greeted him enthusiastically.

"I thought I'd find you up here," he said. "Looks like you're giving a tour." Kayla couldn't take her eyes off him. It wasn't that he was good-looking—though he was ridiculously cute, as she would later describe him to her friends back at the university. It was the easy way he moved, the way he inhabited his body, his voice, an air of confidence. All that and something in his eyes.

Mary introduced him as Ramone Marquez and explained he was a botanist who was working to restore the Hartshorn Ranch on the other side of the Sleeping Maiden. The ranch was an abandoned inholding surrounded by public land and the Forest Service acquired it when it was auctioned for peanuts. Ramone was doing experiments to see if the damage done by fifty years of hard farming could be healed. He explained that he also tracked rare and endangered plants on the mountain and took side trips to see the beavers whenever he could work it in.

Kayla stepped forward. "I remember that ranch from when I was a little girl. I went there with my grandfather. That family had a girl my age. We played on a rope swing and I remember beautiful rose bushes by the front steps to the ranch house. I think that was the one and only time I visited there."

Ramone turned toward Kayla. "Oh my gosh, that's amazing! The old house is still there and I often sit on the steps in the evening and wonder who planted that rose bush. I've tried to imagine the family who lived there."

"So the rose bush is still there?"

"Yeah, they must have deep roots. I should take you out there and show you what's become of the old place. I'd like to know if it brings back memories." He put his hand out and she took it. "I didn't get your name."

"Kayla Burnside." The strap of her pack slipped off of her shoulder and she lunged for it, almost smashing him in the forehead. He ducked.

Olene jumped in. "She's a veterinarian and owns the Jango Ranch." Grace poked her in the ribs with her elbow and Olene stepped back.

It is fair to say they all felt it, a shift in the barometric pressure, an undefined intensity, a hum, a heat. Something magical or something magnetic happened. If it were a Disney movie there would have been bluebirds tying ribbons over the heads of the young couple while butterflies shit glitter and fluttered about on happy wings. Kayla actually blushed and Ramone couldn't take his eyes off her.

They stalled there on the trail and made small talk as long as possible while Kayla and Ramone keyed in each other's information on their phones. Mary grew restless and announced her departure, the rest of them followed close behind her. Kayla was the very last to leave him. As she walked away she looked over her shoulder for one last lovelorn gaze and promptly tripped over a root and face-planted, luckily in a soft clump of rice grass.

Ramone rushed to her in an instant and stood over her, concern etched across his face. She rolled over, spit out a gritty pebble, and ran her hand over her face to make sure there was nothing bleeding, broken, or missing. Then she laughed, laughed until her sides ached and tears rolled down her cheeks. Ramone smiled along, puzzled.

He got on his knees to be closer. He laid his hand on her back. She was beautiful. "Are you sure you're okay?"

She rolled over and looked up at him. She took a deep breath and wiped the tears from her eyes. "Oh gosh, that felt good. Yeah, I needed that. Okay, I'm under control now. No worries."

She stood up and brushed herself off. She bent over and picked up her hat, slapped it across her knee to get the dust out, and then shoved it firmly on her head. "You know what this means, don't you?"

"No, what does it mean?" He was standing now, watching her brush dust off her shoulders and thighs.

"It means I just fell for you." She winked flirtatiously and walked away, wiggling her hips in a seductive parody of a bimbo strutting her stuff.

He laughed hard and called after her. "Then I'm one lucky guy."

Luna felt something walking behind her on the descent to the trailhead. Twice along the trail something touched her shoulder lightly from behind and she turned to find nobody there. She took three deep breaths and tried not to focus on the uneasy feeling that a cold shadow followed so close behind her that it curled around her neck and made her shiver. She listened to the conversations around her and was happy to be among such wise older women with their stories, experience, and opinions they no longer hid. Halfway down she stopped behind the others to find a place where she could duck off the trail and pee.

She had barely stepped away from the path when she looked down to choose her footing and saw his feet next to hers. She knew they were his feet because they pointed in opposite directions, an ability acquired by falling off a cliff. A jolt of adrenaline shot through her and she jumped backwards. She looked up and saw him standing there as plain as could be but with a subluminous tone to his skin.

"Jesus!" She yelped and cupped her hands over her heart.

He corrected her. "No. It's Nolan."

"Your name is Nolan?"

"Nolan Mikesel."

She had never been that close to him. In Rope Canyon he was either behind or below her. "I don't care what your name is, you're that monster who tried to kill us."

"Yes." He paused, then said softly, "That one."

"What do you want?" She hooked her thumbs into the straps of her pack and stuck out her chin.

He didn't answer. He looked needy, not scary. Forlorn, in a typical ghostly way. Pathetic.

She was impatient; she felt she had enough of him when he was alive and now seeing his ghost seemed unreasonable exposure. "Why are you here?"

"I'm stuck. I can't leave."

They stood apart and studied each other. She noticed how the breeze moved through him and some sunlight leaked through him, too. His thin frame of protruding bones held his parched skin like a taut bag tethered to sticks. His once bold tattoos had shriveled so that the cobra that wrapped his biceps had become a mere worm and the screaming skulls on his sunken chest were mute and wrinkled. He was naked and his proud pecker was now a soft pea. Sleepless years pulled his face downward like it was melting. A sourness permeated the air around him. She read him up and down twice, took a deep breath, studied him again, and then spoke.

"Forgiveness?"

"Yes . . . yes."

"Then I forgive you. Now go!"

And he was gone. Poof! Luna was amazed.

"Shit! That was easy!"

She peed, pulled up her pants, and scrambled down the trail to catch up to the others. She acted like nothing happened. She didn't speak a word about it because she had learned a long time ago to keep that kind of thing to herself. Later at home she told Hoppy, who believed her but wanted to know how she could decide so quickly to forgive the being who terrorized them years before.

"I mean, did you really forgive him or were you just uttering magic words to make him go away?"

"I meant it. I was ready and he looked like he had suffered enough. His presence was toxic, so it was better to release him and get that badness out of here, better all around."

"Wow. Good job, Luna!" He put his palm up for a high-five. They laughed. She wrapped her arms around his shoulders and climbed onto his lap.

Later as they settled under the covers of their bed, lights out, the shadows of swaying cottonwoods playing across the ceiling, she took his hand and whispered, "It was wise to forgive."

"How do you know?"

"The moon taught me."

"The moon?"

"We live by sunlight, but too much sun and we would curdle and burn, wither and die. The moon distills the sun's harsh light into a milky balm. It bathes the world in a merciful glow. It heals the day. The moon showed me how forgiveness follows fire."

She closed her eyes. "Goodnight."

He kissed her gently on the cheek and watched her tumble away into the universe of Luna Waxwing dreams. He wished he could follow her there but already she was a bright spark receding into the distant horizon among a billion twinkling lights.

C h a p t e r   5

A benign climate became cranky. The atmospheric rivers of the warming planet grew so turbulent that waves of weather oscillated madly, kicking off monster storms and pitching alternating fits of flood and drought. An epic drought scoured the land around Stony Mesa. Old juniper trees retreated into their roots until the landscape bristled with their bare abandoned limbs, twisting upwards like the skeletal fingers of ghosts imploring an indifferent sky. Whole mountainsides turned beetle-kill-gray and burst into flames. The heat of these new mega-wildfires was so great it baked the life out of the soil. The following spring, torrential rains soaked charred and sterile ground until it slid into valleys, erased roads, and broke pipelines.

Temperatures often spiked too early in the spring so that scant snowpack melted fast and didn't last. The mega-reservoirs of the Southwest receded, freeing a paradise of redrock canyons that were soon rich in dripping seeps and fresh willows. They were the legendary Edens we sacrificed to capture water for profligate use decades ago. Their recovery was a silver lining in an otherwise harsh weather dynamic.

Receding water also revealed mud flats strewn with half-buried boats, rusted outboard motors, Styrofoam coolers, ropes, skis, cans, bottles, tackle, and a million other lost, broken, and wasted manmade bits mixed among layers of toxic silt. There were sewage issues. Civilization's footprint was a plastic-encrusted stain.

Unprecedented aridity punctuated by hard-fisted storms became the new norm. Southwest cities baked. Water rights doubled in price and then doubled again as desperate cities bought agricultural water from ranchers who cashed in, turned off their sprinklers, sold their cows, closed headgates, and moved away. Water-starved pastures baked under the sun and were then hammered by wind into cupped and dusty fields of ragweed and thistle. As the droughts intensified into killer heatwaves, the residents of Phoenix and Las Vegas fled the frying zones of asphalt and cement and headed for the countryside. A migration began. The only thing headed south was real-estate prices in desert cities.

In Stony Mesa, a season of vagrants followed tourist season. They camped just off the road under canopies of cottonwoods. They built fires under redrock alcoves, paused at rest areas and parks to pee and fill up jugs with tap water. Whole families slept in cars. The good citizens of Stony Mesa began to lock their doors.

The more affluent refugees from the slo-mo crash of civilization drifted through town, their necks craning toward real-estate signs in front of vacant lots, abandoned ranches, even swayback cabins with attics full of squirrels. Anything might be up for sale but despite the volume of lookers there were few takers. There was no work to be had in Stony Mesa and it was very far from everywhere. But if you could set up a workstation in your home and phone your work to an office far away there was no lovelier place to live. No traffic or pervasive noise. Clean air and clean water, what was left of it. Spectacular scenery. Stony Mesa was relatively undamaged by the chaos of the times.

People migrating away from heat zones who could work from home over the web usually balked at settling their families in Stony Mesa when they investigated the school system. They were reluctant to place their precious little prodigies in a public school they considered academically anemic and culturally starved. For their part, the locals hesitated to share their precious water with new people who already had their noses in the air.

It was an axial age. Greed, anger, and raving delusions trumped fairness and fellowship. Chaos ruled the nation. The residents of Stony Mesa surveyed the world from the safe distance of their satellite dishes and gave thanks that the turmoil and tragedies they witnessed on screens in their living rooms and dens had not reached them. Or maybe challenges and changes had reached them so incrementally that, like the proverbial frog in a pot of gradually boiling water, they grew accustomed to the annual hundred-year floods, record-breaking heat, vistas of brown forests, the infernos that were possible all year long now, half-empty reservoirs, dust storms, and wind, way too much hot, dry wind. The Apocalypse, Elias Buchman mused, was not an event but an "episodic accretion."

Even so they believed they were still ahead of the fallout, before the flood, still waiting while dreadful pandemics to come whispered in their veins. They looked at the news and worried. If we get cut off, if refugees from the baked cities flee here in droves, what will we do? But for three seasons a year most people were too busy hosting tourists to give those questions the serious thought they deserved. The immediate pushes away the important. Instead of preparing for a likely disaster we make the parent-teacher conference, see the kid play basketball, work a second job, help an ailing parent, volunteer, or respond to a hundred text messages a day and countless Facebook friends.

Like people everywhere who should know better, many folks in Stony Mesa were caught up in an empire of distraction that required them to continually tweet, text, blog, post, and otherwise encounter and tend to the virtual realm. They walked around with their thumbs twitching at little plates of dark glass. Who had time to plan when one is compulsively distracted, walking about obliviously while frantically counting one's buttons? They fed on the clay that was served them because although there was no nourishment in it, it filled them and eased the pangs of anxiety and doubt. Even in remote Stony Mesa, people were becoming their very own zombies. Or, as Luna Waxwing put it to Elias Buchman, they became "soft-robots."

Tourism still drove the local economy. Fewer Americans traveled out of the country anymore, what with terrorism, failed states, serial civil war, ecological collapse, pandemics, mass migrations, and catastrophic storms becoming the new normal. America became America's vacation destination. After so many mass shootings in theme parks and festivals, there weren't many places left where tourists could feel safe and relax. Stony Mesa's nearby national park was one place that seemed to exist beyond the alarming crises of an overheated planet of slums. And you could drive there.

Air travel had become dangerous after the terrorists decided that airports were a legitimate battleground, along with crowded market-places, stadiums, train stations, churches, buses, hospitals, and restaurants. We understood that if a terrorist is willing to die trying, no place is truly safe or sacred. We had finally reached that sick satisfying realization that our paranoia wasn't imaginary after all, but well advised. We became a planet of people who stayed close to home.

The cruise ship industry collapsed in tandem with the failure of antibiotics to stop the new drug-resistant viruses. The consensus on "cruising" shifted abruptly after too many ships arrived at port with a load of puking customers except for the ones in body bags. That form of travel was now regarded as "superbug roulette." Again, Stony Mesa was a clean alternative.

Much of America's classic scenery had dried up, burned up, or was periodically and unpredictably underwater. Coastal tourism suffered sea surges, jellyfish swarms, oil slicks, and blooms of toxic algae. Travelers to the great mountains saw mountainsides of ghostly trees and charred forests. The wounds were unmistakable even to a flat-lander. Our once glorious, robust, and iconic mountain ranges of the American West had become a landscape that required major photoshopping. The desert canyons down the hill from Stony Mesa, however, had already been hammered down to naked essentials and seemed less damaged to tourists and more "natural," whatever that meant. It was reassuring to know that deserts can be so beautiful, since so much of the planet seemed to be headed in that direction.

The one thing Stony Mesa didn't have was water. Tourists didn't like the restrictions, like the ban on washing the mud off trucks, motor-cycles, and off-road toys. Restaurants didn't serve water unless asked to and motels only changed sheets after three nights. Showers had timers. But visitors endured the inconveniences because they understood that water was always scarce in the desert and now even more so.

Kayla Burnside's Jango Ranch was rich with water. Her grandfa-ther was an early settler and developed a spring and tapped the river that ran across his land. He had prior rights to as much water as he could use and more. Over the years, that water had been leased to neighboring ranchers who arrived later. As they gave up and moved on, Kayla secured the water for the Jango and shared water she was enti-tled to with neighbors who were drying up. But those who grew alfalfa were fighting a losing battle. Lucerne, as the old-timers called it, is a water hog and in an era of aridity and an inconsistent supply of water, it made no sense to grow it in Stony Mesa. Ironically, Kayla Burnside found herself in the midst of an epic and perhaps permanent drought with more water than she could use.

Her aquarian advantage occurred to her in the hours she drove between the university and the Jango Ranch, the only time in her life for reflection and review. She wondered what water was worth these days. That answer was buried in the complex, multi-layered, loopholed, arcane architecture that was water law in the American West. But she knew she had the original claim from her great-grandfather, the locally famous Jango Burnside. Today that must be worth something. Finding out how much it was worth was always on her list of things she intended to do but it was never near enough to the top of that list to actually get done.

On a Saturday in May, the value of her water moved to the top of her list when Morris Buttars called her on the ranch's old landline. She was in the kitchen unpacking groceries she brought down from the city when the phone rang. She pushed the vegetable drawer of the refrigerator shut and closed the door.

The voice on the line sounded professional the way announcers and salesmen and lawyers do. It was confident and serious. "Excuse me, is this Kayla Burnside?"

"Yes, who's calling?"

"My name is Morris Buttars and I am with the Nutley Corporation. I'd like to meet you and talk."

"Talk? About what?" Kayla had heard of Nutley. It was an international corporation that made processed food products like candy bars, snack chips, whipped cheese spread, and donuts filled with a sweet paste made of thirty-two ingredients that only existed in laboratories. As a kid, she craved those packaged foods but she gave them up after her first nutrition class as a pre-med student in college. Why, she asked, would the Nutley Corporation call me?

"We have an offer we'd like to discuss."

"Wait a minute. Nutley like the candy bar?"

He chuckled. "Yes, one and the same, but this is not about candy. We want to talk to you about water."

They agreed to meet the following evening. Three men in crisp suits arrived in a Ford Escalade that had never seen the outskirts of a city. When the men climbed out of it they looked around the farmyard like tourists stumbling out of a bus, gawking at a foreign landscape. They carried valises and laptops. Kalya watched them from the living room window. She walked to the front door and waited for them.

They stayed almost three hours and by the time they departed Kayla was late leaving for her job at the university lab. She drove away and dialed Grace Buchman.

"Grace, it's Kayla. I have a favor to ask. Can you ask Elias to do some research for me?"

"Why of course, dear, what is it you need to know about?"

"Bottled water."

C h a p t e r   6

Skip Dunneman was a godsend. He worked hard and had multiple skills. He could solve problems that came up on the job and he was self-directed. To top it off, he had a great sense of humor. Knowing that Skip would be there to help each day took a load off of Hoppy's shoulders and he realized how much stress he had been carrying before Skip showed up at the Desert Rose. Skip made friends easily and built a wide web of relationships in just the first couple of weeks he lived in Stony Mesa. He was tall but not intimidating because he was lanky and stooped with an easygoing demeanor to match his relaxed posture. He was polite with the elderly, solicitous of children, and generous with those his own age. There were times he seemed flawless.

"Too good to be true," muttered Luna one evening after Hoppy listed Skip's wonderful qualities for the umpteenth time. She worried that Hoppy trusted Skip too much.

"I'm glad he's such a great workmate, but be careful."

"About what?"

"I mean don't tell him secrets."

He was hurt for a moment and then indignant. He took a breath and was about to speak when she interrupted.

"I'm sorry. I know you wouldn't do that, I just . . ."

"Tell ya what. I'll trust Skip less and you trust me more, okay?"

She promised. The very next day Hoppy and Skip traded stories as they worked. They started with stories from their childhoods, Skip telling about his pet chicken and Hoppy kicking in the one about skateboarding through the girls' locker room. Stories about outrageous adolescent adventures escalated. Hoppy hopped trains while Skip skipped school. And at last they reached the meaty tales of young men gone wild. Hoppy told him about the time he spiked the Young Republicans' punch with LSD and Skip told about the time he got caught skinny dipping in a golf course pond on a Saturday afternoon. Hoppy told about the time he was stranded on a huge rock in the middle of a flash flood and Skip told about the time he poured sand in the gas tanks of trucks at a fracking well. Hoppy did not reciprocate with his own monkey-wrenching tale. He changed the subject.

Skip was forthright about his politics and his willingness to act on his beliefs. When he described how biodiversity was being shredded or how the climate was thrown into chaos, Hoppy agreed that it was happening and had to stop. It was the how part of changing the world that he was stuck on. Skip claimed he was going to California to help friends who were planning to shut down a refinery. Strategy was not Hoppy's strong suit and lately he was so busy taking care of the Desert Rose, raising a baby, installing solar panels, and keeping up with Luna that the question of how best to save the world was moot.

Hoppy told Skip that Sage was now crawling. He and Luna were rearranging their home to cover sockets, fence off stairs, and move anything within Sage's reach that he could put into his mouth. Sage might put anything in his mouth. He showed less discretion than a cockroach. Luna complained that these days she worried less about his future in a troubled world and more about whether he could get his hand into the toilet again. Crawling is a baby's initial tutorial in gravity and steps, ledges, and edges are hard teachers. They had to watch him all the time.

Skip asked him about the baby. Was he planned? What was it like to become a father?

Hoppy said they thought long and hard about having a baby. They read books and blogs, visited medical websites, read and wrote poems. They practically interviewed young parents they knew. They talked and talked, revisited and reviewed. They confessed their dreams, their fears, and their confusion. Finally, bluebirds convinced them.

Scanning the human landscape fed their doubts. The emotional ruins and scars of broken homes littered the horizon. Hoppy had no doubt that he and Luna could find the happiness he knew in his own family while growing up. His parents might be odd but they loved him, he knew it, and the household was mostly nurturing and secure. Luna had not known that kind of warmth and security. Her dad, he explained to Skip, ditched her mom when Luna was too young to remember much.

Her mother loved her and her father provided economic security but there would always be that wounded feeling. There was this bond that her friends had with their dads that she would never know. Daughters are supposed to reside deep in the hearts of their fathers. Her dad wrote checks.

But the bluebirds gave them hope and showed the way. Hoppy and Luna set up a bluebird house on a pole out of the prevailing wind where it would catch plenty of sunlight, close enough that they could watch any activity from the kitchen window. They wrapped a snake and cat guard around the pole, made sure there were sticks and rails nearby to perch on, checked for access to grass and insects, and made a water source nearby. Soon after they completed their part, bluebird couples were visiting the house. The little birds tried out the nearby perches and examined food and water options. They popped in and out of the bird house as if they were making sure the hole was comfortable because they would be spending days on end ducking in and out, first with nesting materials and then with bugs for babies. If the hole were too large it might admit chick-eating birds. The bluebird couples perched on the roof while downloading the angles of the sun, assessing wind patterns, sensing threats and opportunities.

One couple committed and moved in. Hoppy and Luna watched as they gathered nesting materials. If one was foraging on the ground, the other would perch high and look out for danger while singing a beautiful silver tune. The male was radiantly blue. The baby birds hatched and Hoppy and Luna listened to their plaintive peeping whenever a parent returned with a morsel of food. The male carried away the smelly fecal sacks that might reveal them to predators. Mom and dad hunted all day to feed their brood the insects and juicy caterpillars that swarmed the farm. And all day they sang, looked out for one another, and flashed their beautiful blue wings in joyous flight.

They reminded Luna that there was something powerful and primal about birth and parenting that she did not want to miss. The bluebirds' acceptance of their duties was inspiring and beautiful. They did it with music, singing instead of whining.

"So you're telling me," said Skip, "that bluebirds are your role models?"

"Yes, except for the parts involving the regurgitation of insects. It's hard to explain, easier if you know Luna."

Skip had the opportunity to do just that because Stony Mesa was a small community and they encountered each other at numerous town crossings. He spent a lot of time at the Desert Rose Café and never missed a chance to smile and say hello. Luna was always friendly and polite. She was thankful Hoppy had Skip's help and pleasant company but she held back. One evening as they shared a salad on the back porch, Hoppy asked her why she kept her distance from Skip. She couldn't put her finger on it. "I don't know, he just tries too hard."

Hoppy figured Skip had a crush on Luna and she was defensive. He knew that half the young men in town had a crush on Luna and most of the older men treated her with fatherly regard. He had learned to live with the way she lit men up and he let it go. Jealousy was an unpleasant emotional experience and not useful for keeping the love of your life happy.

Skip came back to the story of pouring sand in the gas tanks two more times in the course of a work week. The first time he told the story he waited for Hoppy to reciprocate. Hoppy didn't bite so Skip brought it up again, this time elaborating on why his destruction of fracking machinery was just and right. Hoppy didn't bite. The third time he asked Hoppy directly if he thought monkey-wrenching was justified. Could Hoppy imagine himself engaging in monkey-wrenching? Was he capable, willing?

"Justice," said Hoppy, "is one thing. Risk is another. I would never jeopardize Luna and Sage. These days I have a hard time imagining myself getting a day off from work, so leading the revolution is not an option for me. Capable, yes. Willing, no. Let's break for lunch."

Over breakfast the next day Luna asked Hoppy, "How's the Skipathon going these days?"

Hoppy hesitated. "I think that underneath that happy exterior Skip is troubled."

"Troubled how?"

"I don't know. Torn. Troubled."

She measured her response carefully. "Well, remember what comes with troubled people."

"What?"

"Trouble."

Chapter 7

Kayla told herself to be alert. Night had fallen and the road back to Stony Mesa was notorious for the deer and elk that crossed the road. They were hard to see until you were right on them and they tended to freeze in headlights, their mesmerized eyes shining as if lit from within. Hitting a deer was bad enough but hitting an elk was like hitting a horse. She knew of accidents where the drivers clipped the legs of an elk and the entire torso came crashing through the windshield as the car rode under the animal.

It was hard to keep her mind on the road. She was tired again, or maybe not again but always. Not just physically tired but emotionally worn out. It was time for a change in her life. Her team at the university lab had accomplished what they set out to do. They developed the most effective coyote contraceptive ever made. There were moments of pride in that achievement but she never got that satisfying feeling of closure she expected to feel at the end of such an exhausting struggle.

She and Ramone agreed to meet for dinner at the Desert Rose Café the following evening. Her attraction to Ramone was another source of uncertainty and one more signal that her life was perched on a tipping point. He wasn't a member of the One True Church and that was an issue she hadn't entirely laid to rest. She was raised with the expectation that she would marry within the church but she found the men she met through the church annoying. They were bossy and presumptuous in that way that men raised in a patriarchal culture could be. They acted as if Kayla should be desperate to end her old-maid status and thankful for their attention. They had little insight into her work and no appreciation for what she had accomplished. They weren't that interested.

Ramone on the other hand seemed to appreciate her for herself with no expectations or assumptions. They shared much in common despite the fact that he was raised in the Midwest and had never set foot inside the One True Church. They both worked in science, both loved the outdoors, and both loved horses though she was the more experienced rider. They had long conversations each evening and when she talked to him she felt relaxed and open. He respected her ideas and feelings, understood her immediately, and was not afraid to let her lead a conversation. They talked for hours on the phone and she felt the floodgates of her doubts and worries open. Ramone was someone she could trust. And someone she desired.

She told him that the project she was devoted to for almost four years now was mostly over and he congratulated her. "You must have feelings of relief and satisfaction."

"No, I don't really and I thought I would."

"Why is that?"

"I thought if we developed some non-lethal means to limit coyote populations the problem would be solved. But there are complexities."

"Like what?"

"Like mesopredator release. Studies of ecosystems where the contraceptive was field-tested showed that when the coyote population was reduced, the number of smaller predators increased because the coyotes were no longer there to keep them in check. So coyotes were no longer eating calves and lambs but foxes, skunks, and feral cats were devastating the songbird populations. When we tampered with the food web we traded cattle for songbirds."

Ramone smiled knowingly and nodded. Then, like a carnival barker he exclaimed, "And around and around it goes and where it stops, nobody knows . . ."

"Yeah, I guess I underestimated how complex those relationships in the food web can be. I suppose the problem of coyote predation itself happened because we took out the wolves that kept the coyotes in check."

He feigned alarm. "Wolves? Did you say wolves? Oh sweet Jesus in the morning!"

She laughed. "Yeah, that's definitely not an option. Wolves are like coyotes on steroids, right? The mention of the name makes my grandfathers' ranching buddies stutter and turn red."

"But seriously, Kayla, I know what you mean. Ecosystems are not only more complex than we thought, they are more complex than we can think. I am humbled by what I am learning while trying to restore just a small piece of troubled ground."

She couldn't stop. "Oh, and rabbits! In one field test the coyotes were virtually eliminated, not through contraception but through trapping and hunting. When the coyotes were gone there was this population explosion of rabbits, both jackrabbits and cottontails everywhere. They devastated fields of grain, so then the ranchers were pissed off about that. It never ends."

She articulated her doubts for the first time, out loud anyway. It felt good to have someone who might understand her listen to her. "Another problem with coyote contraception is that coyote fertility is this amazing dynamic. If the pack's numbers are cut for any reason, be it hunters, trappers, contraception, or even a hard winter, the females come into estrus more frequently and breed faster. So you're up against this mysterious inner biological clock. And if you don't apply the contraceptive to each and every female, say you're doing well to hit half of them, then the females that didn't get the contraceptive make up the difference."

He laughed. "Why does the word tricky keep coming to mind? You can have a similar problem if you kill adults in a pack because more food is available to pups and they're more likely to survive."

Kayla was on a roll. It was so good to unload what she had been holding in for too long and for once she didn't care if the people dining at the next table heard her or not. "And here is another big factor I underestimated. You have all these ranchers and rangemanagers out there who have been calling on the U.S. Wildlife Service for years and years. The service kills more than sixty thousand coyotes every year and that doesn't count the ones killed by ranchers themselves. So there are all these long-established relationships that you might say are self-sustaining. The trappers and rangers are buddies, neighbors, maybe their kids are on the same baseball team, whatever. So they're reluctant to reject the habitual methods in favor of something new that steps on the other guy's toes. I understand that. I grew up in Stony Mesa. Good neighbors don't rock the boat. So as long as ranchers want a quick solution, you could say a quick return on their investment, and as long as there is a service that wants to be employed doing what they have always done . . . well, it's pretty discouraging. There are simple things they could do like putting out guard dogs or removing the carcasses of the cows that die on their own so they don't attract coyotes, but it's easier to let the government do it. You know, the damn government, the one they want to leave them alone."

He waited for her to continue but she didn't. He could hear music playing in another room and tried to identify the band. He broke the pause. "Are you familiar with Michael Soulé?"

"Yeah, they call him the father of conservation biology, right?"

"Right. Well, Soulé says that the price of ecological literacy is that you see the wounds. You don't just see them, you feel them. And you see how complex the world is and that feels overwhelming. But you get to see the beauty, too. The wonder. And I remind myself that I don't have to save the whole world, just my corner of it, just what's in reach. That's all I can do and it's enough. Added to all the others who are saving their little corner, too, we can eventually save the whole enchilada. Sew the pieces back together. Restore it. That requires lots of trial and error. You did your part well, Kayla, and you should be proud."

Around four in the morning she awoke with a swirling head. The dinner with Ramone was perfect. He was perfect and that was scary. This can't be real, she told herself. It is too good to be real. She second-guessed the way she passionately kissed him before she got into her car and drove home. He was surprised but pleased, too.

Ramone was one big reason she wanted to live and work in Stony Mesa instead of spending half her life in the city. How could she manage a move? If she could increase her hours at the veterinary clinic and didn't have to pay monthly rent for the apartment near the university, she could quit her job there and also afford to live at the Jango. It would be tight but possible.

She mulled the options. I could sell most of the water to Nutley and have enough water for my own needs. I'd be set. She was reluctant to go there but she did. She had been quietly building a rationale for selling her water to Nutley. If they decided to build a bottling plant in Boon County, that would mean jobs, and in Boon County even a few jobs made a difference. Most of her classmates moved away because work was so scarce and she knew others who settled for less so they could stay close to family. They worked three part-time jobs without benefits or they got by on seasonal jobs and unemployment. They gave up the chance to have careers and they were over-skilled for the jobs they did.

But it was more likely that Nutley would take the water out downstream. That wouldn't help anyone in Boon County. She wished she knew more of the specifics of what Nutley intended to do. She wished she knew more about water law. She wished she knew a good lawyer she trusted.

She finished a cup of tea and pulled on her boots. Morning chores awaited and feeding her horses was up first. Molly and Star were the one indulgence she allowed herself in a close to the bone lifestyle. Riding on weekends kept her sane. Made her strong. There was something about that connection to animal mind and body, the partnership, the motion, rhythm, the powerful aroma, the touch of skin on skin. She felt better just seeing them. Their hot snorts pulsed across her cheeks when she stroked their powerful necks and she was steeped in that pungent horse aroma that tingled her scalp. The thrill of their lips moving over a palm full of grain healed her after a week of incessant noise and traffic.

I'm getting ahead of myself, she concluded. I must be patient. Pay attention. Look for signs. And then she prayed because she had always prayed. Members of the One True Church bowed their heads in prayer when they got in a car, played a basketball game, ate a meal, began a meeting, or made a sale. Life in her grandfather's church was punctuated by prayer. It became Kayla's way of reminding herself of what was important and what she was thankful for, even if there were no Heavenly Father to listen to her words.

Her colleagues at the lab were embarrassed when they caught her praying quietly at her desk. One friend asked her how she reconciled work as a scientist with such prayerful behavior.

"I'm not asking some supernatural power to intervene in my life, not since I was a kid anyway, it's just that if I can say what it is I need I am more likely to get it because I can feel it. The clarity of prayer is empowering."

"So that's it?" her colleague replied. "A cognitive hack?"

"No! I mean yeah, but more than that. I'm giving you the part of it you can under- stand. The rest of it is about my history. You know, how I was taught. Prayer helped me through rough times. It's personal." Her friends at the lab accepted her explanation because everyone liked and respected Kayla. If she likes to pray, they said, that's her business.

She stood by the corral while Molly and Star nibbled nearby and was not sure of which way to face, whether to close her eyes or look up, whether to fold her arms or clasp her hands. Sometimes she imagined that the signals she tried to push across her brain were slowed by the fat of memory and the gristle of habits. It was an inadequate tool for the tasks she asked of it.

"Please," she whispered, "guide me."

Chapter 8

It was the last straw. According to Bunny Cleaver, who had been feuding with federal range managers for as long as he owned cows, the United States Forest Service was engaged in systematic harassment of himself and other like-minded ranchers. The latest offense happened before he finished his breakfast when a ranger from the Sleeping Maiden Mountain station called to complain. He told Bunny that some women visiting the beaver colony on the south side of the mountain saw evidence of cows where they were not supposed to be. A woman biologist who Bunny guessed was that ol' biddy Mary somethingerother was to blame. The old bat found a cut fence and she wanted Bunny to send a rider and get the cows away from her precious water rats.

Bunny cut the fence separating his grazing allotment from a wilderness study area every year. The aim was always the same: let his herd get to the lush grass below the beaver pond. The ranger on the phone told him that the meadows below the pond were overgrazed and needed to recover.

"Recover from what?" Bunny demanded.

"Look, Mr. Cleaver, we've been over this again and again. When you put too many cows on that grass and leave them there late in the season so the forage has no time to recover, then you have less the next year. You now have twice as many cows out there as the number of cows we figure is sustainable. And that is why you always want more territory for your cows to graze, because you ruin the acreage permitted to you. Then to top it off, you don't pay your fees. It's public land, Mr. Cleaver, and it belongs to all Americans. You're cheating taxpayers and giving all the ranchers who play by the rules and cooperate, which is most of them, a bad name."

"The good Lord put grass there as a gift to man. Cows eat grass, we eat cows." He was baffled by how ignorant these environmentalists were. It seemed to Bunny that they worshipped the grass itself.

"The law is clear on this, Mr. Cleaver. You don't get to decide . . ."

Bunny pushed a button on his phone and ended the conversation. He missed those old landline phones with a sturdy cradle to hold the phone's handset. He had a phone like that back when he first argued with the Forest Service. He missed the way he could slam the phone down when he hung up on them. It sent a startling noise through the line, a satisfying exclamation not possible with so-called smartphones.

Something had to be done to still those federal agents and get them off his back once and for all. Bunny bruised his ankle while wrestling an ornery cow into a squeeze shoot and spent the next few days in his truck listening to talk radio. The angry hosts vented and Bunny sat in his truck and stewed. By the time his ankle was fit for working again Bunny was convinced that something dramatic and bold had to be done. But what?

That night he prayed on it. He kneeled before his bed and bowed his head over folded hands. A clock on the dresser ticked loudly and the digital blue light from his electric toothbrush shining into his bedroom from the bathroom distracted him. He got up and closed the door between the bedroom and bathroom to block the annoying glow. He stuffed the clock under a pillow and resumed his prayer position. A minute into it his wife entered the room with a toothbrush sticking out of her mouth and a towel wrapped around her hair.

"Get out, woman! Can't you see I'm praying?"

She scooted out and waddled down the hallway while muttering under her breath. Dissent in the Cleaver household was limited to half-heard mutterings. The rule was if you don't like it, talk to yourself. She turned the corner and disappeared. He resumed his deliberations.

It came to him. It was not a flash like before. There were no auras or the audible click and buzz in his inner ear that signaled God's voice. It was more like a salve that settled over his shoulders. God spoke silently this time.

Heavenly Father wanted him to seize the Forest Service station near the Sleeping Maiden trailhead. He was pleased and relieved that God agreed with him and directed him to do what he wanted to do anyhow. He reflected on how often he could anticipate what God wanted.

I guess that is why He chose me, thought Bunny, because we're so much alike.

The word went out to the faithful: saddle up, boys, it's time to ride! Yee-haw! But first he had his granddaughter Celestia Prudence download images of the Forest Service station from Google Earth. The Cleaverites studied the layout, which was simple: a gravel parking lot next to the trailhead, a short path to a small lawn, a modest fieldstone house probably built by the Civilian Conservation Corps way back during the Great Depression. They pooled their knowledge of the target. A seasonal employee lived there during the summer but he was gone now. The offices were used by a half dozen rangers and scientists—that crazy witch Mary Handy for one—when they were not in the field, which was most of the time.

"Candy from a baby, I'd say," pronounced Bunny as he leaned forward on a table covered with downloaded maps and photos. "Once we have it secured, we call the media. Get a television crew out there. That's when we call for the people to rise up and take back the land that is rightly ours, our birthright. The righteous will rise and the wicked will be punished when the Lord's plan unfolds. It will be glorious to behold! We will be His avenging angels!"

It seemed a stretch, even to the faithful. Taking over a mostly unmanned ranger station on the far side of nowhere was an unlikely way to begin the apocalyptic battle between the righteous and the damned. Perhaps this was the ultimate act of faith, the time when the true believers separated from the weak ones. But if there were any doubters among the Cleaverites, they didn't speak up. To a man and boy they swore they would follow Bunny Cleaver into the lion's den, even if the lion's den had a public restroom and an orientation kiosk.

When? they asked. Soon, said Bunny.

C h a p t e r   9

Grace and Elias invited Kayla for dinner. Elias could share what he learned about bottled water and Grace had an excuse to share time with Kayla, whom she admired. Grace made beef cubes and gravy, a meal they never ate alone because they ate mostly vegetarian, organic, preferably low salt and gluten free. But Kayla was a meat-eating cowgirl raised in Stony Mesa, so Grace assumed that it was appropriate to serve beef. It was local grass-fed beef, too. Grace asked Elias not to mention how much methane is produced by cows and what a deleterious impact that had in a warming world. Elias agreed they could veer off their dietary track for one evening and he assured her he would be polite and avoid the cow fart lecture.

Kayla arrived in a pale turquoise blouse and tight jeans that showed off a fit physique. Elias was disappointed that they did not have rhinestone designs on the back pockets. He still wondered if they would leave scratch marks on chairs and he figured that tonight would be his chance to find out. Grace asked him to focus.

Over dinner Grace asked about Ramone. Had they gone out to see the old Hartshorn Ranch he was restoring? No, she told them, but they had gone on a dinner date. Grace asked, "What did you think?"

"I think I want to move to Stony Mesa full time so I can find out if I'm wrong."

"Wrong about what?" asked Elias.

"Wrong about thinking he's the perfect match for Kayla Burnside. No kidding, I've never met anyone like him."

"That's wonderful, Kayla, I'm so happy for you." Grace clapped her hands together softly and her face blossomed into a radiant smile.

"Be careful with your heart." Elias, of course, distrusted spontaneous decisions.

Grace cuffed him on the shoulder. "Oh, Elias, love doesn't wait for a second opinion."

Kayla laughed. She loved to watch Grace and Elias banter. It was obvious that they adored one another despite the fact that he regarded

Grace's positive enthusiasm as unsound and she found him annoyingly negative. Somehow their differences were complementary.

Dinner over, they retreated to the back deck to catch the last rays of the sunset as it lit up clouds, first gold, then pink. A lavender hue rimmed the eastern horizon. The Buchmans, like most people in Stony Mesa, had a postcard-perfect view of the canyons from their home. There were many different views to be had in town, each one a little different from the next. This view featured distant canyon walls standing in front of white-capped blue mountains. At sunset the mountains wore a violet aura. They took a few minutes to drink it all in and then it was time for Elias to tell Kayla what he learned about bottled water. They went back inside and settled into the living room.

Elias sat in his easy chair. A laptop sat at his feet and an end table at the armrest was stacked with books and an unruly pile of magazines and journals. He took out a small notebook from his back pocket and flipped through some pages. He perched a pair of reading glasses on the end of his nose.

"Well, first of all, I discovered I didn't know much about bottled water. Because we live in a tourist town we see people with plastic bottles of water all the time. They're a big item at most stores here because the tourists buy them by the case when they're camping. I guess they don't trust our tap water and think bottled water is safer. That's too bad because our tap water is very clean, carefully monitored, and delicious as well. Sweetwater. Mostly pure snowpack filtered through sandstone."

Grace interrupted. "Our water is the best. Elias and I hike a lot so we have stainless steel water bottles that we refill. We take a jug on trips so we can drink Stony Mesa water while we're in the city."

Elias nodded. "And that, by the way, is lots cheaper than buying plastic bottles. In fact, you can refill your own water bottle about two thousand times from your kitchen tap for the price of one bottle of water purchased from a store. And get this: about a third of the bottled water on the market is straight out of some municipal tap anyway. It's just packaged tap water. In taste tests against bottled water, tap water always wins."

"But is it safe? Tap water, I mean." Kayla figured there must be some compelling reason to buy water in plastic bottles.

"Generally speaking, yes, it is very safe. Oh sure, if you live in Flint or some other city where corrupt politicians are poisoning poor people, the tap water is unsafe—but that's the exception. If a hurricane stomps on your watershed, ya know—an emergency—then bottled water is a better bet. Tap water is highly tested and monitored but bottled water is practically unregulated. And there are concerns about how safe and clean bottled water is. Tests show more bacterial contamination from bottled water than tap water because it tends to sit for days as it is transported and then shelved. Sometimes it sits in the sunlight for days. Tap water never stops running but bottled water is stagnant for part of its short life."

Grace wiggled to the edge of her seat. "Tell her about the chemicals!"

"Yeah, well, the bottles are plastic and there are traces of plastic-making chemicals in them. The presence of hormone-disrupting phthalates are particularly troubling. They could be linked to birth defects and cancer. There may be traces of benzene and chlorine by-products."

"I think the worst of it is the waste!" Grace was a fanatic recycler. Elias tried to steer her away from open trash bins she might root through for cans. She carried a bag on their walks in case she found cans hiding in the weeds. This happened a lot because town folk who were members of the One True Church were not allowed to drink, so beer was usually consumed while riding in trucks or ATVs and the cans tossed away so that snooping wives or parents didn't find evidence of alcohol use.

Grace was as close to agitated as Kayla had ever seen her. "Every week, Americans use a half billion plastic water bottles! Can you imagine that, a half billion? In one week? That's enough to stretch around the globe!"

Elias looked down at his notes that were scribbled on a pocket-sized flip-pad as if he were still on the city beat at the newspaper. "About one in six of those plastic bottles gets recycled. Most of those are shipped to Third World countries to be down-cycled into other plastic products, most of which can't be used again. So that's billions upon billions of bottles that go into landfills, get incinerated, or worse— they go into the ocean. That's why so many cities have banned them. And there is pollution on the front end of the process, too, because plastic is an oil-based product. You could run a million cars on the oil used to make plastic bottles and, of course, oil means air and water pollution. And here's a twist: it takes several gallons of water to produce one gallon of bottled water."

Kayla was overwhelmed. "Jeez, Elias, you make bottled water sound like the dumbest thing mankind has ever invented. There must be a reason we want so much bottled water."

"It's a classic example of manufactured demand. There are lots of labels for bottled water, all of them sounding so refreshing, cascade this and spring that, pictures of snow-capped mountains and waterfalls, but really there's just a few corporations behind all the brands. Soft drink companies worried they had saturated their markets and were looking for something new to sell. The key to making us buy water, something we get almost for free, was simple: fear. They spread doubt about the safety of tap water and over time pushed us into the buying habits you see today."

Kayla sat still, gazing into a future that no longer included the option of selling her water to Nutley. If ignorance is bliss, waking from ignorance is a harsh experience.

Elias put down the notebook and removed his glasses. "Kayla, why did you want me to look into bottled water? Is somebody offering to buy your water?"

She was taken aback. "How did you know?"

"Is it Nutley?"

"Yes it is. You're scaring me, Elias—are you psychic?"

Grace laughed so hard she snorted. "Oh, I'm sorry Kayla, I didn't mean to be unkind but, honey, Elias spent a career as a reporter. Did you think he wouldn't guess why you were curious about bottled water?"

Elias added, "I looked into that, too. Nutley is aggressively hunting for water. They're known for that so I figured it was them. They're hedging their bets and looking for more sources because the drought is reducing what they have access to, like in California where they've been shut down because of dry reservoirs and low groundwater levels. I'm sure they'd love to claim their water is from Stony Mesa springs even if only a tiny fraction is actually from Stony Mesa, or if it's a share taken out a hundred miles downstream. Do you mind my asking how much they offered you?"

Kayla shrugged. "We didn't get that far and I guess we never will. I grew up on the desert. Water is life, not a commodity. I know I should think of this in market terms alone—what is it worth and what can I get—but I couldn't live with myself if I participated in something so wasteful and dirty. My grandfathers developed those springs and broke their backs digging irrigation canals because watered land was livable land. Crops and cows. Not even for success, but just to survive. They'd roll over in their graves if their precious water ended up in a plastic bottle sitting in a vending machine in New York or Miami. I'm not sure whether I'll meet them on the other side or not, but if I sold our water like that I'm not sure I could explain it."

"Karma," Grace added.

Kayla looked perplexed. "Karma? Karma who? Oh, you mean . . . yeah, that too, whatever you choose to call it."

Elias wanted to get more of the story. "Do you have to sell? I mean are you in trouble financially?" He knew it was rude to pry but couldn't help himself.

"No, but if I ever want to live here full time I have to find a way to make the ranch pay and water rights are my best bet."

It was Grace's turn to intrude. "Any other offers? Perhaps you could find a buyer that you can live with."

Kayla smiled and shook her head no. They took dessert on the back porch and watched swallows under the barn eaves feeding their young. The adult birds dipped and darted through the evening air filled with flying insects that Kayla could not see. Their acrobatic skills were breathtaking.

"I'm jealous," said Kayla.

"Me too," said Elias. "I wish I could fly like that."

"But you'd have to eat bugs," added Grace.

"Yes," said Kayla, "but at least you would have no doubt about what to do and how it's done. You'd know your purpose. You could find your way home."

C h a p t e r   1 0

Hoppy listened to Skip Dunneman as they installed solar panels on Otis Dooley's garage roof. Hoppy was sorting loops of electrical cables and placing them next to the panels. Skip was sorting boxes of hardware to attach the cables to the panels. Skip could work and talk at the same time. Hoppy admired that because he could not track and match all the numbers in front of him while also dissecting the human condition. Skip was the most articulate person Hoppy had ever encountered.

Skip and Hoppy shared their disdain for industrialism, communism, capitalism, imperialism, racism, sexism, militarism, materialism, consumerism, and all the other isms that seemed to generate what both young men referred to as "civilization." And civilization, according to Skip, was not sustainable or redeemable. Skip had a shorthand name for the all-consuming economic order that they both detested. He called it "the culture of faster-bigger-more."

Skip explained, "The fundamental contradiction is this: they have built an all-encompassing economic engine that requires constant never-ending growth. A contraction of even a percentage point is a crisis that must be avoided. But we live in a finite natural world. There's only so much fertile soil, so much fresh water, and you can only pollute the atmosphere so much before you no longer have a friendly climate. We're learning the hard way that there are consequences for overloading the carrying capacity of the planet. And private property and money drive the system. If you are an owner you can do what you want to your property without any regard for its ecological or social cost. Capitalists look at the world around them and see property, profit, markets, and commodities, never the living land, never an ecosystem of living communities."

Hoppy ate it up. Skip was Darwin, Marx, and Mick Jagger rolled into one. Where Hoppy was content to have feelings about these things and let his intuitions guide him, Skip was taking names and making plans.

Skip had Hoppy in his trance. "They call us extremists to demonize us and dismiss our perspective. What is extreme about clean water and clean air? What is so extreme about wanting to pass a viable planet on to your kids? If you shred habitats and kill off whole species you're not an extremist, but if you stand in the way of someone who is doing that you are labeled a terrorist. Corporations tear up the planet and spew poison into our bloodstreams, foul our lungs, turn the sea acidic, make radioactive waste that will be deadly for thousands of years, and on and on and on. Extreme? Nope, normal. But try to stop the destruction and you are an extremist."

"I hear ya, Skip. It's ass backwards." Hoppy was glad Luna wasn't there to witness his enthrallment. He pumped his fist twice and yelled, "Tell it!" the way he did at the African American church he attended in Oakland when he was a child. This wasn't politics, no, this was that ol' time religion.

Skip knew he had him and wasn't about to let go. "Damn right. This nation was built on slavery and genocide. Abolitionists were the extremists back then but selling human beings was just business as usual. It wasn't genocide that killed all those Native Americans, it was Manifest Destiny. No matter how terrible their crimes, the rich and the powerful rationalize their crimes and turn the story around. Hey, they say, we're just making wood for houses and furniture, not clear-cutting forests and making species go extinct. Look at all the things that you use every day that are plastic, they say. Don't you drive a car? If we are to blame, then so are you."

Hoppy laughed. "Yeah, you're born into a world where you can't go anywhere, like go to school or shop for food without a car. You can't get a job without one. If you were bleeding in this part of the world, you can't get to the doctor without a car. You can't see friends and family, you can't function as a normal person without that car. So even though you had no say in the way the world was put together, you're complicit because you find yourself in it and can't imagine a way to live differently. You're trapped in it but it's your own damn fault."

"You got it, brother, you hit the nail on the head." Skip closed in to seal the deal. "Here's the thing. It's their narrative and we have to break it open, challenge it. We have to blow it up. Empires hide their atrocities against both humans and nature by using words like prosperity and freedom. It's time to call them on their bullshit and show them we're going to fight back."

Hoppy was sure that Skip Dunneman was sane and right. Brilliant maybe. But whenever he ended his rants with a call to arms, Hoppy retreated. He wanted to act on his beliefs, too, and he understood the compelling need for resistance, but he had Luna and now Sage to think about.

"Hoppy, can you keep a secret?"

"Sure, what?"

"No, really, I have to be able to trust you."

"You can trust me."

Skip walked close and leaned in. They stood on top of Otis's garage roof alone. Otis had left for town to attend a fundraiser for the Stony Mesa performing arts summer program, one of his favorite mayoral duties. As far as they could see from their rooftop vantage there was nobody within earshot. Two houses away, Lydia Funk's mutt was yapping at a cat. A whispered conversation from a neighborhood rooftop could not be heard over the Funk dog's bark. Skip quickly scanned the premises for eavesdroppers and leaned over to put his mouth near Hoppy's ear.

"I'm going to bomb the Syngentech offices. I don't have to tell you what pigs they are and why they need the world's attention focused on them. They're pushing a new genetically modified alfalfa. They've already modified corn, soybeans, and other crops so that they can resist Syngentech's main money-maker product, Rid-All. I'm sure you know that Rid-All is toxic and dumping tons of it on alfalfa to get rid of weeds saturates the soil and eventually gets into groundwater. From groundwater to bloodstreams is just a matter of time. Bye-bye butterflies. Clusterfuck."

Hoppy nodded hard. "Yeah, we run an organic farm so I know all about that. If the crap they spray on their GM crop blows our way we won't be considered organic for long."

Skip pushed his hat to the back of his head, sat down on the spine of the roof, and rested his arms on his knees. "They just opened a small office in Boonville and it's an easy target. A salesman and a secretary work during the day. I'll do it at night so nobody gets hurt. Then when they discover the damage I'll release a statement outlining all the damage they do and why they must be stopped."

"Skip, I don't think I want to know about this."

"I want you to help me, Hoppy, I need you to help me."

"Help how?"

Skip looked over his shoulder and back. He lowered his voice. "The new office is small but you can bet there are security cameras because the bastards know how unpopular they've become. Their offices have been bombed and burned all over the country, all over the world for that matter. I'll wear a black outfit and a balaclava that hides my face but I can't drive there and park. I need a ride and a lookout in case someone comes by in the middle of the night. It's unlikely but I can't take chances. After I set the bomb, you pick me up and we drive away. I'll set a timer on it so we have an hour to get away and that's more than enough time. That's the extent of it. It's simple. Your part is easy. I'm taking all the risks and you'll be safe."

Hoppy didn't answer. He went back to work and was quiet for the rest of the afternoon. As they cleaned up the roof top and put away tools, Skip approached him one last time.

"Well . . ."

"I'll think about it."

Dinner was over. They cleared the table and put food away. Luna nursed Sage and Hoppy did the dishes and then dumped the day's compost into a bin they had built together when they first moved to the ranch. Luna sang Sage to sleep and tucked his favorite blanket and a stuffed giraffe under his little arm. She tiptoed out of his bedroom. Hoppy sat on the porch and watched bats swoop and dive for moths that flitted about in the cool evening air as the last rays of the sun faded across the horizon.

He wore a serious face that Luna rarely saw. She tousled his hair affectionately and sat down next to him. She scooted over and bumped his hip playfully. "Whatcha workin' on in there, Mr. Hoppy?"

"I'm thinking about something Skip said this afternoon."

Luna tried hard not to cringe or say something sarcastic. Here we go again, another Skip Dunneman reprise. She worried that the load of trying to manage the farm, the market, and the solar business all at once was too much, so she was pleased that Hoppy had a coworker who could help him with the new solar business. He was dog tired when he came home at night and she missed that callow young man from just a few years before. She was glad he and Skip enjoyed each other's company, too, but Skip's influence on Hoppy was a nagging concern.

"What did Skip say?" She tried to sound more interested than wary.

"He's been talking about the need for direct action against all the forces that are pulling the world apart and destroying life. He thinks it is time to disrupt the establishment narrative."

Luna's hand crept to her heart and she pressed it between her breasts to calm herself and get grounded. She stepped lightly. "Establishment narrative? What's that?"

He tried not to sound defensive. "Well, the rationale for everything they do. It's like the matrix we are all in, like it or not. You know, assumptions and all the things we take for granted that justify the harm we do to the planet and each other."

"Oh, that." It was difficult for her to stifle sarcasm when they talked about Skip Dunneman's daily rants.

"He thinks time has run out. Civilization is collapsing and if we want to save ourselves we need to attack. Change the narrative, he says. Break it open."

She pressed her hand harder into her chest and waited to form her response. Hoppy was waiting, too. He needed to hear her take on it before he could decide whether to help Skip, an option he didn't share with Luna.

She laid her free hand on his arm and then ran her fingers up his sleeve to lightly cup his shoulder. "Hoppy, I understand the need for acts of resistance. We met out on the Sea Ledges and if I remember correctly we were both chained to the gate of a mining site with a bulldozer bearing down on us. That was civil disobedience. We did it openly and accepted the consequences. That made us credible witnesses."

Years had passed since that day and they never talked about Hoppy's sabotage of the mining site. The subject was a hole in their otherwise solid relationship, something they stepped around because they feared they might fall through that hole into a dangerous realm that could swallow their love alive. Hoppy's regret had calcified into remorse but not shame. He still argued that monkey-wrenching is not an aggressive act. It was defensive. Such hardcore acts of resistance were generated by love. His behavior was not wrong but was considered a crime because he alone had done what everyone else who loved the planet and life itself should do but were afraid to do. He could be punished for his courage.

His years as a fugitive taught him that tearing apart the social contract and violating the boundaries set by law was troubling in ways he did not anticipate. His anxiety humbled him. He even acknowledged that he and the gunman in Rope Canyon shared a fundamental breach by taking the law into their own hands. But, Hoppy argued, we cannot be compared because the intent and scale of behavior are so important. I didn't try to kill anyone and I didn't do it for mere money. Still, society viewed his actions through a lens much different than his own and if someday he faced a jury, it wouldn't be a jury of his peers.

Luna searched for words that would not make him defensive. "You know firsthand that if you don't do what you do in the light of day, then you have to sneak off in the night. Look how the damage you did at the mining site backfired on us. We began by making people aware of the dangers of tar sands mining. We confronted that non-violently. We had the moral upper ground because of our civil disobedience. After your monkey-wrenching we spent all our energy denying we were criminals and huddling with our lawyer. Damage control, remember? And how much fun have you had these past years keeping your act of destruction hidden?"

"I know, I know. It's just that I feel I'm not doing my part." He rested his head on her shoulder and put his hand on her hip.

She pulled his chin up with a finger so he was looking right at her. "Hoppy, Skip is very smart but even when I agree with him I don't trust him. I don't know why, it's just a feeling. And I don't know what Skip means about the narrative but we're telling a story, too. Skip can 'break the narrative' as you say, but we're just telling a different story altogether. That's what the Desert Rose is all about. Look at the network we're building here and all the creative energy we've enlisted."

"Making craft cheese is hardly revolutionary, Luna."

"Well if you pull that one thing out and look at it alone it doesn't seem like much, sure, but it isn't just cheese we're making. We're feeding people good food, we put friends to work. Look at the ways we are learning how to live lightly. And joyfully!"

She brushed his hair from his face and ran a thumb across his forehead. "You're gonna get a cramp in your brow if you keep that look going much longer."

He tipped his head back and smiled. "I guess I wish I could do more, is all. Lately I feel too busy and too small at the same time."

"Hoppy, it is not just what we are doing but also what we are not doing. We are not burning coal anymore. We are not eating or serving food contaminated with herbicides or meat raised in feedlots. We are not buying from big-box chain stores. We are leaving an economy that destroys life. Sure, we have a long way to go. It's a transition."

She dropped her hand from her heart and wrapped both arms around him. They swayed softly together. She put his face between her hands. "We're building a community here in Stony Mesa that will make a difference. We created a safe place for others who are telling that new story Skip is so concerned about."

She kissed him gently on the forehead and leaned back. She shrugged. "Maybe Skip is right. The old story is that the world is a machine and a market. Our story says it's a living community. And we're not just telling it, we are living it."

Hoppy brushed a stray lock away from her face. "I know, Luna. I just get frustrated. I think of the future and when I see Sage in it, I . . ."

He choked and couldn't finish. He didn't have to. She pulled him into her arms again.

"I promise you we are building a better world for him. It may not be a dramatic act that demands attention because it takes a while to make it happen, maybe a lifetime, I don't know. If Skip is right and civilization is crumbling, that makes it all the more important to make places where we can live despite that. I love you, Hoppy, and you love me. We have our baby. That's something, too."

Hoppy's overwrought brow relaxed. "You once called it an ark, Luna, and I like that. I like to think we're trying to build an ark."

"Yeah, well I think Skip Dunneman is more like a torpedo. Look Hoppy, I'm glad you and Skip have become good buds and all, but be careful. Me and Sage are depending on you. This doesn't work without you."

Hoppy finished a cup of coffee on his way out the door and squinted at the rising sun. He did not see Skip the day before because it rained and the roof was too slippery. Skip took the day off and Hoppy caught up in the greenhouse. He had hours to review his choice while pinching blossoms off of tomato plants, thinning beets, and washing spinach for the market. He washed his hands when he was done and left for the café to repair a leaking faucet in the kitchen. He was picking up his tools and wiping the floor when Luna came in with Sage on her hip. She lowered him into a baby swing, set it gently to rocking, and then tended to customers as they walked in. She didn't know Hoppy was there and moved unselfconsciously from the reception desk to tables.

He watched how people watched her, the way her smile and bright demeanor captured their attention, charmed them. And that sexy ass of hers. I'm one lucky guy, he told himself and for a moment he thought he might cry. He pulled himself together. A shift was happening that felt hormonal. Maybe he needed more sleep. He watched Luna and Sage and understood how much he had at stake. He ached when he considered the world Sage might grow up to inherit. He ached at the thought of ever being separated from the two people he loved most in life.

He slept fitfully that night and Luna moved to the couch. Hoppy was so busy wrestling the sheets and jerking his limbs spasmodically that he didn't notice her leave. She climbed back into bed when his convulsions subsided. He started muttering again so she spooned him from behind and laid her hand across his heart to still him.

Hoppy woke early. He rolled out of bed softly so as not to wake Luna, and crept out to the kitchen to put on a pot of coffee. Their dog Juniper showed him how pleased she was to see him up so early by thumping her tail where she lay. He stroked her ears and asked her quietly to not thump so loudly. They walked together out the back door and stood in the yard and looked up. Dawn was clear with vibrant oranges, reds, and pinks, a kaleidoscope of colors as solar rays played along the surface of clouds and the contours of the earth itself. The sun broke the horizon and they turned away because it was too bright for their bare eyes to bear.

He straightened up and squared his shoulders, his chin up, neck stiff. Attention! This is a message from the universe! He waited for the signal. Here it comes. The dawn is a beginning. I am beginning my new life. I am proclaiming where I stand. He struck a superman pose with his hands on his hips and his chest expanded to heroic proportions. Juniper nudged his leg and he broke his pose. An hour later Hoppy was out the door.

Skip arrived at the Dooley place to finish the job and saw Hoppy waiting in his truck. His posture indicated that he was resolved. Skip parked and the two men crossed the yard and greeted each other. They unloaded tools and spools of wire for the next set of panels. Hoppy waited for Skip to bring it up. It didn't take long.

"So, my brother," Skip said good-naturedly, "are you in or out?"

"Out. Sorry, but definitely out." He wanted to say he had been there and done that but caught himself and said nothing. A long silence ensued. Skip looked more than disappointed, he looked scared.

"Look Skip, it's like this. To devote myself to the kinds of revolutionary acts you want to do is too much for me. To do it that way you have to be all in. I have a wife, a baby, and three businesses to take care of all at the same time and I can't put any of that at risk."

Skip managed a smile. "Sure. Hoppy, I understand."

A part of him wanted Hoppy to say no and was relieved. Why is that he asked? He had little time to analyze his conflicted reaction because his anxiety spiked hard. Hoppy's refusal to take part in the bombing of the Syngentech office meant that Skip's meeting in the city next week would not go well. He tried to put that out of his mind but it kept creeping back. His heart raced each time he imagined how the upcoming meeting might unfold.

"Hoppy, could you see yourself doing it, I mean monkey-wrenching, if you were not so tied down? Is it that you don't think it's the right thing to do?"

It was a dangerous moment. Hoppy was tempted to tell about his own sabotage of the Sea Ledges mining site. That would make him a credible comrade-in-arms. He hesitated then resisted the urge to tell.

"We could debate that, Skip, and I'm not certain where I'd come out on that. Doesn't matter because I never got that far. Everyone's got a role to play, ya know, lots of niches and all that. I'm a husband, a daddy, and the guy who tends the garden and sticks these panels to this roof. Right or wrong, monkey-wrenching is not an option for me. Sorry to disappoint you."

"No! No, I understand. It's okay." But it wasn't okay. Skip couldn't bomb Syngentech alone. He needed Hoppy as his partner. He thought again about the meeting in the city, about how his contact there would receive the news.

Just before lunch Hoppy noticed how Skip's hand trembled when he held the drill. "Are you okay?" he asked Skip. "Want me to do that?"

"No, it's okay, I'm fine." A lie. Hoppy could tell.

Skip went home for lunch. He parked his truck in front of the feed store and went in to replace a pair of gloves that had worn through. He made his purchase and left the store. On his way back to his truck he saw a strange creature walking his way. It was a slender old woman with an incongruous costume. Her hair was piled atop her head in a nest of braids that featured a centerpiece of wax fruit that wobbled precariously. She wore a faded and moth-bitten tuxedo shirt and jacket. Her ensemble was completed by a pleated lace skirt that fell to the top of leather hiking boots.

He'd seen her walking around town in different outlandish costumes but only from a distance. They called her Crazy Kitty. Her appearance was so amusing that he momentarily forgot his worries. He could use some comic relief in his life. The only other person in the county who thought hiking boots and a prom dress were complementary was Luna Waxwing. He suppressed his smile as Crazy Kitty approached.

He meant to avoid eye contact and pass quickly but she stepped into his path and he almost bumped into her. "I know who you are!" Her eyes were feral and she pointed a crooked finger in his face. "You're a fake! A liar! Traitor!"

This wasn't so much fun after all. She saw his discomfort and flashed a chilling rictus grin. It lasted only a moment but the image stayed with him. This was turning out to be creepy. He struggled to stay calm and step around her. "Really, I'm all that? And who are you, the king and queen of the ball all rolled into one with your tuxedo top and formal gown?"

She ignored his words and captured his eyes with a piercing stare. "I see right through you, boy!" She flashed fierce eyes and spoke in a hissing whisper. "You came into this town as a liar and now you will leave as a traitor. You may fool the others but I see through you."

He noticed a dark blue bag slung across her shoulder and the small head protruding from the opening. It was either a little dog that looked like a man, all jowls and furrowed brow, or a little man that looked uncannily like a wet-eyed dog. Whatever it was, he stared at it and half expected it to speak. Instead the little beast made a gurgling snarl and raised the far corner of its lip enough to expose a single yellow fang.

Skip turned and retreated quickly, slammed the door, gunned the truck out of the parking lot, and drove straight to his cabin. He lay down on the couch and closed his eyes. After a few minutes he texted Hoppy: "I'm not feeling well. See you tomorrow."

He could not sleep. He kept rolling it over and over in his mind, practicing different ways to say it, dreading that meeting.

Chapter 11

On the first Monday of most months, Hoppy and Luna opened the Desert Rose Café for a community potluck dinner. Monday was the one day of the week when the residents of Stony Mesa might be free from the demands of tourists and guests who usually left town on Sunday afternoons. Some businesses were closed on Monday since weekends were long and busy and owners and employees alike needed a break. The dinner was free and open, just bring a dish and your own drinks. Luna believed that people listen better and are more tolerant of others' opinions when they are feeding one another and experiencing pleasure together. The Monday night gatherings were what she called "gastronomical community building."

If you were new in town, the Monday-night dinners were a great place to meet your neighbors and make friends. People who were too busy during the tourist season to keep up on all their friendships valued the get-togethers because they were a chance to see many friends at once and catch up on what was happening in each other's lives. People who played musical instruments were welcome to bring them and play. The hallway was crowded with cases for guitars, mandolins, flutes, violins, and banjoes.

Elias Buchman warned Luna that she should be careful to present it as an informal event that was sponsored privately because otherwise there would be issues with licenses and food handling rules. Training would be required, there were alcohol restrictions, and so on. So instead of referring to the Desert Rose Café , Hoppy and Luna considered using their last names and calling it the Ziller-Waxwing dinner. But Ziller-Waxwing sounded too much like a bird, and dinner in that case might be a fresh caterpillar. After much discussion they decided to call it nothing and let people come and go as they pleased if and when they found out about it. Luna guessed that social media would take care of the publicity for the monthly dinner by itself. They just opened their doors and called it good.

Because members of the One True Church were welcome, the so-called move-in residents of Stony Mesa were discreet about their use of cannabis if not wine and beer. Although the elders of the Church did not attend social functions where alcohol was present or any function that did not begin and end in prayer, many of the church's less adherent members did attend from time to time. They seemed to treasure the opportunity to enjoy themselves without judgmental glances from church patriarchs who hovered over the congregation like shepherds guarding errant sheep.

Even Crazy Kitty enjoyed the monthly dinners and she behaved well enough until someone or something set her off. She scolded those around her for being Chinese puppets and putting fluoride in dog food. You wait and see, she told them, one day you'll all be wearing costumes and performing for rich foreigners who want to see the Old West re-enacted. Kitty herself was wearing fly-fishing waders with red suspenders over an ornate ruffled blouse, which sounds incongruous but somehow worked. Her hair was braided in loops that concluded in a twist atop her head, held in place by a small stuffed monkey. The best thing about Kitty was her wardrobe and most of her fellow citizens in Stony Mesa tolerated her outbursts so the sartorial show could continue.

Luna distracted Kitty from her sudden tirade by asking if she would be willing to give a workshop on accessorizing at the Desert Rose. Kitty looked Luna up and down and noted that Luna was wearing a ballet skirt over cotton hiking shorts and leggings. Kitty decided she was in the presence of a kindred spirit, a comrade of the cloth, and she immediately became calm, even smiled. Luna took her by the hand and walked her to her car. Kitty left peacefully and Luna was admired by one and all for her crazy-lady acumen.

Entertainment in Stony Mesa was a local affair. The town had no theater, arcade, concert hall, golf course, or country club, no venue for entertainment but one saloon and a handful of restaurants. During the tourist season residents flocked to the weekly programs at the Moenkopi Institute, where you could hear a lecture on bat echolocation one week and enjoy a violin recital the next. During the winter, the most exciting thing happening was the blood drive. Sports events were held twenty miles away in Boonville, a larger town where Stony Mesa's kids were bussed to school. Stony Mesa's library was a bookmobile that visited for two hours every other week.

There was satellite TV and the Internet to while away the leisurely hours that were few and far between for Stony Mesa's workers who held down part-time and seasonal jobs to make ends meet. The retirees had the most leisure time, but they were an odd bunch given to obsessive hiking and reading. Of course, residents could text and tweet, post, blog, snap, chat, and e-mail like billions of other humans across the planet. They had a billion cat videos at their fingertips and recorded their lives in minute detail on their Facebook pages. But for live entertainment, they had each other.

Dinner parties were common among the retirees, while younger people gravitated to the local bands that played on weekends at the Desert Rose. Open-mic night was not an opportunity for abundant talent to show itself as it is in the city, but was an expression of limited availability and modest budgets. It was cheap and easy but the audience frequently remarked on the amazing talents of the few musicians who lived among them in Stony Mesa and how generous those musicians were to play so often. Young and old alike looked forward to the community potlucks at Luna and Hoppy's place.

Luna nursed Sage at dawn and then laid him down in his crib, milk-drunk and sleepy. She wanted Olene to post a reminder on her Facebook page about the upcoming potluck. Dixon Kingsley, a local boy who was a banjo wizard, was in town visiting his mom and dad and he agreed to be this month's featured performer. It was too early to make phone calls but she knew Olene was always up at first light. Sunrise, she told Luna, was her favorite moment of the day. She stretched, meditated, and prayed in the sweet morning light before making herself a hot cup of tea and cruising the Internet on her laptop.

The phone rang twice and a familiar voice answered but it was not Olene. Luna was puzzled and glanced down at the screen on her phone to see if she had accidentally poked the wrong number.

"Mom?"

"Yes, Luna?"

"Are you at Olene's?"

She hesitated. "Why yes, I am."

"What are you doing there? It's seven in the morning."

A longer pause. "Well, dear, I spent the night."

Luna was baffled and then shocked. "Are you and Olene . . ." She couldn't finish.

"Yes, we are. Let's talk about this later, okay?"

Virginia Waxwing dressed herself, kissed Olene goodbye, and drove directly to her daughter's house. Sage was waking as she arrived and she picked him up and helped Luna change his diaper and set him in a highchair by the kitchen table. They sat on either side of him and faced each other squarely.

Luna got right to it. She could never tell when Sage would get cranky for the nipple or start to coo seductively so she wanted to talk to her mom while Sage was content to chew quietly on his teething ring or slap himself in the forehead with it. "So you and Olene are . . ."

"Yes."

Incredulously, "You're lesbians?"

"I guess so. I mean I don't guess, I know. Yes."

Luna prided herself on her open-mindedness and liberal leanings. She had gay friends and attended the commitment ceremony for a favorite professor back when marriage was still not an option for gay couples. She was compassionately aware and politically correct to a fault. But her own mother?

"How could I not know this? Am I blind?"

"Well I didn't know myself until recently." Virginia poured two cups of tea, picked Sage's teething ring off the floor for the third time, and put her hand on her daughter's hand. "Let's both breathe first. Okay. There. That's better."

She began. "When I was growing up I didn't know such feelings could exist. Yes, there were homosexuals but that was an aberration and a sin. They say it all changed in the sixties but not where I grew up.

Gay people stayed in the closet or if they came out they were punished. You could lose a job, friends, business, family. In some places it was physically dangerous. You could get beat up. So when I felt attraction to girls, I thought it must be a hunger for friendship because I couldn't be one of those bad people. As for boys, I liked them but it was more admiration and friendship than sexual attraction."

"Admiration?" Luna was light-headed and not tracking well.

"Well, you know, they seemed so free compared to girls. We had more rules, more boundaries. Girls had to worry more about their reputations. Boys didn't have all those obstacles."

"What about my father, did you like him?"

"Mmmm, not really. He was supposed to be a great catch because the family had money and Bo was very smart and ambitious. He had success written all over him. I may have been incredibly naïve about sex but I made up for it in fertility. I got pregnant the first time. So we married because that was what you did then. But sex was never satisfying with him and it wasn't long before we weren't having any. I thought it was unpleasant because he was selfish and didn't care if he met my needs. After the divorce I dated some and tried it again. Do you remember Arthur?"

"Oh my god, Mom, you fucked Arthur? That skinny dude with the pencil moustache?"

"Well, that's rather indelicate, honey, but yes. Or I should say Arthur fucked me. It was awkward and I thought, well, it's always awkward the first time."

"Not for me and Hoppy it wasn't."

"No, I imagine you two had no hesitation. You're both voracious about all aspects of life. Anyway, after Arthur I gave up. I was already so busy working and raising you. Celibacy was easier."

Luna tried to imagine giving up sex and failed, but she took her mother at her word. "So when did you find out or when did you know for sure, or . . . ?"

"In Italy. There are so many beautiful women there. You walk down the street and it seems every other woman you pass is a model.

I couldn't take my eyes off them. There are handsome men, too, but I realized I wasn't turned on by them. It was the women. So I went to a gay bar and met Elena. We went back to her apartment and it was a revelation. Like a missing piece of a puzzle finally fit into place and I felt whole for the first time. Sex finally made sense and was necessary and good."

A piece of Luna's puzzle was missing. "And Olene?"

"Oh, honey, Olene is wonderful. You know that."

"I didn't realize Olene was a lesbian. Did Olene know before you two . . ."

Virginia laughed. "Olene has known all her life and there was no doubt or confusion for her. She's just discreet because she's a very private person."

Luna struggled to make sense of what she was hearing. "Why would Olene move to Stony Mesa? Seems like an unlikely place to meet other lesbians."

Virginia laughed again. "Luna, there are lesbians everywhere, even in little Stony Mesa. Now you're the one who is naïve."

She got up and put her arms around her daughter and kissed her head. Luna rose from her seat and turned to her mom. They stood in the kitchen with their arms wrapped around each other until Sage choked himself on his teething ring and gagged. He pulled the ring out of his mouth and gave it baleful stare, then spit up a small pool of undigested milk, which he proceeded to slap gleefully. They picked him up and cleaned him off. Virginia left to drive Olene to her dentist appointment and Luna was left to wonder how she could be so blind for so many years. Maybe she held on to her childhood ideas of who her mother was for too long. Those notions were never altered by new encounters because they did not see each other for years. They didn't evolve. They were an artifact constructed by her younger self. She thought about how her mother also had to see her daughter in a new light because Luna, Liz then, was just heading for college when Virginia left to travel the world. When Virginia returned, Luna was a wife and mother.

All day long Luna's mind was preoccupied with the news about Olene and her mom. She considered the changes she had lived in the few years since that day she and Hoppy met in the Boon County jail. She thought of their farm, the café, and baby Sage. About how her mom returned to her when Sage was born. About all their new friends. What was it about Stony Mesa? Where do we go next, now that we are staying right here? How do we make a life?

They were all there together. Dixon played his banjo while the good citizens of Stony Mesa milled, chatted, laughed, exclaimed, ate, drank, bounced squealing babies on knees, and admonished older children to be careful where they chased each other. A social cacophony swelled around them as forks clicked on plates, chairs scraped in and out from tables, a kid squealed, babies cried, someone sneezed, and several people laughed together. Voices mixed in a shuffle of half-heard words and fragments of conversations that emerged from the background and then receded when overtaken by a fresh set of stray sentences.

Dishes were passed and aromas savored. There was a choice, as always. One table held vegetarian and gluten-free dishes and the other table was a mix of all the usual potluck suspects like coleslaw, baked beans, deviled eggs, chili, and potato salads. Different varieties of each crowded the table top. Stony Mesa natives gingerly approached tofu and vegetable dishes they had never tried and were astonished to find so much kale on one table. The natives brought salads topped with marshmallows and casseroles made with bacon that the community's vegetarian members secretly lusted after and consumed while excusing their indulgence with rationales about the need to be neighborly and open minded.

Social entertainment in Stony Mesa crossed the socio-economic boundaries observed in cities where there are so many people to choose from that a person could socialize exclusively with others who share a similar class background, work, interests, and so on. But in little Stony Mesa, plumbers mixed with lawyers, retired teachers befriended ex-cops, and doctors invited carpenters over for dinner. One of Olene's best friends in town had only a sixth grade education.

Retirees shed old identities and reinvented themselves as artists, writers, horse breeders, garlic farmers, and guitar collectors. Unbound by the requirements and expectations of former professions and businesses, they became the people they always wanted to be. A middle-aged man wearing a leather vest and a full sleeve of brightly colored tattoos might be a retired broker who is now the president of Bikers for Buddha. A woman with pink hair and a nose ring might have been a NASA engineer. The muleskinner might speak four languages and a masseuse might have a doctorate in French literature.

The old-timers in town found the malleable identities of the move-ins suspicious. Those born and raised in Stony Mesa who worked the jobs their parents and grandparents worked, who had never lived anywhere else, were thoroughly imprinted with family history by the time they started school. They either envied or pitied the newcomers' freedom to invent themselves anew. Wherever Grace and Elias traveled, strangers asked, "Where are you from?" In Stony Mesa the first question was, "Who are your people?" It was not uncommon to get a genealogical synopsis when first introduced to an old-timer. "Hello," he might say, "I'm Vernon Tate but I'm a Taylor on my mother's side and Clarke on both sides." And then he might add, "The Clarkes who spell it with an e," so there was no mistake. Tonight a handful of natives were on hand who seemed to enjoy interacting with neighbors who cared less about kin and clan and just took them as they were.

Grace took Sage from Luna, who was busy greeting people as they arrived, lighting up everyone she encountered with a radiant smile and laughter. Grace carried Sage around the room, showed him the horsey photo, and let him feel a jade plant on a sill. He fixated on the fan for a minute and gurgled and cooed but lost interest when it didn't respond. Grace wiped bubbles from his lips and softly swayed as she made their way around the room, stopping every few feet so someone else could say hi and kiss his little toes, make funny faces, or play a quick session of peek-a-boo. Sage was an easygoing baby who smiled at strangers and giggled on cue.

She sampled the activity around them as they strolled the periphery of the crowded room. Hoppy was picking Don Mossman's brain about how to split a beehive that had grown too large. It was an unusual challenge, as the norm was die-off rather than growth. Hoppy had never made a queen and put her in a new hive. Don was eighty-three and still kept enough bees to keep his extended family in honey with enough left over to sell at the farmer's market. Hoppy often sought advice from the town's old-timers who had a skill set and a knowledge base that was not getting passed on to younger generations. They knew how to make the world work without the aid and intervention of computers or the Internet. They had acquired knowledge slowly and first-hand, before YouTube was available. He called them the pre-digitals.

Kayla took Ramone Marquez by the arm and introduced him to everyone they met. Grace had never seen Kayla so happy and brimming with energy. Skip Dunneman was doing his best to please Luna, not flirting so much as trying to get on her good side, and Luna was doing her best to politely ignore him. "I wonder what that's all about," said Grace to Sage, who squealed and pulled her nose in response.

She completed her circuit of the dining room and saw that Luna was now entirely focused on Lucas Hozho, who had dropped in on his way home to the reservation to see his grandmother. Lucas worked as a counselor in a rehab program for homeless indigenous kids in the city. He drove back to the reservation as often as possible and usually stopped in Stony Mesa to see Hoppy and Luna and baby Sage. The Desert Rose was a favorite way station and there was always room in the old bunkhouse Luna restored. Lucas had lost weight and Grace wondered if his eating habits were healthier or if his weight-loss was a sign of stress.

She walked over to Olene and stood beside her to discreetly listen in on a conversation she was having with Elias. She heard Olene say, "A community isn't a thing like a body or even a set of bodies, it's more like a process, maybe an awkward dance of mutuality or an exchange of essential gestures between people who have decided to trust each other to define each other."

Elias looked at her and nodded, not sure how to follow up on that. Olene's statements fascinated him but he needed time to think them over. Grace suppressed a smile as she thought back to how worried Elias was about whether there would be an intellectual life available to them when they moved to Stony Mesa. "Be careful of what you wish for," she whispered to Sage, who thought that was funny and tried to grab Grace's earring.

"Olene, please pass the salt. And tell me what you put in these delicious deviled eggs." Otis Dooley was a leveling presence and habitually grounded those around him. This habit was honed as mayor while dealing with Crazy Kitty, who complained that Sheriff Taylor was actually a reptile hiding in human form, or when convincing Dex and Chantelle Russell, leaders of the local Constitutional Party, that if property taxes were abolished the town's water system could not be maintained by volunteers. Otis could go on for hours about the physics of nebulae and black holes, but otherwise he was as grounded as the toilets he affixed to floors during his work day.

Virginia Waxwing circulated among the gathered. She was quiet and unassuming. Grace stopped to talk. "Look Sage, it's Grandma!"

Sage bounced up and down in Grace's arms and made a gleeful yelp, excited to see Virginia, who laughed at his enthusiastic response. "Well Virginia, it doesn't get any better than that, does it?"

"No, Grace, it doesn't. My cup runneth over."

Grace completed her circuit and returned Sage to his mother. A group of teenagers stood together shoulder to shoulder while staring at phones in front of them and not conversing. Their thumbs flew as if texting was as natural as chewing gum while walking. Oldsters like Grace tended to stop while texting, their heads bowed, backs bent, brows furrowed as if they were studying the Talmud. The thumbs of the young are fleet. Grace's thumbs were slightly arthritic.

I wonder what is happening to us? she thought. There are so many forces pulling us away from one another. Americans pick up and move for work or to go to college far from our families and we never settle down for long before we move again. Life becomes a succession of strangers separated from one another, housed in boxes, isolated from so many of the communal aspects of living that were primal and necessary for most of our human history. We are disconnected from the earth and each other. Maybe this is how young people compensate for the feeling of community we've lost. They network across the web and form online communities there. From tribe to vibe, Kayla called it.

But tonight she felt deeply connected—so much so that she was moved to tears that she wiped away quickly before she was caught and had to explain what was too hard to describe. Olene is right, she thought, we will trust one another to define who we are, where we belong, and what matters most.

She was glad they moved to Stony Mesa. It felt right, like they belonged there. Sure, she thought, we are recent arrivals. What is Kayla? Third, fourth generation? Not that long really. Even Lucas's Navajo family migrated only a few hundred years before. Not long compared to a rock or a river. There are trees older than that on the far slope of the mountain above town. Most of us here tonight migrated here. We did not come here to seek treasures or to stake a claim to gold or ground. Those days are over. All we can claim now is each other.

Chapter 12

Dang it! Kayla heard the crunch of gravel as the pickup truck drove up and parked in front of the house just as she promised herself she had a rare hour free to kick back and relax. She walked from the kitchen to the living room and pulled back the flowered curtain she had helped her grandmother sew many years ago. She pictured the scene clearly in her mind. Her grandmother leaned over her at the sewing machine. She was generous and patient. Kayla was a child, then, escaping turmoil and sheltering with her grandparents. Her grandmother taught her to sew, her grandfather taught her to ride. They trusted her in a way her parents never did. They treated her as capable and worthy of their trust.

For a fleeting second she thought that Ramone was paying a surprise visit and her heart skipped a proverbial beat. No such luck. She peered out the window and saw a gray pickup truck, immaculate, double cab, diesel. Reverend LaVon Pettybone was paying her a visit. He stepped out of his truck carefully and was followed by two more sets of arthritic knees, bad backs, and grinding hip sockets. The elders of the One True Church tended to be old indeed. They delivered wisdom and doctrine through a haze of pharmaceuticals designed to keep them upright because they suffered high blood pressure, limp dicks, swollen prostates, weak bladders, indigestion, cataracts, skin cancers, toenail fungus, and dementia.

Kayla ran to the mirror in the hallway and straightened her blouse and hair. There wasn't much she could do about the mud-smeared jeans with a torn pocket she had changed into earlier when she went outside to do the day's chores. Why is he here? Why now in the middle of the afternoon?

He knocked and she opened the door. Two other men were standing behind him. She recognized DeeRay Oldroyd and Lester Woodey, both elders in the One True Church. Her anxiety increased exponentially and she no longer felt like the adult veterinarian she had become but the little girl holding her grandfather's hand and walking into Sunday service. She swallowed hard and summoned a welcoming smile.

"Reverend Pettybone, what a pleasant surprise! Elder Woodey, Elder Oldroyd, come in."

They smiled in that condescending way important men smile when encountering the less enlightened subjects of their interest. Kayla was not sure what to do next. The reverend and his top assistants usually visited church members on Sundays after service or in the evening. On such occasions they wore crisp dark suits and carried Bibles with gold leaf lettering on the covers. Today they wore jeans and white shirts with string ties. Reverend Pettybone's tie was fastened with a nugget of polished turquoise large enough to choke a pony.

She invited them to sit and hurriedly cleared the couch of magazines and a sweater she had left there from the night before. "Can I get you something to drink?"

"No, that won't be necessary, Sister Burnside." They smiled and glanced sideways at one another. Elder Woodey studied the room carefully as if he were an inspector looking for flaws. She noticed that DeeRay Oldroyd was holding a slim valise that he placed on his lap as he sat. She hoped it was not an account book of tithings, because she hadn't contributed since she took over the ranch.

"I know how busy you are, sister, so I'll get right to the point." The reverend didn't care much for small talk and because of his authority in the One True Church he didn't feel he had to indulge in the usual pleasantries offered when one visits unexpectedly. His unannounced intrusion was his right as her pastor.

"Sister Burnside . . . uh, Kayla, that is, we've come to discuss some business that is important to both the church and our community here in Stony Mesa." He had known Kayla since she was a child and he served in churchly offices with her grandfather. He imagined he was a fatherly figure to her and his demeanor dripped of paternalistic condescension. It was as if she had never changed, never gone away to college and then veterinarian school. She struggled not to revisit the feelings of inadequacy that were common among the women members of the Church when confronted by a sanctioned patriarch. The other two men folded their hands across their laps and nodded approvingly as the reverend spoke.

"I understand that the Nutley Corporation has made you an offer on your grandfather's water rights. Have you given them an answer?"

"Why no, I haven't." She was surprised they knew about the offer. Stony Mesa was a small pond and news rippled across its confined surface quickly.

"Good. We are here to make a counter offer on behalf of the community. The Church, that is."

"You want to buy my water?" The offer was as odd as it was unexpected. The church was not in the practice of buying water, or at least she was not aware that it was.

"Yes." Reverend Pettybone had rehearsed his pitch and was ready. "As you are well aware, Kayla, the drought is getting worse. Several ranches in the valley have gone dry. Wells, too, are drying up. It's a dire situation. Cattle require more water than is presently available and alfalfa is water intensive as you know. Since you have sold your cattle and are not growing alfalfa, you obviously have more water than you need. Your horses have more than enough. Last week your horse pasture was flooded with water."

She chewed on her lip and looked down. "I know, it was a mistake. I didn't shut the irrigation gate when I should have because I was late getting back from the university."

"Well whatever the reason was, it is a shame to waste precious water when so many others are in need. The very livelihoods of some members of the congregation are at stake. They need that water. We are here on their behalf. Surely, you understand the situation and as a member of the Church in good standing . . ."

"Oh, I see. But I'm sure there's a way to share what I have until the drought breaks. You don't have to buy my water, I am willing to share."

The three men looked at each other knowingly and hid their amusement. The reverend enlightened her. "It doesn't work that way. Water law and rights are very complicated. Ranchers who are members of the church need more than charity. They need the assurance that the water will be there from year to year. We have offered to make that happen if you will help us do that."

Elder Oldroyd opened the valise and pulled out a sheaf of papers. "We have spent several hours with our attorneys on this. As you know, your great-grandfather Jango Burnside developed the water in the springs that feed into the river. He had the original rights to that water and passed that down the line to his heirs. It's a complicated transaction but you can sign those rights over to the Church and keep enough to take care of your own needs."

"More than enough," added Elder Woodey. "And of course we will pay generously for the excess." He smiled magnanimously and the other two men smiled at him and nodded. Look, their faces said, we are one big happy family here.

Reverend Pettybone pressed hard now. "Kayla, the One True Church embraced you as a child. We welcomed you into our homes and hearts. We took care of you—why, I think it is fair to say you were raised in the Church. Your character, your principles, your values. We're a part of you and you are part of us."

Kayla wished she could run from the room, get on her fastest horse, and ride into the sunset. Guilt added to feelings of inferiority is a powerful mix. "And I am thankful for the church's role in my upbringing. I have so many fond memories."

"Memories? Kayla, it sounds like the church is in your past. I sincerely hope that is not so. We love you today as we loved you then."

She waved her hands and her face flushed red. "No, no, I didn't mean it that way."

"Good, I'm glad to hear that." The good reverend smiled again and eased back into his soothing fatherly mode. He talked as slowly as he would to a child. His voice had a mellifluous tone.

She listened closely and nodded and smiled on cue, a good little girl again. But when the sheaf of papers was handed to her with a pen to sign where indicated, she balked.

"I can't do this now because I need time to think."

The elders looked at each other and their disappointment was plain. The reverend spoke. "Take your time, Sister Burnside, take your time. We can leave these documents here for you to study. Please remember that uncertainty is the enemy of ranchers like your neighbors. Like your grandfather. Unless they have a good idea of how much water is available, they can't plan. Knowing how much water you can count on comes first."

She couldn't make eye contact and mumbled. "I may want to have these reviewed by a lawyer."

All three men began to jerk and twitch in their seats like bugs were crawling up their pant legs. The reverend recovered first. "That's a good idea, Kayla. I can give you the contact information of our Church lawyers and they will be glad to go over it line by line if that makes you feel better."

She was on a precipice now. She smiled but it came out crooked and her eyes squinted spasmodically like when she bit into a lemon. She couldn't come right out and say she wanted her own lawyer because she didn't trust theirs. Or could she?

"Is that the way it's done? I mean what if there's something I want to change? Something minor," she added hastily to reassure them.

Frowns of grave concern were now added to looks of disappointment. She felt smaller and glanced down from the chair where she was sitting to see if her feet still reached the floor. She remembered that scene in *Alice in Wonderland* where Alice shrinks down. She hated that feeling. She could no longer afford that feeling. A little voice inside her whispered twice and then yelled into her brain, THIS IS BULLSHIT!

She pulled herself upright and straightened her spine. She lifted her chin and felt a spark of courage ignite. Throughout her life in the One True Church she smiled politely, swallowed hard, and kept her mouth shut. She was a good girl then but now she was a woman. A smart woman. Where, she asked herself, did that capable and articulate woman go when the reverend and his assistants walked through the door?

"Reverend Pettybone, you're so smart about these matters and I have no experience in them. But may I ask, if you were in my seat would you sign without question? Do you conduct your business that way? No review, no objections, no negotiation?"

Pettybone surveyed her from the end of his nose, a judge studying a miscreant. He smiled or smirked, it was hard to tell which one. "No, I am not troubled by doubts or questions because I conduct my business exclusively with members of the Church. I trust the Church implicitly to serve its members. I know my fellow church members are honest because our church teaches that."

That spark of courage was building into a bonfire fed by a lifetime of combustible suppression. "But you sign contracts with members of the Church, too, don't you? Do you trust all of the members implicitly, too? This contract to buy my water isn't found in the Bible. It's an agreement between men and a woman. It's in the fallible realm of human activity—worse, human economic activity. I love the Church and I'm inclined to honor its requests but I also believe God gave me a brain and I want to honor that gift, too."

Elder Oldroyd was stuck on the term "fallible realm," which he repeated over and over silently. Elder Woodey was not fond of the guttural term "God," which seemed vulgar. Church members by habit said Heavenly Father or Our Savior or at least Our Lord. Those terms were more melodious and grand. The word God was a shortcut often used by non-believers who didn't claim any master or personal savior, or it was used by those who doubted divine paternity altogether. One way or the other, it was not a good sign. He looked to the reverend for a signal. Reverend Pettybone decided to beat a hasty retreat. He thanked Kayla for her time, rose, and made for the door. He turned to her before he left.

"I want to add a final word here. The Nutley Corporation is faceless and far away. I doubt you know even a single shareholder. But your neighbors . . ." He didn't need to finish. He nodded cordially and left, the elders following close on his heels.

Kayla returned to the city. She took the contract offered her by the One True Church to a friend she knew from college who had become an attorney for a large corporation. He took the papers and said he would get back to her. Two days later he called her in the evening at her apartment.

"What do you think?" she asked him.

"It's a fairly standard agreement to sell water but the price is way off and you don't even get to control the water they left you. If you want to sell the ranch's water rights you can do much better."

Her heart jumped. She was so hoping he would tell her it was a killer deal and ask her why these folks were being so generous. Instead, here was another hurdle. How do I turn them down or ask for more? I will need to make a case. She asked her lawyer friend, "Okay then, if you had one word to describe this contract what would it be?"

He thought for a long moment before replying. "In a word?"

"Yes."

"Bullshit."

Chapter 13

The city was a three-hour drive from Stony Mesa. Skip Dunneman tried to distract himself with music and then with talk radio. It was no use. He was more than nervous about how his contact would react when he learned that Skip had failed to enlist Hoppy in the bombing of the Syngentech office. A month had passed since his last trip to see his contact and as he drove over the twisted two-lane road through the mountains he realized how the time he spent in Stony Mesa had rewired him. He was accustomed to quiet now and he liked the clean air and sweet water. He liked that there was enough space to feel solitude. The road he was on would descend from the mountains to the interstate and from then on there would be more and more traffic through the endless congested burbs that had metastasized around the city. Noise and bad air thickened as he drove closer.

He was baffled so many people were still driving despite the dire effect of cars on the air and in turn their bloodstreams, lungs, and brains, to say nothing about the weather that had turned sullen and mean. But then here he was in a car, too, trapped like all the others in a man-made world where nobody can stay in place for long. Closer to the city, the burbs were turning back into farms, or at least something like that. Lawns were mostly replaced by gardens big and small, private and communal, some cooperative and some for profit alone. Vacant lots were appropriated by people with rakes and hoes who lived in condos and had no yards of their own. Greenhouses crowded together where parking lots once ruled. Global trade was so disrupted by serial resource wars, failed states, terrorism, corruption, drought, floods, refugee crises, monster storms, super bugs, pandemics, rising seas, and on and on and on, that people planted gardens to back up their uncertain food chain. A funky green patchwork of micro-farms blossomed across the burbs. Solar panels were ubiquitous, too.

He remembered something that hot veterinarian, Kayla, said. He was at an open-mic night at the Desert Rose and she was talking to her friends at the table next to his. The topic was change and how it was happening. One of them said something about how the world was changing in profound ways but not dramatically. The changes sneak up on you, he said. The young veterinarian listened mostly but then she offered her summary. Creeps, not leaps, she said, and everybody laughed. He envied the way they could talk and laugh easily. Unlike him, their behavior was not calculated or dangerous.

He parked a block away from where they agreed they would be safe, a small restaurant downtown, and he walked. He hastened his pace so that he would be punctual. He arrived on time but his contact was not there. It was not like him to be late and another flood of anxiety rushed through Skip Dunneman's nervous system. He took a booth and waited. The waitress asked if he wanted coffee and he asked for water instead because he couldn't imagine pouring acidic coffee into an already upset stomach. Long minutes later, Kent Medal walked into the restaurant and approached the booth. Skip was unsure of how to greet him. Medal didn't smile or offer his hand. He slid into his seat and tucked a leather valise onto his lap.

"Let's make this quick. I don't want to take any chances on being seen with you. What have you got?"

Although he had rehearsed in his mind a hundred times, Skip forgot his lines and twitched helplessly while Kent Medal stared at him and fingered a salt shaker like it was a voodoo doll of Skip Dunneman that he was choking. Skip looked down and worried that his vocal paralysis was caused by the suffocating grip Kent Medal had on that little glass bottle.

Medal slapped the table. "Fuck! You got nothing! I knew it!"

Skip stammered something about needing a little more time but Medal cut him off.

"Bullshit! You've had all summer, asshole!"

Skip pleaded. "I tried to get him to talk. I even told him I thought whoever monkey-wrenched the Sea Ledges site was a hero but he didn't own up. Maybe you're wrong and he didn't do it."

"Oh bullshit, Dunneman! Jay Paul Ziller, Hip Hop Hopi, Hoppy, Happy, Hippie, whatever name that punk goes by now is the one who did it and he needs to be put away where the rest of us can't be hurt by him. And how about the bombing? You failed that, too?"

Skip again pleaded for more time and this time he was saved by the bell. That is, saved by a phone call to Medal that was not so much a ringing bell as a riff of cymbals and dogs barking. Where, Skip asked silently, did he come up with that awful ringtone? Medal put up one finger to hush him and said he had to take the call. He got up abruptly and walked out of the restaurant and stood on the street talking. Skip watched him through the front window. The call ended and Medal tucked the phone into his pocket and stood for a minute with his hands on his hips as he rocked slowly back and forth on his heels. He turned suddenly and marched back in. He slipped into the booth across from Skip and glared at him.

"Okay, this is what comes next. You told me they have a workshop in a barn, right?"

"Yes."

"You are going to construct a pipe bomb. You will use material that Mr. Hop-head Ziller has touched. DNA and fingerprints, got it?"

Skip's face was ashen. "Yes, but I don't know how to make a bomb." He was afraid of bombs.

"Look on the Internet, nitwit." Medal reached into a valise and pulled out a thin sheaf of papers stapled together. "Here it is in a nutshell. It's simple but be careful."

Skip took the papers hesitantly and looked like he might cry. His skin had a flu-like pallor under a sheen of nervous perspiration. "I'm not sure . . ."

"Not sure of what, dickhead? That you have a lot riding on this?" The group next to them had pulled two tables together and was celebrating a birthday. They sang the birthday song and Medal cast an annoyed look over his shoulder and paused. When they finished singing, he leaned across the booth and whispered emphatically. "You get him to touch the parts, you build the damn thing and leave lots of traces in that workshop of theirs, and then you set it off in front of the Syngentech doors. They lose a door and a couple of windows, no problem for them. That dunce sheriff they have down there will call in a forensic team and I'll take it from there. You turn witness and you have a deal. Got it?"

"Yeah, got it." He scanned the room for wastebaskets in case his nausea blossomed into actual puking.

Medal reached for his valise and began to slide out of the booth. "Give me a break, Dunneman, is this how you did your drug deals, all mopey and weak? If you had the balls to do that, you have the balls to do this. And get it right for once." He stood up, turned fast, and hurried away.

The waitress arrived with Skip's glass of water and apologized for being slow. "Sorry, honey, but we're slammed today and one of the kids at the next table spilled a full glass of soda . . ."

"It's okay. My friend left so I think I'll just go now. Really, it's not you."

On his way back to Stony Mesa he considered what would happen if he just kept driving. How long would it take for them to find him? What would they do to him then? Would that be any worse than what he faced now?

He drove slowly, the sheaf of instructions next to him on the passenger seat. The traffic on the interstate thinned. Night fell. He turned off the big highway and onto the serpentine road to Stony Mesa, over dark mountains and down into a vast maze of canyon walls glowing ghostly in the moonlight.

C h a p t e r   1 4

They rode Kayla's horses to the abandoned Hartshorn Ranch. Ramone had been to the old homestead on horseback once before and told Kayla there was an old logging road that hooked up to an old mining road that led to the north swale of the ranch. He took a Forest Service horse that first time but it was skittish and he had to stop several times to remove limbs that had blown down across the trail. It was hard work with a handsaw that was all he could carry on horseback and his palm was blistered under thick gloves. He mounted and dismounted his nervous steed several times. The trip was an ordeal.

Kayla promised him her horses were well behaved. Without all the stopping and remounting to clear blow-downs along the way, this trip would be easier. He asked if she needed help loading the horses into her trailer. She was sure she could handle that by herself but she asked him to meet her at the Jango and help her so they could drive to the trailhead together.

It was easier. The horses were easy. Conversations, the weather, all of it easy. They'd had four days of high wind just before the trip but there were no new obstacles. They talked about that. These days it seemed as if wind was stronger and more frequent. They were thankful that the Southwest did not experience the persistent march of tornadoes and hurricanes that tore up so much of the world. No rising seas, of course. But even in pretty Stony Mesa weather extremes were frequent and four straight days of hot wind, like four days of nonstop rain, can be stressful. Kayla called it Ibuprofen weather. On that day the weather was perfect. Easy.

Ramone told her about his family's colorful past. His great-great-grandfather fled Mussolini to Spain and fought in the civil war there. When the anarcho-syndicalists he joined were overrun by the fascists, he fled to Mexico where he married. The family migrated to New York after World War II and eventually moved to Ohio where Ramone grew up.

His best friend lived on a farm with horses and that was where he learned to ride. They talked about the differences between English riding and western riding. Ramone's parents also divorced but not until he was in college, so they talked about divorce, wounds carried and healed. They talked about music, pets, food, friends, adventures, travel, pet peeves, and movies. They did not talk about God or sex.

Kayla visited the Hartshorn as a kid but her memories were vague. Standing next to the ghostly remains of the ranch house did not help her recall that childhood trip. The yard was overgrown with slim new willows, an alder patch swallowed a broken fence, and cattails filled the pasture. The rose bush she remembered was still vibrant, the only non-native plant she could see. The swing and a tree house were gone, a picket fence and an outhouse, too.

"I had to haul out a ton of debris." Ramone had been making sense of the ranch's troubled ground for a couple of years. The first year he pulled out thistle and cheat grass by hand. The pastures were compacted by cattle and he punctured and chopped it until his palms and fingers bled. The old spring was choked by tamarisk and Russian olives that he hacked and dug away. He showed her a scar from an olive thorn that scraped his scalp above his brow. But the results of his labor were plain. The spring was running again and a wetland was spreading below in what was once a dry meadow. Chattering birds fed on the insects there and Ramone told her it was possible to walk blindfolded across the landscape and find the resilient spring by simply listening. Where there is water you will hear life.

"There's not enough water here for beavers, so I'm the beaver." He showed her how he had constructed crude mats of woven willow limbs to channel and hold the ribbons of spring water that now laced the pasture. "I didn't have to bring in many plants but the cattails needed help and I brought in local columbine and yarrow, some wild iris, bee balm. This year I've seen a big increase in the number of pollinators in here and that was one of my goals. I've identified six species of native bees and, of course, hummingbirds you can see for yourself."

They talked about pollinators and that triggered suppressed desire. She was chomping at the bit to jump his bones and he wanted to put his hands all over her. Caution ruled, however, and they changed the subject from pollination to saddle oil, a subject that also invited erotic thoughts, so they ended up talking about the history of the Jango Ranch. Kayla told him she often wondered while growing up there what the land was like when the first Jango Burnside claimed his ground along the river. Ramone was sure that it was bosque and wetland. She asked him to walk the ranch with her someday and tell her what he saw with his botanist's eye and, of course, he jumped at the chance and agreed.

He found an old plank that was clean and they made an improvised bench to sit and eat their lunches. Kayla brought potato salad and homemade bread that Luna baked and sold at the Desert Rose. Ramone had dried fruit and smoked salmon. He brought a bottle of wine along but was not sure if Kayla could partake since members of the One True Church were forbidden to taste alcohol. He asked her.

"Yeah, I'll share a glass of wine and an occasional beer even though I'm not supposed to. I never touched alcohol until I left for college. I got drunk once but it was such an unpleasant experience that I won't go there again. I break a lot of church rules these days. I shouldn't be here alone with you without a chaperone, for example. The Church always assumes the worst about its members' willingness to control themselves."

Ramone told her he was raised Catholic but became a Quaker in graduate school. "I think it was a reaction to the endless wars in the Mideast. Quakers are pacifists and the ones I met were so sane compared to all the people I saw around me who were caught up in the fear of the times and the endless wars for oil. I got so sick of news about drone strikes against terrorists and the willingness of all sides to kill civilians who got in the way. Then there were all the refugees, just the sheer madness of it all. I'm still a member but I haven't been active for a few years now."

Kayla got brave and confessed to Ramone that her membership in the One True Church was something she carried with her from her childhood but she no longer shared the Church's views on anything. "It's tough," she said, "starting over from scratch when you find that what you were taught doesn't make sense. Thank goodness for an education. At least I know how to think."

She described how upsetting it was to her when she saw animals mistreated and ignored. She read a book about so-called killer whales and was blown away by their intelligence and emotional capacity. Ramone agreed that humanity's cruelty toward its fellow creatures was upsetting but he was more concerned about extinction. "That's the bottom line here at the Hartshorn Ranch. For me, anyway. I figure if you want to do something for animals, save their habitat. Give them a place where they can thrive. Give them a home, or maybe I should say restore their homes. Most people I know would never deliberately kill birds or other animals, never deliberately wipe out bees or butterflies, do things like that. But without any awareness or intent we destroy habitat, which amounts to pretty much the same thing. If you love your fellow creatures, save their habitat."

"Their homes."

"Yes."

Kayla nodded. "It's so hard for me in these past few years to think of the Jango as property or as real estate. What is land but nature? The Jango was where I discovered wild nature, everything from tadpoles to lizards to horses, and in my childhood mind it was all priceless. It was enchanted. Markets are what you learn later on. Olene told me that real estate is a legal abstraction that we project over ecological space. At first I thought, well there goes Olene over the nuthouse wall again, but the more I think it over, the more it seems true. The same thing is happening with the ranch's water rights. That way of thinking says you can rip off a big chunk of living land, measure it in acres, and translate that into dollars. You can pave it, gate it, mine it, fence it, whatever pleases you, and act as if it was never part of something else that is alive and whole."

Ramone simply replied, "Amen."

The horses fell asleep on their feet in the sun. It was time to go if they wanted to get back before evening. They saddled up and moved down the trail. Kayla was hopeful for the first time in weeks. Her challenges looked manageable. Ramone was the best thing that happened to her for a long while. He made her feel confident and worthy. He valued her. Trusted her. He made her feel horny, too, and she had not felt that since . . . she couldn't remember when. It was obvious that he couldn't get enough of her, too, and it felt so good to be wanted.

Back at the Jango he helped her unload the horses and unhitch the trailer. They both had commitments early the next day. It was time to say goodbye. They told each other what a great day it was. There was an awkward pause and then she grabbed his arm and pulled him into an embrace. They held each other for several seconds and then she pushed away enough to cup his face in her hands and deliver one strong, long kiss. Then she turned and stepped away. At the doorway she grinned and made a theatrical bow. "To be continued?" she asked.

"Definitely," he answered.

She watched his truck disappear down the driveway and was unwilling to let him out of her sight until the last trace of dust settled.

That evening Grace called to check on her. "So, honey, what do you think?" she asked.

"I've made up my mind," she replied. "I know what I am going to do."

Chapter 15

Luna reflected on the nature of explosive sounds. It was hard to describe them to someone who hadn't heard them, because explosive sounds are so shocking, fleeting, and infrequent that we are not familiar with their various inflections and haven't developed a vocabulary to describe the differences. She supposed that people immersed in war could distinguish the bam of a bomb, the crack of a rifle, and the muffled womp of a mortar going off but to her innocent ears the sound coming from the barn was simply the loudest bang she had ever heard. It had a sharp initial cast followed by a chest-thumping concussion. The windows rattled so hard she thought they might crack. After that it was all bird squawk and chatter. Horses neighed in the distance. Her first impulse was to check the baby.

The explosion woke Sage from his nap and he began to fuss. She rolled him over and patted his back while whispering in a reassuring tone. He surrendered to sleep; she stood for a minute above his crib and watched him to be sure. The moment she was certain that he was fine, she rushed from the room. She grabbed her phone off the kitchen counter and slipped on the first pair of sandals she found by the back door. She walked quickly toward the barn at an uneven pace as feelings of urgency wrestled with dread.

Nobody was at the farm this afternoon but Luna and Skip Dunneman, and he was nowhere in sight. She called for him but there was no answer. She reminded herself that Hoppy was down at the market selling vegetables and goat cheese and the others who would normally be nearby were at workshops on fermenting foods.

She reached the barn and stopped cold. A premonition like ice water poured down the length of her spine. She took a breath and went to the door. She pushed and yelled, "Hello? Skip?"

The door was stuck. The concussion from the blast had buckled the door frame so that it allowed the door to open about a foot before it jammed tight. An acrid odor wafted through the opening. She butted her shoulder against the door and managed to widen the opening a few more inches. She squeezed herself through the doorway and popped into the unlit barn. On the north side where she and Hoppy had cleared room for a work area and built a small shop and cabinets, Skip Dunneman sat on the floor under the work bench. He was silent and didn't move or even look her way as she approached him. He sat with his legs splayed and he held his right wrist with his left hand. His head was slightly bent down as he stared in catatonic wonder at his right hand. Luna watched him watching his hand and then she saw what held his focus. His hand was covered in blood and was missing fingers.

She ripped a clean rag into tourniquets for his open wounds and made a cursory search for the severed fingers. Based on the voluminous bloody bits of flesh and splinters of bone she saw stuck to the wall, she concluded that they would go to the emergency room unaccompanied by a cooler containing stitch-worthy digits. She got Skip on his feet and helped him walk to the door. She kicked and tugged it open a few more inches and pulled him through. They reached the car door as Skip's knees buckled and he bent over. He wretched twice and she dug a handkerchief from her pocket and wiped his lips. She put him in the back seat and told him to lie down. She ran into the house and down the hall, gathered Sage in her arms, snatched a blanket from the crib, and scanned the room for what she needed to bring. She grabbed a diaper bag and stuffed his pacifier in her breast pocket, unmindful of the fact that she now looked like she had one disturbingly large nipple.

She laid the baby in his car seat, strapped him in, and thanked God he was still asleep. On the way to the emergency room he lay blissfully unaware of the pale young man sitting next to him who was holding his horrific hand. He did not see the man's scalded forehead, missing eyebrows, and the small blister on the tip of his nose. Skip was silent aside from a single whimper when the car rattled over a cattle gate and shook hard.

There was no advantage in calling 911. By the time volunteers were alerted and drove to get the town's lone ambulance, at least a half hour would pass. If the ambulance was already out on a call it could be hours. A sheriff's deputy or state cop might be there sooner but the clinic was in Boonville, about twenty miles and as many minutes away, and she could get him there faster by herself. She drove as fast as she dared and prayed there would be no cow standing in the middle of the road around each bend. She kept both hands on the wheel but let go long enough to hit Hoppy's number and put her phone on speaker. She waited through four very long rings. "Pick up, pick up," she whispered. He answered and she quickly described what happened and told him to call the clinic ahead of her arrival. He called the clinic as soon as he disconnected and then closed the market and ran to his truck.

Luna sped uphill out of Stony Mesa and across a wide grass valley toward the medical clinic in Boonville, the county seat. Skip moaned again, baby Sage gurgled, and Luna's heart thumped so hard she feared it would bruise. As she came into the town, alfalfa fields were succeeded by a matrix of fenced pastures with placid cows grazing the bovine gulag. The clinic was a plain brick building built with a federal grant that allowed for no architectural flare. She pulled up to the wide glass door in front.

She bolted inside and yelled, "I need help! I have a man in my truck who is injured! Hurry!"

Luna was pushed aside by the scramble of nurses and doctors. They wheeled Skip into the clinic to get him ready for an ambulance trip to the nearest hospital an hour and a half away. She sat down and allowed herself to shake and then remembered Sage. She ran across the clinic and almost knocked over DeeRay Oldroyd, who was standing at the reception desk holding his monthly urine sample. She reached Sage just as he stirred from his nap and an instant before Hoppy pulled into the parking lot.

Skip was unconscious when he was loaded into the ambulance. Hoppy asked a nurse he knew as a frequent customer at the Desert Rose what her assessment was. She assured him there was nothing life threatening. After the shock wore off he was in terrible pain, she explained, so they gave him a shot and he passed out. At the hospital a surgeon would clean up his finger stumps and a hole in his palm big enough that you could see straight through. "Ugly as it is," she said, "he will survive and heal."

Sage grew restless and wanted to nurse. Hoppy took his family home. Luna heated leftovers and Hoppy went to the barn to clean up the grisly red spatters on the workshop walls. They made arrangements to go to the hospital to be with Skip the next day.

Skip awoke. He was groggy and saw the world through a dim window of gauze. He was puzzled by his immobility. He was a bug trapped in a spider web, except his web was all tubes and wires. He looked up and saw Luna, beautiful even through his drug-induced haze and the gauze. He tried to say hello but his lips were swollen and it came out *elbow*. He passed out.

He surfaced again and she was still there and so was the web he was tangled in. He squinted hard and tried to bring her into sharper focus. He ran his tongue over his dry lips and cleared his throat. "Why am I saluting?" he asked.

"You're not. You blew off two fingers and there's a hole in your palm so the doctor elevated your arm."

"I blew off two fingers?"

"Yup."

"Which two?"

"Well," she said, "let's just say your pointing days are over and you will no longer flip the bird on that hand."

He turned a shade paler and moaned.

"I know it sucks but it could be worse. Could be your thumb." She hesitated and a smirk suddenly appeared. "Get it? Sucks. Thumb? Or how about this—what would suck worse? Your dick?"

He squinted and pushed his head up from the pillow under his neck. She seemed so odd, so out of character.

"I lose fingers and you make puns?"

"Yes, seems callous doesn't it? Nothing compared to a pipe bomb, of course. Which, I must add, you made in my very backyard even though you know full well how I detest violence."

Luna leaned over him. Sarcasm alone could no longer mute her rage. She yelled in his scalded face. "I have a baby in my house! You made a pipe bomb near my baby!"

She straightened up and lowered her voice. A look of disgust replaced one of scorn. "It's hard to feel sympathy for such reckless stupidity." She stopped and he waited. He knew she wasn't through. "And if you succeeded in building that bomb, then what? Who would be filling the bed you're in then?"

Skip rushed to his own defense. "I wasn't going to hurt anyone, not physically, just property. Safe at night. I planned it so nobody gets hurt."

She wasn't buying. "You didn't plan to blow your fingers off either and yet here we are with your hand hung in the air in a perpetual bye-bye. Hey, maybe that's why your hand is elevated, you're waving goodbye to your fingers."

"Please, no more jokes. I surrender. I'm sorry. Let me go back to sleep."

She stood up and leaned over him again. He half expected her to start pulling out the tubes going in and out of him and wrap them around his neck.

"Here's the deal, Skipper. You're in here for two days and then we will take you home. There will be follow-up visits to the doctor and you will have your hand strapped up like that so you can't feed yourself or dress yourself or drive. We will feed you and care for you while you heal. I will hold my tongue if you hold yours. We will make it work. I'd say we are looking at a month at most. And then you will leave and we will never see you again. Got it?"

"Yes. Okay. I got it."

She was right. One month later he was good to go. The stumps of his missing fingers healed over. They were tender and ached but the doctor said there were no complications. Luna and Skip kept a civil tone throughout his convalescence. He thanked them every time they changed his bandages and applied salve, when they drove him to doctor appointments, and every day when they helped him in and out of his clothes. Luna cooked healthy dishes and made concoctions of herbs for him to drink. She wrapped his fingers in comfrey leaves and frankincense. She washed his clothes for him and changed the sheets. Although she acted with compassion, her face and posture showed distance and formality. He was quiet in her presence because he knew it was best to lay low. He stayed in the guest room where he could hear Hoppy come home, then muffled talk and laughter, the click of plates and shuffle of chairs around the kitchen table. On most nights Luna would sing softly to their baby. Sometimes Hoppy played the mandolin. Skip had never felt so low.

He healed enough to handle a phone call and tried to reach Kent Medal but the number had been taken out of service. He tried not to panic. The first order of business, he told himself, is to get well. Then I can sort out what comes next.

What came next was flu-like guilt and remorse. He stayed in bed for days, tossed restlessly into the wee hours, and suffered a stiff neck and headaches. His jaw ached from grinding his teeth and on too many midnights he awoke clammy. On a gleaming blue and gold morning three weeks into his stay it came to him like a revelation from above: if he was going to recover, he must tell them. All of it. The whole truth.

He rehearsed in his mind for days. He was determined that by the time he left them he would have the courage to tell them. When the time is right, he told himself. But the time was never right and a week later he forced himself to march into the kitchen while they were having dinner.

"I'm sorry to interrupt your dinner."

"That's okay, Skip, no problem," Hoppy said cheerfully as he pulled out a chair from the table. "Here, have a seat."

"Thanks, I'd rather stand." He passed trembling fingers through his hair and cleared his throat.

Luna locked into his eyes and held them. He froze in place. "What do you want to tell us, Skip?"

"I want to tell you I'm sorry for building that pipe bomb so close to your home and your baby. I'm sorry for more than that. I lied to you from the beginning. I was working undercover for a cop who suspected Hoppy was involved in some monkey-wrenching at the Sea Ledges mining site a few years ago. The plan to bomb the Syngentech Corporation offices was a sting. I didn't want to do it but he, the cop I mean, threatened me. I was wrong. I am sorry."

He waited for a response but they just looked at one another and nodded. "I got caught with drugs," he explained. "A lot of drugs, really, and it was the second time for me. I was facing years in prison and this cop offered me a deal. If I went undercover and got something on Hoppy that was incriminating I would get a lighter sentence, maybe get off altogether. I was desperate so I took the deal. I didn't know you when I agreed to do it. You were just a name, a way out. If I had known you, I never would have agreed, I swear it."

Still no response. Maybe they were unable to process what he was telling them. "You don't have to worry because I never got anything on you, Hoppy, and now I'm done with it. I am thankful for what you've done for me and I know damn well you didn't have to take me in and I didn't deserve it. I'm ashamed and I'm sorry."

He was not sure what to expect when he confessed to them, but indifference was not on the list of possible outcomes. They were unnaturally calm. They listened quietly and didn't interrupt or ask questions.

"You don't seem surprised. I thought you'd be shocked and angry or at least upset."

"We knew." She said it as if she hadn't been dying to confront him for weeks.

"You knew? How?"

Luna looked at Hoppy and he nodded. He let her tell it. "You met a man named Kent Medal at a restaurant in the city. One of Sheriff Taylor's deputies was up there to celebrate his sister's birthday and take the kids to the zoo. He sat in the same restaurant with his family. He remembered you from Stony Mesa and he recognized Kent Medal because Medal was at the Jango Ranch when Kayla's grandfather died. He didn't think anything of it until the pipe bomb went off in your hand and then he mentioned it to Dunk Taylor who also remembered Kent Medal. Dunk doesn't like him. He went up there and confronted Medal, who admitted you were working for him. You were setting us up. You were preparing to betray us."

He stammered, "When . . . when?"

Luna was ready. "When did we find out? It was about a week after you blew your fingers off."

Skip was dumbfounded. Why didn't they kick him out of their home when they found out? He wanted to reply but was speechless. She continued. "You're probably asking yourself why you haven't heard from Kent Medal."

He wanted to reply but a guttural noise was the best he could do. She took over. "Dunk brought Elias Buchman with him. Elias had a stack of paper on Medal, everything from performance reviews and medical records to . . . well, his whole personnel file. Turns out you weren't on the books, Skip. Medal's attempt to sting Hoppy was his secret bid to be a hero and save his failing career."

Skip made another guttural noise—words weren't happening for him this evening. Luna resumed. "Here's a juicy bit of news for you. You thought you had a deal to get a lighter sentence, right? Well, there was no deal. As I said, you were off the books. As soon as it went down, he was going to throw you under the bus, as they say."

This time Skip managed to emit a stutter followed by guttural noise. She was starting to feel pity. "I know this is a lot to take in but here's the next part. Dunk and Elias cut a deal with Medal. If he turned in his resignation they wouldn't expose him. He can never be a cop again. Never. He's gone now, moved out of state. You could probably look for him but you're still in trouble. You have a sentencing hearing next month and you are on your own."

His voice returned. "Why didn't you confront me when you found out? You must have felt angry and hurt but you kept taking care of me. I don't get it. Why wait until now to tell me that you already knew all about me and Medal?"

Luna looked at Hoppy to ask if he wanted to take it from here. He nodded back and signaled for her to continue. She turned to Skip. "If we had accused you then you would have become defensive. You would have retreated from your responsibility. This way you had to figure it out. This way you confessed on your own. Your confession is a necessary step if you want to get clear of what you did and go on to do better."

They waited for it to sink in. Hoppy stepped forward. "You didn't just betray us, you betrayed yourself. We love you, Skip, you're a great guy. But you fucked up. Big time. We forgive you, man. You can do better. Much, much better. And you will, I know it."

"But not here, Skip, not with us." She was adamant.

He covered his face with his hands and turned toward the guest room. He walked the first few steps and ran the last half of the hallway. He closed the door behind him and they heard muffled sobs. That night he packed quietly and drove away before sunrise. They never saw him again.

Chapter 16

At the trailhead parking lot they changed into their boots, checked their packs for food and water, and then gathered around Mary Handy. This would be their second hike on Sleeping Maiden Mountain guided by Mary, who welcomed any chance to do outreach and explain the work she and her Forest Service colleagues were doing on the mountain. There was a restroom attached to the ranger station next to the parking lot and they took turns using it.

"Okay," Mary announced, "did we all pee?" They laughed and started out but then waited for Olene to return to the truck where she had forgotten to retrieve her hiking sticks. She explained that she didn't normally use them but her knees were getting older.

The hiking group was an odd mix. Luna and Kayla could be mistaken for athletes. Although Olene, Grace, and Mary were in far better health than most women their age, knees and hips were not what they used to be. Toes ached and shoulders and necks required constant massaging. Kayla called their merry band the "babe and crone patrol."

The trail led straight up the mountain and the first hour was hard. They stopped occasionally to catch their breaths and gulp water. Sleeping Maiden was about thirteen thousand feet at the summit and the trailhead started at six thousand feet. The air was thin toward the top. Mary led them along a slim path through the trees that ended on an escarpment with a spectacular view. They looked out on the land as it fell away from the mountainside into rolling hills that descended into desert canyons. Luna walked to the cliff edge and peered over; Kayla joined her.

Olene gasped. "Girls, please! Be easy on my heart, step back!"

Luna and Kayla grinned at each other but complied. Olene and Grace thanked them.

Mary stepped up on a block of sparkling basalt, an impromptu podium, and began to lecture. "From here you can see the lay of the land and the history of man's use as it is written across the land. The foothills you see rolling out to the far canyons were once grasslands.

Pioneer journals commonly refer to grass that was shoulder-high to a horse. It seemed like a paradise for cattle."

Kayla looked at her feet because she knew what came next. Mary saw Kayla's discomfort but kept on.

"A rail line was built to Junction Corner and hundreds of thousands of cows and sheep were shipped in and set loose. But it wasn't the kind of grass or soil that settlers knew in the eastern places where they came from and the climate was much more arid than they knew. Much more. In the blink of a geological eye the foothills and meadows were overgrazed. The grass was replaced by cactus and thistle. Soil washed away and meadows were reduced to dunes and gullies. Dust storms were more frequent than rain."

The first time Kayla heard this story she didn't believe it because it was so at odds with what she was told growing up. She researched it and Mary was right. This place she loved bore wounds.

Mary balanced on a rock over her backwoods classroom. The lecture was coming to a conclusion. "Similar conditions developed all across the West. The Taylor Grazing Act was passed in 1934 to stop the overgrazing and manage the conflicts over the undamaged land that remained. An era of soil improvement and range management followed the Grazing Act and that made a huge difference. But the grass is mostly gone and you can see how pinyons and junipers have moved over most of those old grasslands."

Kayla pointed to a set of hills that had geometric patterns shaved into its contours. "That's chaining."

Mary explained that chaining was done by bulldozers with anchor chains strung between them. They pulled the taut chain across the ground and ripped up the trees in their path. Then they pushed the dead trunks and limbs into piles to burn. "The rationale was to open space for forage so elk would benefit but you can bet cows got the lion's share."

She winked and laughed. The others chuckled politely. Mary's attempts at humor were rare and her puns and jokes were always more obvious than she suspected. She wasn't known and respected for her wit but for her knowledge. Her passion for conservation was geekishly serious. She continued.

"Actually, in this case lions are nowhere in sight. There are a few cougars left but they stick to these remote islands of forest. Wolves are completely missing. But there are enough coyotes to go around. And that brings us up to the forest we are standing in at this moment in time. This forest is in bad shape. When the charismatic carnivores were eliminated—wolves and cougars I mean, bears to a lesser extent—the whole ecosystem was thrown out of balance. Now there are too many deer and elk and because they live free of predation they hang out along the stream banks where the living is easy. They overgraze the willows and that eliminates beaver and . . . well, you know all about that now. But in this forest the degradation of riparian areas is mostly because of cows."

Olene added, "Their shit is everywhere, which is why giardia is in every stream and spring."

Kayla piped up. "I had giardia. It was terrible. I was riding my horse over by Slickrock Flats and I stopped at what looked like a crystal clear spring bubbling out of some rocks. It was contaminated. I couldn't go more than fifty feet from a toilet for two weeks and I lost ten pounds. I wouldn't recommend it as a weight loss strategy."

Olene wanted Mary to "name names."

Mary was on a limb and had to be careful. "Well it's more of a general problem but in this region Bunny Cleaver is the worst of the lot. He puts twice as many cows on his allotment as allowed and when they chew that to the nubs he cuts fences and lets them loose on the land that surrounds his allotment. Up this high, however, the challenge is this unhealthy forest. Decades of fire suppression let all this fuel build up. Climate change has killed the trees across entire drainages through beetle infestations. Cold winters once killed beetles but now they survive the warmer and shorter winters and their numbers grow and grow. I don't have to tell you about the fires."

"Why not cut all this timber and thin the forest?" Grace's question was sincere and logical.

Mary nodded. "There isn't much profit in the small trees and dead wood. It would require roads and there are already thousands of miles of old logging and mining roads crisscrossing the land. In the past, loggers and miners did a lot of damage to soil and streams. They use bulldozers and other heavy equipment that tear up ground and crush undergrowth."

Grace, always the peacemaker, was concerned about the hostile relationship between the Forest Service and some of the locals.

Mary was eager to address her question. "Grace, I think it's overstated. You are all locals too, aren't you? We seem to be getting on just fine. We have a good relationship with most in the ranch community, too. But there's a hardcore minority that seem hell-bent on declaring war on the evil feds. They get all the attention, of course, and the many partnerships we have with ranchers get ignored. And the ranchers who play by the rules and pay their way get painted with the same brush as the disgruntled ranchers who think they are above the law. That's not fair."

Olene was itching to add something and Mary turned to her. "Give people a safe place and a fair means for working out their differences and they almost always find common ground." Olene was adamant. Mary agreed and cited successful partnerships between the Forest Service and its ranching stakeholders.

Luna raised her hand. "What about Bunny Cleaver, Mary?"

Mary winced. "I guess there are some opposing perspectives that can't be reconciled, especially these days when there is so much troubling news. Sometimes I think one side is in a state of panic about the ecological crisis and thinks the time has come for desperate measures while the other side is in a panic over those of us who are so alarmed we want to make big changes."

Mary's work as a conservation biologist put her in a Debbie Downer role frequently. She looked to Olene, who understood Mary needed an antidote to despair. Olene asked Mary to show them a stand of aspen trees that covered hundreds of acres of ground. She read that the aspens were connected at the roots and could be considered a single giant organism. A friend told her there was an exceptional stand of aspens on Sleeping Maiden. She hoped her enthusiasm would be contagious.

Mary was glad to get away from politics. "That's right, Olene, you can see that stand of trees from here. It's a short walk over the ridge." They walked toward it and Mary explained, "Aspen groves are often referred to as clonal colonies because new trees sprout from a common root system. And, yes, an aspen forest can be considered a single super-organism. The roots are far enough under the soil that they can survive fires so there are many aspen stands that have survived for thousands of years. Roots can go dormant for a long time but spring back to life when the conditions are right. An individual tree may last a hundred years but the root system can be much older. There is one enormous aspen forest called 'Pando' in Utah that may be eighty thousand years old. Ice or fire, no matter what, the resilience of aspens endures."

Olene was already charging uphill toward a soft green cloud of aspen leaves. Their white trunks were lit by sunlight and dressed in a quaking lace of leaves. Luna and Kayla lagged behind as they talked about different ways to crush apples for juice. They were writing a grant together for a mobile apple press so that people in Stony Mesa with backyard orchards and more fruit than they could eat, can, or dry could turn their excess into juice. They talked about starting a cooperative distillery in the future.

Grace asked Mary about the medicinal qualities of aspen wood but Mary didn't know much. "I assume they use the bark and I hear it has aspirin-like qualities. There's an entire encyclopedia's worth of knowledge of medicinal uses of plants that we've lost because the indigenous people who held that knowledge lost it as they were either decimated or assimilated."

The group fell silent as they entered the aspen grove. A million leaves fluttering gently in the breeze made a hushed rustle that was a tonic to the ears. They walked among the smooth white trunks that wore wrinkles like the thin folds of a silk stocking before it is pulled tight. The grove offered cool shade, musky aromas, a balm under a cobalt blue sky. Their conversation paused while some sat and some meandered among the pale stalks, all of them washed by the healing power of the trees.

They departed for the return trip to the trailhead and their vehicles. They walked slowly and quietly for most of a mile down the mountain. Olene broke the spell. As usual she was brimming with thoughts and feelings but she was hesitant to share. Grace saw she was poised on the border of another self-revealing riff and knew Olene needed permission.

"Go ahead, Olene, I can almost hear your thoughts churning."

Once punctured, Olene spilled. "Well, I was thinking about our culture's hyper-individualism and how delusional it is. Look at the aspens. Above the surface they also look like unique individuals but deep at their roots they are one. Humans also emerge from an unseen realm. We share our DNA not only with one another but with animals. Under our own skin we have the same bones and blood that require the same nourishment. We arose together and like aspens we can hold each other up and we can survive together. I think aspens are great role models."

They thought it over, the usual mulling phase after Olene spoke. Kayla responded first. "That's gonna be a stretch for most of your neighbors in Stony Mesa, Olene. The popular saying in my youth was 'what would Jesus do?' What would an aspen do never occurred to us."

The others, including Olene, laughed. Kayla hastily added, "But it's a lovely thought."

"Yes," said Grace.

"Yes," said Luna. "Lovely."

Kayla turned toward Olene and tucked her arm into Olene's arm. "I have a bumper sticker for you and your ideas. Wanna hear it?"

Of course they did. Kayla had a way of summing things up.

"Okay, here it is: Beneath the skin, kin."

They returned to the ranger station. The first thing that drew their attention was all the trucks in the parking lot that were not there when they left. Mary had no idea why there would be so many trucks. She racked her brain to remember if there was an event, some group visiting for a field trip perhaps, that she had forgotten. They approached and noticed the bumper stickers and decals. "Don't Tread on Me" was a popular choice and the others had mostly to do with immigrants, guns, and taxes.

Their focus on the bumper stickers loosened and they looked up and read an unfamiliar sign. A handmade banner was hung across the front of the parking lot gate that read in bold script "Sovereign Patriot Territory." Underneath in smaller letters was "Constitutional Revolutionary American Party." Someone had scrawled "like us on Facebook" in one corner of the banner.

A clutch of young men stood by the walkway that led to the station. They wore camouflage pants and jackets as if they were ready for a day of deer hunting except for the assault rifles they held across their chests. One of the boys leaned back on a fence post and stared at a phone screen. Two taller boys behind him looked over his shoulders in that stoop-necked posture assumed by those transfixed by phones. They reminded Kayla of the look on the young men who volunteered to be hypnotized in a show that played at the Boon County High School when she was a student there. She half expected them to fall to the ground at any moment and flap and cluck like chickens. The young men were startled when they looked up and saw the women approaching.

"Do hunters use that kind of rifle to kill deer?" Grace asked.

Mary answered in a hushed and shaky voice. "No, they don't. Those are assault rifles and they use them for . . . well, for assault." Confusion was now morphing into alarm and she could feel her blood pressure spike under her Forest Service shirt. She walked quickly toward the young men and firmly but politely asked who they were and what they were doing. They looked at one another and waited to see who would answer first but not me was all they saw. Mary was a pop quiz and they hadn't read the assignment.

"Never mind," she said as she pushed past them and started up the walkway.

"Hey, you're not allowed!" shouted one of the adolescent gunmen. He reached out and grabbed her by the sleeve. She yanked her arm away from him and turned to face him. She noticed he had a large pimple growing over his left brow and a mustache of pubescent lip hair. He couldn't be more than fifteen. He looked angry. A pissed-off teenager with a gun that could cut a person in half in two seconds struck her as a bad combination and she swallowed hard and tried to control a swelling feeling of panic.

"The hell I'm not allowed." She marched onward.

Kayla watched one boy who had his index finger curled around the trigger of his AK-47. This could get ugly fast, she thought, and in an effort to defuse the tension she went up to him, smiled flirtatiously, and said, "First rule of gun safety, bro, is to keep your booger hook away from the bang switch." He looked down at his hand and pulled it away from the gun. She smiled again, winked, and switched to a sisterly voice. "Don't throw your life away, kid."

The puzzled boys made only a half-hearted effort to block the other women from walking toward the entrance behind Mary. Luna and Kayla pushed them aside while Olene and Grace followed closely, trying hard not to step on the heels of the women in front of them or look over their shoulders at the adolescent gunmen. The boys watched them go into the building and wanted to stop them but were too disoriented to act quickly. In their imaginations the boys saw themselves in a heroic gun battle with tyrannical federal agents, not blocking the door from three old ladies and two hot chicks.

The Cleaverites planned to alert the media once the Forest Service station and grounds were secure. The men had left the boys outside and were inside the ranger station talking about the logistics and timing of their plan when the women hikers returned. The boys at the gate had not been instructed on what to do if a small band of women pushed them aside.

Luna was eager to get back to Sage and nurse him. Her breasts had started to leak and her shirt was stained with milk. She followed anyway.

"Why was her shirt wet?" asked one well-armed teen after the women had disappeared into the building.

"I don't know," said another. "Shut up and get ready!" shouted a third. The boys at the gate realized they had blown it but figured five women, three old enough to be their grandmothers and one weirdly wet, were not much of a threat. Let the men inside handle it.

The ranger station was filled with a dozen armed men. If they were hunters, they must have been out to bag a tank. The room bristled with gun barrels, not the sleek barrels of hunting rifles designed to kill an elk with one shot but the kind of industrial-strength weapons of war designed to pierce through car doors and building walls or a half dozen human beings at once. The women stopped cold and tried to process the camo-colored scene before them. Bunny and his gang of wannabe heroes fell silent when the women entered the station. They were as surprised to find the women in the room with them as the women were to find them there. The freeze frame only lasted a couple of seconds when Bunny Cleaver stepped forward, stuck out his chest, and began to speak.

"I am Commander Cleaver of the Constitutional Revolutionary American Party and this—"

"Get out!"

He involuntarily took a half step back.

"Leave! Get out now! Now!" Kayla stepped forward and clenched her fists. The nearest Cleaver, seventeen-year-old LaVoy, raised his hands defensively and pitched backward.

Bunny Cleaver blinked and stepped back. He recovered quickly, pulled himself up tall, and continued. "I said—"

"Get out!" This time it was Luna who stepped forward and stuck her chin out as far as it would go. "Get out now! Leave! Now!"

Kayla had an athletic rodeo rider look about her that made her threatening posture credible to the Cleaverites, but Luna not so much. Although Luna was also physically fit she was adorned in her usual wispy scarves and lace that hid her hardened core, her rock-climber muscles, her body honed for balance and stamina. If she had threatened to cast a spell on them, she would have been truer to her appearance. She was not aware that her leaking milk had spread a dark stain down the front of her shirt. The Bunny boys retreated. Maybe it was the milk stains that intimidated them. Maybe her milk was magical. Or maybe they feared she would put them in time-out.

Grace pitched in too. "Shame on you! Shame on you!"

Grace's normal bearing was serene and maternal, so the women were surprised to see her rage. The guns got to her. Elias had an old shotgun left over from hunting trips with his father when he was a teenager. It was buried in a closet and neither of them was sure where. She didn't like guns because she didn't like killing. She was suspicious of people who called themselves gun lovers because it seemed to her that there were so many more life-affirming choices for one's affection than instruments of death. And here in the room were men who couldn't get what they wanted without resorting to threats of horrific violence. She wanted to address them in a more articulate and civil way but found that once she started yelling "shame on you!" she couldn't stop.

Olene stood back, shielded by Grace. She wore an incongruous grin because she had realized that the acronym for Commander Cleaver's Constitutional Revolutionary American Party would be CRAP. It was hard to believe these men could be so clueless that they overlooked such a basic consideration. The emotional temperature of the room rose quickly and Olene decided she would play the role of the reasonable one who alone might guide the startled militia men through the fierce trio of screaming witches. "If I were you I'd go while you can," she said. "I'm sure they mean what they say and can't be stopped. The last time they got this mad . . . well, no need to go into that. I'm sure that man will recover but he may never be able to . . . you know." She held up her closed hand and made her index finger go from limp to pointing up.

The men in front flinched slightly and stepped back an inch. Alma Cleaver, Bunny's youngest son, pulled his pistol from its holster, stepped in front of his father, and turned toward Kayla. "One more step, miss, and you'll force me to . . ."

"Are you fuckin' kidding me? Are you threatening an unarmed woman with a gun? Put that away, you half-wit, before I take it from you and shove it up your ass!" Kayla had never been so rude in her entire life. She was simultaneously appalled and thrilled.

Not only was each and every Cleaverite in the room struck silent by Kayla's loud fury, her fellow hikers were also taken by surprise. Grace would later tell Elias she had no idea someone Kayla's size could be so loud. Luna later told Hoppy, "That cowgirl has balls!"

Mary Handy was the only woman who did not verbally engage the gang. She was a federal employee and this was her domain, but she understood immediately that if the station was being hijacked by armed men, she was vulnerable. Sure enough, Golden Cleaver pushed himself between Grace and Olene. Golden was the son with a deep scar across his forehead from the time he snuck behind the horse his brother was riding and lit a firecracker. He reached for Mary's arm and caught her sleeve. "This one is a ranger! We can hold her hostage and demand . . ."

Mary jerked her arm away from his grip just as her free hand reached toward Golden's face and let go an entire can of bear spray into his lopsided eyes. He screamed and tumbled backwards, clawing at his face. The bear spray filled the small room and everyone began to cough and yell at once. Shoulder to shoulder they jostled through the door and crashed onto the small patch of lawn outside. They gagged and rubbed their eyes. Curses filled the air. As they picked themselves up and recovered, the women continued to confront whichever Cleaverite they found in front of them. One young man with a bandolier of bullets grazing lazily across a generous expanse of flannel belly was backed up to a fencepost by Grace Buchman.

"Guns? Really, guns? You think you pick that up and suddenly you are right? Suddenly you represent someone aside from yourself? Do you think that gun gives you the right to speak for me and mine? Nonsense! If you think you can intimidate me you're wrong! Someone as stupid as you can't be trusted with a weapon. Now give me that right now!" Grace held out her hand, palm up.

He looked for a moment like he might hand Grace his gun. Instead he rolled sideways out of the range of her fury and walked briskly toward his truck. As he turned his head to watch the furious old woman from over his shoulder, he tripped over another Cleaverite who was bent over searching for a pocket full of ammo he had dropped while stumbling blindly through the door. The portly young warrior pitched head first into a brick drinking fountain and was knocked out cold.

Luna also tripped on her way out the door but did a neat shoulder roll despite the handicap of her swollen breasts and popped up above the writhing Cleaverites. She stumbled half-blind to the threshold of the station entrance, turned with her arms out, legs akimbo, and yelled. "You're out now and it's over! Nobody gets back in, it's over!"

"The hell it is." Bunny Cleaver himself, tear-stained, red-faced, and hatless, stepped toward her. All their squinty tear-filled eyes followed him as he took two giant strides toward Luna, stopped short, uttered "oof!" and dropped to the ground in a denim and cowhide heap.

"Shit! That hurt." Kayla held her right wrist with her left hand and flexed the fingers of her right hand open and closed, open and closed. In an afternoon of strange turns, the way that Kayla Burnside dropped Bunny Cleaver cold with one solid punch to the jaw was the most unexpected twist of all.

The entire lawn full of red-faced Cleaverites was silent. Mouths agape and eyebrows high, they stared at their crumpled prophet and the cowgirl who cocked him cold. They could not believe their eyes.

"Holy shit." Golden Cleaver spun on his heels and headed for his truck. Two others knelt over Bunny and tried to bring him to consciousness. They slapped his cheeks lightly and called his name. The prophet sat up and drooled. If the Lord was guiding him, he apparently broke for a nap because Bunny Cleaver was speechless. The militia kid who was conked out by the drinking fountain was dragged away by three of his compatriots, spilling bullets across the gravel parking lot. Bunny coming around and muttered curses as his sons helped him to his feet and steered him to the parking lot. His direct line to the Lord had dissolved into static.

A Cleaverite who was on the phone in a back office heard the melee but was talking to a television reporter for KJETV. He hung up the phone when he smelled the acrid aroma of bear spray and walked to the front of the station to find it empty and filled with harsh air. He wondered where everyone had gone and wandered outside to see the Cleaverite militia in full retreat. He called out to Bunny, "You can't leave now, the television cameras are on their way!"

The men gathered for a brief conference near Bunny's truck. They agreed that they couldn't take back the station without a violent confrontation with the women and that it was better to leave before the media witnessed that or before their retreat was captured on film. Bunny himself was so disoriented and woozy from Kayla's haymaker to his jaw that all he could say over and over was, "The Lord is not with the she-devils, he's with me!" This was not regarded as all that helpful by the other men, who were beginning to realize that ranting and strategy are not the same thing.

His own sons, grandsons, and loyal ranch hands looked down at their boots or off into the distance. Bunny witnessed their embarrassment and he became even louder and more desperate. They nodded and humored, calmed, and cajoled him, and carefully guided him into the back seat of a double cab pickup truck. His grandson LaDon sat beside him and gently wiped spittle from the front of Bunny's Carhartt jacket. He clipped a seat belt across the prophet's shoulders. "It's okay, Grampa, we're going back to the ranch now. You'll feel better tomorrow."

But he didn't feel better the next day, or the day after that. Eventually he retreated into a muttering state laced with expletives. If Bunny was still the mouthpiece of the Lord, one would have to conclude God had a potty mouth.

In the years that followed the retreat from the ranger station, the old man went back to punching cows, cutting fences, and muttering. His warnings that the Constitution lay dangling from a thread and his attempts to rally patriots for an armed rebellion were ignored. Even his own children backed away from his rants. A failed prophet may be mad, but his followers are simply fools. Bunny's wife died and one by one his sons and daughters moved away until Bunny was alone. The ranch was sold, and a bent and busted old Bunny Cleaver was passed by his offspring from household to household, where he wore out his welcome by yelling at their toddlers, kicking their dogs, and spitting while he talked. Nearly ninety, he landed, incontinent and incoherent, at Shady Days Manor.

There, sitting in the nursing home with a fresh diaper, a warm tray of food in front of him, and a television show playing that he could not follow, Bunny Cleaver reviewed his life. He recognized that day at the Sleeping Maiden ranger station as the hinge point in his life's history. Kayla's punch to his jaw undid him. His powers melted like the wicked witch in *The Wizard of Oz* after Dorothy throws a bucket of water on her.

"I'm melting, I'm melting!"

"What is that, Mr. Cleaver?" Nurse Batterwise was accustomed to incoherent outbursts from the patients she attended at the Shady Days Manor, and Bunny Cleaver often conversed with invisible beings.

"That little bitch!"

"Now that will be enough of that, Mr. Cleaver."

That day on Sleeping Maiden Mountain was a turning point for the other Cleaverites, too, who dispersed back to their jobs driving trucks, laying pipe, cutting meat, and praying for another gas and oil boom. One of the grandkids joined the marines and a couple of others went to jail for poaching elk out of season. There was a taxidermist and three mechanics among them, four charges of domestic abuse, three arrests for failing to pay child support, and two dead in auto accidents. Golden Cleaver, the oldest son and rightful heir to his father's Cleaverite movement, ran for county office three times and lost badly, proving to the Cleaver family their patriarch's scornful indictment of the corrupt political system and the necessity of armed revolt to restore the Constitution. Only, they lost their nerve and held back. From a wheelchair in the nursing home, Bunny continued to rant and warned Golden that God would punish him if he failed to do his father's bidding and start the holy war against the federal intruders and their Satan-worshipping tree-hugger allies.

Golden never took up arms against the federal government, but he died by gunfire nonetheless. He was hired to play an old-timey marshal in a fake gunfight that was the traditional highlight of the Boon County Rodeo show. According to the script, a stagecoach circled the rodeo grounds during the intermission and was stopped by two men on horseback with pistols drawn. They wore black hats with kerchiefs pulled across their faces. As the play-acting robbers empty the coach and tell its occupants "hands up," the marshal rides into the arena and confronts the bad guys. Those in the audience who were familiar with the Cleavers thought the selection of Golden Cleaver to play the marshal was ironic given his family's history of defying the law. Most of the spectators thought ironic was something that was at least very hard if not actually made of iron.

A spectacular gunfight with blank bullets ensues, except this time one of the bandit actors mixed up his blanks with real bullets. An investigation revealed that he was shooting at prairie dogs and showing off his six-shooter to his youngest boy when he realized he was late for the show. In his haste to leave he had loaded five blanks but missed the real bullet still lodged in the chamber. Golden was shot through the neck and bled to death in front of the rodeo audience. Half of them cheered, not suspecting the fatal flaw and admiring how real the fake blood looked, and half of the audience gasped in horror as they realized that the show was not so amusing with actual blood. Golden died before the ambulance reached the hospital.

When told of the accident that effectively ended the Cleaverite movement once and for all, Bunny Cleaver, now ancient and demented, his back warped and his hair sparse, an enormous suspicious mole growing on his temple, cleared his throat and spit on the ground. "I told him God would get him!"

Bunny Cleaver thought for a moment and then smiled. It felt good to be right.

Chapter 17

Luna thought Kayla had lost weight since the incident at the Sleeping Maiden ranger station a week earlier. Her eyes looked tired. She hadn't seen Kayla since Sleeping Maiden and she was worried about her, so she had decided to pay her a visit. She drove to the Jango Ranch. How different this visit would be compared to the time she confronted Kayla's grandfather about Juniper's missing toes. She pulled up to the old ranch house and lifted Sage out of his seat. She shifted him onto her hip and knocked on the ranch house door. Kayla opened almost immediately.

"I saw you coming. Hi Sage!" She crouched to look into his face and gently ran her finger under his ample chins until he made eye contact and gleefully yelped recognition. The women laughed and walked inside. Kayla looked tired but Luna was pleased to see that she was in good spirits.

The confrontation at the station had already become the stuff of local legend and the humiliation of the Cleaver clan reinforced their isolation from the rest of the world. Mary Handy wanted to press charges but Dunk Taylor couldn't figure out what charges would stick or how to deliver the charges to the Cleaver compound anyway.

"No harm done, right?" the sheriff asked Mary. "Heck, they left didn't they?"

"But that's not the point, Dunk," Mary replied.

"Yes it is." Dunk told her he had enough to do without tilting at sawmills.

"You mean windmills."

"What?"

"Never mind." Mary's supervisors at the Forest Service were also against pursuing the matter further so she gave up the hope that she could use the confrontation at the ranger station to get the illegal Cleaver cattle off the range once and for all. The four women who were in Mary's group that day were also against an aggressive response. Grace felt badly that they had "lost control" and Luna didn't want her involvement to taint the reputation of the Desert Rose as a safe place where all were welcome. Kayla worried that if Mary pushed too hard, she could be charged with assault and battery for decking Bunny Cleaver. She had enough on her plate. Olene feared the ensuing controversy could jeopardize her privacy.

Luna sat Sage on the floor and pulled his favorite toys from a flowered diaper bag. He had begun to sit up by himself, though even a slight breeze could knock him over. She handed him a stuffed turtle, which he began to gnaw enthusiastically.

"Is he getting teeth?" Kayla thought he was the most beautiful baby she had ever seen.

"Jeez, let's hope not. He's hard enough on my tits without teeth. So what's the latest?"

"I'm making progress. I did my last shift at the university lab and I'll get paid for all those vacation days I never took and some of the unused sick leave, too. That gives me a cushion for a while. I dropped the apartment there, too, so I don't have that expense. I can work more hours at the veterinarian clinic here in Boon County and if I am here all week I can be on call more. I'm boarding at least four other horses now and that helps. So add it all up and I'm going to be okay, but I'm not done yet."

Luna smiled at her and offered a high five. "Yeah, I'm sure you're not done yet. What about the grants you told me about last week?"

"Elias is working on grants with Ramone. They like each other and are a good team but even so it's a long shot. There's so much competition for what's left and everyone everywhere is hurting and trying to adapt, or maybe cope is more like it. With so much breaking down . . . but, you know all about that."

Luna nodded and looked down at Sage playing with his foot. "Yes, sadly, I do. Sadder yet, this boy next to me will know it more. I try not to go there because it breaks my heart."

Kayla put her hand over her heart and tapped it lightly. "Me, too. I can sit around and give in to my despair or roll up my sleeves. First up is to mend this ranch."

"Yes, that's right. And you know Hoppy and I are in this with you all the way."

Kayla took Luna's hand and squeezed it. "Yes, I do know that and I cannot tell you how grateful I am for your support. For all of you."

"And the church, Kayla? Did you . . ."

"No, not yet."

Because she knew it would close the door and she was reluctant to lose what was more than membership in a church. It would be losing a connection to her childhood with beloved grandparents and good friends, so many friendly neighbors, too. She would be losing certainty itself. The last step would be the hardest.

The day after Luna's visit, Kayla called Reverend Pettybone of the One True Church and asked him to visit her alone. She didn't want to handle three of them at once, like his last visit. It was tough enough without being outnumbered. Pettybone was reluctant. The One True Church had a policy that stated male leaders could not be alone with female parishioners. He quizzed her.

"Have you prayed on this, sister?"

"Yes, Reverend Pettybone, I have."

"Good!" She could almost see his smile through the phone and wondered how it felt to be so sure God was on your side. She had a recollection of that feeling but it was lost to her now.

He pulled into the driveway the next morning, as the first light was still crawling through the lilacs that lined the way. Bees were finding the first blossoms of the day and birds were finding their first bugs. A meadowlark was trilling sweetly from a fencepost while a raven croaked far above. The first thin clouds appeared on the horizon and would soon build into thunderheads.

The crunch of gravel as his truck pulled up to the ranch house reminded Kayla of Reverend Pettybone's first visit, when he caught her unprepared. This time she was rehearsed and ready. She knew life rarely goes the way it is rehearsed but she remained confident. She remembered how Grace always said it will all turn out well in the end, and if it isn't turning out well then it isn't the end. Or something like that. Focus, she told herself, focus.

She opened the door and invited him to sit. He took off his hat and leaned forward with his elbows on his knees. He could tell right away this wasn't going to go as well as he had hoped. She was having trouble making eye contact with him.

He put on his most mellifluous voice, the one reserved to persuade listeners that he was kind, patient, and wise. "I am eager to hear what you learned when you prayed, Sister Burnside. I have prayed that Heavenly Father's voice is clear, that you know His intentions."

That threw her off her script for a moment and she considered addressing whether he alone was so privy to God's plans, or whether God even had a plan, or if that way of looking at life on earth even made sense. She stammered, paused, and then got back on track.

"I'm sorry, but I'm not selling my water to the One True Church."

"What then, do you have another offer? We understand the Nutley Corporation . . ."

She cut him off. "No, I turned them down, too."

"Kayla, if you need more time to consider this, well, we didn't mean to pressure you."

"No, it's not that. I'm going to give it back."

The air in the room was hot. Her heart pounded and she struggled to breathe. He didn't get it and she could hear his brain struggling to comprehend, a soft sizzle like bacon frying in a rainstorm. She smelled the sharp odor of nervous perspiration. Is that me? She glanced quickly toward her armpits and sure enough a dark stain had begun to appear. She would have to explain her plan in more detail but wasn't sure she could do that.

She threw it all out there at once. "I'm flooding my meadows nearest the river and letting the alfalfa fields go back to willows. I'll be keeping some land and water to live on, enough for my horses and for a community garden for Stony Mesa. A big one, maybe greenhouses, too. I'm looking into conservation easements. I don't have a complete plan yet but I know what I want. Everything along the river will go back to wetlands and woodlands like it was when my great-grandfather settled it."

He turned his good ear to her so he could be sure he understood what she was saying, but he was as baffled now as when she began. If she told him she was shipping the ranch and its water to Neptune or that she had decided to raise mermaids he would have been as clueless. She gave him a moment to reply, but he was stuck.

She decided to go for broke. "I'm putting a couple of beavers on the feeder stream that comes from the north seep, you know, the chalky one along the canyon wall. It's going to be a wetland eventually like it was when the first Jango Burnside drained it and clear-cut it. I'm giving it back. We used it long enough."

She stopped and looked at him and he looked back with a puzzled expression, as if a third eye had popped out of the middle of her forehead and he was afraid to look away but couldn't accept what he was seeing. She was doing her best to project confident defiance but her jaw trembled slightly and she hoped he didn't see that. Vanquishing Bunny Cleaver was a piece of cake compared to handling Reverend Pettybone.

The reverend found his voice. "Turning your back on the church and the people who raised you is serious, very serious. Not just socially for you but think of Heavenly Father's covenant with his people."

Kayla interrupted. "You didn't raise me, my grandparents did that. You were kind and supportive because I was his granddaughter and I was obedient to the church. I am thankful for your kindness but my grandfather raised me to be independent and brave. He might not understand but he would support me like he always did."

He raised his voice above hers. "And Heavenly Father?"

She raised her voice to match his. "I don't believe in that kind of god, not anymore. I don't want your blessing, I don't need your salvation."

He gasped. She watched shock play across his face, the subtle shift in his shoulders as he pulled away from her ever so slightly. There, she thought, I did it. I did it. She was so relieved she could float off the floor. Or burst into cathartic tears of release.

Now she felt clear, her confidence returned. "You know about the Hubble telescope, don't you?"

The reverend muttered a baffled affirmation.

"Hubble pierced the cataract of our earthly atmosphere and gave us a window on the universe. Its scale is beyond comprehension and it is filled with galaxies like pinwheels and storms of gas and light in every color imaginable. Have you seen the photos of nebulae? Their beauty is stunning. How can you reduce the God of such an awesome realm to a man or to a prophet?"

"What other instrument of God's love is there?"

"There are animals."

He was scornful, incredulous. "So you would have me worship what, a dolphin, maybe, or bears? The Indians had a spider woman. Do you think an insect is a worthy instrument of God's truth?"

"Why not? Why not a God who is manifested in every living thing, not just humans, especially male humans? If that God was the one we followed, we might have too much reverence for his creation to slaughter like we do now. Maybe we wouldn't scrape our way across the land and sea and cause so much damage."

"Sister Burnside, you are way over your head. Every living thing is indeed a manifestation of our Lord. It is proof of his love for us that he has given us such a bounteous world."

Kayla shook her head no. "There is a difference between regarding an elephant as a bounty and seeing her as God incarnate."

"Seriously, Kayla, you worship elephants? You've become what? A Hindu? What would your grandfather say about that?" He aimed to shame. His voice was at once incredulous and disdainful while it also resonated authority. He was good at this.

Kayla was mad now. "You didn't intimidate me when you invoked God, so I don't think invoking my grandfather is going to work either."

"Intimidate? Is that what this is? Oh, please!"

She stepped back and pulled herself up. She resumed in a lower and slower tone. "I do not believe I will be lifted away on celestial wings to some afterlife that's a glittery version of this life. The only circle that remains unbroken is the cycle of energy and nutrients and nitrogen and seasons and stars and everything else that goes round and round in nature. And isn't that enough? Isn't that its own miracle? Sorry, but my salvation is not through obedience to your doctrine. My salvation happens right here, right now. I'm going to save myself by healing the land that I love. You want to touch what is holy? Take off your shoes and walk barefoot on this earth."

Without a further word she walked to the door and opened it, gesturing for him to leave. He hesitated, unsure and out of his element. He had expected the usual compliance and deference that his conforming flock showed their celestial shepherd. He shook his head and smacked his lips, conveying a profound disappointment intended to induce shame. He walked out quietly and nodded politely as he passed. She watched his truck as it disappeared down the driveway. It turned onto the county road and was gone. Just like that, it was over.

The following morning the leaders of the One True Church met in the church's Stony Mesa office. It was a somber affair, not just because they were disappointed Kayla was not persuaded to sell her water to them but because they were sincerely sad to lose a young woman whom they loved and admired and considered kin. Excommunication was ruled out. Give her time, they agreed, and pray for her return to the fold, that she might see the error of her ways and return to our loving embrace.

Kayla wanted to call Luna and Grace and tell them the news. She wanted to tell all of them, especially Ramone, but decided to wait until she could tell them in person. She organized an impromptu potluck at her place that evening. Luna said she would bake bread and Hoppy had fresh greens to contribute. Olene and Virginia promised an appetizer. Grace baked a pie and would bring a jar of jam, of course. Elias said he would make a spaghetti carbonara casserole. Otis said he'd bring his special chili and his telescope in case they wanted to see stars after dinner. Lucas Hozho was in town, too, and so she invited him. Mary Handy said she'd be delighted to join them. Most important of all,

Ramone Marquez said he'd come over early and help her set up the dining room and put an extra leaf in the table. And no, he didn't have to be back the next morning.

She would wake up tomorrow and begin to overcome every challenge and solve every problem that came her way. Ramone would help. Together they could do it. And that evening as she watched her guests celebrate and laugh, comfortable among each other, she realized there would be many more tales to tell as they shared life in Stony Mesa. She was thankful to be home.

THE END

About **Chip Ward**

Chip Ward was born in New Jersey, but forty-three years ago moved to Utah, where he is an obsessive hiker. His past careers have included being a manager at a fishing lodge and a bookmobile driver and deputy director of the Salt Lake Public Library. Though the places he has called home and his careers have varied throughout his life, writing and discussing the conflicts of our time have been mainstays. His two most recent book publications include *Canaries on the Rim: Living Downwind in the West* (1999) from Verso and *Hope's Horizon: Three Visions for Healing the American Land* (2004) from Island Press – Shearwater Books. Other work has appeared in the *Los Angeles Times, Catalyst Magazine,* TomDispatch.com, and *The Boston Globe.*

TORREY HOUSE PRESS

Voices for the Land

The economy is a wholly owned subsidiary of the environment, not the other way around.
—Senator Gaylord Nelson, founder of Earth Day

Torrey House Press is an independent nonprofit publisher promoting environmental conservation through literature. We believe that culture is changed through conversation and that lively, contemporary literature is the cutting edge of social change. We strive to identify exceptional writers, nurture their work, and engage the widest possible audience; to publish diverse voices with transformative stories that illuminate important facets of our ever-changing planet; to develop literary resources for the conservation movement, educating and entertaining readers, inspiring action.

Visit **www.torreyhouse.org** for reading group discussion guides, author interviews, and more.